Praise for Jas

"This is a brilliant modern parable disg[...]
—*Publishers Weekly* on [...] *anches the Future in the Dick*

"[Pargin] once again achieves the perfect balance between sardonic humor and satirical digs at the digital age."
—*Library Journal* (starred review) on *Zoey Punches the Future in the Dick*

"With verve and velocity, the story moves . . . one cinematic set piece after another, strung together with twisty fun and wit."
—*The New York Times Book Review* on *Futuristic Violence and Fancy Suits*

"Like Jonathan Swift for the internet age. His newest is only more proof that he will be remembered as one of today's great satirists."
—*Nerdist* on *Futuristic Violence and Fancy Suits*

"Pargin once again delights with scathing social commentary thinly disguised as an outrageous action novel. . . . This is a feast."
—*Publishers Weekly* on *If This Book Exists, You're in the Wrong Universe*

"*What the Hell Did I Just Read* is reminiscent of Douglas Adams's work, stuffed with layers of absurd pastiche."
—*The Washington Post*

"If you want a poignant, laugh-out-loud funny, disturbing, ridiculous, self-aware, socially relevant horror novel, then *This Book Is Full of Spiders: Seriously, Dude, Don't Touch It* is the one and only book for you."
—*SF Signal*

"Reads as if Bill Murray's world-weary Ghostbuster and sassy Buffy the Vampire Slayer spawned a slacker child—like *Clerks* with monsters . . . Surprising, disturbing, and inventive."
—*Herald Sun* on *John Dies at the End*

ALSO BY JASON PARGIN

ZOEY
IS TOO
DRUNK
FOR THIS
DYSTOPIA

JASON PARGIN

ST. MARTIN'S GRIFFIN
NEW YORK

Published in the United States by St. Martin's Griffin,
an imprint of St. Martin's Publishing Group

ZOEY IS TOO DRUNK FOR THIS DYSTOPIA. Copyright © 2023 by Jason Pargin. All rights reserved. Printed in the United States of America. For information, address St. Martin's Publishing Group, 120 Broadway, New York, NY 10271.

www.stmartins.com

Designed by Steven Seighman

The Library of Congress has cataloged the hardcover edition as follows:

Names: Pargin, Jason, 1975– author.
Title: Zoey is too drunk for this dystopia / Jason Pargin.
Description: First edition. | New York : St. Martin's Press, 2023. |
    Series: Zoey Ashe ; 3
Identifiers: LCCN 2023025179 | ISBN 9781250285935 (hardcover) |
    ISBN 9781250285942 (ebook)
Subjects: LCGFT: Science fiction. | Novels.
Classification: LCC PS3623.O5975 Z43 2023 | DDC 813/.6—
    dc23/eng/20230526
LC record available at https://lccn.loc.gov/2023025179

ISBN 978-1-250-87995-0 (trade paperback)

Our books may be purchased in bulk for promotional, educational, or business use. Please contact your local bookseller or the Macmillan Corporate and Premium Sales Department at 1-800-221-7945, extension 5442, or by email at MacmillanSpecialMarkets@macmillan.com.

First St. Martin's Griffin Edition: 2024

10 9 8 7 6 5 4 3 2 1

For my mother, who gave everything to everyone

HEIRESS, ASSOCIATES AMONG VICTIMS OF EAST VILLAGE BLAST: REPORT

Zoey Ashe, 23, is reportedly among the victims of this morning's explosion in the trendy East Village neighborhood of Tabula Ra$a, along with an unknown number of her associates.

Ashe achieved notoriety as the surprise heir to the fortune of flamboyant real estate mogul Arthur Livingston. There have been multiple high-profile attempts on Ashe's life in the fifteen months since, her father having accumulated numerous enemies over the decades due to his alleged involvement in organized crime. It is unknown why Ashe and her associates were present at the time of the incident and no official announcement has been made regarding their . . .

BLAST MAY HAVE BEEN DUE TO IMPLANTED DEVICE, SAY EXPERTS

The explosion that collapsed an East Village business and reportedly claimed multiple high-profile victims may have been the result of an implanted device, say experts.

The blast occurred sometime after midnight and authorities have so far declined to declare it to be an intentional attack. Law enforcement sources speaking on condition of anonymity say charred human remains recovered from around the blast site are consistent with an internal device, the legs and skull reportedly having landed over two hundred feet apart. Black-market implants, including notoriously unstable augmentations, have recently become the subject of . . .

BELOVED RACCOON BELIEVED KILLED IN EAST VILLAGE BLAST

Bandito, a wild raccoon with over 15 million followers on the social livestreaming platform Blink, is believed to have been killed in the overnight explosion in an upscale neighborhood on the East side of Tabula Ra$a.

Bandito rose to fame last year after an unknown user captured the raccoon and attached a dime-sized Blink-enabled camera on a harness, set to continuously stream its day-to-day activities. Millions of users have since followed the animal's adventures as he has attempted to secure food from trash bins and dumpsters around local businesses while evading predators and Animal Control. Fans are planning a vigil this afternoon outside the . . .

CHAPTER
1

EXACTLY FORTY-FOUR HOURS BEFORE a building would collapse on top of her, Zoey Ashe was shuffling drunkenly around her mansion in a bathrobe, munching Doritos.

She'd actually gotten lost in her own home, dully convinced that someone had switched around all the rooms as a prank. She'd gotten up in search of her favorite drunken-night food (the Doritos in the heated bag that makes them taste like they'd been pulled fresh from a deep fryer) but when she arrived back at the guest bedroom, she'd opened the door to find a chemical-stinking storage room packed with housekeeping equipment, including the pair of floor-cleaner robots plugged into their chargers like a couple of sleeping tortoises. Zoey had gotten distracted for a while, giggling and trying to feed them Doritos, until she'd lost interest in that and stumbled back into the hall. That's when she heard the alarm.

It sounded like it was coming from outside, a robotic woman's voice sternly warning an intruder that terrible consequences were coming their way unless they turned back. Zoey shuffled back toward the main stairwell leading down to the front entrance, only to instead find herself in the foyer at ground level—ah, that's why she'd gotten lost, she was on the wrong floor. She pulled open one of the obscenely heavy, twelve-foot-tall etched-bronze doors, paused to wipe Doritos dust off the knob with her robe, then stepped out into the night, only remembering she was barefoot when she felt the cold cobblestones under her toes.

"You are on a course to violate restricted airspace over private property," stated the alarm voice with chilling robotic indifference. "You have five seconds to turn back or automated countermeasures will be used, up to and including lethal force." Zoey thought it was funny that this kind of computerized warning voice was always coded as female. She had brought it up with the person who'd installed the alarm system and was told that for the type of guy you're trying to deter, a stern woman was the last voice they'd ever obeyed: a schoolteacher, a mother, or whatever female family member had gotten stuck with raising them.

Zoey surveyed the area and saw nothing out of the ordinary, unless she counted the pair of white trucks belonging to the company that was about to install a pool out back, which she had apparently ordered at some point. But they'd been there for days and surely the estate's ingenious threat detection knew that. Then, her sluggish brain finally processed what the robotic schoolmarm was saying about "violating restricted airspace" and she squinted up into the night sky, scanning it for hovering lights.

The last few times she'd heard this alarm it had turned out to be paparazzi—usually drones, once a helicopter—hoping to catch some kind of crime or other depravity occurring at the estate, as if Zoey's people would do that kind of thing out on the lawn. Then she looked down at herself and remembered why the March night felt so much colder than she'd expected: she was wearing a fluffy white bathrobe, but that was it. Her underwear had been discarded in the hallway, the dress she'd worn to the evening's awards ceremony had been left in the car (she actually wasn't certain it was an awards ceremony, it could have been a charity banquet or possibly a wedding reception—she just remembered a lot of tuxedos and mandatory clapping).

The intruder apparently hadn't turned back. The AI dominatrix voiced a new message, stating that they were now officially flying over private property and that countermeasures were being readied. Though, if they were here for photos, they probably had everything they wanted from Zoey's appearance alone. The tabloid media outlets loved to simultaneously describe Zoey as fat and disgusting while also publishing as much of her bare skin as they could steal. One drone had caught her sunbathing on a private beach in an extremely conservative two-piece, then ran the photos under a headline saying she was "flaunting" her chunky horror of a body. The next day, a progressive women's publication pushed back by describing Zoey's choice of public attire as "brave," which hardly made the situation better. The point being, if this was just a flying camera, the operator now had pics/video of Zoey in her rumpled bathrobe, standing on her driveway among the marble statues while holding a Doritos bag, her hair looking like it had spent the last couple of hours being pawed and pulled by a sweaty line cook. She briefly considered pulling open her robe and flashing them but figured tabloid readers probably wouldn't be impressed by that a third time.

The robotic schoolmarm gave a final warning that projectiles were on their way and that if they hadn't yet turned around their aircraft, it was probably too late, so why bother. Zoey still couldn't see the airborne intruder but thought she could hear it, that weird pulsing rush of little drone engines. Then a couple of spotlights kicked on from the yard and there it was: not a drone or a helicopter, but something in between, a personal flying device carrying some idiot over the wrought-iron main gate, then soaring above the hedges and statues along the winding driveway.

A moment later, two of the statues inside the gate—men in armor, on horseback—pivoted and from their eyes flew angry swarms of projectiles that streaked up into the darkness like sparks from a poked campfire. The arms and legs of the flyer were ripped off, whirling to the ground before the torso and flying device tumbled down after them.

Zoey gasped and dropped her Doritos. Had she just watched someone die?

She pulled the lapel of her robe closed, as if worried she was now dressed inappropriately for such a somber occasion. She looked down at the Doritos bag, the animated flaming-triangle logo dancing above a heap of dusted chips, as if looking to it for advice. Receiving none, she started running. She moved as quickly as her current physical state would allow, bare feet slapping the cobblestones. It seemed improbable that someone could survive both a dismemberment and a subsequent fall but, hey, modern medicine could do almost anything. Hadn't she just seen a story about robotic surgeons reattaching a severed head? Or had she seen that in a movie? Either way, there was no one else around to help, so she ran toward the fallen intruder with no idea what she'd actually do once she reached them.

The estate and its defenses had been built by Zoey's biological father,

Arthur Livingston, whom the press described as a "flamboyant real estate developer" or "ruthless organized-crime kingpin," depending on the publication (specifically, on whether or not it was a publication that Arthur Livingston had owned). The system was not designed only to deter burglars, but to thwart a full-on armed assault from some cartel's hit squad. Anyone attempting a breach like this had either done zero research or was just delegating their suicide.

And still, Zoey ran.

A new alarm was sounding now, this one from back in the house, alerting staff to go out and investigate whatever had landed on the front lawn. Somewhere back there was a naked dude in a guest bedroom who was probably squinting drunkenly into the darkness, wondering where he was and if the alarm meant the place was on fire.

Zoey arrived at the approximate landing spot of the flying intruder's various parts. She felt around her robe pockets for her phone—nope, not there. Her bodyguard had gone home; she'd dismissed him after leaving the banquet (birthday party? Funeral?) with the tattooed member of the kitchen staff she'd picked up, the guy having made some slurred comment about how he could protect her if assassins appeared. The only human on-site right now was Carlton the Butler, whom she'd inherited along with the property. And Carlton was, by Zoey's estimate, between seventy and two hundred years old. The wailing alarm was giving her a headache, so she shouted, "WOULD YOU PLEASE SHUT UP?!?" and was amused to find that actually worked. Then she remembered that everything in the house had been set to respond to her voice commands. That's why a misheard phrase shouted in an argument had once resulted in the HVAC system shutting up several ducts.

She first found a severed arm in a bright yellow sleeve, smoldering where it had been detached from its body. She felt an urge to get sick and stifled it. There was no blood, which seemed strange. Then Zoey noted that, where the wrist was revealed between glove and cuff, there was a plastic joint instead of skin. Either the flyer had a prosthetic arm, or his entire body was prosthetic (Zoey's drunken mind needed a few seconds to remember there was a word for that: "mannequin"). She did, in fact, then find a plastic head and torso still strapped to the flying rig a little farther up, next to a fountain made to look like a woman pointing her pelvis into the air, spraying forth liquid (Zoey had replaced much of her father's old decor, but hadn't gotten to the front lawn's water features yet). The flying rig was an oversized backpack, sprouting fins and wraparound arms that ended in control sticks. The whole apparatus was a garish yellow, so eye-wateringly bright that Zoey thought it looked like an angel had pissed on it. The mannequin pilot had been wearing an equally yellow jumpsuit and helmet. She felt relief that was quickly swamped by confusion.

"May I be of assistance?" asked a raspy but dignified voice from behind her. She had never seen Carlton move at a speed quicker than "very old man doing his best," yet she frequently saw him appear in spots that would have required a brisk jog at the very least, if not a dead run. She speculated that Carlton could actually move very quickly when he needed to, but perhaps thought it was unbecoming to be seen sprinting from place to place in formal butler garb.

Zoey said, "It's a dummy."

"I would still advise caution. The system has not detected any dangerous devices, but some dangers are difficult to detect. Previous experience has taught us a hard lesson on that subject."

Some part of Zoey's brain knew this was correct, but what was the point of drinking if you were just going to cling to your inhibitions? The limbless torso was lying chest-down in the grass, so she rolled it over. The front of the yellow jumpsuit was emblazoned with a logo backlit by animated fireworks. Tall block letters spelled out,

THE AMAZING AVIV

Zoey pointed at it. "Do we know what that means?"

"No, but if one were to divine the meaning via context, one would guess that Mr. Aviv is a stunt performer, and perhaps something of a prankster."

"He had us shoot down a mannequin as a prank? It's not very funny, he should have filled it with poop or something."

"Perhaps this was not the prank. Perhaps this was a dry run, to see what happens to intruders who attempt to gain access to the grounds via the air."

"Ah. Well, now he knows."

"Should I call Wu?"

"He's almost certainly already on his way, any alarm from the house goes directly to his phone. If anything, we should message him to not bother. In fact, please do that. I'm going back to bed."

"Very good. And should I notify Mr. Blackwater?"

"I guarantee you he also already knows, and that's assuming he didn't know about it before it happened. I have to try to get some sleep, I have to be up in . . ." she tried to do the math, "four hours?"

She wasn't sleepy; she and the guy whose name she hadn't retained had spent the evening downing what he'd called Dragon Shots: smoldering liquid that, if she blew across the glass, would unleash a puff of flame. It was obvious now that one of the ingredients was some kind of stimulant designed to keep the party going until sunrise.

"Oh, and, uh, in the third guest bedroom, there's a guy up there. Got a lot of tattoos. Wake him up and tell him you've called a car to pick him up. And, you know, actually do that before you tell him." She turned to head back to the house. "What do I have tomorrow? Or later today, I mean? I know I have to get up but can't remember what for."

"First, I believe, is a tour of the new factory with Mr. Blackwater, a journalist, and a number of schoolchildren. It begins . . ." he consulted his watch, "five and a half hours from now."

"Oh, god. Can I get out of it?"

"I, of course, cannot answer that question. I suppose one must weigh the consequences of leaving said children, as well as the public image of the company, in the hands of Will Blackwater."

"Ugh. I have to get my life together. Start going to bed at a reasonable hour, the whole thing. All right. I just have to get through that factory tour, then I can come back here and collapse on a sofa for the rest of the day."

"I believe there are a series of meetings and obligations after, including tonight's debate."

"Oh, right. And then the next night is the thing."

You know how sometimes your life gets into a holding pattern because you're just killing time until a dreaded scheduled event? For Zoey, that event was coming Sunday evening and for weeks she'd been filling her life with distractions, trying to fast-forward through the timeline until the blessed day when it would all be over and done with.

"As for today, it sounds like the biggest challenge will be staying awake for it all," said Zoey in what would turn out to be the most inaccurate prediction of her lifetime.

CHAPTER
2

THE EVENTS DESCRIBED HEREIN take place in the future, in an 85,000-square-mile expanse of a gorgeously hostile territory that people in Zoey's time will call Utah, which you'll note is the same as what it's called now. The difference is that in your present, the southwestern part of the state is home to a number of friendly small towns and some of the best hiking grounds in America. In Zoey's future, a cabal of wealthy real estate developers have bulldozed all of that nonsense and laid the foundations for a gleaming new metropolis called Tabula Ra$a.

Spearheading that effort was Arthur Livingston, an innovator responsible for numerous breakthroughs in the field of committing crimes in ways that cannot easily be prosecuted. Tabula Ra$a was to be a Utopia built according to Arthur's undying belief that if enough capital accumulated in one spot, everything else would just work itself out. His spectacularly violent death at the hands of his rivals would thus be declared "ironic" by some in the press who clearly did not understand the meaning of the word. When a professional shark wrestler gets bitten in half by a Great White, that's not irony, that's somebody getting precisely what they signed up for.

Those are but the broad strokes of the events; the details are all but impossible to know. This is by design. Arthur had famously surrounded himself with a team of four advisors who, according to outlandish rumors that happened to be true, had mostly cut their teeth as "dirty tricks" operatives for intelligence agencies that, it should be noted, considered just shooting their enemies in the back of the head to be an example of a clean trick. Their names were Will Blackwater, Andre Knox, Budd Billingsley, and Michelle "Echo" Ling. Or maybe they weren't; their birth certificates would almost certainly display different names, if anyone were actually able to find such documents. "They are always impeccably dressed," wrote one journalist, "but they do all of their most important work in the dark."

Arthur's team, whom most people in town simply called the Suits, were the subject of endless conspiracy theories (one claimed that they owned an invisible military helicopter to move about the city) and just as many conspiracy facts (they had, in fact, used such a helicopter at some point, but it was a rental). "In a world full of cameras," said one obituary, "Arthur Livingston and his underlings mastered the art of staging a reality that suited their needs." Fringe publications often attributed some kind of occult powers to Arthur and his people, but the truth was they simply didn't need them. Arthur had learned early in life that reality only existed as the collective perceptions of the beings living in it, so if one could manipulate those perceptions, they could effectively control reality. Arthur used this unfathomable power to advance goals that were similar to the goals of most powerful men throughout history: mainly to acquire stupid amounts of wealth and sex.

Upon his death, it was discovered that Arthur had bequeathed his entire empire to a previously unknown daughter who, at the time, was residing with her mother in a Colorado trailer park. This was the equivalent of our hypothetical shark grappler requiring his estranged child to resume wrestling the very fish that had just chewed through his torso. The name of that daughter was Zoey Ashe and, along with that empire, she also inherited the Suits. As for whether this bizarre arrangement was the result of a carefully orchestrated plan or a drunken impulse, it is believed that Arthur took the answer to that question to his grave.

Zoey has since become the subject of many salacious rumors herself, many revolving around the accusation that she has resorted to some deeply unhealthy habits in order to cope with the stresses of her new position. Zoey would be the first to tell you that this is absolutely untrue: her unhealthy habits were doing nothing to help her cope.

CHAPTER
3

ZOEY WAS LEANING ON a huge pillar of quivering beef when she heard the crash.

The noise had erupted from somewhere outside the vast production floor and sounded like a buffalo rampaging through a bicycle shop. She was on the verge of asking if that noise was unusual for this facility when an alarm began wailing, answering the question for her. This was a day for alarms, apparently. Alarms and headaches. There was a handful of white-jumpsuited staff working the factory floor and she attempted to judge the scale of the emergency from their reactions. They were all exchanging looks with each other, apparently trying to do the same.

"What was that?" Zoey asked the man in the black three-piece suit next to her, who was currently directing a withering gaze toward the commotion.

"She cut her way in through the roof," replied Will Blackwater, as if he'd somehow discerned the who, what, and where from a clanging chorus of tumbling metal. It wouldn't surprise Zoey if he had. Will was a man in his late thirties whom the press referred to as Zoey's "advisor" or "puppeteer," depending on the publication. He was wearing the clothes of a man headed for a funeral and the expression of a man who was about to cause one.

The pillar of beef next to them continued quivering.

They were in a cavernous space dominated by stainless-steel pipes and rhythmic squishy noises. It was a "cultured meat" factory owned by a company that had almost sarcastically named itself Montana Skies Beef. Here, tissue extracted from some especially delicious cow was fed with nutrients until the cells multiplied, growing into massive wads of living pink "beef." The wobbly masses were then transferred to these clear vats, each ten feet tall and five feet wide, where they were stretched and then massaged with pulses of electricity, causing the pink pillar of flesh to flex and convulse as if being tortured. Cultured beef was mushy when freshly grown, so this shock treatment would work the muscle tissue to better simulate the natural texture of meat that had spent a few years moving a cow around a pasture. The sprawling facility was packed with these pink pillars, each marbled with carefully calculated amounts of white fat, each shivering in turn, as if a cold wind was blowing across flesh that had not even skin for protection.

Zoey knew all of this, not because she now owned this factory—though she definitely did—but because it had all just been explained moments ago by a holographic cartoon cow that was leading the tour. She, Will, and her bodyguard were taking the tour along with a blond reporter, whose name Zoey kept forgetting, and the reporter's camera operator, who at the moment was using a touchscreen to operate three hovering cameras that were capturing the scene from various angles. One of those cameras was continuously focused on Zoey's face to record her reactions, which unfortunately meant it had captured her involuntary yelp of "ohmygod" when she'd entered the room a few minutes ago and gotten a look at the ranks of twitching, alien meat columns. Will had warned her about them in advance but had completely failed to tell her that they *moved*. When Zoey heard the mysterious crash, her first thought had been that one of the meat slugs had escaped its enclosure and gone on a rampage.

Will asked, "Is she alone?"

Zoey had no idea why he was asking her, or what the question even meant. Before she could ask him to clarify, an answer came from behind her.

Wu, whom the press referred to as Zoey's "bodyguard" or "henchman," depending on the publication, said, "Yes, everyone else is joining remotely. She came in through the roof over the loading bay. Cut right through the steel trusses."

He was fed information like this via a display in his sunglasses, though in that moment, Zoey wished its software was better at noticing threats while they were still a little farther away. No one had discussed even the possibility of them getting ambushed while doing a boring publicity appearance for an acquisition Zoey didn't necessarily remember acquiring. If they had, she'd have gotten less drunk the night before and gone to bed way earlier. She'd also have probably picked a different outfit; she was in a fairly short, off-the-shelf minidress with a pattern of loud splotches of red and white that she'd picked out because she'd thought it kind of looked like meat.

Will nodded and said, "Well, no need to ask if she's armed," which Zoey understood to mean that whatever tools or abilities had allowed this intruder to slice through structural steel would make it equally easy for them to cut Zoey into pieces, if indeed that was their goal. Her temples were throbbing, as if her brain were trying to peck its way out of her skull like a baby bird.

"Are we safe here?" asked Zoey.

"Montana Skies No-Kill Beef is absolutely safe!" exclaimed the holographic cow, the AI apparently thinking it'd detected a relevant question from the tour group. "In fact, there hasn't been a single recall of cultured beef the whole time it's been on the market! The one instance of large-scale contamination was found to be the fault of the wholesaler!"

Will said, "Shut that thing up or I'm going to break it."

The cow went into a silent looping animation, as if that also was a phrase it had heard before and had learned to respond to out of self-preservation. The alarm continued wailing from the other room, until it was abruptly cut off by another metallic crash. That was, presumably, the alarm mechanism being destroyed by whomever had just triggered it and was, Zoey noted, the one noise an alarm could make that was more alarming than the alarm.

The blond reporter, who was not a real reporter but a paid shill hired to put together a puff piece about the grand opening of the beef factory, seemed to slowly realize that she might actually be in position to document history, or at least a spectacular murder, which was almost as good. This was the kind of story that could elevate her to real-reporter status.

"Viewers," she began breathlessly into the nearest hovering camera, "we have just heard a commotion from another part of the facility; it sounded to me like some kind of structural collapse or even an explosion. We do not yet know the cause but I'm hearing there may be some kind of intruder. Zoey Ashe, of course, has been the frequent target of violence since she assumed her current position and, of course, tensions are running high on the cusp of the upcoming elections. Zoey, how are you feeling right now?"

The camera that had been focused on Zoey's face buzzed in a little closer. "Actually," said Zoey, "can we turn these off for now? We'll do this later."

"I do want to remind you that we are live . . ."

Zoey wanted to ask what kind of sick freak was watching a beef-factory grand opening live, but one thing she'd learned is that you can't overestimate how bored people get.

She turned to Will and Wu. "Can you guys loop me in here?"

Will held up a hand to ask for silence, listening intently. Everyone was staring in the direction of the noise, toward a wall in the distance featuring a truck-sized doorway closed with a heavy black rubber flap, like a giant doggie door, presumably to let automated carts full of product roll in and out. From beyond that doorway, Zoey thought she could hear a female voice.

Wu the Bodyguard said, "She's coming this way."

"*Who is?* What is happening?"

"We're still assessing."

Zoey did not consider that an answer. Wu moved to put himself in between Zoey and the threat. On his right wrist was a black band that contained a number of exotic projectiles. In his left hand was what would appear to a casual observer to be a red Ping-Pong ball, or possibly a stolen clown's nose. Wu also had a katana on his back, but that was mostly just for show, both as a warning and as branding.

Zoey turned to the reporter and her camera operator. "Seriously, you guys might want to leave. I have, uh, weird enemies."

The reporter and camera guy actually seemed to be considering this. Just how badly did they want to become real journalists? The job didn't pay much. But Zoey was rooting for them to go mainly because she intended to follow them to the door.

They didn't move, but Wu said, "We need to get Zoey out of the building. The front exit is clear."

All three of the hovering cameras now swung around to focus on Zoey. She knew she would be forever judged by whatever she said and did next. Would she flee from whatever was heading her way, leaving her rank-and-file factory workers behind? If so, that clip would be replayed and used against her until her dying day. Or would she stay and face down the threat like a brave male would? If so, the incident would be forgotten by lunchtime.

She counted seven or eight of the white-jumpsuit-wearing workers, all in the process of checking settings on various screens, some seeming to do pretend work, hitting the same loop of buttons over and over. "You guys, go," she told them. "Out the front. Whatever this person wants, they almost certainly want it from me, not you. You'll be paid for whatever time you miss, I promise."

The staff looked apprehensive, each waiting to see if someone else made the first move. The hovering cameras pivoted to catch their reactions. They, too, were now live in front of an audience. Did they want to be seen leaving this young woman to the wolves? Collectively, they made a silent compromise and retreated until they were closer to the main exit, but without going outside. Technically, they hadn't abandoned their posts, but they still had a clear path to safety should whatever came through that doggie door be the kind of exotic threat the city was famous for.

"As you can see, Ms. Ashe has chosen to stay behind to face whatever is coming," said Blond Reporter. "There has, of course, been a significant investment in this facility and she will not so easily be deterred from her mission to become the Beef Queen of Tabula Rasa."

Zoey was about to say that was absolutely not her mission, when Will interjected, "She's not staying for the factory. She's staying for the kids." He tossed a thumb to his right and Zoey's stomach dropped.

Oh, god, she thought. The kids. Between her pounding headache and looming panic, she'd forgotten all about them.

"We have to get them away from here!"

The meat pillar shivered in response. The children were on the other side of an exterior glass wall to their right, on a grassy fenced-in lawn along with several miniature cows.

The substance in the vats, which the press referred to as "cultured meat" or "Frankenmeat," depending on the publication, had taken something of a beating in public opinion over the last few years. Not that Zoey had known how fierce the resistance was when she'd bought this facility; she'd thought she was doing a good deed, since this beef used a tiny fraction of the land and water as the real stuff, produced an equally tiny fraction of the CO_2 emissions, and involved none of the animal suffering. That last one was a big part of the marketing for Montana Skies and, as such, the grounds outside the factory included a petting zoo with several adorable, waist-high Highland cows lazily grazing under a "Friends, Not Food" banner. Zoey's tour group had thus included a dozen children from a school or an orphanage or something (she hadn't paid close attention to that part of the meeting), and they were currently outside, petting those friendly miniature cows and posing with them for photos. The kids had been diverted out there prior to this part of the tour, as the shivering beef-pillar section of the facility would presumably have been far too traumatizing for them. The glass wall was, of course, only transparent from the inside.

No one responded to Zoey's request to evacuate the children because it was already too late. Everyone had turned their attention to the doggie door, where a woman was stepping through. In any other era and in any other city, Zoey would have assumed she was hallucinating what she saw next: the woman, thin and pale with brown hair and wearing a flowing kaftan, seemed to be surrounded by a cloud of glowing butterflies. This kind of thing alarmed Zoey more than if the lady had walked in toting a shotgun and a meat hook.

"Again, who is this?" asked Zoey under her breath.

"She calls herself Harmonia," replied Will.

"Do we have any idea what she wants?"

"From the look in her eyes, I suspect a rational mind would be unable to comprehend what she wants."

"Don't say that, you can't diagnose mental illness from a facial expression."

"Maybe not, but it's a pretty reliable way to detect zealotry. Look for the whites above the irises."

"So what do we do?"

Will shot a meaningful glance toward the children outside the glass wall and, raising his voice, said, "The same as always: protect the innocent, above all else."

Zoey almost barked a laugh at that, as she assumed Will was being sarcastic. Then she realized he'd said it for the benefit of the cameras. Whatever meager audience of Zoey fans/beef fetishists had originally joined the broadcast, that audience would have grown exponentially the moment word got out that violent tragedy might be on the way. This time of year, that would matter to Will, as at least some of those people were eligible voters.

Harmonia drew closer and Zoey could make out the uncanny smile and glassy eyes that she did have to admit triggered a primal fear response somewhere deep in her brain. The woman's long hair was in braids and she wore a handmade crown of flowers. She moved with soft, elegant strides on bare feet, flowing between the meat pillars, which seemed to vibrate in response. There were maybe ten of the butterflies flitting around her and, from this range, Zoey could now identify them as mechanical drones, each the size of a child's hand, their wings outlined with threads of piercing blue light.

Harmonia stopped, stared at the nearest twitching meat pillar, then covered her mouth and fell to the floor.

"My god!" she wailed. "My god. My god!"

Zoey got the sense that the woman, Harmonia, was playing up her reaction and just then remembered what Wu had said a moment ago, that the rest of her team (or army? Disciples?) were following remotely. Each of those butterfly drones presumably contained a tiny camera, and each feed was being viewed by who knows how many people who were loyal to the cause or maybe just curious to see if this would end in disaster. Zoey also noticed that Harmonia wore what looked like white elbow-length opera gloves. Whatever power she possessed that had allowed her to slice or punch her way through the roof was probably contained in her hands, so the gloves were likely there for protection, made of some kind of high-tech material that would keep those hands from getting destroyed in the process. Unless she'd chewed her way through with her teeth—Zoey had absolutely seen implants that would allow you to do that, too.

"Welcome to Montana Skies!" said the holographic cow, having detected that someone new had joined the tour. "Would you like me to start the presentation from the beginning or continue from where we left off?"

Zoey stepped around Wu to face the woman, as she assumed it wouldn't look great on camera if she just cowered behind her bodyguard the whole time.

"Uh, hi," Zoey began, noticing that Harmonia wasn't quite making eye contact. "I, uh, know this all looks super weird but there's an explanation for all of it. Do you want the cow to explain?"

"It's worse than I thought," said Harmonia. "I had heard rumors, but seeing the pillars of flesh, are you guys getting this? The way they quiver? I feel like I've descended into Hell. I'm being addressed by the ghouls now, you can see them just over there. It's Zoey Ashe, her right-hand man, Will Blackwater, her bodyguard, and two people who I think are journalists. If you look back by the door, you'll see a pack of ghouls in white, either staff or maybe security, ready to tear me to pieces."

Zoey realized the woman was talking to the streaming audience and ignoring her completely, which was going to make negotiations significantly more difficult, if negotiating was even what she had in mind.

"I am approaching the ghouls now," announced the woman to her flock of butterflies. "Whatever they do to me, you shall serve as witnesses."

"Hello," said Zoey, "and that's 'hello' to you and to everyone joining by, uh, butterfly. Welcome to my beef factory! What can I do for you?"

"As you know, Zoey Ashe owns half of the businesses in this city, her wealth inherited from one of the most notorious crime lords in American history."

"Oh, so you're still talking to them . . ."

"In her mansion, her pet cat has its own lavish suite, while the impoverished children of Tabula Rasa sleep in alleys. Under Zoey's watch, her father's operation has become far more depraved. As you can see."

The butterfly woman gestured to the quivering meat pillars.

Zoey said, "So I guess we're both addressing the streaming audience now. What you said about my dad is true. But he's been dead for over a year and the operation is now as legit as you'll find in this city." Zoey always had to throw in that last qualifier; in Tabula Ra$a, this kind of thing had to be graded on a curve. "I realize this is going to lead to a discussion about whether or not all of his wealth is fruit of a poison tree and if legitimacy can be purchased when the money to purchase it wouldn't have existed if the operation had been legit from the start. I've asked that question myself—many times—and the answer I keep getting is that pretty much every fortune has bloody roots so all we can do is try to make it right. Your name is Harmonia?"

"It is," replied the woman, addressing Zoey directly for the first time. Still, she felt like Harmonia's gaze was passing right through her. "Are the rest of your henchmen here? Or are they out orchestrating some new horror for the city?"

The rest of the Suits were not, in fact, present, as there'd have been no reason to drag the whole team along to tour the cloned hamburger distillery. Hell, Zoey was pretty sure Will had only come as an excuse to avoid some other, worse meeting, probably one involving local politics.

"It's just the ones you see here," said Zoey, "and we don't really plan horrors anymore, the horrors that occur now are pretty much spontaneous and against our will. I actually bought this factory as part of that, the going-legit process. One day, I found out I owned a horse-racing track and that felt like a sleazy business to me so I immediately sold it and bought this instead. It's beef without hurting the cows! I know the manufacturing process is weird to look at, but have you ever seen a slaughterhouse?"

"Mute Zoey Ashe."

"I'm sorry, what?"

"You are muted on my feed. For anyone tuning in, your voice will be silenced and a box will appear over your mouth to prevent the reading of lips. I will not allow you to brainwash my followers with your lies." She gestured to her glowing butterfly drones. "My flock, take out her cameras."

The butterflies zipped around the woman, leaving streaks of blue in Zoey's vision. They swarmed the reporter's three camera drones and, one by one, all three banged to the floor, smoldering and stinking of molten plastic. They then fluttered back to Harmonia and now Zoey wondered if Wu had anything on him that would defeat a pack of electrified insect drones.

She looked to Will. Zoey couldn't read his expression, not now or at any other time. In general, if you ever thought you *could* read Will's expression, it was only because he wanted you to, which meant you still weren't doing it.

The cameraman dropped his control pad and sighed. "Those were twenty thousand dollars each."

Zoey said, "We'll pay for them," then turned to Harmonia. "It looks like you're not here to talk, so what exactly do you intend to do here today? And do you mind if we all just take off and leave you to it?"

Without answering, Harmonia made a gesture toward the nearest quivering meat pillar and the butterflies flew over to it. Half swarmed to the top of the glass pillar, where pipes and conduits ran up to the ceiling in bundles. The rest of the drones clustered at the bottom, where metal brackets attached the apparatus to the floor. Next came sparks and the sizzle of concentrated energy slicing through metal, the drones working it from both ends.

"Wait," muttered Zoey to Will, "is she mad at the meat?"

Will only looked annoyed.

The butterflies kept working until the meat-filled glass column shifted and then tilted on its perch. The whole thing fell over, shattering on the floor, exposing the raw cylinder of wobbling pink flesh. Harmonia strode over on her bare feet until she was standing over the pillar, carrying herself with the solemn grace of a mourner over a casket. Her bare feet had come to rest atop several shards of glass and tiny circles of blood were oozing out. Harmonia seemed not to feel it.

"There it is," she said softly to her unseen audience. "This is what they're putting into your hamburgers, your hot dogs, your tacos. Some of you have eaten this already. Of course, they say this . . . *mass* . . . is the result of extracting cells from a healthy cow, then growing them in a lab. But we know the truth, don't we?"

Zoey rubbed her eyes. "Oh, god. I think I know where this is going."

"You!" shouted Harmonia to one of the white jumpsuits around the front door. "What cow did this 'meat' come from?"

The man glanced nervously at his coworkers. "I . . . don't know," he said, barely loud enough to be heard from back by the doors. "You mean, like, its name? That's not information we would—"

"In what region of the country was it raised?"

"I don't know, ma'am, somewhere out in—"

"What type of cow, then? You'd surely know that, just from working here. Hereford? Texas Longhorn? Wagyu?"

"That first one, I think. That wasn't really my area of—"

"Come here."

"What?"

"You heard me. Come here."

The man, a square-jawed guy who almost seemed to Zoey to be too pretty for this job, tentatively came forward. He stopped some distance from Harmonia, warily eyeing her flock of flapping robotic butterflies.

Harmonia gestured to the fallen meat pillar. "Eat it."

"What?"

"Take a bite of the meat. It's just beef, right?"

He wrinkled his nose. "Well, it's raw. And it's, uh, unfinished . . ."

"He will not consume the meat," announced Harmonia to her audience, "because this meat was not grown from the cells of a cow, but of a human."

Zoey said, "Jesus Christ. Why is it always cannibalism with you weirdos? When I was little, the conspiracies were always about child sex-trafficking, did you guys get bored with that? I mean, at least that's an actual problem in the world. I know you're not going to listen to what I say, and I know that your fans can't listen because you've blocked my mouth, so I'm going to ask out of pure, morbid curiosity: *What possible motivation could we have for feeding human meat to people?* What would we have to gain?"

"You get the lower classes addicted to human flesh and they will begin to hunt and eat one other. You will then sit back in your palaces and laugh as their blood runs in the streets."

Zoey took a moment to compose herself before speaking.

"You know my story, right?" She began. "Not too long ago, I was on minimum wage plus tips and government PDR payments. Now, I know you think all of the rich people in this city are monsters, but I've been dealing with them personally ever since I got here and I can assure you *they are actually much worse.* This whole city was built with casino money—did you know that the games don't run on chance? Those slot machines use software, it's an algorithm that picks payouts based on human psychology. It detects right when the player is about to give up and then throws them a minor win to keep them hooked, or makes the spinning numbers look like they *just* missed a jackpot. Big payouts are timed for when the most tourists will see the flashing lights and get tricked into thinking they could be next. And you know who cleans and maintains all of those towers downtown? It's not robots, it's migrant workers who wiped out their life savings for their papers, then got here and were told they had to work for half the promised pay or get deported. Do you see the theme? This whole city was built on false hope dangled to desperate people like a fishing lure!"

Zoey was getting so worked up that she had to stop and restrain herself before the vein on her forehead started throbbing. Wu was now looking at her with some concern.

Harmonia said, "I am well aware of what people like you do to the downtrodden—"

"I don't think you are!" interrupted Zoey, the words painfully ricocheting around her skull. "Just, do you realize how weird it is that the person who owns the land basically controls everything? Or that a person can own land at all? Then when other people build stuff on and around that land, when other humans do work that makes it livable, the owner of the land gets infinitely rich off it even though they didn't do anything! Owning property is an infinite-money cheat code and nobody sees it as a problem! I have no idea what I'm doing and I just keep getting richer! And no, the enemy isn't a few corrupt billionaires. Below us, all of the CEOs and corporate landlords collude with each other all the time, they fix prices, they keep wages low, you name it. Below them, the executives and middle managers run a system designed entirely to protect their salaries. That's why they won't blow the whistle on the monsters, because they'll lose their stock options and their kids won't get to attend one of the expensive private schools that exist only to choke off the pipeline for anybody outside their class of elites. It's all rigged to keep the money flowing upward, but the second the workers try to organize and gain bargaining power on *their* end, these rich vipers send thugs to break up picket lines with microwave beams that cook people alive. Do you understand what

I'm saying? Harmonia, *you don't need to make stuff up.* Hell, I'll join you, give me some butterflies."

At this point, Zoey figured even the huddle of white jumpsuits by the doors should be ready to rise up and seize the means of production. Harmonia, however, still seemed unmoved. Distracted, even.

There was a crash and the tinkle of glass to her right. Zoey turned toward the glass exterior wall and, beyond it, the lawn with the children. One of the panes had been shattered by the butterfly drones. The tour-group kids outside had reacted to the noise, as had several of the tiny cows.

"Come, children!" shouted Harmonia, stepping toward them. "Come and see what the ruling classes are doing with your flesh."

One of the kids, to Zoey's horror, ran toward the opening in the glass wall, a curly-haired boy who seemed thrilled at the promise of chaos. Then, the rest of the children followed him, their little eyes lighting up at the one thing few human brains can resist: the thrilling promise of novelty.

"No!" yelled Zoey.

"Stay out there!" shouted Wu in his most authoritative voice. "It's dangerous! No! Stay back!"

The curly-haired kid arrived and gawked at the quivering meat pillars. "They're alive!" Then he saw the toppled one among the jagged shards of glass and said, "Look! That one got out! Whoa!"

There was no turning them back now. Twelve children and three small cows came wandering in to witness the awesome wonders of the beef factory. One little girl was stepping tentatively among the columns, eyes wide, her little arms wrapped tightly around herself. The curly-haired boy grabbed her, hustled her toward the toppled pillar, and yelled, "I dare you to put your tongue on it!"

The little girl shrieked. Another boy laughed. Another kid said, "I'll put my tongue on it for a hundred dollars."

Harmonia opened her arms. "Gather around, children. Come and see."

Zoey turned to Wu. "Do something!"

It was clear from Wu's expression that he didn't know exactly what Zoey wanted him to do. He had various methods of incapacitating threats, up to and including incapacitating them right off this mortal coil in smoldering briquettes. But the presence of the children complicated everything.

Will set his eyes on Harmonia and, in a voice that somehow seemed bored, said, "I assume you know that if you hurt these children, your movement is dead forever."

"If *I* hurt these children?" replied Harmonia in a quivering tone that implied her outrage was about to cause her brain to boil out of her ears. "These children, who will see their own flesh multiplied and consumed for generations by a civilization turned into cannibals at the hands of a cabal of ghouls?"

"Hold on," said Zoey. "So we're not just manufacturing man-meat here, but we're taking the starter tissue from kids? Why would we do that? Why?"

"Their meat is the most tender."

"How do you know that?"

The children were getting upset, presumably less because they understood the danger and more because they just hated hearing grown-ups fight. One of the fluffy little cows came over and started sniffing the handsome staffer Harmonia had brought forward earlier, the one who hadn't known his beef trivia.

Harmonia approached one of the children, a tall boy with jet-black hair. "You, young man. You seem to have the proper muscle-to-fat ratio for livestock. Did these people here do anything to you? Did they use a needle, or a thin blade, to withdraw a piece of your flesh?"

The boy looked to Zoey like he was hoping she'd provide him with an answer to what had to have been the most confusing question he'd been asked in his young life.

"They did it to me!" shouted the curly-haired boy, who was now sitting on the floor and playing with bits of broken glass. "They took it from me!"

Harmonia's eyes went wide. "Tell me where."

"From my butt!" shouted the boy, laughing.

"No, I mean—never mind." Harmonia faced Zoey. "You're going to take me to the room where you collect the samples of child flesh. And then you're going to show me where you store them. I'm not allowing you to destroy the evidence the moment I leave."

"Well, there is no such room," said Zoey, "so it looks like we're at an impasse."

Harmonia directed her swarm so that the glowing blue butterflies surrounded the handsome staff member. The cow next to him gave a confused little moo.

Harmonia asked him, "Do *you* want to show me where the children's cells are taken?"

"I don't know anything about that!" he replied. "I don't know anything about this place at all! I, I, uh, don't even work here!"

Harmonia faced Zoey. "Take me to the extraction room, or this man dies."

Zoey looked to Will. She prided herself on not having to rely on him in situations like this or, really, any other. But he still had far, far more experience than she did in this kind of thing. There was a long pause while Will looked back and forth from Harmonia to the man she was holding hostage with her butterflies and then to Wu, who seemed poised to cut the woman down if some kind of resolution could not be reached in the next five seconds or so.

The fluffy little cow grunted and licked its snout.

For the second time that morning, Will uttered a phrase that was utter nonsense to Zoey: "Millie wants you to come home."

Harmonia reacted like Will had just pulled a gun.

Through a clenched jaw, she said, *"Are you threatening my child?"*

Zoey felt the familiar sensation of being simultaneously comforted and terrified that Will was, somehow, several steps ahead.

"You take up the cause of 'children' but you have a child in the city who is your own flesh and blood, whom you have not spoken to in six months. She's thirteen, these are her formative years. She needs a mother, to teach her how to be a woman. You, not her father's carousel of young girlfriends. You've invented this cause to cover for your own failure, for your own cowardice."

"If you speak of her again, I will kill you. You may not think I am capable, but I am."

"I know you are. You received implants from the same supplier that made your moth swarm. That's some expensive hardware. Who paid for it?"

Harmonia was purposefully working her fingers, as if activating the tiny machinery threaded through the muscle and bone. Zoey noted gleaming, diamond-shaped panels on the palms of her gloves.

Zoey said, "Whoa, everybody calm down. This actually seems like the world's easiest problem to solve. Harmonia, take a sample from any of these beef towers. Or all of them. Take it to an independent lab and let them test it. If it doesn't come up human, boom, problem solved. Right? No need for violence. There's no difference of philosophy or morality here, this is just a misunderstanding."

"All your offer tells me is that every lab in the city is on your payroll. Otherwise you wouldn't have suggested it."

"Then take it out of the city, send it to a lab in Europe, wherever. Don't you want proof?"

"If it came up negative for human cells, it'd just mean you swapped the samples during shipping."

"I don't understand, what would serve as proof for you, then?"

"Show me the tissue extraction chamber, like I asked."

"*It doesn't exist.*" Zoey was trying to keep the frustration out of her voice and failing spectacularly. Her headache had reached a point that she was frankly surprised wasn't fatal. "Do you want to tour every room of this facility, to prove to yourself that it doesn't exist? We can do that."

"That would only mean the entrance is hidden. I'm done listening to your lies."

The woman grabbed the little boy who'd claimed he'd had his butt sampled and yanked him to his feet. "You. Show me where they took you, to extract the tissue."

"No!" yelled the curly-haired boy. "You smell weird."

Will said, "I know you didn't pay for this gear yourself. You got fired from your job at the real estate office three months ago, after ranting to customers about human meat in their burgers. The divorce came a week later, right? How much has this cost you, this obsession of yours? What would it mean if it turned out you were wrong this whole time? About this? About everything? What if it turned out that you're being used, that some power-hungry schemer is playing you like a, well, not a violin, that's too sophisticated an instrument. Like a squeaking dog toy."

Harmonia set her jaw. "No. I don't need to see the facility! I have him. I have a witness. Come on."

She started to drag the child away, as if intending to leave with him.

In a panic, Zoey stepped forward and yelled, "Hey! You're not taking him out of here!"

Harmonia kept walking, yanking the child along. And then, chaos ensued.

First, Zoey felt a hand wrap around her bicep. That was Will, restraining her. Enraged, she ripped her arm free and lunged forward, grabbing the hostage kid by his free hand, trying to separate him from Harmonia. In the following few seconds, two distinct images were imprinted on Zoey's brain:

The first was Harmonia, who'd pivoted and raised her hand toward Zoey, a hand that held no weapon because, Zoey knew, it was itself a weapon. Lines of bright blue pulsed across the diamonds in her palm. The second image, spotted just at the outer boundary of Zoey's vision, was Will Blackwater's face. Just moments ago, she'd had the thought that she could never read his expressions. Well, the alarm he showed now was genuine; what was happening was absolutely not what he had been expecting.

There was a flash and instantly Zoey was blind. She fell to the floor, blinking dark orbs out of her vision while chaos erupted all around her. A little girl shrieked. Zoey smelled sizzling meat and hoped it wasn't from a human child. She kept blinking, trying to restore her sight.

Everything was unfolding via a series of vague shapes between her and the windows, a play acted out by thrashing shadow puppets. There was a tall dark figure that she thought was Will, hauling the screaming curly-haired boy away from Harmonia. She saw Harmonia raise her hand as if to fire off another blast of whatever she was summoning from her implants. Before she could, Wu flicked the red ball he'd hidden in his left hand toward the woman. This, Zoey knew, was a nonlethal weapon she'd been briefed on months ago, a shell containing a sticky goo that was like industrial-grade marshmallow. If it hit an armed assailant, the goo would expand several thousandfold to engulf their arms and torso—it would also presumably disable, if not ruin, whatever weapons they wielded.

At the moment the goo capsule impacted Harmonia, she was standing in front of the fluffy little cow. The ball exploded into a pink mass, causing the woman to stumble backward until she fell into the cow. The goo then glued her to the animal, which panicked and took off running toward the opening in the glass, mooing and dragging the now screaming woman that was stuck to its flank. Everyone on the factory floor watched dumfounded as the lowing, shrieking mass went galloping out onto the lawn and into the distance.

The woman's flock of butterfly cameras watched her go for a moment, paused, then slowly followed her out. Several of the children applauded.

Zoey was on her hands and knees, staring at the floor and watching her fingers come into focus. Wu was asking if everyone was okay. She felt a searing burn in her scalp and touched her head. She had a bald streak of raw skin where whatever beam Harmonia had fired at her had missed her brain by millimeters. She looked over her shoulder and found where Harmonia's beam had struck: there was a charred wound in the quivering beef pillar, a tunnel of seared meat that ran all the way through. Zoey sat back and tried to recover while Will and Wu conferred with staff and some security people who had finally arrived (where had *they* been?). Then Will took a call and, after a five-word conversation, walked over and saw the path scorched through Zoey's scalp.

She watched a strange transformation play out on his face: There was initial shock as he realized for the first time what exactly had occurred and, more importantly, what had *almost* occurred. His mouth fell open a little bit, his eyes went wide. Then, after exactly two seconds, his lips snapped closed and he swallowed. Then it was gone, just like that. He'd flipped a switch in his brain and his normal implacable expression took over.

He said, "Can you brush your hair over from the side? We have another meeting."

"What? No, Will, we don't."

"We do now. Something has come up. Another of the girls has gone missing. Come on, security will mop up here."

Zoey had no idea what "girls" Will was talking about or why they would be missing. But it was also one of the few combinations of words that would force her to move. Somewhere, someone was in danger.

Zoey groaned and lay back on the floor for a moment, staring up at the pipes and ductwork crisscrossing the ceiling.

"I need a minute. Are the children from the tour group okay?"

"The staff will tend to them. It'll be easier if we get out of their way before the press gets here. Come on, let's go. Echo will be here in under a minute."

He pulled her to her feet. There was a time in her life when she'd have been shocked by Will's callous desire to press on with the agenda, but she knew the real urgency on his part was about getting her into the car as quickly as possible. Zoey's body had a history of going into shock any time she was nearly killed in spectacular fashion, and Will clearly wanted to get her moving before that could happen. She stood on her own, feeling like both of her legs had been replaced by vibrating Frankenbeef.

"I don't know if I can make it all the way to the car. I may have to lean on you as we go."

"You shouldn't. There are always cameras out there and that's bad optics."

CHAPTER
4

"IS IT BAD?" ASKED Zoey, examining her head wound with her phone's camera.

"It's pretty bad," said Echo Ling, who'd picked them up at the beef plant for the ride back into town. "You have a bald streak right near the crown of your head. It really stands out with your black hair."

Echo, whom the press referred to as Zoey's "technical advisor" or "mysterious Filipina operative," depending on the publication, had almost certainly gotten less sleep than Zoey. You wouldn't know it to look at her, though, thanks to what Zoey attributed to an incredibly unfair distribution of genes and also the fact that Echo wasn't just constantly treating her body like a trash can. She was wearing a black jumpsuit with a keyhole neckline that made it seem like twisting at the waist would cause a boob to pop out. She'd had her hair cut short a week ago, something Zoey felt like she should be arrested for, leaving her with a messy pixie cut that just drew more attention to her stupidly perfect face. Zoey considered Echo her closest friend and Echo probably considered Zoey to be her seventh- or eighth-closest. When they were out in public, people looked at them like a famous model was walking her pet warthog.

Zoey grunted. "Surely somebody can fix it, right? Follicle implants or something?"

"Nope, that's going to be bald forever," replied Echo casually. "No one will ever love you."

"Shut up."

"Zoey, you almost died. We're not worried about your hair."

It's true that you can't judge an individual's personality based on their profession, but the fact that Echo's previous job had involved cheating casinos probably said quite a bit about hers. Her path had crossed Arthur's in one of his joints when she was caught winning at blackjack with a partner and some novel tech that *almost* defeated the most sophisticated anti-cheat system ever devised. Arthur was so impressed by Echo's prowess, audacity, and symmetrical facial features that instead of dumping her in the desert along with all the previous cheats, he offered her a job. There had been some friction between her and Zoey when Zoey had first taken over, but it's remarkable how two women can form a bond over something as simple as surviving a helicopter crash together.

Zoey studied her wound as if she could heal it via sheer concentration. "I have to do a public appearance tonight and then tomorrow, the biggest, most terrifying public appearance of my life, or anyone's life. And everybody's going to be staring at my head."

"It'll give you an interesting story to tell. You know what cures anxiety? Having cool stories ready for the crowd."

"Or," said Will from behind a glass of Scotch, "you could use your old man's method, just tell interesting stories regardless of whether or not they actually happened. Was this the only vehicle you could summon on short notice?"

"No, Zoey specifically asked for it."

They were rolling toward the city in a mobile café that appeared to be shaped like a giant, bus-sized sushi roll (it was technically kimbap, Zoey had been told, the Korean version without the raw fish). There was a single chef behind the counter at one end of the vehicle serving a variety of fast food from the region, including stir-fried spicy rice cakes and weird, dark sausages that were too exotic for Zoey. She was having an Inkigayo sandwich, four thin slices of impossibly soft white bread with alternating fillings of egg and potato salad, coleslaw, and at the center, a thin layer of strawberry jam. It was like a bunch of cool, creamy flavors nesting in a pillow. The interior of the vehicle was coated with screens that could be programmed to create the illusion that the dining commuters were having a nice brunch in Seoul. The displays were off today, so all Zoey saw was Tabula Ra$a's creeping traffic outside. Her people always wanted to be able to see if, say, a vehicle rolled up next to them and started peppering the wheeled kimbap roll with projectiles.

At the moment, they were inching their way toward Tabula Ra$a city limits, which at this particular exit was marked by a giant animatronic statue of a mostly nude woman, straddling all eight lanes and beckoning the drivers forward. It felt more like entering a weirdly horny amusement park than a major city in Utah. Zoey figured tourists loved stuff like this, but the thousands of migrant laborers coming in to work on the city's hundreds of active construction projects probably saw it differently. Though she supposed the giant woman's gesture ultimately meant the same to both: "Come, and be prepared to leave a part of yourself behind."

"So is that Harmonia lady still stuck to the cow?" asked Echo. "Is it just wandering around a pasture somewhere with her screaming on its back?"

"Security team picked her up," muttered Will over his Scotch, as if impatient to change subjects. "They fried her implant, it's a pretty hefty price to get it replaced. I doubt we'll be hearing from her again."

The obvious question for an outsider at this point would be: Why not call the cops? But everyone in the rolling kimbap knew that the police in Tabula Ra$a were just barely there. Those in Zoey's world usually had other, better options. For example, she happened to own the largest rent-a-cop service in the city, and her biggest business headache at the moment was trying to make the concept of privately owned police seem less dystopian to the public than it clearly was.

Zoey said, "If our security team killed her, just tell me."

Will shook his head. "That would have been the wrong move. Her people would have made her into a martyr, claimed we were afraid of what she 'knew.' In fact, her benefactors may have been hoping we would kill her, for that very reason. To stop a movement like that, you need to make it socially radioactive, make it clear that anyone who joins is instantly lowering their own social status. She came off like a clown and the moment was captured on camera for all time. That's a better outcome, in terms of nullifying the threat."

"What group was she with, again?"

"Soylent Black," answered Echo.

"It has something to do with soy? I don't understand."

"There was an old movie," said Will, "about an overpopulated future where they start grinding up people and secretly feeding them to
the hungry as a supplement. In the movie, the human food was called
Soylent Green. Soylent Black is just a play on that, tweaked to sound
scarier, I guess. They're obsessed with human meat in the food supply.
But that's not who paid for those augmentations and the butterflies; I
think that was a gift from a certain politician who's looking to make
headaches for us. Speaking of which, if this situation with the missing
girls is what I think it is, then we're on a ticking clock, and at the worst
possible time."

"Okay, can I have one minute to catch my breath before we rush to this
next thing? My left hand is shaking and I can't make it stop."

"You've got the whole ride over there to get your head right. Those of
us who've been in a combat zone know that's more of a break than you
often get. Sometimes it's more than you want. It's better to move on to the
next task than dwell on the bullet that missed you."

"Oh, no," said Zoey to Echo. "Will is using war metaphors again. Is it
that bad?"

"Her name is Rose," replied Echo. "The missing woman, I mean. She
worked at Chalet."

"Ah, when Will said another 'girl' had gone missing, I thought he
meant a child." Part of Zoey's inheritance was a small army of sex workers
of all types and genders, whom people within the industry had a habit of
referring to as "girls." "She was an escort?"

"These aren't escorts," said Will. "Escorts go to parties with you, these
are prostitutes."

"And there's been more than one? And they're getting, what, abducted
and murdered?"

"Not necessarily. It might be more complicated. Axolotl will know
more. If she's been killed, that's bad, obviously. But if someone is holding
her and the other two who've gone missing, that might be worse."

"Worse than dead? Worse for who, them or us?"

"Everyone." He shrugged. "The world. Everything, what happened
just now, what's about to happen—we have to look at it through a political

lens. That's just the situation right now, everything that comes our way could be carefully crafted to shape public perception."

In her time in the city, Zoey had been making a heroic mental effort to never think about local politics, as the office of mayor of Tabula Ra$a was like the hood ornament on a car that was trying and failing to ramp a volcano. She knew the election was important—or at least, she heard the men in her life constantly telling her it was—but if three women were tied up in some predator's makeshift dungeon, Zoey cared less about the electoral implications and more about getting someone to find that dungeon and kick the door in.

"If this is the third to go missing," asked Zoey, "why am I just now hearing about it?"

"The first," said Will, "wasn't necessarily news, sex workers go missing, it happens. When the second failed to show up to work a week ago, that was enough to get it on our radar, but it's three that officially makes it a pattern."

"Well, it's good to know there's a rule."

Wu, in a tone that was unfamiliar to Zoey, spoke up for the first time. "As eager as you are to move on to the next crisis, please allow me to circle back for a moment to the one we just left. I am very interested in how that woman was able to get into such close proximity to Zoey without us knowing about it until the very last minute."

It was only then that Zoey realized that Wu had been stewing in a silent rage for the entire commute. He was fixing a cold, unwavering gaze on Will.

Zoey said, "Yeah, that was my big question, too. Also, does anybody have a hat I can wear?"

"My guess," replied Will, "is that she showed up last night and hid on the roof until morning, inside a duct or HVAC housing. Then when she heard us come in, she cut her way through."

"That's your 'guess'?" asked Zoey. "That's oddly specific."

"That's what I'd do. The grounds are secured before any visit—Wu was on-site for that—but I doubt the roof gets that close of an exam." He flicked his eyes toward Wu. "Right?"

"The issue," said Wu, making a clear effort to keep his voice even, "isn't the woman's physical presence at the building, but that we some-how had no intel about her plan. This was an orchestrated stunt. Did this fanatic's followers really not know in advance the broadcast was coming? And if her fans did know, how did *we* not know?"

"Do you have any idea how many active threats against Zoey are pending at any given moment? And what tiny percentage turn out to be genuine? The challenge isn't detecting them, but filtering the noise. Budd manages threat assessment but he probably thought 'hippie robot-butterfly attack' was not plausible enough to cancel the tour."

Zoey took a bite of her sandwich and watched Will carefully. Echo was drilling her gaze into her phone, looking like she wished she could eject herself from the vehicle and be spared the tension.

"To be clear," began Wu, "you were well-familiar with Harmonia be-fore today. You knew her whole life story—her daughter, her divorce . . ."

"She's been out there for a while, making noise, one of the many cra-zies trying to make a name for themselves by chewing on Zoey's ankles. We have profiles on all of them, it's the list of names I run through to keep myself from sleeping at night."

Zoey and Wu shared a glance. She strongly suspected that Wu was thinking the exact same thing she was.

She said, "You knew she would be there today."

"No," replied Will evenly. "Of course not."

Zoey felt a sensation she only felt around Will Blackwater: the sense that she was *almost* detecting a lie. It was maddening, like thinking you saw a fly but being unable to catch it in your gaze. Wu shifted in his seat and Zoey was sure that, at this moment, he wanted to knock Will's teeth out.

"And another thing," she said, "why was that beef worker so hot?"

"*What?*"

"The guy in the jumpsuit, the one Harmonia interrogated who didn't know anything about cows. He didn't work there, did he? The guy had plucked eyebrows, a spray tan, and a haircut that probably cost more than mine."

"None of them worked there," said Will, as if this was old, irrelevant information. "We hired them to play the role of staff for the event today."

Zoey wanted to demonstrate her anger by throwing her sandwich down, but she didn't want it to come apart, so she wound up kind of gently setting it on her plate, just a little faster than normal.

"*Why didn't you tell me?*"

"I'm sure it came up in the briefing. Andre oversaw all of that, we brought them over from that pornographic dinner theater you own. And why does it matter? It was just part of the window dressing for the tour."

"You brought in fake staff because you knew there was going to be an incident."

"We brought in fake staff because a lot of the resistance to vat beef is that it puts a whole bunch of people out of work up and down the supply chain. That building used to be a meatpacking plant that employed seven hundred, this operation can be run by six. Not six hundred—six people. It's all automated. We're trying not to advertise the fact that those other workers lost their jobs."

"Why didn't we just, you know, not fire them?"

"If you want new world-saving tech to be cost-competitive enough for adoption, this is how it happens. Labor is expensive, if you're rooting for tech to get cheaper, you're rooting for people to lose their jobs. When cars were invented, a whole lot of people in the stagecoach industry had to find new careers, it's the circle of life. And let me point out that the meatpacking industry in America averages about two amputations a week: fingers, hands, arms ripped off by machinery. We're not only doing them a favor, but we're likely *reducing* the amount of human tissue in the nation's hamburgers."

Wu put up a hand. "We're getting off the subject. See, another thing is I couldn't help but notice that while you could have written the book on high-pressure negotiations, you made no effort to de-escalate here. In fact, you just kept provoking that unstable woman until she flew into a rage."

"Of course I did, she was trying to stage a moment on-camera to advance her interests, I staged one to advance ours. I knew you had the tools to stop her from getting away with one of the hostages. It only went wrong when Zoey lunged in."

"Wait," said Zoey, suddenly losing her appetite. "Wait. Just . . . wait. It was your idea to have the children there."

"I recall it was more of a group decision, but that's your next generation of customers, you want them to feel—"

"No," interrupted Zoey, "that's not what I'm saying. You made a point of telling Harmonia that if any kids got hurt on-camera, that her movement was dead forever. She knew you were right."

Will didn't reply. He was going to make Zoey state the accusation out loud.

"So you knew that having the kids on-site would limit her options," continued Zoey. "You knew she was coming, you arranged for the children to be there. You used them as human shields."

It was clear Will had been fully anticipating this allegation. He didn't set his drink down or bother to make meaningful eye contact. "Not everything that plays out in our favor is due to some Machiavellian scheme on my part. Finish your sandwich, we're almost there."

"Don't tell me what to do," said Zoey, biting her sandwich. "You work for me."

Wu gave Will a humorless grin. "No matter what you do, you just have endless faith in your ability to smooth it over afterward, don't you? As long as we keep focusing on the next thing, we'll never stop and examine what happened before. Ever forward, right? Like a bullet train."

The two men stared at each other in silence and Zoey felt the tension in her guts. Then Will pulled up something on his phone and made it clear he'd moved on. A hologram of a woman's head appeared over his screen, maybe one of the missing women. Zoey turned her gaze to the window.

They were exiting onto an off-ramp that wrapped between two towers, each of which was covered head to toe in video screens. At the moment, they were displaying opposing advertisements: On the left was an ad for mayoral candidate Leonidas "That Surely Can't Be His Real First Name" Damon, whose slogan was "Take Back the City from the Scumbags." On the right was a less bombastic, if equally flashy, ad for his opponent, "Megaboss" Alonzo Dunn, whose slogan was "Twenty Dollars Off at Any of My Stores, With Proof of Your Vote for Me."

Zoey looked to Echo and sighed. "Please tell me you have some headache medicine on you."

CHAPTER
5

LEGITIMIZING SEX WORK IN the USA was, to put it mildly, a tricky business. The customer base was almost entirely male but only about ten percent of men nationwide have paid for sex at any point in their lives, and only some tiny fraction of those are frequent customers. So in a city in which full-service sex work is effectively legal and allegedly without stigma, how do you go about attracting that massively untapped sector of the market that is the other ninety percent? Do these curious outsiders want to feel like they're taking a walk on the wild side, into something seedy and exotic where the illicit danger is a turn-on? Or do they want it normalized and comfortable, the way aboveboard massage parlors try to soothe away clients' inhibitions about being touched?

The answer that Zoey's father had come up with was that there was no single answer. He instead opened a whole series of bordellos geared toward every class of customer. There were seedy brothels with entrances hidden in alleyways or in the backs of legit businesses, often "exotic" joints full of incense and silk that gave off the vibe of an old-timey sailor's favorite haunt on shore leave. On the opposite end of the spectrum were "Business Professional" establishments like the Chalet Intimacy Parlor, fronted by a smiling, cute-as-a-button receptionist behind an oval front desk with a trickling fountain looming behind her. Its location couldn't be more public, on the middle floor of a twenty-story vertical shopping mall shaped like a giant crystal donut tipped on its side, one of more than four hundred businesses at a tourist landmark that served more than a hundred thousand customers a day. Chalet's location, nestled among all of those bustling shops and restaurants, was a crucial part of the strategy.

After all, just because nobody was getting arrested for selling sex in Tabula Ra$a didn't mean the customers' spouses or partners would be okay with any particular transaction. A man spotted on Blink entering a "massage parlor" in a seedy part of town could only be there for one reason, but a man visiting a shopping mall could be there to, say, buy a new necklace for his loving wife. Thus, once in the building, there were numerous ways to get into Chalet without attracting special notice, including via a narrow entrance tucked away in the hardware section of the mall's largest department store next door. Even a man spotted taking that route had plausible deniability: on the way to the parlor there were restrooms, vending machines, water fountains—he could have any number of reasons to be back there. Secrets, Will liked to say, are the fragile threads that hold all of society together. Zoey's people, on the other hand, walked right in through the main entrance of Chalet as if they owned the place, because they did.

The receptionist was playing a game on her phone and, without looking up, began to say, "Welcome to . . ."

Her words died when she saw Will. She reacted like he was wearing a vest made of dynamite.

She dropped her phone and sat bolt upright in her chair. "Hi. Hello. What can I do for you? Can I get Axol? I think they're—"

"Yes, please," said Will. "Axol called us. About Rose."

"Oh. Oh, yes. Sure. Of course."

The receptionist reached for her phone and seemed to be trying to remember how it worked. One of the escorts came out from the back, saw Will, froze, then pivoted and quickly went back the way she came.

The receptionist finally punched a button and said, "Axol, Will Blackwater is here to see you." She glanced up and nervously scanned the visitors. "And Zoey, and Echo Ling, and Zoey's, uh, guy. With the sword."

They all stood in awkward silence until a pair of high heels came angrily clomping down the hall. Axol stepped into view wearing a spectacular wig the color of a sunlit oil slick and a skin-tight dress that appeared to be made from the scales of a mythical lizard.

"What took you so long to get here?" shouted Axol. "Rose could be in a basement or in Heaven, either way she ain't here and her clients don't take substitutes. Rose had that Farm Girl look, hair down to her ass, you don't just replace that kind of wholesomeness overnight. That business is just lost, gone."

Will glanced back at a customer who'd just cautiously ventured in, then asked, "Can we take this somewhere private?"

"What, you afraid I'm intimidating the clients? You know there's an Asian dude with a samurai sword standing behind you. Well, come on, then."

Axol led them back to an office and closed the door. There was a smoldering cigarette in an ashtray and a rack of several dozen wigs behind the desk.

"Do you remember the conversation we had about your outfits?" asked Will. "What you wear here isn't the same as what you could wear at the Den. The guys who come here are looking for middle-class professional."

"This is the most middle-class professional outfit I've got, William. Doesn't show anything. You ask me to fill in, I fill in. You want to hire somebody permanent so I can go back to my joint? Go out and find some madam who dresses like a lawyer, one of those ladies that's always got a scowl on her face so you know she's not one of the pros. Now, do you wanna talk about dress code for the rest of the day or do you want to address our crisis?"

Zoey said, "What you said when we came in, you phrased that like we're worried about the lost business. I just want to make it clear, that's not what we're concerned about here. So you don't have to frame it that way for us."

"Who are you?"

Zoey was left speechless for a moment. "I'm . . . Zoey Ashe."

"She owns this establishment," said Will. "And several hundred other businesses in the city and around the globe? Arthur Livingston's daughter? She inherited Arthur's sprawling empire after he was murdered by rivals? In an event that resulted in the destruction of several buildings? Last fall she survived a public assassination attempt at a Halloween parade? Then the destroyed parade float won first prize for Best Float because the organizers didn't realize that wasn't part of the show?"

Axol waved a hand. "I don't keep up with office politics. You shave that streak through your head on purpose? Never mind, I don't wanna know. This ordeal with Rose, I tell you, it's those religious nut jobs. The fundies with the angels? They've been running off all the customers since January."

Zoey looked to Will and then Echo. "Who are they, again?"

Echo said, "Members of an activist group who call themselves the Liberators. They were doing protests outside the brothels, shaming customers coming in. They wear white robes and masks. It's unsettling, to say the least. They have drones that look like avenging angels, hovering above to remind people they're being watched. They became active right around the time the election started heating up."

Axol nodded. "You should see 'em at night, how they light up. The first time I saw it, thought it was the Rapture. I was like, 'There goes seventy-five percent of our customers, sucked up into Heaven.' It turned out to be this gang of puritans. Had a similar effect, though. On the business, I mean."

"And we think these people are kidnapping the girls now?" asked Zoey.

"Don't know. Rose didn't come in, roommate says she got a visit from some folks the other night, but didn't have details as they have an unspoken agreement not to pry into each other's private affairs. I been up for thirty hours, trying to track down any crumb of information. Everybody's upset, everybody loved Rose. Absolute sweetheart. And she makes three."

"I'm dumb about the business at the ground level so I'm going to ask a question that is probably stupid, so just bear with me: How do we know she and the others didn't just quit and/or leave town for their own reasons? Doesn't this job have a really high turnover rate?"

Axol's face showed that this question wasn't just stupid, but also offensive.

Before Axol could answer, Will jumped in. "It'd actually be very surprising if all three just left without notice. Girls go missing for violent reasons often enough that it's an unspoken rule that you let somebody know if you're looking to change cities or careers. They keep a lookout for each other. And of course, DeeDee keeps track, when she can."

"And you think they're all being abducted by these religious types? And what? Killed? Held prisoner somewhere? That doesn't sound like the Christian thing to do."

Axol stared at Zoey. "Bitch, have you ever opened a history book?"

Will said, "We don't know anything yet. These people are at the top of our list, let's leave it at that."

"Do we have a picture of Rose?" asked Zoey. "And the others?"

Will got a look on his face like he wasn't sure why Zoey would need this. It wasn't like she was going to personally embark on a manhunt. Still, somebody shot them over to Zoey's phone. She pulled up holograms that were clearly from the Chalet promotional materials, each of the three women depicted lying in bed, apparently naked, giving alluring looks to the camera. Rose was the kind of woman guys would call "plain," meaning she had hair, teeth, skin, and a figure that most women would kill for, but kept her makeup subtle and her hair dye natural. Just a notch below perfect, enough that customers could convince themselves her smile was genuine, as if she was pleased with their attention. Zoey imagined that face buried under the sand outside of the city, getting eaten by bugs. Or filthy and bloody, in the dark of some basement, maybe one within walking distance of where she was sitting. She quickly swiped the images off her phone, the holograms dispersing into pixels like smoke.

She met Axol's eyes. "Whatever the reason, wherever Rose is, she's going to be the last to disappear."

"Oh, I believe you mean that. Your daddy was the same way. Nothing got him riled up more than when customers broke the merchandise."

"That's not what I—"

"I've messaged Budd to jump on this," interrupted Will. "With any luck we'll have actionable information in the next few hours."

This was the second time in half an hour that Will had referenced Budd Billingsley in his capacity of Man Who Knows What Our Enemies Are About to Do. Will had once said that US intelligence agencies have sophisticated software to scan social media for overheard conversations and suspicious actions in order to build an intricate map of national security threat vertices. They could have saved the money, he'd said, just by hiring Budd.

"Is there anything else?" asked Will, who stood without waiting for an answer.

"Is that a serious question?" replied Axol. "Because if it is, you people still need to fix our vending machines. You push the button, nothing comes out."

"We're not doing this again. The machines aren't broken. If you want coffee and sandwiches to come out, Axol, *you have to put money in them first.*"

"That sounds broken to me, considering what my people go through for this company. Especially in light of what we just discussed. All that stuff should be free."

"We tried that. Once. You know what happened? One enterprising young lady finished her shift, pushed the buttons over and over until the whole machine was empty, put it all in a box, and went up and sold it in the mall's food court. Then she bought weed with the money. The stuff she didn't sell, she threw in the trash. If you give anything away for free without limits, you're automatically setting it at the wrong price and the market will adjust. The cost isn't due to greed, it's to make sure you value the sandwich enough to actually eat it. And these sandwiches aren't five hundred dollars, they're five dollars, anybody can afford that."

Axol looked to Zoey. "Will here, and the other guys in suits, they all meet at your office?"

"What? Uh, yeah. I mean, it's at my house."

"And if they ask for something to eat or drink, from your wet bar or what have you, do you charge 'em for it?"

"You know she doesn't," interjected Will wearily.

"Because everybody involved is rich enough that you don't have to worry about them abusing it, right? So we give away free stuff based on how much you *don't* need it. Interesting."

Zoey said, "We'll make the machines free. If they have to be restocked more often, fine."

Axol smiled and looked back to Will, "Oh, you should bring her along every time you visit. I like this dynamic." She looked back to Zoey. "He can't say no to you, can he?"

"I'm his boss, so, no."

"You think that's the reason, huh? All right, we're wasting time. As soon as you know something about Rose and the rest, I want to know it five seconds later. Now get on outta here."

CHAPTER
6

ZOEY ASSUMED THAT SOMEDAY in the future, she would be able to approach her own property and *not* feel like she was an intruding peasant who was about to be chased off by a pack of mean dogs. That day had not yet come.

It didn't help that negotiating the path to her home did, in fact, look a lot like sneaking in. While the front was marked by a huge set of ornate gates and a winding path through some very expensive (and lethal) landscaping, she never went in that way. Getting to the rear garage entrance of the Casa de Zoey meant driving past the turn that led to the estate (Livingston Boulevard) and continuing for a few miles beyond the point where Zoey's sprawling lawn became a patch of man-made woods. Then, they turned down a gravel road that led directly to a pond and simply ended, as if it was parking for visitors who wished to stop and feed the ducks. In reality, it was the beginning of what her people called the *kūlgrinda*, named after the ancient hidden roads that lay under the swamps of Lithuania, forming paths that were safe for locals but lethal to invaders. The sedan drove directly into the pond, as a few inches under the mossy water was a polymer bridge anyone could drive across if they knew the irregular S-shaped path (if not, their entire vehicle would wind up submerged, with the front end wedged into the thick mud at the bottom). Any vehicle would be watched along the way by the resident mallards, most of which were not real, but rather mechanical decoys with cameras that would alert house staff of any unauthorized visitors attempting the crossing.

Once safely across, the path through the woods was winding and narrow and, at three separate points, appeared to come to another dead end (one of which was a fallen white-fir tree that, upon recognizing an authorized vehicle, would lift itself out of the way). If you made it through, you would arrive at what appeared to be a mossy boulder the size of a house. When an authorized vehicle pulled up, the rock would rise and reveal the downward ramp to the estate's parking garage. Or you might show up to find that the entrance was already standing wide open, as was the case when Zoey's armored sedan rolled up today.

"It must not have closed behind us," said Wu, studying the yawning entrance for signs of ambush. "Wait here."

Zoey, Will, and Echo waited while he ventured on foot into the garage, Zoey browsing through Blink feeds on her phone. This wasn't that unusual of an occurrence; a sensor was supposed to automatically close the rock behind them upon leaving, but sometimes pine needles blew in front of it, making it think there was an obstruction. Wu returned and gave the all clear and they rolled down past two dozen gleaming vehicles that Zoey had never driven. That had been her father's thing, exotic sports cars that could go nearly three hundred miles an hour and whose tires alone probably cost more than any home Zoey had ever lived in as a kid. She needed to do something with those cars but wasn't sure what. Auction them off? Give them away? Put a brick on the accelerators and watch them fly off a cliff, one after the other? Just another of the thousand things on her to-do list.

Zoey, Will, and the rest of the team had been scheduled to gather for a noon meeting at the house, but not to discuss the beef-factory ambush or the missing sex workers. This meeting had been scheduled in advance of both incidents, to discuss the two huge events that had been dominating Zoey's time and energy for the past couple of months: the music festival in the desert—complete with the Sunday-evening appearance Zoey had been so profoundly dreading—and the stupid mayoral election on the following Tuesday.

When Zoey stepped out of the elevator (it opened behind a sliding bookcase, keeping with her father's ridiculous design philosophy), she told Echo she'd meet everyone in twenty minutes. Then she veered off down the hall and up the huge twin staircase in the foyer, finally stopping at the bedroom belonging to her cat, Stench Machine. Zoey had no idea how the press found out Stench had his own room, but she'd never heard the end of it. What difference did it make, if the bedroom already existed and would otherwise sit empty? She got on the floor and took time to apologize to the cat for leaving the house, which was one of Zoey's habits that he found intolerable. Then she stopped by the bedroom of her other, newer cat, Knockoff, thinking that if the press found out she had *two* cat-dedicated rooms, they'd crucify her. But the truth was this was done out of necessity; the cats hated each other due to a series of bitter differences that would seem irreconcilable even to a UN arbitrator.

Back in the hall, she ran into Carlton, holding a basket of laundry.

"Ms. Ashe," he said as a greeting, "I can't help but notice your hair. Is that . . . on purpose?"

"A crazy lady shot me with some kind of direct-energy weapon. Can you get me some ointment or something? It burns."

"Of course. Shall I make an appointment with the doctor?"

"Not yet, maybe it'll heal on its own. I don't think it burned all the way down to my brain but we'll see if I'm missing any memories or motor skills."

"Very good."

She arrived at her own bedroom, which was just one of the guest bedrooms that she'd had remodeled rather than using the elaborate master suite that her father had built (it occupied almost the entirety of the third floor, she almost never went up there). She shuffled in, closed the door, kicked off her shoes, then pulled her meat-pattern dress over her head and flung it aside. Then she crawled into her bed, curled up, pulled the comforter up over her face, and started shivering.

It was uncontrollable, less like a chill and more like electrocution, like all of the tiny muscles under her skin were rioting.

It passed, eventually, mostly. Then Zoey got up and checked herself in the mirror. The wound in her scalp was worse every time she saw it, not because it was actually getting worse, but because in between glimpses she was convincing herself it surely wasn't as bad as she remembered. It looked like somebody had glued a thin strip of raw bacon to her head. She pulled her dress back on and fixed her makeup. She went to the door, went out into the hall, turned around, went back into the bedroom, closed the door, grabbed a pillow, put it over her face, and screamed with everything she had. Then she flung the pillow aside, went back to fix her makeup again, and left for the meeting. In the hall, she glanced back to notice Wu had, at some point, silently fallen in behind her.

Zoey had spent her youth bouncing around various public housing units, often moving before the stuff had even been fully unpacked from the previous move. She had thus never dreamed of living in a giant, rock-star mansion; her "wouldn't it be nice" fantasy was a cozy little apartment in New York City, maybe overlooking some water or a park, within walking distance of cute little cafés and a bodega that always had a cat sleeping on the counter. She'd thought it'd be a place where she could raise a kid—in particular, a daughter—and have the kind of horizon-broadening cultural experiences that Zoey had only ever watched on a screen. It was her last long-term boyfriend, Caleb, who'd informed her that in real life, those cute little apartments now go for twenty grand a month and are rented exclusively by well-heeled professionals and trust-fund kids. So even that dream became the equivalent of hoping to someday walk on Mars.

Now she slept in what to her was a vast fiefdom that felt like the manifestation of a neurosis: the man who insisted he needed this much house was objectively weirder than one who, say, insisted that his dinner consist of two hundred ice-cream cones. The mansion was surrounded by acres of lawn as manicured as a major-league outfield (she shuddered to think about how much irrigation it took to keep it looking like that in this part of the country), with strategically placed groves of what Zoey thought of as Christmas trees (blue spruce, according to Carlton). She used that land for absolutely nothing and told herself it was at least acting as a nature preserve, though she had no idea if the grounds security would allow something like a mule deer to even set down a hoof without triggering an alarm. The Casa de Zoey itself encompassed some 60,000 square feet, including eight bedroom suites, fifteen bathrooms, a giant kitchen that could supply an upscale restaurant, a small indoor swimming pool, a sauna, a trampoline room, a ball pit, a cigar humidor, a movie theater, and a number of other rooms Zoey hadn't set foot in since just after moving in, three of which she was certain were haunted. There was apparently about to be an outdoor pool in the courtyard, or maybe it was a koi pond? She had forgotten what she'd asked for and figured she'd let it be a surprise.

If she'd had to rank all of the rooms, the Buffalo Room (formerly the salon, or drawing room) was definitely in the bottom five, down there among the haunted ones. It was so named by Zoey because of a stuffed buffalo head mounted over the gigantic fireplace (which was fake, just holographic flames over hidden electric heating elements). The room was all wood paneling and leather chairs, the kind of cigars-and-brandy room rich jerks loved to sit around in while complaining about how the poor work ethic of immigrants caused the Great Depression. These days, it was one of the rooms in which the public assumed the Suits met to pull the strings on the city's proverbial puppet show and, well, they weren't entirely wrong.

It was in this room that Zoey had met the Suits as a team for the first time, and she would not be the last person to take one look and assume they would not be leaving the room alive. It was also in this room that, months ago, the team had gathered and hammered out a very specific and foolproof plan to rig the upcoming election in favor of their guy, "Megaboss" Alonzo Dunn, whom the press referred to as an "alleged crime lord" or a "confirmed crime lord," depending on the publication. This had involved boosting a very weak opponent in the primaries, a local tycoon by the name of Titus Chobb, who had the exact charisma of a dripping garbage bag and a vast array of closet skeletons that could be strategically surfaced during the second-round runoffs between him and Alonzo. Everything had played out according to plan until six weeks ago, when Chobb landed in the hospital after a bout of what can only be called an outburst of Blimp Rage.

Chobb had famously run his companies from an office on board a black dirigible that floated around the city. Another billionaire had moved to town and decided he liked the idea and so bought his own, larger blimp. One day his blimp was parked on a rooftop docking port that had been reserved for Chobb, prompting Chobb to order his airship to ram the other. This, unfortunately, caused the passenger hold to dislodge and plummet to the streets below, leaving Chobb's body a twisted wreck that would require months of recovery. The announcement that he was dropping out of the race was delivered on-camera by his son, possibly against his father's wishes. This triggered a wave of conspiracy believers to blame the incident on the Suits, possibly because "incapacitate opponent in a slow-motion blimp duel" is exactly the type of plan Zoey would have come up with. But all this did was allow the party to swap in the next-closest finisher from the primaries, Leonidas Damon, a man who had none of Chobb's weaknesses and for whom the Suits had no active plan of attack. He was also boosted by voters who rallied around the fallen Chobb, again under the assumption that his injuries were due to evil machinations by the opposing party and not his impulsive decision to risk his own safety in a violent airborne blimpdown. This was what outsiders never understood about the Suits, even going back to the reign of Zoey's father: there usually were plans in place but, in the end, the endemic chaos of the universe would always have its say.

Zoey headed directly toward her lone addition to the Buffalo Room, a giant beanbag chair that now occupied easily a quarter of the floor space (they'd had to move out a leather sofa to accommodate it). It was six feet high and she could fully disappear into it; she thought of the crater her body created in the beanbag as her own private office. On the way, she was blocked by the broad body of Andre Knox, whom the press referred to as her team's "public relations manager" or "iron-fisted enforcer," depending on the publication. He was wearing a green suit and tie that Zoey thought made him look like a huge, bald, Black leprechaun.

At the sight of Zoey, he said, "Damn, you shaved a kwahom into your hair."

"A what?"

"Reverse mohawk."

"I didn't shave it, a witch fired a curse at me. It barely missed."

"Yeah, I heard, I was just giving you a hard time. You're handling it well."

"You knew I almost died and you decided to make fun of my hair anyway?"

"This is how we show love where I'm from! You know that! Take a seat. Not in the beanbag, you won't be able to see from there."

Echo had already taken the only other comfy chair, the unofficial prize for being early. Will was leaning against the mantel and sipping his drink. He had once told Zoey that he sometimes preferred to stand in order to easily see everyone in the room, but she suspected he just had lower back problems.

Once Zoey was seated, Andre began. "Budd is chasing down the Rose situation, he may stumble in at some point, but we're not going to wait."

He dimmed the room and a hologram flashed out from a projector on the ceiling, sculpting a model of light that covered the floor. It was a 3D representation of the music festival setup just outside the city: A ring of six massive stages faced outward, forming a circle. Outside the stages were six circular platforms that would each generate a 20x-scale holographic representation of whatever was happening on the stage nearest to it. Inside the circle of stages were the main campgrounds and food tents, at the center of which was a looming structure made to look like a beehive, with tiny dots buzzing around it, as if it actually housed insects. Oozing around the floor of the glowing model was a carpet of squirming pixels, like an ocean of maggots.

"All right," announced Andre, "Day Two of the Desert Catharsis Music and Art Festival, held in Utah's scenic West Desert, five miles outside city limits in lovely Beaver County. A hundred and twenty acts, twice that many vendors, and ten million headaches—"

"Can't we just skip this part?" asked Zoey. "We already know this, it's been the subject of, like, a hundred straight meetings. Or are you doing the intro again just to show off your laser-light model?"

Andre glared across the holographic beams. "Do I disrupt the energy of your meetings? It's hard enough for me to speak in front of a group, I have to be heckled while I do it?"

Echo said, "We can skip right to talking about the election, if you'd prefer."

"Oh, god. Yeah, Andre, talk about the concert as long as you want. And the hologram looks good, you even animated little people in there."

"Those are not animated. This is a live look at the current position of all two hundred and thirteen thousand, five hundred and twenty-nine human beings on festival grounds. Sorry, twenty-eight, one guy just left.

This includes live biometric data of every single individual, including their current heart rate, level of agitation, and intoxication."

"We can even tell you which of them have full bladders," added Echo. "And we obviously didn't make this for the meeting, it's a visualization feed from the live-monitoring software."

"And as far as the election goes, the two subjects are not unrelated, which is what we're here to talk about, as I would have explained had Zoey not so rudely interrupted me."

"Sorry," said Zoey.

"Too late, you're now dead to me. If anybody else interrupts, I'm canceling the whole festival. Now, as you all know, we have one goal, which is to prevent a whole bunch of kids from having to get hauled away in ambulances or in whatever truck they throw you into if you're already dead before the ambulance gets there. That, of course, is the main challenge of Catharsis every year, but this year, the music festival ends Monday morning and the mayoral voting begins twenty-four hours later. So now we've got slimeball candidate Leonidas Damon doing a surprise voter-registration drive right there on the campgrounds—we were unable to dissuade him—and that means Alonzo will have his volunteers doing the same by this afternoon, and both parties will bring their own security. You can see where this is heading: The alcohol, hormones, and music are already whipping the crowd into a frenzy. You throw political tribalism into the mix and you've got yourself a powder keg."

Zoey muttered, "I think I need a drink."

Zoey's company organized and sponsored Catharsis at a tremendous loss every year—the tickets cost less than a bottle of water at other music festivals. Her father had believed that this type of thing was another kind of investment, figuring that being known as the fun oligarch could be useful should the time come for the people to elect a government that was actually capable of, say, regulating local businesses. Last year, there were two fatalities: one when an audience member jumped off an amp tower, incorrectly assuming the crowd below would catch him, and another when a pyrotechnic malfunctioned onstage, killing a bassist. The first twenty-four hours of this year's festival had been unblemished, but no one had taken that as a reason to relax. In theory, the presence of the mayoral candidates shouldn't have changed the equation (since when do a bunch of college kids on hallucinogens care about municipal politics?), but Leonidas Damon was a celebrity, a Blink pundit famous for his rants about ridding the world of filth and immorality. So, no, the festival kids didn't care about the office of mayor, but they had *very* strong feelings about Damon and his movement. The smirking kids who wore his bombastic T-shirts generally knew not to wear them to certain neighborhoods.

As for Zoey, she was scheduled to appear onstage on Sunday evening, right before the headliners would usher in the festival's climax. This had been the big red circle on her calendar, the event she'd been dreading so much that she'd spent months frantically changing the subject every time it came up. The idea that, instead of her brief, generic statement of appreciation, she'd possibly have to stand up in front of a quarter-million human beings and issue some kind of apology or condolences for a fatal incident was too much for her to even contemplate. She physically did not have the capacity to feel that kind of anxiety right now.

"And with that," said Andre, "I pass the baton to Echo, to explain why the situation is even worse than what I just said."

Echo stood with her feet in the middle of the hologram, making it appear she'd just crushed five hundred tiny people under her heels. While it's true that roles within the Suits were ill-defined, event planning would definitely not be in Echo's job description, if she had one. But this particular event was just a means to an end and those ends are what required Echo's unique set of skills.

"As you know," she began, "the goal is to have just enough visible security to deter violence without reaching the threshold where it starts to ruin the vibe."

A scattering of wiggling green and red dots appeared, interspersed among the crowds.

"The green dots are where security personnel are positioned. The red are where we need people but don't have them because one of the security contractors dropped out. That left us a hundred short, so we put out a call for volunteers after the gates opened. That did *not* go well."

"Nobody answered the call?" asked Zoey, genuinely shocked by that.

"In this city? No, that's not the issue."

"Oh, right. Too many."

Echo nodded. "Too many who think a glowing security vest is a blank check to break jaws with impunity. Weeding out applicants is a nightmare when you're trying to find ones who can start immediately. Especially when half of the applicants are claiming to have strength enhancements, as if that's a selling point and not the biggest and reddest flag."

Zoey imagined an overenthusiastic guard grabbing a drunk reveler and tossing him over a fence two hundred feet away. "Yeah, I can see that getting out of hand."

"And then there's the issue with the trash," said Echo as a collection of orange dots appeared, some of them blinking. "Remember when we arranged to have those new receptacles brought in, the ones that suck the refuse down into an underground chamber and burn it? It turns out half of them don't work and so we have to arrange for staff to do collection on the bins, which they're struggling to keep up with."

"It seems like we're now getting into minor details that other people can worry about."

"Actually, the buildup of garbage ties directly in to the political aspect," replied a new voice from the door, "and I don't just mean that in a metaphorical sense."

Budd Billingsley had appeared at some point, wearing a cream-colored suit and cowboy boots, holding a Stetson in both hands. Budd, whose role within the organization the press referred to as "ambiguous" or "a dark secret," depending on the publication, spent most of his working days talking to people. Not having meetings, necessarily, just . . . talking to people. He possessed an ability that to Zoey was as astonishing and unfathomable as the gift of prophecy: he could walk into a room of hundreds of strangers and walk out three hours later knowing every single name and face, having internalized a thumbnail sketch of each personality. When a particular individual appeared on the Suits' radar as a potential threat or ally, Budd could, with a little investigation, all but create a map of their inner mind. It could look like telepathy from the outside, but it was simply a matter of having the right conversations with the right people. And those people weren't the power players, but the power players' secretaries, drivers, and personal chefs. And most of all, their sex workers. For as long as sex work has existed as a profession, the powerful have been using prostitutes as captive audiences for all the anxieties and dilemmas they can't share even with their closest advisors or spouses.

"The amount of trash buildup is a key ingredient in any riot situation," continued Budd. "It's a visual cue that order has broken down, you see, and also provides projectiles if people get rowdy and start throwin' things. And if chaos breaks out to the point that the news is full of actual bloody corpses being hauled out of the festival . . ."

"Then the law-and-order candidate gets a big, free campaign ad for the election that's coming just two days later," finished Andre.

"And the law-and-order candidate is a Nazi," added Zoey. "Got it."

Will shook his head. "Leonidas Damon is not a Nazi. But no, he can't be allowed to win."

"It's no secret that Damon has national ambitions," said Echo. "He wants to tame Tabula Rasa to demonstrate he can do that for the nation. He fully intends to be running for president two or three cycles from now."

Zoey closed her eyes and pressed her fingers into the lids. "So what you're saying is that it's entirely possible that whether or not America has a fascist president in ten years may depend on how quickly we can empty these trash cans this weekend?"

"Welcome to the wonderful world of politics," said Budd. "A vocation you can't do when drunk but can't cope with when sober. The polls show Leo Damon with a lead of around eight points. But polling is notoriously difficult in this city."

"Wait, the Nazi is *winning*?"

"He won't win," said Will. "And he's not a Nazi. A Nazi is someone with very specific beliefs and Damon diverges in ways we can't ignore."

"How do you know he won't win?"

"We'll do what we have to do. But that just brings us to the business with the missing girls."

"It does? How?"

"I said back at Chalet that the situation may be more complicated than it appears. I think Damon is going to try to pull a Monday Surprise to swing the vote. There's no secret these anti-prostitution groups and Damon's campaign want the same thing. He may be using them."

"For what purpose?" asked Zoey. This was the kind of diabolical thinking she could never quite wrap her head around, but Will seemed to find it alarmingly easy.

"I'm not sure," answered Will, "but I'm going to go way out on a limb and predict that Budd was running late because he has news, and that this news is that Mr. Leonidas Damon wants to meet with us."

Budd smiled, nodded, and said, "He wants to meet, but only with Zoey. And he wants to do it at his home. Just her, at his place, or no meeting. He'll do it today, before he and his people have to go set up for tonight's debate."

Zoey felt her mouth forming the words "absolutely not" but knew that would only end in Will explaining in clear, irrefutable logic why she couldn't say no to meeting with maybe the one person on planet earth she most wanted to never share a room with. Not if they wanted to find Rose and stop whatever convoluted machinations this snake had dreamed up in his snaky brain.

Zoey touched the stinging bald strip on her scalp. "Would I be safe there? He's saying I can't even bring Wu, right?"

Will said, "It wouldn't serve his purposes to physically attack you, no. Not directly."

"But he may attack me indirectly?"

"I believe he already did. The lunatic who gave you that burn on your scalp somehow got two million dollars' worth of augmentations and she didn't put it on a credit card. Our best guess is she got the procedure done gratis and that the clinic was reimbursed on the back end with dark money funneled from Damon's side."

"Hold on, so this morning was an assassination attempt? Why don't we just assassinate-attempt him right back?"

Budd shook his head. "It's doubtful he specifically intended that outcome, it's more about creating headaches for us."

"Was that a pun, Budd?"

"Not at all. See, that's another example of an unintended consequence."

"The point is," said Will, "there's no reason your safety would be particularly at risk in this meeting." He turned to Budd. "Tell him she'll be there at two." He looked to the rest of the room. "Anything else?"

"Yes, actually." That was Wu, speaking up from the back. Everyone turned. This was literally the first time Wu had ever spoken up at a meeting and it had clearly unsettled everyone a bit. "This morning, there was something glaringly missed in our threat assessment regarding Zoey's safety. Everyone else seems satisfied to simply move past it, so let me ask this: Aside from what was just discussed, are there any threats I should be aware of? I'm not asking for a list of those who would benefit or profit from her harm, that's just handing me the city's census report. I am asking about plausible, actionable threats in the immediate future. Including anything being planned around her appearance at Catharsis tomorrow night."

"Have you heard anything, Budd?" asked Will.

"There actually is one," replied Budd. "The Amazing Aviv has put Zoey on his target list."

"Who?" asked Andre.

"He flew a mannequin over the gate," said Zoey. "Or tried to, the automated defenses shot it down. It was last night, we think it was a dry run to find out what happens if he tries it for real."

"He's got a huge following on Blink," said Budd, "calls himself an anarchist performance artist. He's the guy who flew a glider into the Super Bowl a few years ago, dumped a bag full of squirrels on the field. He's not coming to kill you, though. For him, it's all about bringing whimsy into the world."

"No," rebutted Will. "He's all about undermining power. That can be worse, in the long run."

"Worse than killing me?" asked Zoey.

"Worse than *trying* to kill you. Harder to stop. We need to keep an eye on him."

Zoey stood. "Great, lots of good information there. Good meeting, everybody. We need to break up my sense of impending dread. Budd, tell a joke."

"Ah, well, I don't have one ready at the moment. Something embarrassing did happen to me, though. This morning, my wife asked me to get her lipstick, I accidentally gave her a glue stick instead. She hasn't spoken to me since."

"Okay, well, let me know when you think of one. Will, do we have time for me to crawl into a bathtub and disassociate for about thirty minutes?"

Will looked at his watch. "If you start running the water now."

CHAPTER
7

IN EVERYDAY LIFE, MEN tended not to notice what Zoey was wearing unless it made her look far more or far less attractive than her baseline. In high-stakes business meetings with powerful sociopaths, however, the decision about what to wear was supposedly much more fraught.

Will relentlessly reminded her that these meetings were full of subliminal dominance signals that Zoey still barely understood, rules these guys apparently learned in business school or while apprenticing for their rich and powerful fathers. Those rules were, by design, incomprehensible to outsiders. Strivers projected power with tailored suits, while billionaires showed up to those meetings in sweatpants, projecting that they didn't have to put out the effort. Overt status symbols are a minefield because, by definition, they only work on those below you—no billionaire is impressed by a celebrity brand—so showing them off can play like an insult rather than an attempt to put your best foot forward. And so on.

As a result, Will was obsessed with how whatever Zoey wore represented the company or her mindset, how certain jewelry signaled "new money" or how a color of shoe would imply to any women in the meeting that she was there to steal their husbands. Will knew a hundred of these rules but seemed to not know the most important one: when Zoey was meeting with a certain type of man, there was simply no winning. If she dressed to look her best, emphasizing her chest and squeezing things in the middle to give her some kind of feminine shape, they'd immediately think, "This devious temptress is trying to brainwash me with her cleavage!" If she dressed as a businesswoman in a pantsuit that turned her body into a shapeless tweed sausage, they'd either treat her as a stodgy spoilsport or act like she was invisible. What Will couldn't or wouldn't grasp was that, among those men, Zoey's body was her outfit; they interpreted intentions via the possession of shapes. "Of course she wanted me to treat her like a piece of meat, why else would she have left the house with those boobs and that butt?" So today she pulled on her favorite pre-inheritance black jeans because they were comfortable and a cream cable-knit sweater because it was chilly outside. If the signal this sent to Leonidas Damon was that she didn't particularly care how he thought she looked, well, that was perfect.

The contingent to accompany Zoey to the meeting was Will and Budd, and of course, her bodyguard, Wu, with the understanding that all three would have to stay in the car once they arrived. The car, incidentally, was white. This was a new development and itself had been the subject of multiple meetings. Her father had a preference for armored black sedans with tinted windows, letting it be known to bystanders that the vehicle contained a celebrity, a captain of industry, or a crime lord (or in Arthur Livingston's case, a combination of all three). Zoey, on the other hand, felt like those were the vehicles of Hollywood villains and that intimidation shouldn't be the goal of her public presence. She had lobbied for garish pink for the new car, but Will had said that would draw too much attention. Wu had agreed and the compromise was a new pearl-white sedan that looked dignified and stately but that also could, in an emergency, unleash death in a dozen different ways. Even if everyone in the vehicle was killed, the car's automated defenses would keep going in the name of vengeance and/or spite.

They were in view of the towers downtown when Budd, studying his phone, announced, "There may be news soon, on the missing girls. It sounds like they may have a statement from a supposed perp, some kind of video."

"That's bad news," said Zoey, "considering the only *good* news would be finding the women alive and unharmed. Right?"

"Information is incomplete so I don't wanna speculate, but, ah, you might, in fact, want to prepare yourself for the worst."

Will rubbed his chin, thinking. "Well, let's hope we see it before we get to Damon's place, I don't want him knowing the score before we do. The worst thing that can happen in a meeting like this is an information imbalance."

"That doesn't make sense," said Zoey, "we're literally going there to ask him for information."

The sedan had rolled up to an intersection. The stoplights, as usual, blasted holographic advertisements, words floating across the street announcing that there were better ways to travel. Rent a helicopter! Or a luxury massage van! The ads never promoted walking.

"Remember, Damon has no motivation to give us the truth," replied Will, "unless it weakens our position. If it's information that alters the leverage in the situation, it would be better to know and play ignorant."

"What's this guy like? Behind closed doors, I mean?"

"Has a wife and four kids," said Budd. "He made his name as a political pundit, doing streams from crime-ridden neighborhoods around the country, making speeches about the rot of civilization. He moved here to raise his profile, as he reckoned no city does violence and vice like Tabula Rasa. As for what he's like in private, in my experience, guys like this just switch one mask for another."

"What's his wife li—"

Zoey was interrupted by a warning alarm. A series of red messages flashed across the windshield in front of Wu.

Budd leaned forward, peering through the windshield. "Well, there's somethin' you don't see every day."

A trio of heavenly figures were descending over the intersection. They were wearing flowing white cloth with ribbons that undulated even though there was no wind, like they had built-in fans to achieve the effect.

"Those are the angel drones the Liberators use," explained Will, in case anyone in the vehicle thought that they were being visited by real heralds of the Lord.

Zoey asked, "Are they armed?"

Wu was examining a diagram on his windshield. "They're rigged to throw projectiles."

"If their plan is to hurl holy hand grenades at us," said Budd, "they'll succeed only in destroying all of the bystander vehicles while we're barely inconvenienced. That is, unless the vendor was lying about this car's capabilities."

The drones floated down and encircled the sedan. Where their faces should be were black glass spheres that Zoey found terrifying. Then those spheres filled with holographic faces, young women whom Zoey recognized: these were their missing sex workers, portrayed as avenging angels. Then their mouths opened and their voices rang out in a chorus loud enough to shake the ground:

"OUR BLOOD IS ON YOUR HANDS! OUR BLOOD IS ON YOUR HANDS!"

Over and over.

Zoey said, "What blood? We don't even know that they're dead."

"What are our countermeasures here?" asked Will.

Wu shrugged. "I can knock any drone out of the sky with the push of a button."

"What measure are we countering?" asked Zoey. "They're exercising their freedom of speech. The weapons in this vehicle are to thwart assassins, not critics."

"OUR BLOOD IS ON YOUR HANDS! OUR BLOOD IS ON YOUR HANDS!"

The angel directly in front of them hurled a red object in their direction and for a crazy moment, Zoey thought it had chucked a tomato at the windshield, like hecklers used to do in old-timey cartoons. It impacted and a splash of crimson sprayed across the glass. If it wasn't blood, it was a perfect imitation. Another hit them from the side. The angels were hurling capsules that burst on impact, covering the white car in vivid arterial splatters.

Wu had seen enough. He tapped a button on the dash and a pulse was generated from somewhere deep in the vehicle, an invisible wave that made the hair on Zoey's arms stand on end. Each of the angel drones fell to the pavement. The light turned green and they rolled through the intersection, the sedan crunching over one of the angels. Zoey wondered if the missing woman's face was still on its display when their tire shattered it. The windshield automatically cleaned itself, giving them a nice view of the red-splattered hood, which looked like they'd just plowed through a herd of elk.

Zoey said, "They're telling us the missing sex workers are dead, right?"

"We just got the video," replied Budd. "It's, well, there she is."

He gestured out the window, at the row of towers along the streets ahead. The buildings were skinned with screens that ran a synchronized broadcast that scrolled from one skyscraper to the next. What it was displaying now was a mass of gore in the shape of a person, pixelated just enough to make the titillated viewer want to go look up the uncensored version on Blink. The mass of gore was screaming, the female victim still conscious as parts were being extracted.

Zoey looked away and said, "Is that Rose?"

"No, it's the first one that went missing. Name is Violet." The significance of that name wouldn't register with Zoey until later. "The video was posted anonymously. The killer was careful not to include anything that indicates location or identity. The full video supposedly goes on for over an hour, during which he peels off her—"

"Stop. I swear, men get such a thrill out of describing every little detail of a mutilated female body."

Will said, "Still, we want to see the actual corpse, if it's found."

"Yeah, you guys go do that."

Budd studied the garbled viscera on the passing towers. "Got to assume it will turn up before long. If the guy is making a show of it, he'll turn the body into some kind of display, probably put it somewhere public. Street streamers are calling the perp the Sex Butcher, because the first name they come up with is always the one that sticks, so in the race to be first they never have time to make it creative."

"But this isn't the work of these religious weirdos, right? They're not sex butchers."

"I am ninety-seven percent sure that it was some of those Liberator people who went to see Rose at her apartment before she vanished. As for what that means, or how we got from there to here," he gestured at the lurid horror splashed across the skyscrapers, "that's the conundrum."

"Conundrum," muttered Zoey. She looked into the side mirror and saw the blood dripping down the door panel. "Can we get this stuff off the car?"

"You want me to stop at a car wash?" asked Wu.

"No. I guess I was hoping you would push a button and a little robot would come out and squeegee it off."

Will said, "I'm going to take a wild guess and say this is the visual Leonidas Damon wanted, that he'll have a camera ready to capture us rolling up to his gates in a blood-soaked luxury car. Political imagery tends not to be a study in subtlety, and arranging that little ambush would have been as simple as him telling the Liberators we were coming. But we'd lose a solid hour stopping to get it cleaned, at the minimum. He could use that against us just as easily, pointing out that while he was waiting to meet with us about the crucial issue of sex worker safety, we were off polishing our armored sedan."

"Just take me to the meeting," said Zoey. "All things being equal, I'd just choose not to play his stupid game."

It was clear Will had something he wanted to say about that but was choosing to stay silent. He actually didn't need to say it, because he'd said it many times before: some games, you're playing whether you choose to or not.

The boundary of Leonidas Damon's subdivision was marked by modest gates and a bored guard in a booth, neither of which would have much to say about their armored sedan if they decided to ram their way through. Gates like these were more a declaration of status, which was the real deterrent: "Rob or vandalize *these* homes and there'll actually be a price to pay." The subdivision was close enough to downtown to see the towers but far enough away to be spared the noise (and, Zoey figured, most of the crime). These were the homes of corporate attorneys, surgeons, hedge fund managers; people Zoey would have considered fabulously wealthy just a year and a half ago but who now couldn't afford to even attend her fundraisers.

Budd said, "You see the water? All these houses are connected by one big community swimming pool, like a creek that snakes around behind 'em all."

The gatehouse was on a little bit of a hill and she could, in fact, see bits of the pool winding behind the tightly packed houses below, like a turquoise ribbon tossed on a floor.

She muttered, "Cool."

These gates were as far as Will, Wu, and Budd could go; they had been told that someone would come to pick up Zoey, so now they were waiting. She knew without being told that Leonidas Damon's demand to meet at his home was a power play and that this wait was just a part of it. An invisible boa constrictor was squeezing her chest, what Zoey had come to call her Anxiety Snake. It showed up any time there were too many proverbial alarms sounding from too many directions. She tried her relaxation breathing exercises and Will noticed her doing it.

"Your role here is minimal," he said. "You're not going to get anything out of this guy that he doesn't want us to know. He'll have something to say, whether it's true or not. Just listen, say as little as possible, and we'll figure out what it actually means later."

"You still have this little confidence in my ability to have a conversation with a power-hungry turd, even though that's pretty much all I do, all day, every day?"

"That's not what I'm saying. Damon's entire campaign depends on selling himself as the lone solution to the city's chaos. He'll probably try to antagonize you into acting rashly, doing something that proves him right. He may try to take credit for the missing girls even if he had nothing to do with it. He may try to bait you into threatening him. I'm saying you *want* to keep your role minimal, as a strategy."

"So all I have to do is not take the bait. I can do that."

"It's the hardest thing in the world, in my experience. Remember, if your father had been better at not taking bait, he'd probably still be alive. As always, go back to the basics: How does the other party want to project themselves into the world? Figure that out and you're ninety percent of the way to predicting how they'll act."

"And this guy wants to rid the city of crime."

"What? No. Zoey, listen, because this is everything: There's nothing in Damon's platform that involves preventing crime from happening. His promise is that *he will inflict harm on the bad guys*. Big difference."

Budd added, "It's like the old joke about the hunter and the bear."

"I don't think I know that one," said Zoey.

"It's kind of blue, if you're okay with that. A hunter goes out into the woods, finds a bear, shoots at him, and misses. The bear lopes over and says, 'You just tried to shoot me! Now there's gonna be consequences. I'm gonna bend you over this log and have my way with you.' So he pulls the hunter's pants down and does just that. The next day, the hunter comes back with a bigger gun, a big ol' elephant gun. He finds that same bear, shoots, and misses again. The bear pounces and says, 'You never learn, do ya? Just for that, I'm gonna force you to give me a blow job.' So he does just that. The next day, the hunter comes back with an even bigger gun, a bazooka. He shoots, not even close. The bear comes over, grabs the hunter and says, 'You don't come out here to hunt, do ya?'"

Instead of laughing, Zoey said, "I'd need the rest of the day to figure out how that applies."

"The point," said Will, "is that if all crime disappeared from the city tomorrow, people like Damon would have to find a way to bring it back. The harsh measures are the ends, not the means. But right now, it means you just need to stay cool." He nodded toward a golf cart that was rolling up to the gates from the other side. "Looks like they're here."

CHAPTER
8

THE CART THAT CAME to pick up Zoey was driven by a woman in her forties wearing a pantsuit the color of a clear sky and the expression of someone who finds all sky colors disappointing. The iron gates slowly rolled shut behind Zoey as she went for a handshake.

"Hi, I'm Zoey Ashe, I'm here to see Leonidas."

The woman did not shake her hand, just nodded to the passenger seat and said, "I'll take you to him."

Well, this was off to a great start. Zoey climbed on board, trying to figure out if this was Damon's wife. She'd seen her in political ads and at campaign appearances but Zoey wasn't great with faces, especially when she was used to seeing them wearing that inhuman, alien smile political wives defaulted to when the cameras were on. They were rolling down the middle of the street and only then did Zoey notice that there were no cars here. The electric carts were parked here and there but the streets were mostly pedestrians and bicycles.

"Oh, I love the car-free neighborhoods," said Zoey, trying to fill the silence. "If it'd been up to me, the whole city would be like this. I always pictured the perfect city as being like a big college campus, all the stuff you need connected by sidewalks, with green areas where people can lounge under trees and read a book or throw a Frisbee around."

The woman said nothing.

Zoey tried again. "I don't think I got your name?"

"The house is just ahead."

They rode in silence the rest of the way. Once at the house, instead of being let inside, Zoey was led around the side lawn to the backyard. It was a narrow strip of perfect grass leading to the community pool, a crystal-clear man-made creek about thirty feet wide and extending in both directions until it curved around the neighboring homes.

"He'll be out in a moment," said the woman before she abandoned Zoey on a patio with some lawn chairs.

Minutes passed. Again, she was being made to wait. Will said they like to watch you while you wait, see what you do. Are you a fidgeter? Do you pace around, inspect the surroundings? Will's rule: Sit and appear totally unperturbed by the delay. They get ten minutes. If they don't arrive by then, leave. It doesn't matter how badly you need the meeting, you don't give them the satisfaction of letting you dangle on the hook. So Zoey had a seat in one of the lawn chairs, rotating it to face the back door so Damon wouldn't have the pleasure of sneaking up on her. Don't pick at your clothes, she thought. Don't pull out your phone. Don't reveal how much it enrages you that this petty wannabe tyrant is using your concern for the missing women against you because he himself is incapable of feeling any such thing. Find something to think about to distract yourself.

Zoey decided she would pass the time by pondering just how much she hated politics.

It was an arena in which everyone lied, all the time, because lying was required, demanded by the voters themselves. And because Zoey had money, it meant she had no escape. The snakes hit her up for campaign donations, they hinted at their ability to grease wheels she needed greased, they dropped implied threats about how they could make the machinery of commerce grind to a halt if she didn't play ball. But the worst part was that, despite all this, politicians had an insidious ability to make you like them. Zoey thought of them as a species of mind-controlling aliens that could somehow exude power and humility at once. The talented ones could flash a smile that said, "I have the power to crush you, but I will not, because I am here to crush others on your behalf."

Zoey heard splashing from behind her and turned to see a man was swimming up to the edge of the pool. Out from the water emerged Leonidas Damon, whom she recognized from his ads. What was not featured in the ads was a whole lot of body hair that was now plastered to his wet, pasty torso, and an above-average penis, which was also visible on the completely nude man.

"Oh, good, you're here," he said as he strode casually over to a stack of towels on a patio table. Instead of wrapping one around himself, he began drying his hair, his genitals jiggling with the motion. "Always dry yourself from the top down. Attack the source of the problem, otherwise the water keeps trickling down and you have to keep wiping, again and again."

He finished, tossed the towel aside and, his hands on his bare hips, said, "I always try to get in a swim on debate day. The water is frigid this time of year, it's like a jolt through your muscles, your whole body comes alive." He nodded toward her hair and said, "Did you do something to offend your hairdresser?"

Zoey fought to hide her discomfort and failed. "Can you put some clothes on?"

"Why? Do you feel threatened? Would you feel threatened if I was a woman? Or do you feel that there is danger inherent to specific sex organs?"

"You apparently do. You're doing this because you know it makes me uncomfortable. You'd feel the same way if you were ambushed by a strange naked man. Especially if he was six inches taller than you and outweighed you by seventy-five pounds."

Damon looked Zoey up and down. "I don't think I outweigh you by that much."

"I swear, guys like you, it's like you have this radar for people's insecurities so you can zoom right in. I have messed-up teeth, too. Go ahead and get that one out of the way."

"You started it, by commenting on my body. All I did was say hello. Hey, would you like to go in and make me a coffee?"

"Ah, because I was a barista. Funny. Somehow, you've told me nothing about yourself but managed to tell me everything I need to know. And you're not worried that what you're doing now looks bad to the voters? Waving your genitals at a notorious woman? You know there are cameras everywhere, right?"

"Nothing here is new to my neighbors or my constituents. I have nothing to hide, I lay bare all of my mind and body for judgment, as everyone should."

Zoey decided to just move on to the subject at hand. "I'm here because we have employees who are going missing. Which you already know. Three, so far."

"Sex workers, you mean."

"Yes, that's the type of work they do."

"I'm not surprised to hear they're going missing, it's a dangerous job."

"It's dangerous work because certain people make it dangerous. Your anti-sex work protestors or whatever they are showed up and, soon after, women started going missing. This last one who disappeared, Rose, was seen talking to your activists right before."

"*My* activists? Did they tell you they work for me?"

"You've built your campaign on banning the brothels, these people all wear your campaign buttons, they have front-row seats at your rallies. They're yours whether you claim them or not. You're both part of this movement to reclaim our streets for Jesus."

"Ah, I see your confusion." Damon grabbed a robe off the back of a nearby chair, apparently feeling like he'd made whatever point he was going to make with his exposed reproductive organs. "You think I want to ban the whores because they offend God. I want to ban them because they're objectively terrible for society."

"Again, it's only terrible because people like you make it so. It's the same as how you just made fun of me for working in a coffee shop. You want coffee, you want coffee shops to exist, you want people to work there, but then you have open disdain for the very workers you just admitted you need. What is that? This requirement that people—especially women—have to do their jobs and then, on top of that, have to be a receptacle for your rage?"

"Oh, so you see those two jobs as equivalent, do you? What would you charge to let me have sex with you right now? Would you do it for a thousand? You've got a wide jawbone, that means high testosterone. Hair on your arms. Got that big ass from your Armenian father. I bet you can really go to town."

"Ah, you're back to the misogynist playbook. Okay."

"So you agree that the suggestion that you would have sex for money is inherently insulting. You can feel it in your gut that it's wrong. You'd be sick at the thought of your daughter doing it, or your sister, or your mother."

"My mother did do it," said Zoey, her plan to say as little as possible already falling to pieces.

"I bet she doesn't now, since she has your money to live off of."

Zoey took a slow, deep breath.

"You and I both know," she began quietly, "that this kind of work is going to go on no matter what we do or what we think about it. The only difference is if we keep the workers safe or force them underground. So getting back to the point, are you saying you know nothing about the missing women, or the group that was in suspicious proximity to the events in question?"

"Have you ever seen Will Blackwater put his dick in a cow?"

Zoey heard herself say, "What?" before she could stop herself, revealing that he'd thrown her off-balance, which, of course, had been the point.

"Have you ever seen Will Blackwater penetrate a cow?"

"You've clearly got some bit planned, so instead of making me answer, why don't you just get on with it?"

"Last week, when that tabloid drone caught you people having thousand-dollar steaks at that rooftop joint downtown, the place where they boil the filets in three-hundred-degree butter? I bet that meat didn't come from a vat. It came from a living cow."

"I have no idea what that can possibly have to do with the subject at hand but I'm sure you're just bursting to tell me. Are you comparing our sex workers to cattle?"

"I'm saying it's interesting that you think having intercourse with a cow is disgusting but it's not disgusting to cage and kill one. What are you trying to protect, its bodily autonomy? You think the owners ask a cow before inserting tools into its orifices to inseminate it? You think these animals get to choose what partners they mate with, what they eat, how they spend their time? How they die? So why do we look down on the cow molester but not the cow eater?"

"Because one of them is a pervert satisfying an urge and the other is just hungry?"

"No," said Damon, looking like he was ready to spring the trap. "It's because society needs sex to be valuable, and to be valuable, it must be scarce. If you catch a man having intercourse with a cow or a sheep or a sex doll, we hold him up for ridicule, shame them out of the behavior. See, that way, they have to get it from a woman and that preserves women's power as sexual gatekeepers. The value and scarcity must be maintained. Therefore, you shun the cow molester. And the John."

"And the gays, right?"

"In a perfect world, yes."

"So knowing this is your position, how far would you and those activists who totally don't work for you go to discourage sex work? Have all of these women been butchered like the one we saw earlier?"

"I don't know. And what is happening isn't something I can stop. You say sex work will continue no matter what we do and to some point I'd agree. But I say the hatred of the whores will also continue. Women hate them because they rob them of their power, the power of withholding sex until they get what they want. There is a reason the men—the ones who aren't customers anyway—hate prostitutes and see them as subhuman. Sex is normally won by achievement and status, with women handing it out to the men who do the most to keep civilization going. Prostitutes short-circuit the sexual marketplace. If you want to keep these women safe, there is exactly one way to do it: get them out of sex work."

"I would laugh if that wasn't so grotesque. Did you drag me out here just so you could dump your Theory of Everything on me? I swear, in my time as a business owner, that's the most common fetish I've run into. Men spraying their pet theories onto my face."

Damon opened a miniature refrigerator on the patio and withdrew a bottle of water. He didn't offer Zoey one. He sat in a lawn chair and positioned himself so that he was facing her. As soon as he sat, Zoey stood. Again, they were almost certainly on camera and any single frame of this conversation could be presented out of context. She was fine with people knowing she'd met with this man, but intended to make it clear with her body language that the meeting was not friendly.

"If these activists don't work for you," she said, "and if we find they have hurt these women, you understand that we will do what we have to do. These women *do* work for me, I'm not ashamed of it and I'm not afraid to claim them as my own. And we will protect our people."

"And I will protect the people your people exploit. I am going to win on Tuesday. Shortly after, the whorehouses and drug dens will be closed down. Shortly after *that*, you and your comrades will stand trial and you will go to prison. Thank you for stopping by, unfortunately my wife had to take the cart to the pharmacy up the street, but I trust you can walk yourself back. You look like you could use the exercise."

Zoey, as a rule, was never to walk alone. She was one of the world's most valuable kidnapping targets and would remain so until the day she had kidnappable children of her own. So while forcing her to walk the four or five blocks back to the main gates—most of it uphill—was petty, it was also a clear breach of her personal security practices and Leonidas Damon absolutely knew that. This was yet another power play and, once again, Zoey suspected she was being watched. Would she request her people come inside the gates to escort her out? Would that make her look weak?

She glanced up to the sky. "You hear me?"

In her nearly invisible earpiece, Will replied, "I do, but there is currently a gun pointed in my face so I apologize if you don't have my full attention."

"There is?" Zoey began to head toward the gate at a hurried pace. "What's happened?"

"Wu told the gatehouse guard that he was going to come through the gates to escort you back to the car, the guard said he had strict orders to prevent that from happening. Wu restated his position in clearer terms and the guard has now drawn his sidearm and appears to be calling in help."

"I'm coming that way. Can you see me?"

"Not directly, but the feed is up on the dash."

Zoey looked up again. Wu had monitored Zoey from the moment she'd left the car via a tiny drone the size of a sparrow, one with a camera powerful enough that it could watch her from a mile in the air if it had to. She had no idea how high it was flying at the moment but she definitely couldn't see it, even against a clear sky.

"Watch to make sure nobody is converging on me. If you can distract yourself from the guy with the gun in your face."

"There is only one person walking toward you, it appears to be a teenage girl. She's in a Liberator white robe and mask and is between you and the gate. I think she was waiting for you."

"Okay. Don't get shot before I get there. And don't kill anybody."

"Wu now has the security guard's gun, but two more have shown up. Discussions are ongoing. It appears Budd may know one of the guards, it's unclear if that makes the situation more stable or less."

"Tell everyone to calm down! We can't have a shoot-out right in front of the Damon compound, he'll turn that into a campaign commercial."

There was a rustle and some grunting on the other end of the line, then Will returned to say, "I now have one of the other security guard's guns. Negotiations are continuing and they are considering our most recent counteroffer." He paused as if to check something. "The white robe is making a beeline for you. And she has something in her hand."

"Don't worry about me." Zoey could now see her heading her way, marching down the sidewalk directly in her path—a masked figure that did, in fact, have the build and manner of a teenage girl or a petite woman. "If she tries something, the drone will swoop down and stop her, right? It's all automated?"

"She *is* going to try something, analysis of her stride and posture implies bad intentions."

"I can see that with my own eyes." This was Zoey's first time seeing the full Liberator costume and while the white robe just looked like something from a church choir, the mask—a smooth, white angelic face—was giving her the creeps. The approaching figure was hunched over and advancing like she'd just caught Zoey with her boyfriend. "Does she have a gun?"

There was shouting from Will's end and Zoey thought she could hear Budd saying, "I just want you to think about this, now. Think about what you're about to do . . ."

After a moment, Will came back on. "No gun, but . . . hold on, two more guards have shown up. It seems clear the security staff were anticipating this encounter. They also seem quite certain that we will not take lethal action and I am beginning to think wc may have to demonstrate otherwise."

Will had likely said that last part for the benefit of everyone holding a gun on him up at the gatehouse. Zoey still wasn't close enough to see what exactly was transpiring up there, the street made a curve as it ascended the hill and a tall house was blocking her view. The approaching Liberator walked like she was trying to kick her robe to death. She conspicuously kept her right hand behind her back. It probably wasn't a bouquet of flowers back there but Zoey had no idea what to do. Stop? Run away? Cross the street? There were no good or dignified options, it was either face down this stranger or run around in the street in circles with the teenage Liberator chasing after her.

"Will, the robe is right up on me, what does she have behind her back? I kind of need to know."

"Hold on, we're preoccupied at the moment."

A gunshot rang out, from up at the gate.

Zoey flinched and came to a stop. The Liberator stopped to glance back over her shoulder at the noise, then turned back and ran toward Zoey.

"Hey!" shouted Zoey. "Calm down, whatever you're about to do—"

The Liberator pulled her hand from behind her back and in it was a red glob that Zoey once again mistook for a tomato, right up until she chucked it, splattering it across Zoey's face and chest. She braced herself for the sensation of, say, acid eating through her skin. Instead, the cold liquid just dribbled down into her shirt. She tried to wipe it from her eyes.

"THEIR BLOOD IS ON YOUR HANDS!" screamed the Liberator in a teenage girl's voice. "You offered them up to predators like a buffet! All of them! Rose! Violet! Iris—"

There was a pulsing buzz from above, Zoey's security drone swooping down. Then there was a snap and a hiss, and then the Liberator was thrashing on the pavement, blue sparks popping from her shoulder. The drone had hit her with a pair of stun darts.

"No!" screamed Zoey, running over to the girl.

And it was just a girl—her mask had flown off, revealing a young face full of freckles.

"Go away!" shouted Zoey as she waved her hands like she was shooing away an aggressive bird. "It's just paint! I'm fine!"

"It's not paint!" grunted the girl around her clenched jaw. "It's blood!"

"It's just blood! Whatever it is, I'm fine!" She looked down at the girl. "Are you okay? The darts shouldn't harm you but the fall to the pavement is no fun."

Zoey plucked the darts out of the girl's shoulder, the tiny barbed hooks pulling up the skin until they popped free.

In her ear, Will said, "Wu is through the gates and on his way to you."

"Tell him I'm fine!"

The teenage Liberator sneered up at Zoey. "Look at all the protection you have! Where was that for Rose? Where was it for Violet? You could have protected them and you didn't."

"I don't disagree! At all! But it's a real stretch to say I killed them—"

"The killers paid to kill them! You let them do it! Everyone knows!"

"What? No—"

The girl sat up and spat in Zoey's face. Then she struggled to her feet and stumbled down the sidewalk, heading back downhill.

"Hey!" yelled Zoey. "You should sit down, you're going to fall again!"

Zoey started to follow her, but then Wu's hand was on her shoulder, urging her back toward the gate.

"Come on, we have to go before this turns ugly."

She followed him up to the gates, where four security personnel were holding guns on four other security personnel in identical uniforms, as if Will and Budd had somehow convinced half of them to join their cause against the other half. Will, meanwhile, was sliding into the backseat of the bloodstained sedan with an impatient look, as if Zoey and Wu were making him late for an appointment. Budd was already in the front passenger seat.

Zoey ducked into the back and Wu slid behind the wheel. The car was moving before he even closed his door. The security guards were now too occupied with menacing each other and barely noticed them leaving.

Will said, "The drone got a facial scan of the girl who accosted you, we'll know her name and where she lives in about ten seconds."

Zoey waved him off. "Forget it. Just take me home."

Pedestrians were stopping to gawk at the blood-splattered sedan. Zoey felt blood trickling down her neck.

Budd asked, "Somebody got a towel?"

Zoey waved him off, too. "It's fine. Take me home. That's all I want. Take me home."

Wu asked, "Are you hurt?"

"That girl seemed to think the killer paid for the privilege, like, if you go to one of the brothels and pay enough money, we let you murder the sex worker. And I don't think she meant it like a metaphor, I think she thinks we actually offer that."

Will grimaced. "It's just another conspiracy theory. Secret Menu."

"Wait, it is?"

Budd nodded. "The theory goes that joints like ours have a formula in mind for the lifetime earnings of a pro and that those numbers are used to set a Secret Menu for the rich clients. That if they pay enough, they're allowed to take a pro and not bring them back."

"And no," added Will, "we've never had such a program, not even when your father was in charge. No matter how low your opinion of him or his organization, it wouldn't make sense. The entire draw for a brothel or escort service is safety. Even the rumor that we were offering them up for death by torture would ruin it. The girls would be better off going independent."

"Wait," said Zoey, thinking her way through it. "Hold on. What were the other two victims' names? Rose and who?"

"Violet and Iris," said Budd.

"They're all flower names. That's weird, right?" This felt important to Zoey but she couldn't fathom why.

"Well, that's not their real names, they all work under pseudonyms."

"Okay, but do all of the sex workers at Chalet use flower names?"

"No," replied Budd. "They don't."

"So could this guy be targeting victims based on those names? Doing, like, a serial-killer pattern?"

"We cross-checked times and dates with the positions of known serial murderers in the city, all of 'em came up clean."

"That wasn't funny."

"That wasn't a joke. We checked."

Will said, "I don't think this is the work of a serial killer. In fact, I don't think the girls are dead. Or at least, not this way."

"We just saw a butchered corpse, Will. Splashed all over the skyline."

"No, we didn't. We saw a video, broadcast to the public. Which means we only saw what someone wanted us to see."

"I don't understand."

"Neither do I. But I will. Budd, has Violet's corpse turned up?"

"Not yet."

Zoey studied her hand, which was smeared with the blood she'd wiped from her face. Her cream sweater was soaked at the shoulders. She wondered where they'd gotten it from. Was it cows' blood? Pigs'?

"I think I did wind up threatening him a little bit. Damon, I mean, I think it's reasonable to say that he did, in fact, successfully bait me. He did his bit about how sex work is ruining society, I gave him the line about how we're just giving the market what it wants but things kind of went downhill from there. I'm not sure how well I came off. He popped out of the water with no clothes on, did you see that? I'm trying to imagine if I pulled something like that, what people would say."

Staring at the passing traffic, Will said, "You think the stuff about the market is just a 'line'?"

"It definitely didn't sound as convincing hearing myself saying it as when you say it to me. I mean, yeah, how much choice do these women really have? Do you ever sit down and think about that?"

Will shrugged. "You can think about it all you want, you can sit around and pontificate about why gravity goes down instead of up, why people can be tricked into thinking wine tastes better just by raising the price, or why every civilization on earth independently invented the dumpling. Knock yourself out. But nobody out there, up in those offices and down on these corners, is sitting around pondering the unfairness of the universe. Markets are about giving humans what they want in the most efficient way possible. It's hard enough just to do that."

"The fact that half of these sex workers are doing it to support drug habits doesn't bother you?"

"That's why drugs are destructive, they disrupt the marketplace by skewing demand. Arthur hated the drug trade. But so what? When they say prostitution is the oldest profession, they're not joking. The moment the species was capable of comprehending possessions and trade, sex was almost certainly the subject of the first transaction."

Zoey's hands were getting sticky. Budd handed her a towel and she absently wiped blood from her fingers, one at a time.

Budd said, "A few decades ago, some scientists trained a bunch of capuchin monkeys to use money, taught 'em that these little metal rings in their pen could be exchanged for food. As soon as the monkeys understood the concept, a male monkey paid a female monkey for sex."

"Is that real or a joke?"

"Real as my hat. Look it up. They also learned how to gamble and, at one point, figured out how to break into the bin where the trainers kept the tokens. The damned things planned and executed a heist."

"The point," added Will, "is that the demand is there and always had been, in all times and places, in all cultures. Where you find demand, you find people willing to fill that demand."

"And that's all that matters," said Zoey, trying to wipe blood off her neck. "The marketplace. The marketplace excuses everything. Forget about all of this other stuff, love, humanity, emotions . . ."

"Yes, it's all a marketplace, a series of transactions. Every conversation you've ever had, every relationship, you're offering something in exchange for something. Companionship, social status, sex, validation, security, whatever. You think it's tasteless to refer to it as a marketplace, most women do. We can pick a different word if that will make it stop clouding your thinking. But right now, there's a billion unhappy marriages in this world because both partners secretly think they're getting the short end of the stick, that they're putting in more than they're getting out. They'll express that resentment in a thousand different ways, up to and including slitting their partner's throat in their sleep, but they don't dare refer to it as a 'transaction' because god forbid you use such distasteful language. Well, with sex work, everything is crystal clear. Here is exactly how much the romantic companionship is worth to me, if that's not enough to convince you to give it up, fine, I'll go elsewhere. When the market is allowed to work, everybody wins."

Zoey closed her eyes and sat back in the seat, thinking vaguely that somebody was going to have to wipe the blood off the upholstery later. "I think that's more naive than anything I've heard a lefty college kid say."

"And yet, if you reached back two hundred years and grabbed some fancy aristocrat and brought him here and gave him one of the middle-class apartments in this city, complete with climate control and movies and ten thousand restaurants that will deliver to his door? He'd murder you before he let you send him back. You can thank markets for that."

Zoey tossed the bloody towel onto the floorboard and said, "So what now? We keep trying to track down these women, praying they're alive and that this is all some kind of a hoax?"

Budd said, "I've got people on it. Nothing can stay hidden in this city for long. Not from me."

CHAPTER
9

ZOEY'S SHOWER WAS DESIGNED to be a sanctuary. The glass enclosure was soundproof and could be set to display anything from a peaceful sunrise to a surreal otherworldly landscape with alien birds undulating in the distance. It could also be set to a scroll of stock tickers and headlines, but Zoey could feel an anxiety attack coming the moment she even imagined being the type of person who couldn't shampoo their hair without monitoring their share prices. This was, after all, just about the only peace she got. Today she set the enclosure to the ambiance of a simple, candlelit room. The shower's nozzles boasted fifty different settings that could simulate everything from a pulsing aqua massage to rough sex with Poseidon, but by far the best feature of the shower, in her opinion, was that it had a stool. A press of a button made it pop up from the floor and you could sit and shave your legs or just close your eyes and let the water pummel your back as Zoey was doing now, watching diluted red swirl around her feet. Occasionally some water would splatter up and hit her wounded scalp, stinging like a cigarette burn.

It seemed impossible that this day was only half over. The itinerary had originally consisted of 1) going on a beef-factory tour and silently pretending to be interested for the cameras 2) attending a boring meeting about music-festival logistics while not even bothering to appear interested in that 3) taking a long afternoon nap 4) sitting through a tedious mayoral-candidate debate while wearing an "I'm extremely interested in this!" expression and planning what, exactly, she would drink once it was over and finally 5) pretending to be sober while sitting through a hopefully short briefing about what was on tap for tomorrow, the day she'd actually been worried about. On the calendar, it had promised to be long but boring. In retrospect, Zoey should have known that days such as these were where your real problems hid, so they could jump out and punch you in the gut.

Zoey's people were all in the conference room cobbling together a new security protocol with Wu, since the day thus far had been a string of spectacular failures on that front. She had wanted no part of that meeting, not just because she was totally uninterested in hearing Will and Wu take turns deflecting blame, but because the whole thing just drove home how, based purely on allocation of assets, the company believed Zoey's life was simply more valuable than any of her employees', including the sex workers'. They couldn't even argue that her extra protection was due to her public profile making her a target; these women were objectively in more danger and they would never have Zoey's around-the-clock protection, purely because they didn't have Zoey's net worth. As such, it was now occurring to her that the subject of the missing sex workers and the city's de facto legalization of vice was going to come up in the debate, which meant Zoey's actual name could come up, which meant she was likely going to be asked by the press to comment afterward, which meant answering questions about the seared wound in her hair as well as her views on cannibalistic conspiracy theories.

The invisible boa constrictor pulled itself tighter around her sternum.

She didn't want to get out of the shower. She did her breathing, reminded herself that statistically, she was probably one of the safest people on earth in this moment, that her home was a fortress, and that when outside of it, she was protected by some of the most devious minds in the city, if not the world. Go out, she told herself, meet with your people and arm yourself with the information you need to face the danger. It's your enemies who should be losing sleep, not you.

She told the shower to shut off and let the air jets blow her dry. Then she strode confidently out of her bathroom and immediately came face-to-face with a towering figure dressed in black.

Zoey was too startled to scream. She gasped and tried to cover herself with her hands.

The figure was easily six inches taller than Zoey. On its hands were gloves of gleaming black metal that formed the fingers into wicked, pointed claws. The intruder wore a black cloak and under it, a form-fitting suit of armor in an hourglass shape that suggested femininity. It was covered with a pattern of what appeared to be serrated shark teeth, looking like brushing a hand over the surface would shred your palms. Over the figure's face was a dark cowl featuring only a pair of yellow eyes with vertical pupils.

With a primal shriek, the figure uttered a series of words.

Those words were, "Oh, my god! You're naked! I'm sorry!"

It spun to turn its back to Zoey.

"What are you doing here, DeeDee?" yelped Zoey. "You almost made me piss myself! Actually I think a few dribbles of pee actually came out. Jesus Christ, I'm going to have a heart attack . . ."

"I let myself in, I was waiting for you to get back. I wanted to talk to you, not your people. I heard you showering but I thought you would, I don't know, I thought you'd have a robe or something."

"I thought I was alone! Why would I put on a robe?!?"

"I do! I don't even let my dogs see me when I'm not dressed! Are you still naked back there? What's happening?"

"Hold on, I'm trying to find something. What if Wu had been here? He'd have tried to kill you."

"If he'd been here, I'd have changed my approach. Your people are all huddled in the conference room."

Zoey pulled a bathrobe from a hook on her door and cinched it closed up to her neck. "My god, how is this the second straight meeting where someone was naked?"

"What? What was the last one? Are you dressed?"

"Yes."

"Are you sure?" DeeDee cautiously turned back toward Zoey and pulled off her mask, an operation that was somewhat delicate considering her fingers were talons made of a rigid, exotic material that could rip through a car door.

Zoey had met DeeDee through DeeDee's uncle, Alonzo Dunn, the aforementioned candidate for mayor opposing Leonidas Damon. DeeDee had worked security for Alonzo when he was merely a local businessman/

crime lord, depending on your perspective, but wanted no part of this election nonsense. She was thus in the process of going independent and Zoey's team had actually helped get that terrifying black costume made, among other things.

"What do you want, DeeDee?"

She held out her gleaming clawed hands, her fingers extended. Then she curled her fingers in just a little, like she was about to slash someone's face off.

"That's as far as I can close my fingers."

"What do you mean?"

"Your implants, I can't make a fist. I can't even hold a cup unless it's a big one. I have to drink with both hands, like a toddler. It started a few days ago, it's getting worse."

"I can ask Echo. She might be able to help if it's a software thing. If it's something to do with the surgery or how the parts were, uh, installed, you may be in for a bit of a wait. The surgeon who did yours isn't in the industry anymore."

"Isn't 'in the industry'?"

"In the industry of being alive. He got exploded when trying to install one of the little power packs while it already had a charge on it. Or something like that. The point is, we'll have to find somebody who can do it."

"I can't make a fist. How can I punch these bastards if I can't make a fist?"

"You can karate chop them or something, it looks like that would still hurt. Or slap 'em around."

"This isn't a joke, Zoey."

"We told you there were risks, all this stuff is experimental. We'll get it fixed. Is that the only thing you came for? You had to know that I'm not the person in this organization who knows the most about augmentation gadgets."

"You're the one person in this organization who tells the truth as an initial impulse. And the one who won't instantly stonewall me on this."

"On getting your implants fixed?"

"On going to see Rex Wrexx."

"Is that . . . a band?"

"Of course, you don't even know who Rex Wrexx is. I should have guessed."

"Maybe I do know, I'm not good with names. Or I should say, I thought I was good with names, until suddenly my job required me to remember five million of them."

DeeDee gave a spiteful little nod. "Will hasn't told you about him."

It wasn't a question.

"It's possible he has, DeeDee, I have a lot of meetings. Remind me what his deal is again?"

"He's the one taking your sex workers. I'm sure of it."

This stopped Zoey. "He is?"

"He burned the face off of a woman last year, just because she was spreading rumors about him on Blink. The rumor she was spreading was that he was getting off on murder fantasies. All the red-flag behaviors. So it was one of those cases where the reaction to the rumor confirms the rumor. When the first one turned up missing—Violet—his name should have come up and it should have stayed at the top of your list until somebody went and arrested and/or killed his ass."

"No, my team has never talked about him."

"Zoey, I can assure you they have. They just didn't talk about him around *you*."

"I'm sure there's a reason. I mean, why haven't you gone after him?"

"Ask your man why. He'll tell you. Or maybe he won't."

"Don't tell me this Rex guy works for me."

"He doesn't. It's not that simple. But let's just say he's considered untouchable. Take me to Santa's Workshop, if it's a software thing I can reload it myself, the process is automatic. Come on, before your people show up. But, ah, after you put real clothes on."

The local press was full of ridiculous rumors about Zoey and her sprawling estate. "Zoey's cat has his own luxury suite" was the big one and, of course, only half true: Stench Machine's room was just a standard guest bedroom with a couple dozen pieces of cat furniture and a litter box (then again, her other cat had a similar room, so the half-truth was double what the press thought, so maybe that made it one whole truth again?). "Zoey has a padded combat room where she pays desperate homeless people to fight to the death" was true in the sense that there was a padded room full of fighting stuff, but she'd never had anyone fight to the death in it. The weapons were colorful rubber batons and other harmless sparring gear (incidentally, Zoey had found that guys she brought back to the estate *loved* the fighting room; she'd take them in there and smack 'em with a foam sword, then watch their eyes light up). The rumors of a secret basement vault were entirely true and came with a whole cottage industry of people speculating what was in said vault, all of whom were wrong (it was empty).

But the strangest and least plausible rumor by far was that in Zoey's ballroom there was a nano-accurate parts fabricator that could crank out implants and accessories capable of giving any human the destructive powers of a minor demigod or, at least, a tank. This one was one hundred percent true. Or two hundred percent true, as she actually had two of the fabricators now, in the room they'd code-named "Santa's Workshop." There were many frivolous and unnecessary rooms in the mansion, but this was definitely not one of them.

The augmentations like those wielded by the crazy meat-factory lady weren't legally available off the shelf, thank god. They were instead offered in a few shady facilities in the city, to varying degrees of quality, and it should be noted here that the drawbacks of a poor-quality device were horrific. Ruptures and/or explosions of the tech's tiny little power plants were the most common outcome, an event that looked like the user tried to poop an entire storm's worth of lightning all at once (well, that's what you'd see if you slowed down the video of such an accident; at full speed, it was just a flash and then the sound of charred meat landing in the distance). Others suffered software malfunctions that caused the victim's limbs to go thrashing out of control with enough force to smash holes in brick walls or overturn nearby cars. One guy with strength implants in all four limbs had them malfunction in a manner that knotted him into a screaming, bloody pretzel. Near the end of Zoey's father's life, he'd bought a business and with it, the rights to this technology, for reasons that could probably be boiled down to boredom. The end result was, in retrospect, inevitable, but at least he'd thought to make a will first.

Nonetheless, the high-powered human augmentation horse was out of the barn and, as Will was fond of saying, if you can't make a dangerous market go away, then you'd better damned well try to corner it. So in a ballroom that had once hosted opulent charity functions and private art showings (or whatever it was rich people did with such rooms), there were now two humming industrial machines the size and shape of Mechagodzilla's turds. The segments of the cylindrical machines represented stages of a manufacturing process that assembled components with circuits and switches too tiny to be viewed even under a conventional microscope, using raw materials that, in some cases, cost several million dollars an ounce and could only be shipped in special armored containment trucks.

Zoey, already on her third outfit of the day, led DeeDee to the ballroom and to the machines waiting on the floor like a pair of giant, sleeping, black caterpillars. The room always stank like burnt chemicals and that was just one of the reasons why Santa's Workshop would forever be Zoey's least favorite room in the house. If it was up to her, the fabricators would be transported off-site, but the security features were so thorough that any attempt to move them would cause the machines to self-destruct. Zoey hated getting too close to the fabricators, but DeeDee strode right over to the nearest, woke up the control screen, and pushed around some holographic modules until it seemed to be doing what she wanted.

"It just has to reinstall," said DeeDee, "it'll only take a couple of minutes."

Over the last year, the Suits had endured an influx of inquiries from those who desired augmentations and they'd thus had to develop a system of red-flag checks to filter the applicants. It was a three-strike system and the mere desire for superhuman abilities counted for two. A willingness to ignore the potentially horrific side effects got you most of the way to Strike Three (one viral clip of a man's augmentation malfunction could be described as *literally* gut-wrenching—it took a special type of person to just shrug it off). So far, only DeeDee had met the criteria.

She glanced back at Zoey. "That wound on your head looks painful."

"It just throbs, mostly. But whenever I accidentally touch it, it's fire. And I think when it turns into scar tissue, no hair will grow in that strip. What does it feel like? Having the implants, I mean?"

"It took me a while to identify the facial expressions and tones of voice

I was getting back from certain men I encountered. Then I realized, for the first time, what I was getting was respect."

"Respect, or fear?"

"With these particular men, they're the same thing. Haven't you noticed that, since you took over this whole operation? People looking at you different?"

"I guess. It's weird, because in some ways it's made it much easier to get the truth out of people and in some ways it's made it much harder."

DeeDee nodded. "Sometimes I think I just get different lies."

Zoey had met DeeDee about five months ago. DeeDee was not a people person but, it turned out, had developed a method over the years for finding like-minded friends: she attended meetings of powerful men and sought out other women who looked as fed up as she was. The series of meetings in which Zoey and DeeDee had encountered each other had involved a public relations crisis, the transfer of ownership of multiple corporate entities, and Zoey accidentally kidnapping a child and getting briefly set on fire during a parade. Afterward, DeeDee had directly sought out Zoey for strength-augmentation implants and Zoey had unilaterally given the approval. They'd done the procedure a month ago, a lattice of exotic materials woven around bones and ligaments. DeeDee had left the operating room in extreme pain, wincing as she walked out to the street, grabbing the rear bumper of an unmanned delivery truck and lifting it effortlessly with one hand. Zoey had watched as DeeDee just stood there, holding the ass end of the truck over her head, quietly weeping tears of joy.

"Maybe this is too personal," said Zoey, "but have you noticed it's harder to get dates? I don't know what genders you're into but I assume it's weird for everybody."

"Well, these gloves come off, along with the rest of the costume. I don't disclose up front that I can crush their skulls, the ones who are looking for that in a partner aren't the kind of—"

DeeDee stopped and turned at the sound of frantic footsteps from the hall. Echo came sprinting into the room, skidding to a stop a moment before Wu came flying in after her.

Zoey spun to face them. "It's fine, guys, calm down."

DeeDee said, "It's just me," and neither of the new faces relaxed at that statement.

Echo said, "The moment you got in proximity to the machine, alarms blasted in the conference room."

"Did you let her in here?" asked Wu.

DeeDee responded, "I didn't have to let her in, she lives here."

"It's fine," said Zoey, "she was in my room when I came out of the shower. Fully dressed. Everyone was fully dressed the whole time. Don't bother asking how she got in because she's not going to tell you, just as she never told you any of the other times."

"You left your garage door open," said DeeDee, her attention already back on the control screen.

"Her implants aren't working right, we're reinstalling the software. Everything is fine."

Wu didn't seem to agree. "The estate's security system should have identified an intruder regardless of how she got in."

"She went into the system and added herself as a resident," said Will, who came in the door behind them, holding a drink. "She did it one of the times she visited with Alonzo." He looked to DeeDee. "Right?"

"Why haven't you told Zoey about Rex Wrexx?" asked DeeDee.

Will's face didn't so much as twitch. "He's a D-list celebrity scumbag in a city full of them. He hurt a prostitute, he was banned from further services and forced to pay restitution. We've had no problem with him since."

DeeDee scoffed and, well, she didn't so much *smile* as bare her teeth. "I'll be curious to know what Zoey thinks of that antiseptic summary, once she sees the photos."

The screen on the fabricator chimed and DeeDee examined it, swiped away some messages, then tried to close her hand. She still could not make a fist. She cursed under her breath.

Zoey said, "She needs a surgeon-slash-augmentation mechanic."

"We're still trying to find one," replied Will. "It's a specialized practice and a lot of them are getting scared off because of the danger and lawlessness involved, plus some seem to think the entire concept is spitting in the face of God. It won't be cheap. Are you okay with that?"

Zoey said, "I'll cover it."

Will didn't seem to approve but said nothing.

DeeDee said, "You want to handle Rex, or you want me to do it?"

"That," replied Will, "depends on what your 'handling' entails."

"That depends on how quickly he tells me the truth."

"We'll talk to him."

"When?"

"Soon. Tomorrow. The schedule is full tonight, with the debate and everything else. Can you hold off until then?"

"What if he snatches another victim?"

"If another girl goes missing," said Will, "that won't mean Rex is behind it. Go stake out his house, or put a Blink tracker on him. But don't confront him, you'll just make everything worse."

"And what if I choose to do it anyway?"

"Then the violence gets pinned on Alonzo, since you're connected to him and he has that reputation, then Leonidas Damon wins the election. Is that what you want?"

"And what if I decide the lives of these women mean more than your politics? What will you do if I disobey your order, Will?"

"Everybody's here!" shouted a new voice before Will could answer. Everyone turned.

In from the hall sauntered Zoey's mother, Melinda, a woman whom the press described as "striking" or "the elegant original of which Zoey appears to be a defective bootleg copy," depending on the publication.

"Hey, DeeDee!" she shouted. "Love how the outfit turned out! So scary! Can you sit down in it? It looks stiff."

"Hello, Ms. Ashe."

"Call me Melinda! My daughter is Ms. Ashe. Oh, Zoey, your head is looking better."

Zoey had just flat-out lied to her mother about how she'd gotten the wound, saying in a text message that it was an accident at the beef factory, a result of her goofing around with the equipment.

"Come, everybody," said her mother, "we're going to be late for dinner. We're having it early so you can take off for the debate, remember?"

Zoey said, "I'm not hungry. Which just tells you what kind of a day it's been, normally I can eat through anything. DeeDee, are you gonna be at the debate?"

"We can talk about that over dinner," answered Zoey's mother. "Both of you."

"I really must be going," said DeeDee. "But thank you for the offer."

"You do must be going! To dinner! Right now."

Zoey sighed. "Just give in, DeeDee, there's no arguing with her."

CHAPTER
10

ZOEY ALWAYS ATE IN the giant kitchen (her favorite room in the house) because the alternative was eating in the cavernous dining room with its absurdly long table (Zoey's second-least favorite room). Well, that's where she ate when she wasn't just taking food back to her bedroom or, more likely, eating the entire meal during her walk back to that bedroom. Everyone was thus piled into the kitchen at Zoey's insistence, some at the bar in front of the ovens/grill/deep fryers where Carlton was working his magic, others across the room at the other bar, which was dedicated to beverages—fully stocked with liquor and a gleaming espresso machine that, when she was in the mood, Zoey could play like a fine instrument.

"What are we eating?" asked the tall, bald woman wearing the obsidian suit of shark-tooth armor.

"Ah, everybody orders what they want in advance," said Zoey. "Echo is having a protein shake made of those banana things everyone is eating now."

"Enset," said Echo.

"Will is having some kind of grain alcohol with a side of glass, Budd and Andre brought barbecue from Andre's restaurant—"

"Best in the state," interjected Andre.

"Which, I'm now told, is the best barbecue in all of, uh, Utah. Wu always brings his own meals, his wife makes these adorable little boxes with the veggies and stuff all neatly arranged in compartments—he can't stand to have his foods touching each other. But Carlton can make almost anything you ask for, though sometimes I think he has stuff delivered and then plates it as if he made it himself."

"That you save your most profuse compliments for those meals," said Carlton, "is most hurtful."

DeeDee asked Zoey, "What are you having?"

"Oh, ah, this is weird but he's making one of my comfort foods from when I was a kid: cracker flitters. I actually feel like the name is racist somehow but crackers are pretty much the only ingredient. See that pale mush in the big glass bowl over there?"

DeeDee stared. "Okay, I have to know more."

"It was my mom's grandmother's recipe, she said it came from the Depression. You take a whole bunch of saltine crackers, soak them in water until they fall apart, drain off the water, mix in an egg, make them into patties, and then deep-fry them. That's it. Then you eat them with maple syrup, like pancakes. They have zero nutritional value but they taste like a lazy Sunday morning."

"That is what my grandma would've called a 'struggle meal.' I'm in."

After the food was made and distributed, everyone ate in silence for about two minutes until Zoey's mother looked over at DeeDee and said, "So how's the vigilante business?"

"That's not my full-time job," replied DeeDee, "it's more of a community service. The cops in this city barely show up and when they do, they seem to pick what calls to respond to based on what's easiest. Private security only protects those who can afford it. You said the costume is scary, but I'd make it scarier if I could. I can't be everywhere but if I show up in these dudes' nightmares, I don't have to be."

Zoey said, "She protects the sex workers."

DeeDee shrugged. "I try to be there for anybody who works off the books and doesn't feel like they can go to the cops, or won't get a response if they do. In this city, yeah, it's the sex workers most often. A lot of the other off-the-books laborers, the big gruff construction workers, they look out for each other, I suppose. This is really good, by the way, I'd ask for the recipe but fortunately I was able to memorize it."

If she was being honest, Zoey had spent the days after DeeDee recovered from the surgery waiting to hear about some prominent local lowlife having been punched so hard that his lungs landed on a rooftop several blocks away. Most of the augmentation applications had come from individuals with a specific score they wanted to settle; DeeDee, however, had always insisted that it was simply about correcting an imbalance. A lawless society was one in which women were destined to be prey unless they huddled under the umbrella of protection offered by some strong man whom they were now shackled to in one way or the other. She wanted to be strong because in this world, strength was freedom, independence. That alone, DeeDee had said, made the surgery worth it. Still, it seemed inevitable to Zoey that somebody was eventually going to get their lungs punched out.

"Someday we'll have police around here," said Zoey's mother, and Zoey felt herself tense up. There was no more sensitive subject than this.

Every business acquisition was a gigantic headache for Zoey, but her purchase of the largest private security firm in the city was like a migraine that somebody had tried to cure with a drum solo and a nail gun. First, she found she was employing a large number of violent sadists and/or lifelong bullies who mainly wanted a blank check to crack skulls and look cool. So the first change she'd made was to make the company uniforms pink; anybody who instantly quit rather than wear them was someone she didn't want on staff anyway. But they all just went to work for rival companies (or, in some cases, got hired by the actual Tabula Ra$a PD), and the competing security firms had started to act as rival gangs, especially those in the employ of actual criminal organizations. Pitched battles had been known to break out.

Zoey just muttered, "Well, good luck to whoever tries to get that going."

"It's crazy," her mother said to DeeDee, "that nice people like you are forced to get violent just to keep things tolerable."

"It's all violence," replied DeeDee. "Violence, or the threat of it, is the only reason any of us can do anything. If you have a home, the only reason a bunch of scary people can't just come and take it from you is that promise of violence from agents of the state. Money only has value when it's backed by a government and there's no such thing as a government without guns."

"In any case," said Will, "the hard part is making sure you're getting it right. You punish the wrong people and everyone loses faith in the system real fast."

"And by the wrong people, do you mean the innocent, or the ones who have the power to kick back?"

"Let me put it this way: since you've started patrolling around the red-light districts, has business for the sex workers gone up, or down?"

"I don't keep track, that's not my area."

"I'll answer for you: it's gone down. Way down. Because for every one scumbag you scare away, you run off ten normal customers who are terrified they'll get falsely accused and torn to pieces by the Obsidian Avenger. And since there's no due process or trial, they know they'll never get to prove their innocence."

Zoey asked, "Are you guys arguing about that Rex Rex guy again? Somebody tell me what his deal is."

"Rex Wrexx," corrected Budd.

"What?"

"You said Rex Rex, his last name starts with a 'W.'"

"We are saying it one hundred percent the same way."

"You seriously can't hear the difference?" asked Echo.

"Are you guys messing with me?"

"When you look at the women who've gone missing," said DeeDee impatiently, "what do they have in common?"

Zoey was eager to show that she knew this one. "They all have flower names."

"No, when you *look* at them."

Zoey brought up her phone and scrolled through the trio of holographic heads. "Ah, let's see. They're all under thirty, looks like. Different hair, different eye color . . . they're all conventionally attractive."

"They're all *white*."

"Oh. But that's most of the city, right?"

"That's half the city," said Echo, "but only twenty percent of the sex workers."

"Three white ones tells me the perp is targeting them specifically," said DeeDee. "Which means he was probably a customer."

"Or," rebutted Will, "whoever is behind it is media savvy and knows what sort of victims make headlines."

"We know Wrexx visited Violet at least once. And I bet he saw the other two off the books."

"But who is he?" asked Zoey. "You said he's famous?"

"Famous for being famous," replied Budd around a barbecue rib. "You've seen him out and about, he lives in that bus with the clear walls, calls it the Fish Bowl? Lives his life in front of a live audience, streams it all. Not even the toilet is blocked off. He's also an activist for a whole lot of causes pertaining to the legalization side of things. Got a lot of fans, particularly among women, been doing a whole lot of heavy lifting in terms of registering the vote."

Zoey groaned. Pieces were starting to fall into place, and they were forming a picture of a giant dog turd.

Andre nodded. "If Alonzo beats the polls and wins, it'll be due to last-minute deciders, the folks who haven't really gotten into election stuff until the final days. That's the kind of votes Wrexx can sway, the casuals."

"Did you just call him by his first or last name there?" asked Zoey.

"Last."

"I swear, I don't hear it."

"We have statistical models that show it's pretty much impossible for Alonzo to win without Wrexx's support," added Echo. "Understand, it's not just him, he has a whole network of influencer friends who'd fall like dominos if Wrexx turned on Alonzo."

DeeDee said, "Not that this is relevant to your precious electoral strategy, but Wrexx had a favorite sex worker, named Lyra Connor. Gorgeous red braids. He almost killed her during a session. She went into a private Blink group that night, warning other pros that this guy may not stay in the fantasy stage of his murder fetish much longer. But of course, that message didn't stay with the sex workers, it leaked to everybody, including the press and people on the opposite side of Wrexx's politics. He wasn't too happy about that. Then one day, Lyra is walking to work and a drone swoops down. It sprays this sticky liquid in her face, then a jet of sparks to ignite it. It was basically napalm. Her whole head lit on fire. Left her mostly blind, deformed. Burned off her eyelids, her nose, her ears, her lips."

Zoey put down her fork.

"And then," said Will, "Rex paid the girl two million dollars in compensation, plus paid for surgery to fix her up."

"Under the table," said DeeDee. "Nothing admitted publicly, nothing done legally. He denied all involvement, at least whenever there was a camera on. The man has a fetish, Will, for hurting women—really hurting them, I'm not talking about some slaps on the ass. And nothing will come between a man and his fetish. That's all most serial killers are, men whose brains have short-circuited to connect sex and murder."

"For one thing," rebutted Will, "he has an alibi for at least two of the missing girls—"

"Unless he hired someone to snatch them up," interrupted DeeDee.

"And two, the body we saw on display today was butchered. That was never part of his thing."

"Rage against women is his thing. His whole thing. That's what I saw up there, on those screens, splashed across the buildings. Rage."

"You saw what someone wanted you to see. If I thought Rex did it, I'd send you after him myself."

"No, you wouldn't. Not with the election coming."

"Well, I'd send you after the votes are in."

"Enough!" shouted Zoey's mother. "No more talk about dark subjects at dinner. Zoey, tell me about your day. Aside from the bad stuff."

"Uh . . . oof, aside from the bad stuff? Hmm. I met some fluffy little cows."

"Ooh! Did you get pictures?"

"No, it seemed like it'd be in poor taste under the circumstances."

"DeeDee, how about yours? What did you do this morning?"

"Nothing interesting."

"Do you think I'm asking you because the answer might be *interesting*? People don't talk to entertain each other, they talk to connect! Come on! Bore me!"

DeeDee thought about it. "I'm growing a little herb garden in the window of my apartment. Got six little pots, all but one of them has sprouted so far."

"See! That's great! I kill every plant I touch, it's like I put out a toxin or something. I always heard they like music but apparently I'm playing the wrong bands."

Zoey said, "I think the cat was peeing on them."

Wu said, "Mei has taught her chinchilla how to hold small objects in its tiny little hands. For a while anyway, before he starts eating them."

"That's good," replied Zoey, who didn't understand most of that. She was pretty sure Mei was his wife, though.

Andre said, "My oldest son beat me in chess last night. First time ever. I didn't let him win, neither."

"You have children?"

"Is everyone clear on what to do at the debate tonight?" asked Will. "It's me, Zoey, and Andre. Echo is prepping at Catharsis, Budd is chasing down leads on the three girls. And yes, DeeDee, if I could spare more people for that, I would. I assume you'll be staking out Rex's bus, but if you stumble across any other leads, please let us know."

"I'll be clear on what to do tonight," said Zoey, "right up until a reporter asks me political questions that have no possible right answers."

"I'm not worried about that."

"Do you remember the last time a reporter put a camera and microphone in my face and asked me about politics? When I had been drinking and was eating that mango?"

Zoey's mother barked a laugh.

It had been at the open-bar reception after a ribbon-cutting ceremony for a new clinic. A food stand was serving chili-dusted spears of mango that were dipped in boiling sugar and then dunked in ice water, forming a sweet glaze around the fruit that made a loud crunch when you bit into it. Zoey, who had begun drinking while the ribbon was still intact, had been in the middle of chewing a piece when the reporter asked her a question. She had held up a finger like she was requesting the reporter wait until she finished chewing, but then she just took another bite. The reporter kept asking questions and Zoey just kept eating her noisy candied fruit, making eye contact the entire time.

"We remember," said Andre. "We've all seen the video. Many times."

Will said, "That's why I'm not worried, there's nothing I can advise

that would improve on that. But there's a lot of standing around and mingling before and after, that's where you can get into trouble. You know
the rules for that?"

"No smiling," said Andre. "You've got to wear a serious face the whole
time. You never know when you'll accidentally be smiling at some opponent or other unsavory character."

"Do you think you can handle the no-smiling rule, Will?" asked Zoey's mother with a devilish smirk. "You think you can avoid breaking into
a giggling fit?"

Will didn't reply.

Zoey said, "I can't imagine finding anything whimsical about the event,
no matter what anyone says or does. It's two people lying to an audience
that is demanding they lie while also lying to themselves. The whole thing
is a dour slog from start to finish. Where is it being held, by the way?"

"On a pirate ship," replied Andre with a completely straight face.

Zoey chuckled. No one else did.

CHAPTER
11

ARTHUR LIVINGSTON AND THE other founders of Tabula Ra$a chose its location for two reasons: 1) it was positioned to intercept eastbound tourist traffic heading to Las Vegas via high-speed rail and 2) the city's whole "let's see how things work when we barely have a government" ethos appealed to Utah's state leadership at the time (the promise of a frankly jaw-dropping number of new jobs and tourist dollars didn't hurt). And while the location had other bonuses, such as some of the most spectacular natural landscapes in the world, what it did not have was beaches. This shortcoming inspired one of the most lavish, ill-conceived, and obscenely expensive construction boondoggles in the history of the city, and thus the world.

The Atlantis Recreation Complex, colloquially the "Tourist Boiler," was pitched as a clear dome about twice the size of any current NFL stadium that would cover an artificial indoor lake. The lake would be encircled by a white-sand beach dotted with cabanas, restaurants, and gift shops. Waves would be generated for surfing and the waters stocked with exotic fish for viewing by scuba-diving tourists. In the center of the lake was to be a half-scale replica of the *Titanic* (still some 400 feet long), featuring period-accurate cabins, dining, and entertainment. The ship was rigged so that, once a month, it would sink, hydraulics slowly lowering the whole thing into the water while giggling guests boarded lifeboats and took selfies. Tickets for the sinking event would start at ten grand apiece.

It would wind up taking twelve years to complete the Atlantis complex, at fifteen times the original estimated cost. The entire exotic fish stock died due to an inability to keep the water at the proper temperature (they were all replaced, then died again, in a process that would have to be repeated five more times). The original design of the glass roof was unintentionally such that, when the sun was in a certain position, all of the light would be focused on one spot, turning it into a heat ray—something that was only discovered when a tourist's paddle boat was set aflame (thus the "Tourist Boiler" moniker). The press had a field day with the cursed nature of a project with "Atlantis" in the name and a *Titanic* in the center; puns about the venture "sinking" were exhausted before ground had even been broken on construction. Still, once it officially opened, everyone agreed the facility was one of the marvels of the modern world and the *Titanic*-sinking event reservations were booked three years out. No one could have predicted that, six months after opening, hydraulics failures would cause the replica ship to unexpectedly sink off schedule, resulting in the drowning deaths of five tourists.

The entire *Titanic* exhibit had therefore been removed long before Zoey arrived in town, replaced with a generic pirate ship–themed restaurant and venue that was designed to remain firmly above water at all times. When the two mayoral candidates were negotiating their terms for the debates, they agreed on two dates, with each candidate picking a venue. Leonidas Damon asked for a debate in the park, surrounded by the city's tent-dwelling homeless population, one month prior to election day. Alonzo Dunn said he wanted his on the weekend prior to the vote ("You know nobody is paying attention before that!") and demanded it be held on the Tourist Boiler pirate ship so he could have some rum afterward. "And maybe during," he'd said, "it depends on how the debate goes. I find all of this mess pretty boring."

Zoey, for her part, hated the Atlantis Recreation Complex and wouldn't even look at it whenever they drove past. She'd grown up in a town in which the tallest building was the water tower and hated huge man-made structures in general. Somebody told her the term for it was "megalophobia," but to her, the dread they inspired didn't seem irrational at all. Buildings that big simply shouldn't exist. These megaliths looming overhead, reaching up and stealing a piece of the sky—it was like witnessing mankind's hubris in action. When she saw skyscrapers, she always imagined them toppling down on everyone below (and it wasn't like she hadn't seen that very thing happen before).

Rational or not, nothing had ever triggered that feeling in the pit of her gut as strongly as the interior of the Atlantis Complex when they all stepped inside for that evening's debate. The entire night sky had been replaced by an incomprehensibly massive dome constructed out of thousands of triangular windows that Zoey could imagine raining down and impaling people like stilettos from the heavens. Attached to the ceiling was a framework of lights and a ring of gigantic video screens to broadcast whatever event was happening down on the pirate ship. Zoey thought about somebody having to change a lightbulb up there and got so dizzy that she had to just look at her feet the rest of the way.

They were quickly ushered across the narrow beach that formed a ring around the indoor lake and, to Zoey's horror, led toward a small ferry to taxi them out to the ship. She'd known they'd have to cross the artificial lake but for some reason had assumed there was a walkway or tunnel or something. As they bobbed across the choppy water (the fact that the waves were artificial infuriated her for some reason), she looked back at the tourists hanging out on the fake beach around their cookouts and bonfires. She found herself envying them. Not a care in the world. She leaned over a rail and couldn't see the bottom of the "lake" below her. She had no idea how deep it was, aside from that it had to be deep enough to 1) allow scuba diving and 2) drown in, since those were the two things she knew for sure happened here. Zoey was exactly as good a swimmer as she appeared to be, which was not at all.

Once they were safely off the ferry (after having to step precariously over a terrifying, foot-wide gap between the ferryboat and the wet stairs that led up to the pirate ship's deck), Zoey was greeted by one of the few sights she found even more chilling than massive buildings or deep water: a bunch of rich people in suits, mingling. Though this was the first moment Zoey was thankful that her team had shot down her request to come dressed as a pirate, in favor of stuffing herself into a pantsuit that made her look like she was going to a Halloween party dressed as a stock-photo businesswoman. She was actually wearing a fancy hat for maybe the first time ever; it was a white beret thing that covered her head wound and looked so stupid on her that she giggled every time she caught her reflection.

Zoey scanned the crowd, then turned back to Will and Andre.

"So when does this thing start, again?"

"Not soon enough," said Will, who had produced a flask from his inside pocket. He took a drink and then, before he could put it away, Zoey grabbed it and took a nip of her own. She knew Will secretly hated when she did that, which she supposed was much better than Will secretly loving it.

She found the pirate ship itself disappointing. It had all of the stuff you'd expect, the masts and the sails overhead (the biggest sail bearing a giant Jolly Roger), along with weathered-looking ropes and anchors here and there. But the illusion was ruined by the inclusion of all of the modern features that revealed it to be nothing but a very expensive theme restaurant: sound equipment and lights around the stage, plus all of the fire extinguishers and red EXIT signs that were probably mandated by law. Still, it seemed like a great place to have a kid's birthday party. To the left of the stage was the raised back end of the ship that Zoey was pretty sure was called the poop deck, which apparently housed the kitchen. Servers in tuxedos were bustling in and out of swinging doors with drinks and hors d'oeuvres. None of them were dressed like pirates. To be honest, that was the part that she found the most disappointing. *How was no one dressed like a pirate?*

"Hold on," said Zoey. "Is my whole sense of balance off or is the floor rocking slightly?"

"Well, it is a boat," said Will.

"It's not a real one, though."

"It's still a free-floating structure," said Wu. "Just chained to the floor to keep it from drifting over to the beach." He delivered this like he knew Zoey would receive it as bad news.

"Okay, you need to point me to the nearest bathroom I can run to if I get seasick. I'm not puking over the rail while everyone films and laughs."

Before she'd even finished speaking, the mingling business people started alighting on them like flies on a dead elk. A guy who looked like a young tech billionaire approached Zoey, shook her hand, and thanked her for her support during "that whole thing in the press." She had no idea who he was or what he was talking about but nodded, remembering to keep her face serious. A woman in an evening gown that made it clear that either she or Zoey had misunderstood dress code came up and hugged Andre, who asked her how the kids were doing.

"Why, it's Will Blackwater," said a voice from behind Zoey, "the man who will be responsible if one day my car spontaneously explodes."

Zoey turned to find that Leonidas Damon, visibly made-up for the cameras, had approached with an entourage that included a few young assistants with tablets, all looking stressed out of their minds.

Will looked bored to see him. "I'm curious, do you think the introduction of prohibition and black markets increases or decreases the number of people getting blown up in cars?"

"I agree there is less crime when everything is legal. Where we disagree is on whether or not the suffering of innocents increases or decreases."

"What we disagree on depends entirely on whether or not our conversation is conducted on-camera. And the only reason you or anyone else think crime is rampant in this city is because the worst of it gets splashed across everyone's feeds in real time. The media pours snuff films into every eyeball until the citizens grovel at authoritarians' feet and say, 'Please, please take away my freedom.'"

"And you want me to believe that rehearsed little speech *wasn't* for the cameras?" Damon gestured around to indicate cameras that Zoey couldn't actually see but she had no doubt were there. They always were.

Wu, appearing to have little interest in the conversation, glanced around and said, "This venue is a security nightmare. They're not checking anyone coming in."

Damon said, "The boat is VIPs-only, all of the staff have been thoroughly vetted."

Wu nodded toward the tourists carousing around the artificial beach encircling said boat. "*They* haven't. But of course, we're still completely safe unless it turns out mankind has invented some kind of weapon that can kill from a distance."

"Well, all I can say is that if your girl here is under such a dire threat from the common folk, maybe she should stop making so many enemies. Me, I invite my enemies to come sit in the front row. Enjoy the debate."

He went off to go mingle with some other powerful sociopaths and Zoey felt about three percent of her tension ease. On the way, Leonidas stopped to talk to a woman with four children—two boys, two girls—and gave her a kiss on the cheek. His wife. She was, in fact, the rude woman who'd picked Zoey up at the gates of their home earlier in the day. The kids looked like they had been promised a pirate-ship party and gotten a crowd of stuffy grown-ups instead.

Zoey muttered, "He can't really win, can he? I don't care if the cameras hear me say it, I smell sulfur when he's around."

"YARRRRGHHH!" shouted Andre suddenly, to seemingly no one. "AVAST YE MATEYS!" He gestured at the venue staff. "So no pirates?"

"I know, right?" replied Zoey. "I'd assume a place like this would hire only amputees so that they can all have the peg legs. Hey, they could hire the former meat processors."

Will showed a microscopic grimace. "So that's how long it took you to forget you're on camera, huh?"

Andre said, "Give me a YARGH, Alonzo."

He was addressing mayoral candidate Alonzo Dunn, or "Megaboss Alonzo" as he was known in the underworld, who had just arrived with an entourage made up of four stunning women and one giant, terrifying dude.

"Come on, I can't be seen acting foolish next to unsavory types such as yourselves," said Alonzo. "This is a serious occasion, now, I have to be dignified. You know that accent isn't even real? I mean nobody in history actually talked with a pirate accent, it was invented by the dude who played Long John Silver in *Treasure Island*, about a hundred years ago. Isn't that crazy, a whole culture from history gets overwritten by one British actor who probably made it up on the spot. Same with witches, they were never green until *The Wizard of Oz*, all because that's the makeup they decided to use that day. Speaking of lying little trolls hiding behind the curtain, I see you've met Leo Damon. Do you feel like you need to go take a shower now?"

Zoey said, "That guy is a turd in my teeth. As for his politics, the only thing I like is that he wants to hang rapists from bridges, I'm actually fine with that part."

"You are? I'm kinda surprised to hear you say that."

"It'd be nice to send a message to all of the other predators."

"I've known a whole lot of predators, Zoey. Done time with a few, worked with a few, got rid of a few. One thing I'll tell you right now: they don't get that message. These guys, the way their brains work, they don't think they're gonna get caught. That's their whole thing, they can't conceive of a future beyond satisfying this desire or that. Threaten them with death, threaten them with torture, it don't matter. You know why?"

"Because they're sick? Mentally ill?"

"No. Or, you know, that's not for me to say. No, the reason they don't think they'll get caught is that *they're right*. You do a crime with no evidence left behind, no witnesses, victims who can't talk to the cops—you're free and clear. Some of these guys prey on girls their whole lives, hundreds of them, before they die or just age out of the behavior. So people like Damon say, 'What we're gonna do is, the rare bad guy we actually catch, we're going to go way over the top in punishing him, to set an example.' But it doesn't work, people have been trying it for thousands of years. I mean, maybe it deters good citizens, the ones who wouldn't dream about raping anyway. So the only purpose it serves is cruelty. Remember, Zoey, cruelty is more addictive than any drug ever sold on these streets. Your average citizen just wants a righteous excuse before they dose."

Another speech, Zoey thought, for the cameras. "So what are you supposed to do?" she asked. "To stop the crime, I mean?"

Before Alonzo could answer, an assistant whispered in his ear and he said, "Find your seats, the show's about to start."

They did. Zoey had about three minutes to try to relax before Wu shifted forward, suddenly paying close attention.

Will noticed and asked, "What is it?"

"Boats. Some of the beachgoers have started paddling their little fishing boats and rafts out, to get closer to the ship. The venue assured us nobody would be allowed to do that. So now not only are the tourists not vetted, but apparently they'll be able to come right up to the hull."

Zoey asked, "Do the cannons work?"

"That would be bad PR," said Will without even a hint of a smile. "Either way, security will stop anyone who tries to climb on board. Hopefully."

Wu's eyes were flicking back and forth, scanning data from inside his glasses. "I'm not worried about someone climbing on board. I have six different devices inside this suit that can deal with some crazy who rushes the floor. I'm worried about—"

Someone shushed them. The candidates were coming out to the twin lecterns to polite applause. A moderator followed them out and took a seat with his back to the audience. He, also, was not dressed like a pirate.

Everything got quiet enough that even whispers would be heard, so Zoey pulled out her phone and sent Wu a text:

WHY ARE YOU SO NERVOUS?

He pulled out his own phone and typed,

NO ESCAPE ROUTE OFF THIS BOAT.

Wu always sent everything in all caps, so she wasn't totally clear on the level of alarm he was trying to convey.

"Gentlemen, it is time for your opening statements. Alonzo, you were allowed to go first last time, so let's give Mr. Damon the first shot today."

The man flashed a shark's smile and started in.

"Thank you. Look, can we put aside all the rhetoric and slogans for a moment? Here's the honest truth: Nobody likes getting a speeding ticket, or a visit from the cops for a noise complaint, or to be accused of a crime committed by someone else who happened to look the same. It's a hassle, right? From the time we're little kids running amuck in the nursery, we fantasize about a world without rules, without grown-ups ruining the fun. But the only way that works in the real world is if every single citizen governs themselves. I would love to live in such a world, in which no one wants to rob or deceive others, in which no one is enslaved to drugs or forced by the powerful to trade their bodies and their dignity for food and shelter. A world in which no one lives in fear. But that is not our world and, I'm sorry to say, *that is not our city.*"

Zoey typed,

Are we in danger?

Wu:

STAY ALERT.

Then, after a moment,

ONE CRAFT IS A CONCERN.

Zoey gave him a quizzical look but Wu was now transfixed by whatever the threat-assessment software was streaming across his glasses. Will was sitting on the other side of her. Zoey elbowed him and showed him the text exchange on her phone. He just gave a quick nod, as if he was already aware.

". . . I say that laws are not tyranny," warbled Damon from the stage. "A neighborhood where you're scared to walk to the corner store out of fear that you'll be mugged or raped, that's tyranny! 'Freedom' isn't an addict with a gun in your face; you're under the tyranny of that gun and he's under the tyranny of his addiction. Laws and police are freedom from the tyranny of the street thug!"

He was interrupted by applause, both from some of the VIPs on the boat, and faintly, from the tourists back on the beach. The moderator asked the audience to remain silent, per debate rules.

Damon resumed, emboldened. "I say, only a devil would try to flip that on its head, to turn black into white. And please notice that the people in suits you see down here in this very audience, the ones who rail against the very concept of the law, *they* don't subject themselves to the tyranny of the street thug—*they* have bodyguards and gates to hide behind. My friends, you all saw it today: we have women getting snatched off of our streets *and butchered like animals*. But is it any surprise? If you re-create the lawless filth of Whitechapel, why wouldn't you get a Jack the Ripper? When you cater to perverse appetites, the monsters that dwell inside men come slithering out. The Sex Butcher isn't the first and he won't be the last."

Zoey's phone chimed again but this time it was a text from Andre, who was seated on the other side of Will. A little hologram popped up over her phone: a looping animation of a horse pooping.

Wu studied the info in his glasses and typed.

Wu:

CAN YOU SWIM?

Zoey stopped breathing.

Zoey:

NO!!!!!!!!!!

And then,

ARE WE GOING TO DIE?

After a moment,

Wu:

STAY ALERT.

". . . this city was built on blood spilled by a gangster, his people sit in this room right now," said Damon, gesturing toward Zoey, "all scrubbed and dressed up like they're ready for court, funneling money to my gangster opponent. But when you see their casinos and skyscrapers, their lavish music festivals and self-congratulatory charity dinners, you should be imagining a roomful of predators who grind up the underclasses and feed them to tourists. Make no mistake: that is what is really happening here. Thank you."

More applause. Zoey vaguely noticed that Damon had just slipped in a nod to the stupid human-hamburger conspiracy theory, but that was now the least of her concerns. She peered behind her, trying to make out what was happening down on the water. It was impossible see anything without standing up and making a spectacle of herself.

"Thank you, Mr. Damon," said the moderator. "Mr. Dunn, your opening remarks."

Alonzo smiled and spread his hands behind the podium. "I'm just gonna say it: If you elect me mayor, I promise you that within a month, you will forget this election ever happened. Within a year, *I* won't remember I'm mayor. I will be invisible to you, because damn it, I have a life to live. I've got a business to run. I say government should be like a hot-water heater: if it's working right, you never even think about it. Now, see this dude over here? The whole problem with him is that *he wants to be mayor.* Hell, he wants to be president. That's the problem with our whole system, our whole society: power goes to the ones who want it most and the ones who want it most tend to be more conniving and diabolical than any of the supposed street thugs they're trying to scare you about. Well, I pledge to you today, I don't want to be mayor. Never did. You can browse through everything I've ever been caught on-camera saying and yeah, you'll hear some inappropriate sentiments, quite a few in fact, but you'll find I have never expressed even a fleeting desire to hold this office. So why am I running? To keep this guy out! This guy and all the other ones like him. The ones who want to stand up on stages like this and give pretty speeches and try to—"

A clap of thunder hammered Zoey's ears, followed by a roar of debris raining across the water. Everyone bolted up from their chairs. Someone was screaming.

A man in a suit ran out in front of the lecterns and shouted, "EVERY-ONE INSIDE! THIS WAY! THERE IS A SAFE ROOM!"

He was ushering them toward the poop deck and the kitchen. Instead of following, Zoey turned to Wu.

"What do we do?!?"

"Someone blew a hole in the hull."

"But we can't sink! This isn't even a real—"

The floor tilted. Suddenly the water was in view and Zoey felt gravity trying to pull her down toward the railing. There were gasps and shouts from everywhere, including from the tourist-packed beach across the water.

Nothing about what her body was experiencing made sense, it was all happening too fast. The boat wasn't so much sinking as *falling*, like it was being yanked down by a kraken. Chairs slid across the floor around her, people were stumbling and falling to their knees. Some were still scrambling toward the kitchen, trying to run along a deck that was suddenly on a thirty-degree incline. That was stupid, Zoey thought; if the whole thing was going under the water, that enclosed space was a death trap. Up on the stage, Alonzo was clinging to his podium but quickly realizing it wasn't really affixed to the ground at all. He and it were both scooting down toward the rail—and the water—along with everyone else. Leonidas Damon was nowhere to be seen but Zoey spotted his wife clutching two of their children, screaming for someone to help as they all skidded down the deck.

Zoey fell on her butt, then tried to use her palms and feet to keep from sliding down. She kicked off her shoes, figuring her bare feet would have more grip. There was nothing to grab on to, the floor was smooth and the surrounding furniture was nothing but light folding chairs that were already tumbling down past her.

"If we go into the water," shouted Wu from somewhere nearby, "hold on to me! I'll keep us afloat!"

From behind them, Will yelled, "Keep her out of the water!"

"She'll be fine," said Andre from somewhere else in the chaos, "she's more buoyant than any of us."

"Don't assume that what just happened is the only stage of the attack!" replied Will, as if that had been a serious rebuttal. "Whoever did this could be down there waiting to unleash stage two. Try to—"

"WATCH OUT!" someone screamed. "IT'S COMING DOWN!"

For one horrifying moment, Zoey had thought her nightmare scenario had come true and the glass ceiling was crashing in on them. Instead, she looked up to find the main rigging was falling over, the mast of artificially aged wood ripping itself free from the deck in a cloud of splinters, pulled down by the weight of the enormous canvas Jolly Roger sail.

The rig fell across the deck and smashed through the railing. Debris splashed into water that was now right at deck level, lapping up onto the floor no more than twenty feet from where Zoey was trying to use butt friction to overcome gravity. Flailing bodies were piling up down at the railing, having slid as far as they could go. At least three were already in the water, splashing around in their fancy attire.

Meanwhile, the huge Jolly Roger sail was laying itself gently down onto the surface of the water. It was this that triggered a scream.

A child's scream.

It was a little girl in a red dress, thrashing in the water right where the sail was about to land. The sheet of canvas, big enough to completely cover a baseball infield and probably as heavy as a car, was about to push the girl under and hold her there.

Zoey scrambled to her feet and made a tumbling, awkward run down the tilting deck, toward the girl who, as Zoey ran, vanished under the rippling skull and crossbones. The child's screams were silenced as she lost access to her air. Zoey reached the partially submerged railing and plunged in, feetfirst. The water was so cold that it punched the breath out of her chest, her entire body convulsing in shock. She pulled herself along the railing toward the edge of the canvas, took as much of a breath as she could, and pushed herself under the heavy cloth, under the water.

She tried to reach out and snatch the girl's arm, or dress, or something. She pushed farther in, into total darkness, feeling water burn its way into her sinuses. She tried to open her eyes but all she could make out was bubbles and chaos. Then she thought she spotted the thrashing shape, the flowing red of the girl's dress, still just out of reach. Zoey was still clutching the rail. She couldn't swim, couldn't even keep herself afloat without help.

She tried to push herself farther along the rail, toward the red blur that was the little girl but found she couldn't move forward now, for seemingly no reason. It was nightmare logic: there were no obstructions, yet she couldn't progress and her air was running out. And then she was going backward, being pulled even though there was no current. This was madness. All of it. Zoey had been completely safe and dry no more than five minutes ago. Now the whole universe was cold, liquid, dark. Her hands and feet had gone numb. Her suit jacket was bunched up around her armpits. She had lost all sense of direction, unsure if she was still even right side up.

Then there was light—she had been yanked out from under the canvas sail, pulled backward by her suit jacket. She thought for an enraged moment that it was Wu, rescuing her but leaving the little girl to die. She turned to tell him to get his hands off her, that a child was trapped and drowning, only to find Leonidas Damon, his wet face expressionless, his fist clutching Zoey's collar.

"A LITTLE GIRL IS UNDER THERE!" shouted Zoey, spraying water from her nose and trying to blink it out of her eyes. "I'M TRYING TO REACH HER!"

He didn't react, just held tight. Then a figure flew into view, diving expertly into the water, curling under the fallen sail to retrieve the child. It was Damon's wife, who'd shed her jacket and shoes and was now pulling the girl out from under the canvas. The girl was, Zoey finally realized, one of the kids the woman had been tending to earlier. Leo Damon's wife held their daughter above water long enough for the terrified child to suck in a huge breath and start wailing. Then Damon let go of Zoey's jacket and the cold calculation he'd just made became horribly clear: he had not wanted Zoey to be seen on-camera rescuing one of his children.

It was apparent now that the pirate ship was going to roll entirely over onto its side. It was leaning at a forty-five-degree angle and nearly everyone who'd been on deck had now been spilled into the sea. Wu appeared, having gotten separated from Zoey earlier when the mast fell. He was managing to stand on the angled deck and reached down as if to draw Zoey out.

"Don't bother, I'll just fall back in! Where's Will and Andre?"

Wu pointed back at the poop deck, where Andre was pulling people out of the angled doorway, the ones who'd taken shelter there back when that had seemed like a safe option a few minutes ago. Will was presumably inside, chest-deep in water and helping victims up to the door.

The tourists in their boats—the spectators who had made Wu nervous earlier—were arriving at the scene now. That was good news overall, but in the near term they were stirring up waves that were slapping Zoey and threatening to pull her off the sinking railing. The shipwrecked victims around her were treading water and they made it look easy, but Zoey had no idea how to do that and all she felt was the depths sucking her downward. She was about to ask Wu to find her some piece of debris that looked floaty when she felt something churning up the water behind her. A paddleboat shaped like a giant swan pulled up, being pedaled by an elderly man in a fishing hat. He grinned and extended a hand.

"Get the kids first!" yelled Zoey. "And anybody who's hurt. Is anybody hurt?"

"They're getting the kids," replied the old man, "but it looks like you're the only one here who can't swim."

He wasn't wrong. Zoey let him help her aboard. A flat houseboat with several drunk college kids pulled up next to them and they fished Megaboss Alonzo out of the water.

He grabbed a beer from a girl in a bikini, threw both hands into the air, looked toward the crowd of gawkers on the beach and yelled, "AVAST, YE MATEYS!"

CHAPTER
12

"IT WAS A TINY remote-control pirate ship," said Andre. "Had little sails on it and everything. It blew a hole in the hull, which wasn't hard because the floating venue isn't exactly built like a real boat, but it floats on these two pontoon things under the surface and I guess the explosion detached one of them, made the whole thing roll over."

Zoey was sitting, wet and shivering, in a concrete staff-only tunnel that ran underneath the artificial beaches. They'd given her a giant, fluffy towel and she was trying to dry her hair while carefully avoiding the raw skin up there. Workers in tropical hotel garb were hustling back and forth with carts of dirty dishes and trays of fruity drinks. Some nervous guys in suits had come by a minute ago and seemed to be trying to get a sense of their legal liability in all of this. Zoey had been texting with her mother, reassuring her that she was fine, that she'd never really been in danger, that she'd just gotten a bit wet. It was, however, becoming clear that incidents were piling up faster than she could invent comforting cover stories.

"Guys," said Zoey, "just tell me: Am I just destined to die in some whimsical assassination attempt?"

"That wasn't an assassination attempt," said Will. "That was an attempt at whimsy that almost killed you anyway, which I suppose would be an even worse way to die."

"The little boat had a flag on it," added Andre, "with four letters: A-V-I-V."

Zoey's brain was so scrambled that she actually needed a moment to spell it out. "Oh, the prankster guy."

"He wasn't trying to kill you, he was trying to dump everyone in the water, so you'd all look silly flailing around. All the rich people in their suits and nice hair, all wet and looking foolish."

"Yes, I'm sure that traumatized little girl is having a good laugh about it now."

"I think Damon agrees with you," said a booming voice from behind Zoey. It was Alonzo and his pack of assistants and/or bodyguards. "I have it on good authority that he's put out a hit on this Aviv character. I don't mean that in a figurative sense, I mean he's let it be known behind the scenes that there will be generous rewards and immunity from prosecution for anyone who puts the dude in the ground."

"If so," replied Zoey, "I don't think it's potential harm to his child that he's trying to avenge. I'm pretty sure he just physically restrained me from saving her from drowning just so I wouldn't be seen on-camera doing it."

"Well, now, that's just smart politics," said Alonzo.

Will took a sip from a drink he must have stolen from a passing waiter and said, "Humiliate a narcissist and you've unleashed a wild animal."

"I came over to make sure everybody was all right. I feel responsible, since it was admittedly my idea to hold the debate on the indoor pirate ship."

Zoey shivered. "We're fine. Though I like how in this city you can wind up on a hit list for getting a politician wet but if you murder three sex workers all you get is 'We'll look into it.' Can you imagine if it was three politicians? Or three cops? Why are we even here, instead of trying to solve that?"

"You're not wrong," replied Alonzo, "but I bet you a thousand dollars they're not murdered."

"You didn't see what they broadcast along the skyline today? The woman getting her guts ripped out?"

"I did. Looked to me like somebody took an already dead body and hacked it apart. Then did a little digital trickery to sell it. Our supposed Sex Butcher is putting on a show."

"What are you, a crime-scene expert?"

"He's seen his share of butchered bodies," said Will over his drink.

"I feel like you guys don't want them to be dead. Like you have reasons for not wanting this to be true."

"If that's your reasoning," said Alonzo, "then you should also ask who *does* want it to be true, or who wants it to seem to be true."

"If you're right," replied Zoey, "I'm glad they're alive, if that's what it means, but also the idea of using their deaths, fake or not, as some kind of a viral political stunt is so disgusting that I don't even want to think about it. Women's bodies shouldn't be props."

"If you get all caught up in what should and shouldn't be, versus what is and isn't, you'll just drive yourself crazy. Thanks for coming out, guys, sorry again for the trouble."

He moved on, his people muttering to him all of the news that came in while he'd stopped to talk. Apparently politics was just hustling from one dishonest conversation to the next, for every waking hour of the day. No wonder only the crazy people want to do it.

Wu approached. Earlier he'd gone off to yell at the venue security, possibly just to make himself feel better.

"They sealed off the building," he said, "our prankster isn't on-site, though there was no reason he had to be. The toy boat was sneaked in days ago, maybe weeks for all we know. There are pirate treasure chests under the water for the scuba tours to look at, the boat was hidden in one of those."

Zoey looked to Wu, then Will. "Is this when you two start arguing over whose fault this was?"

"No argument needed," replied Wu. "It was mine. I should have gotten you off the pirate ship as soon as they started letting spectators out onto the water. Security is my job, not optics, but it was optics that kept me from getting you off the boat."

"No," said Will, "this one is on me. Zoey had no business being here in the first place, I should have wiped the public-appearance schedule after this morning's incident. It'd have been a fine excuse, optics-wise, and we could have just regrouped and focused on the big stuff. Nobody was going to change their vote based on whether or not Zoey turned up tonight."

Andre, who had been sitting and wringing water from his socks, looked up. "Can we just agree to blame Zoey? Our lives were all much simpler before she showed up."

"Sure," replied Will, "but typically we wait until she's out of the room to do it."

"Well, there is some good news," said Zoey. "This day is finally over."

Wu suddenly looked concerned, glancing at Andre and then Zoey.

Zoey said, "What?"

"We're expected at the festival site tonight," replied Wu, "to do a walkthrough of tomorrow night's appearance and the security protocols. Echo is waiting on us. Remember?"

"That sounds like it could be an email."

"We've talked about this. You need to go on-site, you haven't even been out there yet."

"Well, I'm not doing it tonight."

"The prep has to be done tonight," said Will. "We have a truck full of gear to set up that's intended specifically to keep you from getting swarmed by the crowd, should they decide to rush the stage."

"They're music fans, not zombies. You guys go set up your stuff, you can explain it to me in the morning. I'm going back home."

"Wu has to be at the festival grounds—"

"Yes," interrupted Zoey. "Go, all of you, go. Wu, too. I'll be fine. But I'm done for the day."

Will and Wu looked at each other, like each was silently pleading to the other to get their girl under control.

"Zoey," said Wu, "I really think—"

"I. Am. Your. Boss. I'm saying that to both of you and I'm not going to say it again. Take me home. If somebody tries to get at me, the house security will cut them to pieces. I'll be fine."

"But you have to actually stay in the house for that to work," said Will with a stern look.

"I know."

"Because sometimes you don't. Sometimes you go out, and don't tell anyone."

"I won't. And if I do and get killed, I officially absolve you of responsibility. Take me home."

Zoey soaked in her bathtub and tried to get the ringing in her ears to stop. She'd told the tub to play music to drown it out but the faint, piercing whine was still there, lingering in the ether. She thought she could *feel* the sound, humming through the tub and her bones, vibrating her brain. Had she finally endured enough trauma that it had just fried her nervous system? Was this permanent? She imagined being discovered in a fetal position on the floor, ranting in a puddle of blood, having pierced both ears with a knitting needle. She supposed she'd need to take up knitting first.

Zoey pinched her nose and lowered her head under the water. She held her eyes open, watching the ceiling rippling above her, and imagined herself drowning under a Jolly Roger. And still, the ringing remained.

A white cat's face appeared above the surface, Stench Machine having hopped up onto the lip of the tub to see if the evil bath had finally claimed his pet human. Zoey pushed her head back up and tried to stroke him, but he flinched and launched himself away—even her wet hand represented too much bath for the feline. She heard Knockoff meow from the hall, maybe inquiring about the quarrel between Zoey and Stench, hoping this would be his opportunity to move up and become Favorite Cat.

Her plan of letting the tub soak her anxiety away had usually worked in the past, at least temporarily, but Zoey thought part of the problem tonight was that she was using water to soak away water-based trauma. She had no other ideas, her body was crying out for something that she couldn't put her finger on. This was especially maddening considering that literally everything was available to her: she could summon a massage, she could work out, she could order an entire fancy wedding cake and eat it with her hands, she could have Carlton make her an extravagant cocktail, she could, if the press was to be believed, pay two men to fight each other to death in her padded room. None of it sounded good to her. It was a now-familiar sensation, the sense of an itch she couldn't scratch, starving while wanting nothing on the menu. Worst of all: there was no one on the planet who would feel sorry for her. She reached for the bottle of red wine on the floor next to her and found it empty. Cats must have drunk it.

On the floor next to the bottle was her phone, above which hovered the text conversation she'd had earlier while running the bath.

Echo:

Will & Wu are sharing Zoey anecdotes and laughing, they both seem too happy and I hate it.

Zoey:

I don't believe you.

Echo:

Well, they're not laughing but they are sharing anecdotes.

Zoey:

They're uniting against me.

Echo:

Want me to come by when we're done? I can bring junk food from one of the stands here.

Zoey:

No, I'm ok. You don't have to babysit me.

Echo:

. . .

Zoey:

That last message sounded mean but I really am ok, just ran out of energy.

Echo:

Andre is eating what he's calling cow sushi, it's a little strip of toasted garlic bread, topped by some kind of creamy white herb cheese with a strip of charred ribeye laid on top of that. It's three separate foods I can't eat!

Zoey:

No, just going to take a bath and go to bed. Have a good time at the security rehearsal.

Echo:

Have you ever had that split cream cheese garlic bread? They literally dip it in butter to soak before baking, it's a heart attack in the palm of your hand.

Zoey:

Ha, no, I'm good.

Echo:

. . .

Zoey

Thank you for checking up on me, I mean that.

And that's where they'd left it.

Will's warning about not leaving the house wasn't out of fear that she'd go slop it up at some dive bar—well, it wasn't *just* that—but that she'd go off on her own and try to do something about the missing women. But to do what, exactly? Track them down? Rescue them? It's the kind of thing that works in a movie, you just bribe some bartender and he tells you, "Oh, yeah, that broad was in here just before she disappeared, she was with a dude in an eye patch and a spider tattoo on his neck." But Budd and his minions had spent days doing that kind of thing to no avail and Zoey wouldn't even know where to start. She'd wind up letting the car drive her around the city for a bit and then, yeah, she'd wind up at the first drinking establishment she could find where nobody knew her name.

She got out of the tub, dried herself off, almost walked into the bedroom but then stopped to grab a robe first. She then put on her aqua-green socks. They were the pair given to her at the mental health facility she'd done time in after a nervous breakdown the previous year. The socks were her favorite, they were thick and cushioned and had little rubber nubs on the bottom. Will had all but scolded her for wearing them in view of a camera once (they were literally branded with the name of the facility) but that had only ensured that Zoey would never, ever throw them away. She hadn't been able to find an equivalent pair for purchase anywhere so if she ever lost these, she'd presumably have to check herself in again. Hell, if you thought about it, they were probably the most expensive item of clothing in her wardrobe.

She padded downstairs and found her bag of Doritos in the kitchen, but it was practically empty. Exactly seven chips and a puddle of warm crumbs remained. There were no more in the house. She could have some delivered with a single voice command and they'd be at her door before her hair was even dry, but she didn't want more Doritos. She wanted to be mad about how she didn't have any. And the ready availability was making that impossible, which made her even angrier. Apparently when you're rich, true self-pity is the one luxury you can't afford. It was in one of these moods that she'd bemoaned not having a pool to float around in on sunny afternoons, clearly intending to cling to that as a way in which she was being deprived. But, within days, the trucks had shown up with digging equipment and she was told that soon, work crews would follow.

Then she'd have her pool and wouldn't be able to complain about that, either. What kind of Hell was this?

Even worse than that: somehow, down here on the first floor, the ringing in her ears was even louder.

She wandered around the kitchen and then the dining room, finding that the noise changed depending on where she was standing. Did tinnitus work like that? It didn't seem right. After a little more investigating, wandering the halls in her robe with her nearly empty Doritos bag like a slovenly ghost, she realized the noise was not, in fact, coming from inside her head. It was coming from the vents. She thought maybe it was something broken deep inside the HVAC system (the mansion's geothermal unit was a constant source of aggravating problems) but, after pausing her crunching long enough to take in the sound, she thought maybe it was a trapped animal. She could now detect that it wasn't a steady noise but rather came in fits and starts, winding up and then relenting. Maybe it was a raccoon stuck in a stretch of ductwork beneath her feet. Maybe she could get it out and keep it as a pet. Could that be the one thing her life was missing? Surely it could.

She moved down the hall, focusing with her ears to find the exact spot where the noise was loudest, finally arriving at the library with its walls of fake leather-bound books and antique armchairs. It also contained the hidden entrance to the basement vault. There, she thought she could feel the floor vibrating through her socked feet and she sensed that if she'd had a little less wine in her, she'd have probably been alarmed by this. Previously, the vault entrance had been hidden under a hologram of a koi pond, with animated fish swimming around in midair. Catching the right one would open a hatch in the floor (Zoey's father had loved stuff like that). It was extremely frustrating to use, however, and the vault no longer contained anything of value, so they'd simplified the system: now the hatch was simply covered by a fancy rug and, after pulling it aside, you just had to verbally state a six-digit passcode, which, due to a misunderstanding, was "Just pick a random number, I don't have time for this, one of the cats puked on my bed again."

Zoey said that sentence and a circular hatch lid rose from the floor. The noise that Zoey had mistaken for a ringing in her ears upstairs was clearly audible now, less like a raccoon scratching at a vent and more like, say, a failing fan on an AC unit that was going to cost more to replace than a new Mercedes. She descended the spiral staircase in her robe and psych-ward socks as if she was going to diagnose and repair the machine herself. At best, she told herself, she could do something to make the noise stop. Maybe turn it off, if there was an obvious off switch. But even in that case, the only sensible course of action would be to ask Carlton. That she might actually be heading toward something dangerous was a thought that was lurking somewhere in her brain but not in the same part that operated her feet.

The noise was growing louder and it wasn't just because she was closer; the mechanical violence that was generating the noise was rising to some kind of climax. She descended into the vault room, stepping down onto a floor tiled with gold coins (they weren't real, but re-creations of gold coins from Great Britain featuring a young King George V, because apparently her father had thought he'd looked like him?) and the dormant vault that was standing empty, with its comically thick door wide open. The noise was originating here, vibrating through the walls and floor, but it was difficult to tell where it was coming from. She couldn't see any HVAC parts or anything like that, aside from a couple of the usual vents in the ceiling . . .

And then, all at once, the world came apart. There was a grinding howl like a giant fork being dragged across a plate the size of Montana. Zoey covered her ears and hot dust filled the room, jetting in from the wall opposite the vault. *What in the possible hell was happening?*

Her immediate thought, after dismissing an infiltration by Satan himself, was that some huge piece of equipment for the house—a furnace or something—was slowly exploding, or melting down, or flying apart. She scrambled back toward the spiral stairs, covering her ears from the noise but unable to cover the other holes in her face that were being assaulted by the acrid dust particles filling the room. Then there was movement behind the dust cloud, like the wall itself was swirling, and Zoey's brain had no context whatsoever for what she was seeing.

She reached the top of the spiral stairs and found the hatch had closed behind her. It always did that, it required the same passcode to open from this end but in her panic, Zoey couldn't remember the exact phrasing and instead just shouted incoherently, slapping at the hatch with her bare palm. The noise grew and grew into a crescendo of tumbling rocks. Then there was only the whirr of a powerful electric motor. A spinning machine had entered the room, a cylinder about four feet in diameter and some undetermined length. It penetrated the basement for a few feet and rolled to a stop. On the front end was a dizzying vortex of whirling, spiky gears and bits.

It was a damned tunneling machine.

A device beeped from inside the room and powerful fans began whooshing the concrete dust out of the space. Zoey knew that her urgency to escape should only have grown. This intruder machine could explode or fill the room with nerve gas or open up and unleash an army of little killer drones. Instead, she just stood there on the stairs, then started descending, getting a closer look at the device. Her curiosity was telling her that there was safety in knowledge, that if she could diagnose who or what had breached the estate, she'd be better able to deal with it. She absently wondered how many humans this instinct had killed over the centuries.

The machine's motor wound down until it became still. There were some clicks and scrapes from inside and then the whole front end opened and swung around, revealing the interior of the tube: a lit, padded space just large enough for a man and his gear. It was easy to estimate that because that's exactly what it contained. A man crawled out and he kept coming for a while—he was tall. He was dragging with him a bright yellow duffel bag that said something on the side Zoey couldn't yet make out.

A moment later, there stood before her a man in a garish jumpsuit that matched his bag, a flashing logo blasting across his torso branding him as THE AMAZING AVIV. He had dark hair so thick that it looked like a wig. He squinted in the rapidly dissipating dust, coughed several times, then brought out a small camera drone, like he was about to start filming. He surveyed the room, looked to the stairs, saw Zoey, and flinched so hard that he almost fell flat on his ass.

"WHO ARE YOU?!?" he yelped. "I'm sorry, there isn't supposed to be anyone here! Do you work—"

He blinked through the dust, tried to make sense of what he was seeing and, eyes wide, said, "Oh, my god. You're Zoey. Oh, my god. I wasn't—this wasn't part of the plan, you were supposed to be—why are you here?"

"*I live here!*"

He started to reply, then was seized by another coughing fit. Concrete dust was truly horrific stuff and if you ever find yourself having to breathe a lot of it, either you're working in construction or in proximity to some kind of catastrophe. Zoey hated how familiar with it she was, the smell of ruined structure.

She pulled her robe as tightly closed as she could, then said, "Listen to me. Whatever you're planning to do to me, whatever little video you're going to make, I'm saying to you, from one human being to another, one who wants to avoid causing suffering whenever possible, that you should strongly reconsider. My people are going to be down here within the next two minutes. I don't know how fast your little drill there can go in reverse but you should absolutely be gone by the time they get here."

"Your people are at Catharsis. All of them. I just checked them on Blink."

"My butler isn't. And he'll call the others. He's probably already at the hatch, in response to all of the alarms you've no doubt set off by destroying my basement."

"Carlton? He's also at the music festival. You *all* were supposed to be there, everybody, including your mother. You were overheard discussing tonight's meeting in public three different times. It was to be the only time the house was completely empty in the last five years. Trust me, I checked. Zoey, you're really not careful enough about what you're caught saying on-camera, I was able to create a calendar of your entire staff's schedule, almost down to the minute, just by piecing together your overheard jokes and complaints."

"Why would Carlton be there? He wouldn't be part of the prep."

"He's not working, he's at the Boneless Giraffe show. His girlfriend is a huge fan."

"No, I'm talking about Carlton, my butler. He's, like, a hundred years old."

"Yeah, and he has a girlfriend who's twenty-six. And she's a Boneless Giraffe fan. He put in his request to take tonight off months ago."

"How do you know that, if I didn't?"

"I know his girlfriend. Or rather, I got to know her, so I could get that intel. These stunts take months to put together!"

"Why am I even talking to you? I could have been maimed by your drill. And your 'stunt' at the debate tonight almost killed children."

"Oh, come on. The boat has two licensed rescue divers on duty at all times, it's required by the insurance. One little girl was in the water for a total of fifty-five seconds. I'm sure it seemed longer."

"You set off an explosive in a crowd."

"There was no explosive, the remote ship had a compressed air cannon, it created a shock wave that shattered the hull. The only people who got injured were some tourist boaters who got too close and took splinter shrapnel, and they weren't supposed to be there. Ninety percent of my planning on these things is making sure nobody gets hurt."

"Yeah, well, none of that matters now. Messing with a public event, making politicians look foolish, that's one thing—they're restrained in what they'll do in retaliation, due to public opinion and all that." She gestured to the one-man drill and her ruined concrete wall. "My people, Aviv, have no such constraints."

"And you're okay with that? Your 'people' torturing me to death because I made a hole in your basement that your insurance will pay to fix? You think that punishment fits that crime?"

"That's not how the world works. If we let you get away with it, that rolls out the welcome mat for others with worse intentions. Not that I'm convinced your intentions right now still aren't the worst possible."

"If it's all about sending a message, then it wouldn't even matter if I was guilty, would it? They might as well just choose and destroy somebody at random, it'd have the same effect."

It must have been warm inside the drill, Aviv was covered in beads of sweat. He wiped his face with a sleeve and unzipped his jumpsuit.

"So what was your plan?" she asked. "To break into the vault? Well, there it is. The door is standing wide open. We haven't used it in months."

"I know that. This isn't a heist, it's a stunt. But the whole point, as I said, was that you weren't supposed to be here. God, my eyes are burning, your air filtration isn't doing its job fast enough."

"Sorry for your inconvenience. So what were you going to do? Film yourself going through my things? Poop on my bed? Find evidence I'm a slut or a cannibal or whatever the rumor is this week?"

"I was going to pet your cats. It's a running joke on my channel, that I don't care about you or your organization but that I'm obsessed with Stench Machine and just want to pet him. And the other one, if I can. So the big joke was that I spend six months planning how to get into literally the most secure private property in the USA, take all of these huge risks, go up and pet your cats for a few seconds, and then just leave."

He pulled down his jumpsuit to free his arms, tying the empty sleeves around his waist. Like he was making himself at home. He wore under it a tank top that was also bearing his brand, only in a reversed color scheme (guys like this need to always be showing off a variety of merch followers could buy). The lack of sleeves showed off sweaty arms that were the beneficiaries of both genes and gym.

"But the real point you're making," said Zoey, "is that you could have done so much more. Men love that joke, don't they? 'Isn't it funny how I have the power to hurt you, but I'm choosing not to right now?' The goal is still intimidation, to make it clear that I'm not safe in my home."

"No! No, nothing like that. That's not my thing. It's all just, you know, thumbing my nose in the face of power. You tell me what your people are capable of and you say it's *me* who's trying to be intimidating? I say these pranks only hurt you if you try to rule by scaring people. It makes them want to see that illusion shattered. This kind of thing can actually help someone like you. It humanizes you to everybody who thinks you're this dragon hoarding gold inside a castle. But now that you're actually here, I have no idea what happens next. I can't believe I'm actually talking to you. I drilled into your basement and we're just, having a conversation. It's kind of cool."

He crossed his arms and leaned back against the wall, a pose that he probably liked because it made his biceps pop. Zoey sat on the stairs and pushed her hair out of her face. The air was mostly clear but everything felt gritty, the dust having left a layer of filth on everything.

"It isn't cool. None of this is. What you did at Atlantis, what was supposed to be the point?"

"That it's all phony. The whole process, the campaign and the voting, it's as fake as that stupid pirate ship. One guy wants to make the city friendlier to white middle-class tourists and rich Mormons from SLC, the other wants the government in disarray so he can keep getting rich off vices. Both of them are lying about it. Is that really the only choice we have? Why do we have to keep up this charade? No, toss them in the lake. All of them. And here's the thing: I know you agree with me. I can see it every time you make an appearance with these fools. You say what you're supposed to say but you don't do a good job of making your face do the right thing when the fools are talking. That's what everyone likes about you. Nice socks, by the way. I have a pair just like them at home."

Zoey stared like she was trying to set Aviv's face on fire with her mind. "Is that supposed to be a joke?"

"Nope. I have a pair just like them. Almost two years old. I'd buy more but you can't find them anywhere. Did your room have those weird, flat doorknobs? You know why they're like that, right?"

"So you can't use them to hang yourself."

They just looked at each other for a moment.

"Oh, I get it," said Zoey. "I see. Okay. You knew I'd be here. Somehow. And your goal isn't to 'pet my cat,' it's to get me into bed. Then you'll, what, stop halfway through and pull out your camera? Go do a video on how gross and fat I am? Tell people I smell bad? 'Pet my cat.' Real funny."

"You can't possibly believe what you just said. I'm an activist and performance artist, not a sex predator. I've been a public figure for ten years, you won't find a single person of any gender with a story of me treating them that way, not even once. And you're the one who greeted me barely wearing anything at all, I'm trying to be a gentleman and not stare."

"I'm wearing a big, fluffy bathrobe. I could be fully clothed under here."

"Zoey, I'm not trying to be crude but with the way you're sitting, it is very obvious that you are not."

She quickly stood. "And you insist you're not a pervert. I swear, you're all alike. You're literally in mortal danger, my people could be back here at any moment, and you're trying to flirt with me."

"I'm really not."

She padded up the spiral stairs and told the hatch its pass phrase.

"All right," she said, "let's go."

"Where are we going?"

"Upstairs."

"What's upstairs?"

"My cats. You can film yourself petting them, then you have to go. If Will and the rest come back and find you here, god help you."

"Really?"

The hatch rose and, as she climbed up, Zoey said, "I have to get this concrete dust off me, I think it's bad for the skin. I'm going to jump in the shower real quick. You probably should, too."

Forty minutes later, Zoey was staring at the guest-bedroom ceiling, letting the sweat dry.

Next to her, Aviv said, "What am I doing? I can't believe we did that. Your people could be here at any minute! They were supposed to be back before now. Am I gonna die?" He got up on his elbows and seemed to be trying to remember where his underwear had landed.

"It's always fascinating, watching men transform from werewolf mode back into human after the fluids have left their body. It's like all of the reason and anxiety comes flowing back in."

He sat up on the edge of the bed. "I—I want to say this again, you know I didn't plan this, right? You know I didn't break in here to try to sleep with you."

"You're not sleeping here."

"You know what I mean."

"This wasn't your choice, it was mine."

He got up and looked around the room. "I have to go. And I *do* have to go, right? Your people could show up at any time, couldn't they? Do you know something I don't?"

"Hell," she said, "they could already be here, this house has thick walls, they could be walking down the hall right now and you wouldn't hear them. What would they think, if they burst in and saw me lying here like this, with the man who just tried to drown them all standing over me?"

"Are you messing with me? You're crazy! You know that? But just so we're clear, we're in agreement that I didn't plan this."

"You wouldn't brag about this on-camera. If anything, you'd deny it if I told people we did it. They'd make fun of you if they knew you'd been with someone who looks like me."

He stopped and looked down at her.

"Come on, you're going to fish for compliments even now? After what we just did? I know of at least one porn star with your exact body type."

"The things men say that they think women will find reassuring is just *jaw-dropping*. Your clothes are still in the bathroom, I think one of your socks landed in the toilet. And stop rushing around, it's making me nervous. My people can't get through the gates unless I let them in, you're fine."

He went into the bathroom and gathered clothes from the floor. "I know more about you than you think," he said while fishing out his toilet sock. "I don't mean intel I looked up to pull this job, I mean I know where you're coming from. I know your mentality."

"I don't doubt that you *think* you do."

"How's this: You hate that men find you most desirable when you're naked. Because it makes it seem like none of your choices matter, that everything you've done to express yourself, the hair, the clothes, the attitude, isn't enough to drive a man crazy, that the kind of attraction men show you would be the exact same if your personality vanished and you were just a Zoey-shaped sex doll."

"Jaw-dropping."

"But it's more than that," he said, stepping into his underwear. "Because it's really about power. If a woman is hot, I mean the kind where she can walk into a room and instantly change the vibe—"

"Like Echo."

"Yeah. Their world is full of men who *wish* they could have them but *can't*. That's real power, it follows them everywhere. It means that any man who has her, or is just allowed to be around her, instantly has social currency. She's proof of his success, his worthiness—she dictates status by who she grants her company to. You think what you have just isn't the same, right? It's power over guys who want to get with you but it's the kind of power a cheeseburger has over somebody on a diet, it goes away as soon as it's sated. I bet you hate how when you're dating, they always have little suggestions about how you should dress, wanting you to hide a little more."

"I once had a boyfriend tell me a shirt I was wearing made me look pregnant," said Zoey, still staring at the ceiling. "He said it like a joke, but it was also clear that he meant it. But what I know now, but didn't get then, was that he wasn't worried about how the shirt made me look, but how being with me in that shirt made *him* look. When did the world get like this, where everyone is obsessed with how their lifestyle looks to everybody else?"

Aviv sat on the edge of the bed to pull on his jumpsuit. "I don't know, but I bet even back in olden times, those mousey religious house-wives were more scared of their neighbors than God. Who knows what they were like behind closed doors. But you know, when people talk about how they wish they could live in the past, when they fantasize about the knights and castles era or the Old West, I think that's what they're wishing for, to be rid of that pressure. They'd be willing to give up modern medicine and clean water for a chance to be free of all of this, the nonstop performance that comes with knowing everything you do, day and night, is for an audience."

"And yet, I'm here with somebody so desperate to get famous that he literally risks his life on ridiculous stunts for publicity."

"I guess I figure if I embrace it, then at least I've got some control, you know?"

He put a hand on her bare shoulder and she flinched away.

He said, "Hey, uh, I want you to know . . . what I'm doing, right now, I realize it's a privilege and I do appreciate it."

"Well, I've definitely never had a guy phrase it like that before."

"I don't mean what we just did, I mean this. I don't think going to bed with Zoey Ashe is nearly as big a deal as getting one, long, sincere conversation with her."

"Ha, I bet that line really works for you."

"I would ask why you did this, instead of just calling your people to come torture me to death. But I already know the answer."

"Of course you do. You've made it clear that sounding like you have the answers is your whole thing."

"My lady, you are *bored*. I can see it in your eyes. You joked about how men come back to themselves in the aftermath but as soon as we were finished, you were looking up at the ceiling, like, 'Well, *that* wasn't what I wanted, either.' It's so incredibly clear that you find all of this tedious."

"Oh, Jesus. I almost died three times in one day. I have enemies all around me. I'm so stressed that I feel like I'm juggling greased land mines."

"No, that's not how boredom works," he said, zipping up his jumpsuit. "I'm talking about real boredom, boredom of the soul. Being busy doesn't save you from that. You think soldiers in a trench don't get bored? I have veteran friends who say that's the worst part. There's stuff happening all around you that demands your attention but it's not *your* stuff. You didn't create it, you don't control it. That's what real boredom is, this hollow feeling of not living with your own purpose. What did you want out of your life? Before all of this," he gestured to the room, the mansion, "what did you want? To be raising a baby? Instead, you're putting out a bunch of fires you didn't start, for people who don't appreciate it? Just to uphold an empire you didn't build, that you wouldn't have built? If you went out back and grew a garden of your own, the satisfaction you'd get from seeing the first tomatoes come in would beat anything you did today. Because it would be *yours*."

"When you're using that drill thing to dig tunnels, do you ever worry it'll break down halfway through and you'll just be entombed underground until you suffocate?"

"Well, I wasn't worried about it until you said that. But I have people I can call. You don't think I work alone, do you? You think I built that thing in my garage? Nice job changing the subject, by the way."

"How did you get past the house security? Even now, there should be alarms screeching not just here, but on the phones of every single person who works for me."

"Doing that was the whole task. You think I drilled all the way here from outside the grounds, crossing all of the sensors and cameras? Your property is huge, that'd have been literally twelve hours of drilling, I *would* have suffocated in that case. No, I came in from the front yard, right out there. The company you hired to dig out your new pool, and those trucks out there with all their gear? One of 'em had my digger in the back. Your people even inspected it, decided it looked exactly like something you'd use to dig out a swimming pool. Like I said, you're not being careful enough."

"But you still had to get yourself past the walls, even if your drill was already here."

"I was inside the drill when it arrived. I've been living out in the truck for the last few days. I've got a toilet out there and everything, just waiting for you guys to leave. Remember when you shot down the mannequin? I was controlling it from inside the truck, I watched you come out to look at it. I figured you'd double down on checking for airborne intruders and never guess I'd be coming from down low."

"Well, whatever. The real security isn't the gadgets. It's the fear of what will happen if you try something."

"Uh-huh," said Aviv as he tied his shoes, "and based on your day today, how would you say that's working for you so far?"

Zoey was getting cold. She pulled the comforter over her. "Will plays the long game. You might win today, but . . ."

Aviv stood. "Can I ask you a question?"

"Is it going to be the same question everybody asks as soon as they talk to me for a little bit? How can a nice girl like me work with a devil like Will?"

"It does seem like a weird pairing, from the outside. Do you know how much speculation there is out there about you two? About your relationship and the, ah, nature of it?"

"I thought you'd researched us. A minute ago you were making it sound like you knew every synapse in our brains."

"Researching *you* is easy. Researching Will is a pitch-black labyrinth of ghosts and mirrors."

"You should try knowing him personally, it's even weirder. Imagine trying to shop for his Christmas gift."

"Is that a thing you actually do for each other? Are you close friends?"

"Why do I get the sense that's not the question you're really asking?"

"Is it unreasonable for me to ask if he would have, you know, some kind of feelings about what you and I just did?"

"I can't help you there. Nobody knows what Will is feeling, probably not even Will."

"Can I ask how you feel about Will?"

"Nope."

"So how about I ask a more basic question that I also haven't been able to get an answer to: What does Will Blackwater *do*?"

Zoey, who was suddenly very sleepy, closed her eyes and, after a moment, said, "About a hundred years ago, there was a rebellion in the Philippines and the American government wanted to put it down, for the usual reasons. The CIA, instead of just killing everybody, had an idea: they would fake a series of vampire attacks. I guess the people in the villages there had all these vampire legends, so the CIA would put puncture wounds in the necks of rebel corpses they found and leave them for the villagers to find. One guy, they kidnapped him, punctured his neck, and hung him upside down to drain on a busy trail, so he'd be discovered dangling over a pool of blood. This apparently freaked out the rebels and sympathizers enough that they got too scared to even go into certain territory. Within a couple of years, the whole rebellion fell apart."

"That's, like, PSYOPS, right? Psychological dirty tricks?"

"They never stopped doing it, all over the world."

"Will was CIA?"

"I get the sense that they paid him under the table, so there's no paper trail or anything. He says it's the most merciful way to fight, that the right lies can save lives. My father ran into him years ago and just hired him away to do the same for him."

"And that's why you stick with him, you think smoke and mirrors is better than a pile of corpses."

"I guess. But sometimes I can't stop thinking about the fact that in the Philippines, to really sell the illusion, they had to snatch up a real guy and drain his real blood. And then you think, maybe those villagers weren't ignorant, maybe they saw that and realized one of two things was true: they were either being stalked by a vampire, or by something much worse."

She sat up.

"I hear Stench Machine out in the hall. Get what you need and get out of here."

CHAPTER
13

ZOEY WAS IN THE crater of her giant beanbag chair, so she wasn't able to see the faces of Wu, Echo, Andre, Budd, and Will as she told the story that next morning in the Buffalo Room. The silence that had fallen afterward seemed fairly expressive, though.

"And to be clear," said Wu, the first to finally speak, "after this, he just left?"

"Not in his drill, no. It's still downstairs, you can go look at it. I let him out of the front gates."

"You didn't even offer him a ride home?" asked Andre. "That lonely taxi back at three in the morning can take you to a dark place."

"Is he going public with it?" asked Echo. "I'm not seeing a video yet . . ."

"He's leaving me out of the video," said Zoey. "It's just going to be him getting in and petting the cat, like he planned. We just did the one, Knockoff ran away from us, I think he didn't approve of being used as a prop."

"You couldn't talk Aviv out of that part?"

"He made a convincing argument that it was actually a PR win for us, that it would humanize me or something. I don't know, it sounded good at the time."

There was another pregnant pause, presumably as everyone in the room exchanged exasperated looks with one another.

"The problem," said Wu, "is that he has established a blueprint for how to get inside the property."

"Yeah, I brought that up. He had an answer that was really convincing but I don't remember what it was." Zoey really, really wanted to just go back to bed. She believed that she would soon be diagnosed with a terminal condition previously unknown to science, the Permanent Hangover.

"I don't completely disagree with him on the PR angle," replied Will, instantly making Zoey think she'd misheard. "The message he's put out there is that infiltrating our walls requires six months of planning, a multimillion-dollar custom-built machine, and no intention of leaving with anything of value. Also, anyone will assume that this particular method won't take us by surprise in the future."

"It shouldn't have taken us by surprise in the present," replied Wu.

"Let's get on with the meeting, since we have between two and three brewing crises that have nothing to do with our break-in but aren't totally unrelated to Mr. Aviv. Budd, do you want to take us through the crises?"

Budd's voice, sounding the farthest away from Zoey, said, "Sure. Leonidas Damon held a press conference this morning claiming Mr. Aviv's stunt was arranged by his opponent, Alonzo, in an attempt to drown his family. This, as you can imagine, has turned up the temperature on the tensions that were already hot enough to dry out our city's proverbial pot roast. A couple of Alonzo's campaign offices were vandalized by Damon supporters, a third was burned down."

Zoey said, "Let me guess: he's publicly putting out a call for Aviv's arrest but it's actually a call for his abduction or murder via bounty hunter."

"As is tradition in this town, yes."

"So why doesn't Alonzo come out and disown the guy? This wasn't his idea, his people got dumped in the water just like Damon's."

"Alonzo isn't nearly as upset by it as Damon is," replied Will.

"Why?"

"You said it yourself a few minutes ago."

"Ah. Because he thinks he comes out of it looking better. That it humanizes him."

Will didn't respond but, oddly enough, Zoey thought she could hear him nod. It was an affirmative kind of pause.

Budd said, "Regardless of party or faction, in most elections, you've got an order candidate and a chaos candidate. They use different words—

safety, freedom, what have you—but it usually comes down to order and chaos. I won't insult you by implying you need it clarified which candidate is which, but Alonzo was spotted after the boat-sinking having rum on the beach with a pack of supporters. He had a toy cutlass stuck in his belt."

"Your likely next question," said Andre, who sounded like he was in the middle of chewing something, "is whether or not Alonzo did, in fact, arrange for this stunt to happen, or paved the way for it, and the answer is no, he did not. He actually did want this debate to come off, being behind in the polls and all."

"Okay," said Zoey, "so Alonzo's offices getting smashed up, that's the crisis?"

"No," replied Echo, "that's the catalyst. There is exactly a one hundred percent chance that Alonzo's supporters will retaliate. And that kind of thing is going to continue through the day, then tonight we will have the headliners in a music festival involving more than two hundred thousand intoxicated or otherwise impaired young people who already have irrationally strong feelings about Damon's victory or defeat. *That* will be the crisis."

"Ah. By the way, did you know that Carlton went to the concert last night? He has a really young girlfriend, apparently."

"Her name is Katja," said Carlton, who, it turned out, was in the room. "We met at a poker tournament, believe it or not. She enjoys live music, I simply turn off my hearing aid and absorb the vibrations."

Andre said, "You two should go on a double date with Zoey and her stuntman sometime. Take a camera, the rest of us can watch."

"That brings us to the other crisis," said Will. "Budd heard from Rex Wrexx this morning. You remember him? The quasi celebrity who DeeDee thinks abducted the girls? Well, he claims he's being stalked by DeeDee and he's not happy about it. He wants to meet."

"Can we just say no?" asked Zoey. "If he didn't do it, like you say, then I have nothing to say to him. If he did do it, like DeeDee says, then I definitely don't have anything to say to him."

"But you care about who wins the election on Tuesday. Which means you care about keeping Rex Wrexx happy."

"Oh, god. And is now when you try to convince me he's not a scum-bag, so I'll be nice to him?"

"Oh, he's a scumbag," interjected Budd. "He's been known to take trips abroad, to places like Bali. Always makes sure there's no cameras. Let's just say there are rumors he made some cases go away. The stuff you can get away with there, with the girls, I mean? Well, it's become a play-ground for certain types."

"You mean like sex tourism?" asked Zoey. "Is that still a thing?"

"In the case of Indonesia," said Echo, "they have something like a quarter of a million sex workers and they're not exactly in a position to call the police if they get abused by a tourist. The government has been trying to crack down on it for decades but, you know. The money always wins."

"Yeah, I've heard. Can we have Wrexx come here?"

"I'd prefer not," answered Will. "He wants to stream the meeting, I'd prefer we do it at his place or a neutral site."

"If he's the slimeball you say he is, I definitely don't want to be alone with him. It needs to be in public."

"Well," said Echo, "I think that means we're going to his place, since he lives in what is scientifically the most public private residence in the world."

Pun-loving local headline writers spent their days praying Rex Wrexx got into a car accident, so maybe it was for the best that he lived in a moving vehicle. The Fish Bowl, as he called it, was a luxury tour bus with com-pletely transparent walls that for most of the day could be found roving around the city. Inside, Rex spent his time with a rotation of friends, girl-friends, hangers-on, and fellow influencers, having a series of zero-stakes adventures. In the evenings, the bus would park at some scenic spot out-side town and Rex would cook an elaborate dinner while watching the sunset. At its lowest, live viewership was around the fifty-thousand range (usually when Rex was sleeping), then the numbers spiked into the mil-lions whenever someone in the Fish Bowl was having sex or fighting, nei-ther of which were infrequent occurrences.

Zoey and Echo wcrc to meet with Wrexx while Will and Wu would trail in the sedan in case this wasn't one of the rare meetings that ended peacefully and according to plan. All four were in the now-clean white sedan, heading for the rendezvous point they'd been given by Wrexx's people. There, his security would make a big show of hustling Zoey and Echo onto the bus. The goal was ostensibly to keep them safe from the rabid fans who always congregated whenever the vehicle stopped moving, but Will pointed out that it was, of course, just part of the show: it needed to be made clear that Wrexx was a very important person who had very important guests.

"And what are we trying to get out of him, again?" asked Zoey, using all of her concentration to avoid touching the itchy wound on her skull.

"Nothing," replied Will. "This meeting is to placate DeeDee so she doesn't murder the guy in his sleep. Be tough, but don't expect anything. The more you appear to put the screws to him, the better chance she'll be satisfied and hold off until we can actually resolve this."

"So I just have to annoy a man for several minutes and then leave? I have some experience with that."

Wu said, "The concern is that this is going to be the most public of meetings, in a transparent vehicle that is very easy to track. Your angelic protestors may decide it is a good time to make a scene. They shouldn't be there waiting for us, but every minute you spend on board increases the likelihood they, or someone else, will show up."

"And then everything gets stupid," added Echo. "But Wrexx wants to keep us happy, he wants this thing with the missing women to go away. There's no reason to be anxious about that part. He'll be over-the-top nice, if anything."

"My problem," said Zoey, "isn't that I'm anxious about this meeting, the problem is I can't get anxious enough about this because there are too many other things to get anxious about. This meeting isn't even the big nightmare on the schedule, that's coming tonight, at Catharsis. And between here and there we have to, I guess, try to solve a serial kidnapping? I mean, are we doing that before or after lunch?"

"Humans have eyes that face forward, like any predator," replied Will, in a tone like this was a classic axiom and not something a serial killer would say while chasing you through a lair full of mannequins. "We're designed to focus in on one target, one goal at a time. If too much is going on, it plays against our strengths, just from an evolutionary point of view. Our brains are terrible at multitasking. Juggling threats causes a unique type of stress and most dysfunctional behavior you see today is just humans doing a bad job of managing it."

"Okay, then why do people like that crazy butterfly lady make up dangers instead of dealing with what's actually in front of them? Back in my old trailer park, I had a neighbor who found out she had a mass in her lung, then spent the whole time she was dying obsessed with conspiracies about secret government mind-reading drones."

"It's counterintuitive, but that person likely reduced their total amount of anxiety by focusing on that belief. They're trading a hundred tedious internal fights for one, big, external battle. It actually takes the pressure off."

"I'm not seeing how that applies to my situation, though."

"For people in our position, survival is all about prioritizing dangers by what actually needs attention, not by what happens to be engaging our emotions in the moment. You're upset that we're not dropping everything to find the three missing girls but there's a reason for it, which is that there is exactly one, long-term threat that needs to be addressed above all else. Solving any of our other problems has to be done with an eye toward stopping Leonidas Damon."

Zoey watched passing traffic for a moment before saying, "I have a question. If Damon supported our business interests but still had all of the other beliefs, still wanted to ethnically cleanse the country, all of that— would you be supporting him for mayor?"

"Only if I could find a way to rationalize it. I mean, do you know where the rare earth minerals in your phone come from? Do you know what the conditions are like in those mines? Or what kind of governments are propped up by the exports? We make deals with devils all the time, Zoey. It's all about mentally distancing yourself from it."

Echo said, "And this has been today's edition of 'Will Blackwater Tries

to Make Someone in Distress Feel Better by Triggering an Existential Crisis.' You always know just what to say, Will."

Before he could respond, Wu said, "We're here."

"Welcome to la casa!" shouted Rex, who struck Zoey as a thirty-five-year-old body being remote-controlled by a hyperactive teenager. "Have you eaten yet? I'm making syrniki!"

Zoey sat with her back against the glass side of the bus, Echo opposite her, both positioned so they could see what was occurring outside. Their seats were clear plastic stools that had automatically folded into position when they approached. Everything in the interior of the Fish Bowl was designed to offer as little obstruction of the view as possible. Zoey thought about all the pedestrians outside watching her big squished butt roll by.

"I'm not hungry," muttered Zoey. "Things are really stressful right now."

Will hadn't seemed to think there was anything challenging about this meeting, but it was quickly becoming apparent that the unspoken rules for this one were more convoluted than any she'd attended so far. She felt no need to hide her visceral disgust for the man who had burned the face off a woman and who would, in any kind of a sane society, be sitting in a prison cell. So, no, she wanted no part of any food he'd prepared. But why hadn't she just said that, instead of claiming the reason was a lack of hunger?

"How about some water?" he asked and, without waiting for an answer, retrieved a pair of clear glass bottles from an equally clear glass refrigerator. He held them out to each of them and, as a reflex, Zoey and Echo took the bottles. They both knew the alternative was creating an awkward moment where Wrexx held out the offering and they refused as some kind of passive-aggressive gesture. Things would have just degraded from there, with thousands of Wrexx-loving swing voters watching it occur in real time.

He looked Echo up and down. "Good Lord, you're like a touched-up photo in real life. Do you remember the first time a guy called you beautiful?"

"No," replied Echo, "but I remember the first time I realized a compliment can come from a place of hate."

"Ha, I definitely know what you mean," replied Wrexx, and Zoey felt her anxiety snake coil around her ribs. "You say you're not hungry," he said to Zoey, "but it's animals that eat when they're hungry. Humans eat for the experience! I know you like simple, rustic breakfast foods—have you ever had syrniki? I have to get the farmer's cheese imported from Russia. Costs a fortune, but worth it."

At the front of the bus, where a driver would be if it had one, there was a currently dormant DJ setup with turntables and lights. With a swipe of Wrexx's hands, it all folded up into the wall and was replaced by an oven and a range. Another swipe caused a shelf full of cookware to descend from the ceiling.

"Everything in here is designed to maximize space," said Wrexx for the camera and also his guests, if they had cared. "My bed is above you, at night that coffee table in front of you folds out of the way and the bed drops down so I can get my beauty sleep. How is your scalp healing? I have some ointment, my girlfriend gets it from Tibet. It'll heal anything, totally natural ingredients."

"No, thank you, I'm getting treatment for it."

From the refrigerator, Wrexx pulled out a tub of white cheese and a carton of eggs.

"Guys are gonna like that scar, I'm not even joking. Dudes go for dangerous chicks. This is a Russian dish, my guests love it for brunch. Think of it as a fluffy mini cheesecake, only not as sweet or fatty, more savory. Topped with cream and fruit. You're gonna be at Catharsis tonight, yes? To kick off the headliners? Word is it's gonna be straight-up tit-chili."

Zoey had never heard that expression before yet somehow was in complete agreement. "We're really pressed for time, can you say what you asked us here to say?"

Rex had dumped the clumps of soft cheese into a mixing bowl and was now separating egg yolks and whites, the former going into the bowl with the cheese. Outside, vehicles were slowing alongside them and onlookers—mostly girls—were waving and yelling at the Fish Bowl. They were shouting some kind of catch phrase that Zoey couldn't quite make out.

"I'm being stalked by one of your people," he said, never taking his eyes off the eggs. "She wears gleaming black armor and rides a motorcycle and likes to lurk in the shadows near wherever I happen to be. I mean, what's the point of stalking someone who lives their life so openly? What can I have to hide? Last night when we stopped for our dinner experience, I even asked her to come join us. We were cooking pheasant over an open fire while she was parked on her motorcycle off in the darkness, those yellow eyes lit up like a panther. It was scaring the guests. I call her over and she just yells something rude and drives off. What kind of way is that to behave, especially now, when what we need above all else is unity?"

Echo, who'd sat her unopened bottle of water on the glass coffee table between them, said, "So you're saying you have no idea what that's about."

"She seems to think I'm some kind of secret psychopath. Someone who preys on women."

Zoey thought he'd added a little dramatic lilt to the line, like he was getting interviewed by the cops in an old TV show. His being accused of murder was just the new plotline in his rolling broadcast. While he spoke, he was adding sugar and salt to the cheese mixture, measuring by eye and instinct. In the acting world, they call this giving the character "business," some kind of physical activity to make the scene more dynamic.

"But you have hurt women before," said Zoey.

"Absolutely not. I've never hurt anyone who didn't hurt me first. I've only ever acted out of self-defense."

"So the woman whose face you burned off, *that* was self-defense?"

"I did no such thing and would never dream of it." Rex mashed the thick, pale mixture together with his bare hands, squeezing it through his fingers. "That whole situation was unfortunate. Some fans took it upon themselves to act in response to what Lyra was doing. Now, I will say that I do believe in karma and, unfortunately, Lyra got back from the universe the ugliness she was putting into it."

He sprinkled flour into the bowl, along with a handful of golden raisins.

"So you personally had nothing to do with the attack?" asked Echo. "You didn't tell fans to do that or imply that it would be good if they did?"

Wrexx was now forming the mixture into pucks, coating them in flour. "Do you know the backstory here? I went to Lyra once, as a customer. It was average. So the next morning, I did my normal video review—"

"Wait, you reviewed the sex?" asked Zoey.

"Do you not follow my streams? I do sex-worker reviews every Tuesday," he said as he added pats of butter and some cooking oil to a hot skillet. "These girls do massive business off my reviews, I get thousands of requests from them, begging me to do them next. I gave Lyra a four. That's out of ten. She showed no enthusiasm, had poor hygiene, including very bad breath, which is inexcusable for what she charges. And she did this fake laugh every time I made a joke. Like she was mocking me. She acted like she didn't want to be there and was condescending to me when I tried to lighten the mood. The physical act itself was forgettable."

He added nine syrniki cakes to the pan, each sizzling as they made contact. The scent of melted butter filled the bus and Zoey's brain issued a primal command to her salivary glands.

"To get revenge on me," Wrexx continued, "I find out she uploaded a video of her own, full of kink-shaming and all sorts of other ugliness, telling other sex workers to stay away from me. She tried to kill my reputation, which means she tried to kill me, since reputation is all a man has. I did a response video to hers, calling her out, saying she needs to learn how to accept criticism. Then things unfortunately escalated from there. But I had no direct involvement and if the guys who did it had asked me, I'd have told them to cool it."

Echo leaned forward. "But you do understand that—"

"Hold on, this next part requires concentration."

Wrexx watched as the cakes finished cooking, then plated them in trios, topped with a scoop of sour cream and bright red cherry jam, which added a splash of alluring color that dribbled down the white cream. He carefully placed two plates of grilled cheesecakes on the low glass table. The plates each looked like a photograph from a restaurant menu and smelled like temptation. Wrexx returned to his own dish in the kitchen, ate a forkful of a cake, and gave an exaggerated, "Mmmmm!" for the cameras.

Echo, not even glancing at her food, said, "You understand there seems to be a substantial gap in your story. You make it sound like nothing that happened would trigger even a psychopath to permanently disfigure this woman. Do you have a lot of fans like that? The type who are capable of that kind of violence with no prompting whatsoever? If so, it seems like you'd want to be extra careful about not saying anything, even on accident, that might activate one of them."

Zoey looked down and was surprised to find she'd cut into the syrniki with her fork. It had just a paper-thin crust that gave way to a cushion of pure, wholesome fat. She told herself not to actually eat it but she was already doing it. The dish tasted like something you should only have once, on vacation, then you would spend the rest of your life telling people about it.

"I don't know that they needed me to say anything," replied Wrexx before his words were momentarily interrupted by his own fork. "I think they acted based on what they saw Lyra doing to me. I mean, if you saw your mother being raped, would you need to wait for her to tell you to act or would you just act?"

Echo was momentarily speechless. "Are you the . . . raped woman in this example?"

"The Wrexx Army is passionate. We have a code. We believe in bringing beauty in the world, in stopping ugliness wherever we can. Someone like Lyra, they can be beautiful on the outside but full of ugliness inside. I said on my video, the world would be a better place if you could just look at people and see what they are inside, if what you saw could match what's in their soul. Sometimes when you put a thought that powerful into the universe, it can't help but become real. I feel sorry for Lyra, I do. I feel sorry that she has so much ugliness inside her."

"Just to summarize," said Zoey, "you criticized her, she criticized you, then she had her face set on fire and lost most of her eyesight. And you think the ledger is balanced."

"More than balanced. Even though the attack was not at my hands, I donated two million dollars to her recovery, just because my heart went out to her and her family. Whether that will do anything to affect the ugliness inside her is anyone's guess."

"So if I paid you two million dollars, would you let me burn off your face right now?"

Echo shifted in her seat. She was backdropped by three lanes of traffic. Some kids on a scooter were waving frantically at Wrexx, trying to get his attention.

"That's not the question," replied Wrexx, unperturbed. "The question is, if you did that, or if you allowed your vigilante to do it, what would the universe do in response?"

"And by 'universe' you mean your crazy fans."

He shrugged, an exaggerated motion for the cameras. "I don't want that to happen, of course. I don't want any of it to happen. I want everything to be beautiful, all of the time. But some people can't handle that."

Echo asked, "Is Lyra the only sex worker you've had this kind of interaction with? Where something went wrong and through . . . karma, they wound up getting hurt?"

"I know you think I'm the Sex Butcher," he said casually. "My heart goes out to the victims. But when all three went missing, each time I was right here, in the Fish Bowl, in full view of everyone. Mind, body, and soul open to the world."

"And you never implied to the Wrexx Army, through roundabout language, that the butchering of these women is something you wouldn't mind having happen, or that it should happen?"

"Absolutely not. I understand why your mind would go there. After all, if my empathy caused me to pay out two million for Lyra, what would I pay out to you people for three completely dead girls? You see someone like me, somebody with money and a big heart, and your eyes light up with dollar signs."

Zoey stared at Wrexx's stupid face and imagined having DeeDee's power, the physical strength to grab a guy like him by the throat and just crush bone and tendon like squeezing a beer can. She thought about how DeeDee *had* restrained herself and the even more incredible strength that must have taken.

"So let me be super clear," said Zoey, about to demonstrate somewhat less restraint. "If we find out someone has killed these three women, we're not going to be asking them for money. Whatever debt they have to pay will have to be settled between them and their god. We'll just send them to that meeting."

Echo, before she could stop herself, put her head in her hands.

"You sound just like Leonidas Damon," said Wrexx. "Maybe you should be backing him instead."

Echo, trying to steer the encounter back into some kind of productive exchange of information, said, "What Lyra said that made you so mad, you're saying it wasn't true? The thing about how you like to role-play murdering women?"

"Role-play is fantasy. To get to a sexually satisfying place, I like to embody the most visceral experience I can imagine, to fully put myself into that position mentally and spiritually. Death, the threat of it, the knowledge that your partner holds its power, it reminds us of the value of life and the value of life is expressed via sex. It's no secret, I've done it in here, in full view of everyone. But fantasy is fantasy."

Zoey had already decided that she was personally done with the meeting. It felt like the bus hadn't moved in a while. They were heading down Winner's Circle, the main gaming district featuring a cluster of themed casinos, each a spectacular display of truly impractical architecture. They had already passed the medieval castle–themed casino Fort Fortuna and were coming up on the Lucky Cat hotel, a fifty-story-tall golden cat with a left paw that waved slowly in the air like it was hoping to swat down an airplane. Across the street was a tower designed to look like it was in the process of being crushed by a giant snake. It was closed—it had been built as a tie-in with a blockbuster movie that had come out a year earlier but that nobody had gone to see.

"So if you're not ashamed," said Echo, "why did you find it so insulting when she talked about it?"

"She misrepresented it. She said I was going to reach a point where I would only be satisfied with real murder. It was a lie, intended to destroy me. And now look: I stand accused of these other crimes because of it! The ugliness she put into the world just grows and metastasizes. Hopefully, she'll see all of the turmoil she's caused and learn from it. That's all we can do."

He focused on finishing his brunch.

"You call your fans an army," muttered Zoey, staring out of the transparent wall of the bus, already feeling drained by the day. "But if you were gone, are you sure they wouldn't immediately forget about you and glom on to some other personality?"

"I get messages every day from fans saying I saved their lives. Just by being a voice, a face, a spirit they can look to and lean on. They live by my code of bringing beauty into the world, of opposing unfairness and injustice in their everyday lives. Your people can kill me but don't think for a moment that they can kill the movement, the positive energy my people represent. You want to talk about power? That's real power. Don't mess with it."

He came and collected Zoey's plate, noting that she'd eaten one of the cakes and part of another. "It's good, right? Look, guys, we're all on the same team, aren't we? We all want to see Alonzo win on Tuesday and to keep this city free. And, more importantly, we have the same obnoxious enemies."

He was gesturing toward the back of the bus. A flock of angel drones were buzzing their way.

Echo said, "We're done here anyway. Can you find a place for us to disembark that won't turn into an incident?"

Wrexx took a bite of Zoey's leftover syrniki, pointed with his fork, and said, "No worries. The Wrexx Army's got your back."

Six of the flowing angel drones were flying in over the stopped traffic, accusations and lamentations booming from their speakers. Under their angelic shouts, though, was the sound of boos and hectoring from the bystanders. It was clear that the fans in the nearby vehicles weren't just coincidental passing traffic; they knew the route and had been following the Fish Bowl convoy. Others could be found on the sidewalks, either having spotted the bus from blocks away or having just tracked its position on Blink. A flash mob of Wrexx Army members had materialized and they were in no mood to have their morning ruined by a bunch of sanctimonious hobby drones.

Somebody chucked a shoe at one of the angels. Somebody else threw a full cup of coffee. Now the angels, three of them bearing the faces of missing or dead women, were being pelted with trash and Zoey was watching it happen while, as far as any witnesses were concerned, she was enjoying brunch inside the luxury tour bus of a known predator.

Before Zoey could say it, Echo stood and said it for her. "Open the doors. We're getting off."

"But you haven't even touched your food," said Wrexx.

"Two women are in a closed space with you and demanding to leave. Demonstrate now, for the world: Will you comply with that demand, or will you keep them locked in, against their will, to gratify some fetish for exerting power?"

They stared each other down for a moment, then Wrexx ordered the doors to open.

CHAPTER
14

"BEFORE WE GO ANY further," said Zoey, "I just have to ask: Is there a political faction in this city that *doesn't* have any weird creeps in the upper echelons?"

They were back in the sedan, having taken a right turn to get away from the Fish Bowl convoy. They hadn't gotten far, thanks to traffic that really was even worse than usual. Ever since moving to the city, Zoey tended to laugh out loud at action movies and cop shows that portrayed the heroes just instantly teleporting to the next thing via a single edit. In the real world, all it took was one stalled vehicle, or some stupid standoff between two road-raging drivers, and you'd feel the effects for eight blocks. It was a miracle, Zoey often thought, that society functioned at all.

"This nation was built by weird creeps," replied Will, dipping into his vast arsenal of deeply alarming reassurances. "People who don't care about social norms get things done. Unfortunately, you can't perfectly tailor which norms they're going to adhere to and which they're going to break. It was a problem a thousand years ago and it'll probably remain a problem a thousand years from now. Ambition comes from voracious appetites and appetites come in all flavors. I mean, that's the basis of our business. I'm not saying the people at the top are all sex predators, but they're all predators of some sort."

"The existence of those people isn't as scary as the fact that they have loyal fans."

"It's all the same," said Echo. "Wrexx has built a life for himself where he's not bound by rules. Certain people see that and their imagination dazzles with the possibilities. 'What if I, too, could actually follow through on my worst desires, unimpeded?'"

"So you're saying no scandal or bad publicity can ever bring him down."

"Oh, I'm sure his fans would abandon him if something truly bad came out, but they'd dismiss any accusation as heresy against their god. He'd have to do it right in front of them and it'd have to be *bananas*."

A chime sounded. DeeDee was calling in, a foot-tall hologram appearing on the car's center console.

As a greeting, she said, "I tried to watch your meeting live but frankly I can't stand to listen to that man talk."

Echo said, "Zoey and I are both measurably worse people for having spent time with Wrexx. But for what it's worth, I don't think he did it. The three missing sex workers, I mean. We established that he probably *could* have done it, maybe even that he'll inevitably do it someday, but I don't think pursuing Wrexx will lead us to Iris, Violet, and Rose."

"Why? It seems to me like he intentionally picked when to make his move, knowing that the political situation would keep us off his back."

"Honestly? He just doesn't have time. I've scoured his schedule and it's true that he's not on-camera twenty-four hours a day, but this kind of killing takes more spare time than he has. Not just what he'd be doing with the victims, but the stalking, the planning . . ."

"Then where are they?" asked DeeDee's digital ghost. "They need to be found and this whole thing really feels like a side project you people are squeezing in between meetings."

Will shook his head. "No, it's all connected. The way this has been staged, the way the information is rolling out, it's all about influencing public opinion. They showed us one supposed victim yesterday, the election is in two days, so I'd be shocked if we didn't get something new by—"

A new call chimed in. Echo asked DeeDee to hold and swiped a new hologram onto the center console. It was Hank Kowalski, a former detective who transitioned to doing security work for Zoey's organization when the city's checks started bouncing. He was bald and wearing aviator sunglasses that didn't hide the fact that he clearly enjoyed breaking horrific news to people.

"We've got a corpse here," said Kowalski in a tone a normal person would use to announce a pizza delivery had arrived. "It was dumped in the square, right in the middle of the street, in front of the tourists. It's one of your three prostitutes."

Will, looking genuinely surprised, sat his drink down and asked, "Which one?"

"Iris. Second one that went missing. So they're coming in the same order."

Will crinkled his forehead, considering how to ask his next question. "And what condition is the body in?"

"Perfect, now that you mention it. Got her sealed up in a box. How quick can you be here?"

They were, in fact, in sight of the square. Well, Zoey thought, at least now they knew what was holding up traffic.

Will glanced around at the other passengers. "We can actually be there in a few minutes, if we walk."

They arrived to find the Tabula Ra$a PD had made a rare appearance, roping off one lane and part of another, which Zoey figured was probably enough to stall traffic well into Kansas. Gawkers were gathering outside of the police tape (exacerbating the blockage in the process) and drone voyeurs hovered overhead. Most of the street streamers had turned up, the self-proclaimed citizen journalists who appeared in the aftermath of violence or, if they were fortunate and their intel was good, during it. Zoey recognized all of them but one, an elderly woman in a gray trench coat and a red wide-brimmed hat. She had a drone hovering in front of her face and seemed to be summarizing the situation for . . . somebody. Her grandkids?

Zoey, Will, Wu, and Echo had made the walk to the crime scene relatively undisturbed, with only one guy shouting at Zoey, asking if he could pet her cats (so that was a meme now apparently?) and three males who did a double take at the sight of Echo, which was the normal amount. They ducked right through the yellow police tape without so much as a disapproving look from the street cops. At the center of all the commotion was a single detective kneeling over a glass box containing a woman's body.

The woman—Iris—was nude and free of visible wounds. She lay flat in a box that was smaller than a coffin, barely big enough to contain the petite woman inside, as if it had been custom made. The body was being presented like a piece of merchandise and, just in case the onlookers didn't make the connection, on the side was an oversized supermarket label that said,

1864 Oz

Clearance $6.16

Followed by a stamped expiration date—today.

The detective kneeling over the glass box was, in fact, Hank Kowalski, who was in no way employed by the city of Tabula Ra$a. Zoey didn't know if he had used the Suits' influence to commandeer the investigation or if he had just jumped in after no other detectives showed up. He was feeling around the edges of the box, trying to find some seam or other way to open it. None were apparent.

Will glanced over the box and said, "You're not worried there's a bomb sewn into the abdomen? Maybe this is designed to lure us all in and then blow us to pieces with polymer shrapnel."

"I like to live dangerously," grunted Kowalski.

"How did it get here?"

"A truck stopped, open the rear doors, tipped it out, and drove away."

Zoey said, "And we weren't able to track the truck, in a city with twenty million cameras and thousands of drones swarming around?"

Kowalski nodded sideways. "It's right over there, parked on the sidewalk. No driver, it drove itself here. It's flashing the logo of a local meat company that doesn't exist. I think our perp here fancies himself to be a performance artist. Cops will take it and dust it for prints, they've got it roped off to keep the tourists away."

Zoey leaned over the box and looked the girl in the face. Iris had black hair, like Zoey's, puddled under her skull. She wore a peaceful expression;

she could have been asleep to a casual observer. Zoey looked over Iris's naked body and wondered what parts of it she had hated in the mirror. Then she was suddenly aware of the spectators and drones and all the other curious cameras. Eyes on top of eyes, all around them.

She asked, "Is there any evidence to be taken from the outside of the box?"

"So many tourists had handled it by the time I got here that it'd be hopeless, even if the perps had been careless," said Kowalski. "Whatever we get, we'll get from the corpse inside."

"The tourists were, what, taking pictures with it?"

Kowalski gave her a strangely offended look. "They were trying to get it open, Zoey. To help her, if they could. This city is full of weirdos but they're not monsters. But yeah, they were also taking pictures with it."

Zoey turned back to Will. "Give me your jacket."

"Why?"

"If you get a call one day that they've found me out here, in the middle of a crowd, naked, what would you do? Would you just let people stare?"

He took off his jacket and laid it over the box, covering the top half of the woman's nudity. Wu, without a word, removed his jacket and covered the bottom half.

Kowalski stood. "We've gotta load it up and take it somewhere we can cut into it without damaging the corpse. It's not gonna be easy to get in, which I'm guessing was part of the point. We've got those saws and that laser thing they use to cut victims out of car accidents. But now, Will, you've got me all paranoid about this thing being booby-trapped—no pun intended—because if so, then back at the station would be the perfect place to set it off. Maybe the Sex Butcher's got a grudge against the department. Got a bunch of unpaid parking tickets or somethin'."

Zoey kneeled by the box, taking Kowalski's place at the dead woman's side. "I didn't see any marks or anything at all on the body. Did he suffocate her in here?"

"Not likely. There's no bruising or broken nails where she'd have tried to kick or claw her way out. Maybe an injection to stop her heart? They clearly wanted her preserved. I'd guess she was alive as recently as two or three hours ago, there's no sign at all of lividity."

"Of what?"

Before he could answer, Echo said, "There's always a bruising at the bottom of a corpse soon after death, where blood settles after it stops circulating. She has none, it was the first thing I noticed."

Zoey looked closely at Iris's face. "Is it possible that they—"

The woman's eyes snapped open.

Her mouth went wide, gasping for air like a stranded fish. Her eyes darted around, trying to make sense of what she was seeing, to understand what nightmare she'd been abducted into.

"SHE'S ALIVE!" screamed Zoey, pawing around the box as if she was suddenly going to find the opening mechanism the veteran professional detective had missed. "GET HER OUT! SHE CAN'T BREATHE! GET HER OUT!"

The gawkers gasped in response. The old woman streaming the event whispered to her audience with extreme urgency and gravity. The men around Zoey stood frozen, seeming unsure of what to do. There was a large rock and a hunk of broken pavement nearby, apparently what the bystanders had used to try to crack open the case before the cops got there. The only evidence of their work was some white scuff marks in the middle of the box.

"We don't have to get her out," said Echo, "right now we just need to make holes so she can breathe."

Kowalski spun around to one of the beat cops. "One of these vehicles has got to have tools in it!" He pointed to the rows of stalled traffic around them. "I see a van for some kind of contractor, and there is a tow truck—somebody's gotta have a saw, a blowtorch, something! Go! Go!"

The woman slapped and pressed on the box in a blind panic.

Will said, "Considering they make some polymers stronger than titanium, it would be a ridiculous stroke of luck if anybody had something capable of penetrating it."

"If you've got ideas," grumbled Kowalski, "I'm all ears, chief. If this is made of what I think it's made of, you'd need a military-grade railgun to crack it."

Will nodded to Wu, who took off running in the direction they'd come.

Kowalski asked, "Where's he going?"

"To get our military-grade railgun from the trunk of the car."

The sedan's autopilot had been set to just keep creeping along in traffic until it reached them, so in theory it should've been at least somewhat closer than when they'd left it to proceed on foot.

Zoey put her hands on the box and shouted, "Can you hear me?!? You need to calm down and preserve your air! We're getting something to open this!"

Kowalski muttered, "I don't think this is gonna work. Whatever your guy comes back with, if it's enough to crack this thing open, it's also enough that the shock of the impact will pulverize the contents. That kind of energy would be like a big boot kicking a beer bottle across the street. You got a cutting tool? Or I guess what I'm really asking, do any of your people have some kind of energy-based cutting tools embedded in their bodies?"

He was looking at the running Wu when he said it.

Will shook his head. "Not to our knowledge."

"We have stuff at the estate," said Echo. "How long will her air last?"

The woman had not, as far as Zoey could tell, taken her advice to calm her breathing. If anything, she seemed to be hyperventilating. She screamed for help, but barely any sound escaped the box.

"She won't last long enough for you to go and come back. And we don't even know how long she's been in there."

"Can we hijack a helicopter?" asked Zoey. "Scoop up the box and race it to the house?"

Will shook his head. "If she dies in our custody, they'll say we murdered her."

"I don't give a shit!"

Soon, Wu ran up carrying the railgun, a gadget spat out of Santa's Workshop that looked like a combination of an assault rifle and a giant prehistoric centipede. It was designed to release an ungodly pulse of electricity along a rail that carried with it a thin projectile that would then fly out at several times the speed of sound. If fired at a car, the vehicle would barely slow down the projectile for whatever thoroughly doomed target was behind it.

Wu, who had clearly been thinking about this during his sprint back from the sedan, said, "I can adjust the power, we can try it lower and if it doesn't crack, go up in increments."

Kowalski said, "That projectile has to go somewhere, if it ricochets into this crowd of bystanders, it's gonna paint the street with their guts."

"THEN WHAT DO WE DO?" shrieked Zoey. These people loved to tell you why your ideas were bad without offering any of their own.

The imprisoned woman's eyes locked onto Zoey's, pleading. Tears were streaming down her temples.

Will studied the box, narrowed his eyes. "Have you tried looking underneath it?"

Instead of answering, Kowalski kneeled and said, "Help me tip it on its side."

Will and Zoey joined in trying to get their fingers under it.

"We're going to roll you over," said Echo to the boxed woman. "Protect your face, okay?"

Iris showed no sign that she'd heard. Wu got on the other side and braced the bottom of the box with his shoe. Everyone else lifted on the glass—

Iris shrieked. Then there was a wet, muffled *pop*, and the top third of the box became a splatter of red. Bits of gore dripped down the interior of the glass. All three of them flinched so hard that they recoiled, dropping the box back to the pavement.

The woman's bare limbs thrashed once, then twitched, then went limp.

Everyone froze in stunned silence. Echo stood with her hand over her mouth. Wu held his useless alien gun. The crowd stared and let their cameras record but no one spoke, aside from a few people in the back muttering to ask what had happened.

Finally, the old woman who'd been streaming the crime scene said, "Oh, sweet Jesus."

Kowalski said, "They, ah, they must have implanted some kind of charge in her skull. In her sinuses, by the look of it. Goddamn."

Iris's face was like a fully bloomed rose. At least, that's what Zoey took in during the one second she spent looking before turning away. She bent over and put her hands on her knees. The box had been rigged, apparently, to kill Iris if they tried to move her. To kill her right in front of them.

Will's reaction, as was often the case, was infuriatingly out of step with those around him. He stood, his hands on his hips, glaring down at the bloody box with an expression of annoyed curiosity that Zoey thought should be carved onto any memorial statue made of the man.

He said, "Let's go ahead and turn it over."

"Why?" asked Zoey.

Will turned to Kowalski. "You examined her for how long before we got here?"

"Probably thirty minutes. Maybe more."

"And that whole time, you never noticed she was still breathing?"

"She wasn't breathing. I mean, she'd have been fogging up the box."

Will shook his head, annoyed. He went about lifting the box once more. Everyone joined in, tipping it all the way over until it was face-down. The bottom of the box was revealed to be flat black metal, the only side that wasn't transparent. Will got down on the ground, looked into the side of the box, stood up with a "that's what I thought" expression and picked his jacket off the street. He didn't say a word as he brushed off the dust and put it back on.

Zoey got down to see what he had seen.

The corpse should, of course, have tumbled around inside the box, land-ing on its ruined face. Instead, it remained in the exact position as before, defying gravity, the body stuck to what was now the top of the box. Zoey thought for a moment that the killer had glued or otherwise attached the woman to that surface, but not even the black hairs lying across her fore-head fell as they should. The blood and bits of exploded bone dripped the wrong direction. It was like gravity inside the box had been reversed.

Zoey said, "What the . . . ?"

"I thought maybe it was an animatronic," answered Will, "but it's not even that. It's five screens, synced to create a 3D image. The box is empty."

Kowalski said, "I'm gonna be frank, this would have pissed me off less if it'd just been a regular ol' corpse in a regular ol' box. I swear, the crime in this city is getting too stupid for me to keep up with. I mean, what could the prosecutor even charge here? Obstructing traffic? Disorderly conduct?"

"A psychopath with a knife just wants to kill women. Whoever is doing this is trying to change the world. It's objectively scarier."

"This setup wasn't cheap, either," added Echo. "So now we're dealing with someone who has resources."

"Hold on," said Zoey. "Is Iris dead or not? I mean, I know we don't have a corpse here, but what we saw in this box, was this a live feed? Is there a body on a table in some guy's basement with five 3D cameras pointed at it?"

"That's certainly what they want us to think," answered Will. "But ask yourself this: If the killings were real, why go through all of this trouble to keep us physically separated from the corpses?"

"Preventing us from collecting forensic evidence would be one reason," said Kowalski.

"Do we have somebody who can do an analysis on the video? See if it's a live feed or a special effect?"

Kowalski lit a cigar. "I got a guy."

"Good. Get it to him. Let us know as soon as you know something. We've got a—"

"If you say we have another meeting to get to," said Zoey, "I'm gonna steal one of these cars and run you over with it."

CHAPTER
15

ZOEY HAD EXPECTED AN avalanche of messages from her mother inquiring about her difficult day of increasingly surreal horrors, but had received only a single message, cryptically asking if Zoey was interested in a coupon for a free waxing appointment. Her mother did, in fact, have a job (as a sexuality coach, which had always triggered relentless mockery from Zoey's friends in school). This wasn't because she needed the money, obviously, but because otherwise worrying about Zoey would become her full-time job. There was an unspoken rule that she would not obsessively follow news of her daughter's adventures via Blink, but whenever anything big happened, friends and coworkers always turned up to deliver the news, usually in the most alarming way possible. Instead of getting into all that had occurred, Zoey just replied to the free waxing message with a crude joke, which would hopefully indicate that she was unharmed and in good spirits.

The entire team was gathered in the conference room back at the estate for what Will insisted was not a meeting but a debriefing. Andre had brought coffee from a joint down the street called Beansomnia, which was a sore subject around the estate. They charged twenty bucks a cup and yet still made an espresso inferior to what Zoey could craft in the kitchen's machine, if she had the actual desire and energy to do so. Nobody else cared, because they were getting exotic flavors with ten different ingredients, covering the fact that the espresso was bitter from overextraction of the grounds. The joint was running their machines too hot, or too long, or using the wrong grind, or *something*. Sometimes when

Zoey wanted to escape reality, she daydreamed of buying that shop and whipping them into shape. Today, she was actually dreaming up details about how she would decorate the interior, deciding she'd turn half of it into a fancy Swiss chocolate shop. Then the meeting kicked off in earnest and she forced herself to pay attention.

"Budd has suggested he's hit the jackpot in terms of information," Will was saying, "so he gets to go first."

Budd set his cowboy hat on the table in front of him and said, "Right off the bat, I have an answer to the question of the three working girls' names, all of them being flowers. It turns out Violet, Iris, and Rose knew each other, and I mean before they got into this field of endeavor. They kept their friendship private but all three were doing soft-core shows on Blink, with aspirations of modeling or acting or what have you, then moved out here with the promise of getting jobs waiting tables at one of the high-end joints. They'd bought the old fantasy that high-roller tips alone would make them a white-collar income, get them in touch with studio executives and the like. Then they found that those big tips only came when, let's say, bonus services were offered, and that a lot of those tips are paid in the form of Iso or whatever flavor of opioid is on tap this week. And that right there is your ambitious-young-dreamer-to-sex-worker pipeline. The three all got jobs at Chalet, came up with their aliases together, and agreed to keep an eye out for one another."

Zoey said, "But that doesn't tell us anything about what happened to them, does it? Unless you're saying they all knew the killer . . ."

"One month ago, all three attended an off-the-books, exclusive, underground get-together in Las Vegas. No cameras, no phones, everyone signed an NDA. At least seventy people in attendance, including our friend Rex Wrexx."

Echo said, "Well, there it is, then."

"Is it?" asked Zoey. "Because I thought your last update was that those Liberator nuts had talked to them right before they disappeared."

Budd nodded. "They did. Along with virtually every other prostitute, escort, and masseuse we employ. Their strategy is to just blanket the city with their message of salvation. So that connection might not be meaningful. And of course, it's possible that neither is."

"Then I don't see how this information is helpful."

"All information is helpful, even if it's not yet apparent how. But I also knew that wasn't enough to drag everyone into a meeting, so I do have more. I had a little visit with Handsome Cho—"

"Who?"

"A tattoo artist. I won't bore you with the details of how I found him— basically I followed a chain of about a dozen lowlifes who repeated the same rumor until I arrived at the source—but five days ago, Handsome Cho was hired to tattoo a corpse. Specifically, he was told to apply Violet's tattoos to a dead body, and was paid very well to do the job and to stay quiet about it."

Budd moved his hat, summoned a series of stills onto the table's built-in display, and zoomed in to specific body parts. Zoey noticed he'd carefully cropped around any blood and gore. He narrated as he swiped through four tattoos.

"Butterfly on the wrist, a set of paw prints on the left buttock, a red band around the left ankle made to look like tied string. They even had him do the tiny cartoon devil on the nape of her neck. That one not only isn't visible in the torture video they made, but I can't find anyone who even knew about it. Where it was placed, it'd have always been covered by her hair."

"Meaning," said Echo, "they were making a fake Violet body, but may have had access to the real thing."

This yielded a moment of silent consideration at the table, but Zoey thought it just muddled the picture even further.

"And before you ask," added Budd, "no, our tattoo artist never interacted with his employer directly and never saw any faces or heard any voices. He showed up, the body was there, he did the work, left. I'm guessing that what we saw in the mutilation video was Violet's screaming head digitally wrapped onto an already dead corpse, one made to look just like her."

"So Alonzo was right," said Will. "And that's two fake murders, done at some expense. Thank you, Budd. Andre, you're up."

Andre was taken aback. "I didn't even tell you I had news!"

"You get this eager expression on your face when you've got something to share."

"See, this is why everybody hates playing cards with you. But yes, I do have news. A fight and/or riot broke out a bit ago downtown, between a group of volunteers registering voters for Alonzo and some pro-Damon types. Nobody dead, but three in the hospital. It seems worth pointing out that all of the Damonites were from out of town. Not long after that, one of Damon's mobile campaign trucks—you know, the ones that drive around town blasting slogans at everybody—got flipped over. Not by a crowd, but by one guy."

"Somebody with implants," said Will. "We knew that was inevitable."

Someday, Zoey thought, there would surely be a book written about the augmentation-implant subculture as it grew up around the city. So far, the overwhelming majority of the augmented were men and fit a particular profile. Virtually all relentlessly promoted their abilities on Blink in an effort to parlay them into some kind of notoriety and, as a group, there seemed to be a shared belief that they were destined to be the true power in society, if they weren't already. In their videos, they ranted about what needed to happen with taxes, and crime, and abortion. They'd melt iron bars with their hands while they talked, as if to say, "See? My opinions matter now. *Please listen to me.*" They would make vague threats to politicians, even the president, acting as if possessing the physical strength to tear their way through the fence around the White House meant they had a proverbial seat at the table, as if that had been the only thing holding them back before. That first wave of implants had, it seemed to Zoey, attracted those who had a child's idea of what power was and how it worked.

The second wave of customers would, she thought, be people like DeeDee who sensed an arms race coming, those who didn't want to be left behind in a world in which this first group of crazies had become common. There were still only a few hundred augmented vigilantes in the city, but knowing that the next man who grabbed your arm might just be able to squeeze the limb in half with his fingers had been enough for DeeDee and others to line up for implants. But what Will was referencing was the Suits' looming fear that the augmented community, particularly the subsection of the community who were dumbasses, would collectively decide they needed to intervene in the election in the only way they knew how.

Echo said, "We've had to eject three of them from Catharsis so far." The festival was a no-implant zone, nobody wanted a mosh pit where one dude's swinging elbow could decapitate three people at once. "One was just a fan, two were volunteering their services as security."

"How nice of them," said Zoey.

"So then," said Andre, making it clear he wasn't finished rattling off his stream of alarming news, "Leonidas Damon decided to make an appearance at Catharsis, turning up in the infield campgrounds to shout politics at the kids. He got mobbed by fans, then they got mobbed by nonfans, then security came over to break it up and, again, it turned out one of our security volunteers had implants he didn't disclose. He picked up one dude and threw him at another dude. Several broken bones there. Then that went viral on Blink and a bunch of idiots 'retaliated' by going after one of Alonzo's voter-registration convoys. They overturned a car, it caught fire, things got rowdy, and six people wound up hospitalized, one of 'em stabbed pretty bad."

Zoey said, "Please tell me there are no more crises, because I'm already finding it a little hard to breathe."

"I don't know that this qualifies," replied Echo, "but Aviv's video went up. About the estate break-in."

Zoey had, incredibly, forgotten all about that. "Did he keep his word? About leaving me out of it?"

"I, uh, don't see you in the video. I mean, he did title it, 'I Drilled Zoey Ashe's Basement,' but . . ."

With a strange expression she couldn't decipher, Will asked Zoey, "Did he mention having any more stunts planned leading up to election day? Anything for, say, in the middle of the vote?"

"We didn't get into it, beyond him guaranteeing he wouldn't mess with me while I was onstage tonight."

"Did you get into who he wants to see win the election?"

"He thinks both candidates are trash and that the whole process is fake. I didn't disagree."

"Everybody thinks that, including the candidates. But when it comes down to it, one of them is going to win and so everyone eventually has to choose. Did you get a sense of how he's leaning?"

"No, Will. Why are you asking?"

Will, in his infuriating way, responded by not responding.

"Wait, you don't think he's behind this thing with the three women, do you? Even if it's a hoax, it's not *his* kind of hoax."

"But we don't know where the hoaxer is going with it. We don't know what punch line they have in mind."

"So you think he would traumatize these women's families in the name of some kind of performance art?"

Echo said, "Can you ask him?"

"Guys, we didn't exchange contact information. If anything, we should be thinking about how this last 'body' was dumped within shouting distance of where we happened to be sitting in traffic, a block away from where Wrexx dropped us off."

Will said, "All that required was knowing our schedule. And your man's entire basement-drilling operation was based on knowing it in extreme detail."

"He's not my—"

Zoey's phone chimed with an incoming message. She pulled it out and checked it under the table.

It was Aviv:

Did you see the video???

Keeping the phone out of view, she replied,

Not right now, in a meeting.

Echo, steadfastly ignoring what Zoey was doing, said, "Well, whoever is behind it, they've made a mistake: their operation is too big. Budd just proved that. This is the work of a team and that team has had to make purchases over the last few months, including farming out tasks to outside crews. With Aviv, he doesn't care if you know who pulled it off and, in fact, that's the whole point."

A new message came in.

Aviv:

Ha I bet you have the weirdest meetings.

Zoey didn't send a response. A few seconds later:

Aviv:

Have they filled in the hole yet? If I come to see you can I use that same one or do I have to drill a new one?

Zoey:

MY PEOPLE ARE SITTING RIGHT NEXT TO ME, STOP MESSAGING!

Will said, "Here's what I can't get past: If it was Wrexx, why would he want to make the bodies public and swing the election toward the candidate he openly opposes? If it was the Liberators, why would they stage this last one so that we would be first on the scene? All they got was the whole city watching us trying to save the victim. How does that feed the narrative that we don't care about these women?"

A new message chime notified Zoey that Aviv did not obey her request for silence.

Aviv:

Are you ashamed of me? Afraid Will wouldn't approve? Invite me to dinner, I'll wear a suit and slick back my hair, tell him my intentions are honorable.

Zoey had no response for that.

Echo said, "Well, they wanted us to look helpless, right? So how about this: The 'killer' keeps taunting us and pulling public stunts until the election is over. And then, if Damon gets elected, his new police force—or whatever authoritarian nightmare he has in mind to subdue the city—will rapidly catch the killer and end their reign of terror. There you go, a perfect demonstration of his law-and-order prowess."

Aviv:

Would it help if I came and filled in the hole? The machine has a reverse button on it and I assume that's what it does.

Will rubbed his chin, as if it contained a little wheel that made his brain work. "That's the obvious move. Too obvious, I say. A straight false flag to boost the anti-crime candidate? Feels bush league."

Zoey looked up at him. "You think somebody spending hundreds of thousands of dollars to stage a serial-killer hoax is too straightforward of an explanation? Jesus, I have to get out of this city."

While she was speaking, she was typing a reply.

Zoey:

My people think this thing with the missing women is one of your pranks.

A moment later,

Aviv:

How much spare time do you guys think I have? The pirate ship and drill thing took months, that's all the stunts I had in me.

After another moment:

Aviv:

Ok maybe one more. But no I have not faked the kidnapping of multiple women from a historically vulnerable and exploited community.

"Also," said Andre, "it runs the risk of getting found out, all it would take is one of these supposed-to-be-dead girls going to the press. That would sink Damon. He doesn't mind looking evil or abrasive, but this would make him look silly and incompetent."

Zoey shoved her phone in her pocket to cut off her temptation to respond to any further messages.

"Okay," she said, "everybody back up. What if I care less about the organization pulling the stunt and their hypothetical goals than I do about the actual physical condition and location of these actual three human beings? Even if they're still alive, there's no guarantee their captors plan to keep them that way. Like you said, they can't be allowed to go public with their experience. I personally consider that to be the ticking clock here, not the stupid election."

Budd nodded. "We're working on it."

"All right. So this meeting was all bad news and we made no progress on anything. Is that it?"

"I have a question," announced Wu from his spot in the doorway. "At what point does the situation at Catharsis become too volatile for Zoey to attend?"

Zoey immediately felt a rush of pure, hopeful joy. Could this be the excuse she needed to not take the stage tonight?

Will said, "She should be there, everything we've been doing has been about establishing her as the new face of the organization."

"But it's her choice, since she is our boss."

"All I do is advise, Wu. She'll do what she wants, you know that."

They both looked to Zoey and her little flicker of hope was snuffed. The order for her to skip the appearance could come from someone else, but not from her, she wouldn't feel right about it otherwise. Will clearly knew this.

"No," she muttered in a defeated tone, "I'll go. I'm not gonna run and hide."

She heard her phone chime with another message and was proud of herself for keeping it in her pants.

"Do you have finalized text of your remarks?" asked Will.

"It's not gonna be a speech. I'll thank everyone for coming and make a joke and walk off."

"What's the joke?"

"I'll just say something."

Will was visibly alarmed by this. "Budd, can you work with Zoey on the joke?"

"Come on," she said, "what's the worst that can happen?"

Andre shrugged. "You create a viral scandal that propels a psychopath to power, he slowly takes over the world, and humanity descends into a thousand years of darkness?"

"Oh, right. Are we finally at the end of this nightmare of a meeting?"

"One last thing," said Will. "If by some odd chance you should hear from your—from Aviv—try to see if he does, in fact, have some kind of stunt planned for tomorrow or, even worse, Tuesday for the election. This whole situation is combustible, the last thing we need is him causing some kind of chaos."

"I'll let him know if I run into him." Zoey looked at her bare wrist as if there was a watch there. "I am absolutely going to need to get some drinks in me before this thing tonight, how much time do I have before we have to leave?"

"Pardon me," said Carlton, who'd appeared at the door. "Ms. Ashe, you have a visitor. DeeDee Dunn wishes to speak to you. She is in the foyer."

Everyone around the table exchanged glances.

"She wants to speak only to me?"

"That is correct."

Zoey stood. "Well, I hope she's fine with me drinking while we talk."

As soon as she was out of the room, Zoey succumbed to temptation and checked the last message she'd missed.

Aviv:

See you at Catharsis tonight! I got an all-access pass.

Zoey stopped dead in the hallway.

Zoey:

Tell me you're kidding.

Aviv:

I am not.

Zoey:

You literally have a bounty on your head. The festival will be packed with Damon's people.

Aviv:

Are you worried about me?

Zoey:

I'm worried about the festival turning into a hellish orgy of violence.

Aviv:

How would that be any different from previous years?

Zoey:

I'm serious.

Aviv:

See you tonight, will you be in the Artists' Trailer Park?

Zoey:

Leave me alone, I'm busy.

Zoey found DeeDee pacing by the huge bronze doors in the foyer in full gleaming black vigilante garb, minus the mask with its glowing yellow eyes. Her hands were at her sides, locked into flat paddles by her glitching implants.

As a greeting, Zoey said, "We have more information but it doesn't point in one specific direction—"

"Someone wants to meet with you for lunch. There's a noodle bar on Sixty-First, right in the heart of Rich Tourist Hell. Let's go."

"Who is it?"

"You'll see. You can get on the back of my motorcycle."

"No, I can't. Wu needs to come and he needs to scan and prep the area in advance. Everybody yells at me if I go off on my own. Now, if they want to meet here, they can—"

"She doesn't want to meet here."

"Tell me who it is."

"It's Lyra Connor."

DeeDee gave Zoey a hard look, like she was daring her to not remember the name.

Zoey said, "The woman whose face Wrexx burned."

DeeDee nodded.

"We'll meet you guys there," said Zoey. "It's the noodle place that's all open, with the waterfall, right?"

"You're telling me that your employees dictate your decisions?"

"I'm telling you that I try to be a good boss and not make their lives harder. And that I've been guilty of thinking of Wu as this silent accessory who just hovers around. But he's actually a human being and, while he wouldn't put it this way, he actually cares what happens to me. He worries. So, no, I won't go without him. But I do have one important question: Does this place serve alcohol?"

CHAPTER
16

THE NOODLE BAR WAS an upscale joint called Nagashi Somen that, according to the sign, was a replica of a famous restaurant in Kyoto. It was an open bar facing the street and sidewalk, backdropped by a two-story-tall hologram of a waterfall spilling over emerald hills. A single chef stood on a platform above the diners, making thin rice noodles and placing servings into one of ten twisting stainless-steel slides flowing with ice water, which would deliver them to one of the customers at the bar. Each patron was to snatch their lump of noodles from the slide, dunk them in a bowl of broth, and quickly eat them before the next portion of noodles came racing down. If you missed yours, they fell into a trough and were swept out of view, unless someone farther down the bar was able to snatch them. It was, in Zoey's opinion, one of the most stressful places to eat in the city.

Lyra was waiting for them next to two empty stools (Wu must have slipped the chef a fair amount of cash to jump the line; this place never had empty seats, especially this close to lunchtime). DeeDee took the other stool, though made no effort to pick up the chopsticks and Zoey wasn't sure how she'd even do it with her non-working fingers. Wu stood behind them, watching for passing threats.

As they situated themselves, Lyra said, "Have you been here before? We only have twenty minutes to eat, then the chef sends down a serving of pink noodles to signal that it's time to give up your seat. They have warabi mochi for dessert but you can grab it and eat it on the sidewalk."

Her speech was a little hard for Zoey to understand, certain words turning into wet hisses and slurps by lips that struggled to form them.

Zoey knew that Lyra had suffered a truly gruesome injury and also knew that she had walked away with money to get repair work done by a top surgeon. She had thus assumed the woman would look fairly normal, with maybe some scars or wrinkles here and there. That was not the case. It appeared, in fact, that Lyra had not gotten any work done at all, or at least, nothing that was intended to make her look like herself again. In the three seconds Zoey allowed herself to linger on the woman's face, she registered that her gorgeous red curls started halfway back from her scalp, the front half of her skull splotchy and bald. One eye was half open behind a drooping eyelid, the other a milky white ruin. She had a section of missing lip that exposed her teeth. The skin in between each of those features was wavy scar tissue, like a sculpture done by clumsy, shaky fingers.

Wrexx had asserted that Lyra's gruesome injuries were a reflection of the ugliness inside her but it occurred to Zoey that they were literally a manifestation of the ugliness inside Wrexx. This realization made it hard for Zoey to speak.

"Oh, that was yours," said Lyra as a bundle of noodles went zipping down her slide, into the trough in front of the bar. "They go fast! It's like they're swimming past because they're scared of being eaten."

Zoey unwrapped her chopsticks but had absolutely no idea what to say. "Thank you. How have you been?"

Stupid question, Zoey thought. Stupid, stupid.

"Good," replied Lyra as she mopped up broth that leaked through the burned-out gap in her lips. "Considering. My mom moved to the city, to help out while I was in recovery."

"I'm sorry," said Zoey, "about what happened to you. Is there anything we can do?"

"DeeDee says you talked to him this morning."

Zoey hesitated. They were in public, which meant they were on-camera. How diplomatic would she have to be here? How diplomatic could she tolerate being?

"Things are tense right now," said Zoey as she stabbed her chopsticks at another speeding bundle of noodles, missing. "He insists the whole incident was just a matter of him saying some innocuous stuff on-camera, then his fans going nuts with it."

"That's his line, yeah." Lyra snatched some noodles and dunked them in the broth. "This broth they have here is incredible. Tsuketsuyu. I'm probably saying it wrong, I couldn't quite say it even when I had my old lips." She glanced over her shoulder at Wu. "I have a question. If somebody came and attacked me right now, would your guy back there with the sword stop it? Or does he only stop it if they come for you?"

"I would stop it," answered Wu. "Not in my capacity as Zoey's personal security, but as man in position to do something."

"Interesting. How does a guy like you get into a job like this?"

Wu smiled. "Do you want the short version or the long?"

"You choose."

"I joined the army, based on a promise that I would learn a marketable skill, which I believed would assuage my worried parents. I also held a secret belief that it would make me seem like more of a man to all of the girls back home who, without exception, saw me only as friend material. I wound up getting sent to South Korea as part of the peacekeeping force there, once it became clear the mess in the north was going to spill over. The joke was that we were there to be the corpses they could show on the news to justify a full military intervention, but it was one of those jokes that was also true. I did, in fact, discover a lucrative skill, though it was not the one my parents were hoping for, or what any parent wants for their son, I suppose. Once I was out, I took a job as a bouncer at a club. I went viral on Blink for an altercation in which I subdued several men. The rest is very uninteresting history."

"I doubt it's uninteresting," said Lyra, "but I know we're short on time. One more question: Were the other soldiers weird about it, like, were there racists who thought because your family is from China that you were a secret traitor or something?"

Wu smiled. "There was a very heavy push inside all branches of the military to try to root out that kind of thing, but yes, it was there. Some had identified me as an easy target for bullying and had to be taught that their radar for detecting weakness was badly in need of calibration."

"So you arrived already knowing how to fight."

"Oh, yes."

"Because that wasn't your first time running into that kind of bully."

"There is a long and complicated history behind that statement. I can see from Zoey's face that she is eager to get to the point of your meeting but in short, I learned quickly that the advantage of bullies isn't in their strength but in what they are willing to do, being unafraid of consequences or of breaking the rules. What they each discovered about me was not just that I knew where to strike a man to bring him to his knees, but that I was willing to deliver that strike. As I have grown older I have become frightened of how much of an advantage that grants a man in this world."

Lyra nodded. "Thank you for that. So," she addressed Zoey, "our friend Wrexx. DeeDee went back and watched your discussion with him and said I needed to tell you my side. What happened was he made his video, about how I was ruining his reputation, ruining his life, destroying his career, all that. He was actually crying, talking about the trauma I caused him, by me telling people that I almost died during our session and that he got off on it, which was one hundred percent true. So then his fans went about digging through every single word I had ever typed online, every single thing I had ever been caught saying on a camera, including conversations overheard in restaurants and department stores by strangers with Blink cams. They mined the records for every bad joke or offensive comment, every burst of anger, until they could build a profile that made me look like a liar and a psychopath. Then they blasted that message over and over, that I was a toxic person who had set out to destroy Wrexx, that I was a predator, that I was trying to bully him into suicide, or get him arrested, or killed, or trying to extract money. The fans whipped themselves into a frenzy until there were entire Blink groups devoted to nothing but fantasizing about my death by torture. They made digital animations of me getting gang-raped. All of this, within a week. That's how long it took them to go from zero to crazy, just pumping up that rage until someone was finally pushed to take action. It couldn't have ended any other way. Unless, of course, Wrexx had told them to back off. Which he didn't."

Zoey said, "Well, can we find the guy who did the actual attack? If nothing else, there's no way that freak should be walking around free."

"They coordinated it as a group," answered Lyra as another batch of noodles whizzed past Zoey like they were whee-ing their way down a slide at a water park. "They crowdfunded the money to buy a drone, they worked together to look up how to make the flammable goop and how to 3D-print the spraying and ignition gadget. They crowdsourced their stalking, figuring out when I left my apartment to get on the bus, pinpointing the exact right time to strike. They made several attempts before finally pulling it off. As for who actually took the controls on the day . . ." She shrugged. "The police couldn't pin it down and said they didn't hold out much hope they ever would. But does that matter?"

"It has to matter, because otherwise everybody just gets away with it. Wrexx can factually say that he didn't directly cause it or specifically order it. Each fan can say they only played one tiny part, that it all would have happened without their individual participation. At what point does somebody take responsibility?"

"I just don't think that's the world we live in. Why don't you just hold your chopsticks in the water, then the noodles will run into them no matter what?"

"That feels like cheating."

"It wouldn't if you knew what you were paying for this meal. I bet you don't even have to look at prices when you shop. That must be weird, living in a world where suddenly everything is basically free."

"You know what it's like? It's like if one day you went out to your yard and flapped your arms and just suddenly started flying and realized, in that moment, that everything you'd been told about gravity is fake. I remember all of the movies about miserable rich people I saw as a kid and let me tell you: for the most part, they're having a really, really good time. There's a whole party scene here in the city that I mostly avoid, but it's all these rich kids competing with each other on who can throw the biggest and best. We're talking mountains of food from five-star chefs, orgies on pleasure-boosting hallucinogens you've never even heard of, decorations that turn the venue into a totally immersive environment—a space station or a Roman bathhouse, that kind of thing. If you knew how much sheer *pleasure* these people have in their lives, you'd go burn their mansions down."

Lyra nodded. "I knew one of the high-end escorts who used to go to parties like that. And when I say high-end, I don't just mean she looks like a supermodel, I mean she looks like a supermodel *and* speaks five languages. She's funny. Radiant. She said she doesn't even have sex with them, they just pay her to be there and light up the room. I don't know if that's less weird than what the rest of us do, or more."

Zoey caught some noodles, dunked them, and felt like an apex predator as she chewed. The broth was a wonder, ten layers of flavor that would require a poem to describe. They both just ate for a moment, the bustle of the sidewalk behind them, Wu and DeeDee no doubt drawing stares from tourists.

"When it happened," said Lyra as she patted her chin dry, "I thought the drone had just sprayed something disgusting in my face, raw eggs, or maybe paint. There was this moment when I was like, oh, this is gross, I have it all in my hair, it's all sticky, I have to go back up and take a shower now. Then the drone made this weird sound and I guess it was the sparks, it had, like, a little road flare or something, and the feeling was cold at first, like, I couldn't even tell what was happening. Then I couldn't breathe—you know, the fire was taking all of my air—and then everything was pain. I swear, I could feel it boiling my eyes. The scream I let out was just a whistle, like a teapot. I couldn't hear myself doing it at the time. I only know because I've seen the video, over and over, from Wrexx's fans sending it to me."

Zoey stopped eating.

Then, quietly, she said, "No, they can't just get away with this. The guys who did it, no, I'm sorry, I don't accept that."

"They have," replied Lyra, "and they will. You know what's weird? After that, it's not that my face changed, it's that the universe changed around me. The way people treat me. I instantly became invisible to society. Everyone quickly glances away. Except for kids. Kids stare. The way men used to hold doors open for me, hold elevators, offer to help get things down from shelves at the grocery store, the way they would constantly invent reasons to talk to me, to keep the conversation going long after it was over—that's gone. Just like that. It's like my face, that was my whole humanity, my whole value to society. I mean, I knew my face had value, every woman knows, but you don't think of everyone on the planet suddenly deciding you're a totally different person, or not a person at all. My *family* treats me different. My doctor. The pastor at my church."

Lyra stated all of this matter-of-factly, without so much as a tremble in her voice. She paused as if expecting Zoey to have questions but Zoey had become transfixed by the empty bit of counter in front of her.

"I haven't spent the money from Wrexx. I gave a lot of it away. My mom had a lot of debts. But I'm dipping into it more and more now. My body is the same, so I could still make money in the business—catering to a different customer base, you know—but I've tried to get regular jobs, waiting tables or front desk at one of the casinos. Absolutely not. You know they make you attach photos to those applications? You can't stick an old one on there, either—they want a time-stamped, full-body shot. You know, to make sure you haven't gotten fat since the last pic. And these are jobs that would require me to live with five roommates to make rent in a bad neighborhood here. But if I just live off of Wrexx's payoff money, then I'm, what? A professional victim? I'm connected with him for the rest of my life?"

"I'm trying to ask myself what I'd do."

"If it happened to you," said Lyra, "your people would have snatched up Wrexx before the flames were even out, then fed him into a wood chipper, feetfirst. And I know everyone eavesdropping on this conversation is waiting for me to ask you to do that, but how would his crazy fans react? What would they do to you? To me?" She took a sip of her tea, carefully using the intact side of her lips. "Afterward, he made little jokes about it, constantly. Subtle, like it was an inside thing among his fans."

Zoey turned to DeeDee. "I've been thinking this privately for a while now but I realize I should say it to you: the restraint you have shown in not going after Wrexx is *astonishing*."

DeeDee didn't answer.

"I'm glad we could talk like this," said Zoey, turning back to Lyra. "But what *do* you want me to do?"

"DeeDee says you guys think he may have had something to do with the three missing sex workers."

"Do you?"

Lyra reached into her purse on the ground next to her stool. She brought out a loop of thin, black wire attached to a tiny box, like a buckle, with one end of the wire protruding from it, like you could pull it through and tighten the loop.

"So my session with Wrexx that started all of this? As soon as he got there, he put this around my neck. Feel this wire. It's incredibly strong, I don't know what it's made of. Then he touches this button on his phone and the loop constricts, choking me. This little box here, there's tiny machinery that pulls it tight. I start panicking, trying to get it off, but it's like a garrote, you know, like assassins use in movies? That's how tight it is, I can't get my fingers under it. And he watches me flail around trying to pull this thing loose, then he hits a button and it loosens itself. Then he does that a few more times, until finally he leaves it tight, tells me I'm going to die. I black out. When I come to, he says it's all a joke. But then he says he's going to leave it around my neck forever, twenty-four hours a day. So if at some point he decides to choke me out, he'll just turn it on and I'll never know when it's going to happen. He says if he turns it up all the way, it'll slice right through the skin, the tendons, the bones. I start screaming at him, I start crying, I beg him to get it off me. He laughs, says it was all a joke, and takes it off."

"Did you tell your boss at the Chalet? I thought their entire job was to keep stuff like that from happening."

"I did. And they do keep a blacklist of banned customers, anyone who's gotten abusive or demanded their money back, anything like that. I told the manager, he listened, then nothing happened. So Wrexx keeps making appointments. I confront the manager about it, he finally tells me that Wrexx can't be banned. Because he's untouchable, he's a celebrity, all that."

Zoey groaned. "And that's when you made your video."

"Yeah. It was the only way to try to keep the others safe. Then all this happened," she gestured to her ruined face, "and yeah, they finally banned him then, but . . ." She shrugged.

"And if they'd done a better job protecting you, this feud doesn't start and you don't get hurt. But they didn't want to lose the revenue."

"My complaint wasn't the first, either. They knew exactly what Wrexx was like. But the risk wasn't just in losing his business but in his ability to steer other business away. With his reviews, you know."

"That's why you wanted to meet with me."

"That's why I wanted to meet with *just* you. Not your people. You're frustrated that it's hard to pin down the blame for something like this, that there were too many people involved from start to finish. But there was only one player in this game who had the power to step in and stop it before it started and that's your company, your people. I'm not saying I don't blame Wrexx, I do. But he's got something broken in his brain, he can't stop, won't stop, until somebody stops *him*. Your people, on the other hand, made a rational choice not to step in based purely on the bottom line. I don't know if you know this but out here, in the world, they don't talk about the Suits, they talk about the Suits and Zoey, as two separate things. Because people believe you when you say you're different, that you came in from the outside, that you're not from the same world as Arthur's scary old henchmen. So when I think about how much I hate your people, I try to keep you separate."

Zoey rubbed her eyes and put her elbows on the bar, watching another clump of noodles zip past. "I feel like my head is going to explode. All I want is to find the three women, alive or dead, I want to find them and get them to safety, if that's still possible. I don't care about solving this convoluted mystery, we can work out who needs punishing after, I just want to help the three human beings who my company failed to protect. But every step I try to take in that direction, it's, like, oh, here's several more layers of subterfuge and conflicting information. Meanwhile, my team keeps talking about what this means for the election and the future, but I *just want to find the women*."

"If you're hungry," said Lyra, "you'd better snatch some of these, we're almost out of time. Plus, I think the chef is getting annoyed that you and DeeDee are making a mockery of his whole operation. Just one more thing, then I'll let you go. There's always been rumors that Wrexx goes on these sex-tourism safaris, people like him have those countries pinned on a map. One rumor is that last year, a teenage sex worker in Bali was beheaded, at a time when Wrexx would have been in the country. This is before the thing happened with me, understand? So it's weird that, prior to my thing, the rumor was that the beheading was done with a wire. But if you try to look up anything on it, you just hit a brick wall."

Lyra snatched a bundle of pink noodles from the slide, ate them, then began gathering up her purse.

"I know you've been wanting to ask," said Lyra as she allowed the next customer to take her stool. "No, I haven't gotten reconstructive surgery yet. Maybe I will, eventually. Maybe I won't. But for right now, I want people to see me. All this press they put out about how Tabula Rasa is this fun, lawless playground? I want the tourists to see what that really looks like. Thanks for your time."

DeeDee left with Lyra and Wu hustled Zoey toward their next destination, trying to minimize the time spent on a crowded sidewalk.

"Do you have any thoughts?" asked Zoey as they moved briskly toward a tower on the next block.

"I have many, are there any specific thoughts you're asking about?"

"I don't know, about this case, how we're handling it?"

"I think that if we were serious about solving this, we would be doing what the police would be doing if they had the manpower: knocking on doors, talking to the victims' neighbors, sifting through thousands of hours of Blink footage to find the one lead that would get us closer to the truth."

"I thought that's what Budd and his minions were doing."

"His people don't have subpoena power, they're going around and offering wads of cash in hopes that somebody associated with the bad guy will flip. Until that happens, we're in a completely passive role, waiting to see how and when the third victim is shown off to the public."

"I hate that what we're dealing with here is ultimately just a show. It's all being doled out as fodder for the stream audiences to gulp down."

"If so," said Wu, "then you agree with Will that we can predict the perpetrators' next move by simply asking what would draw maximum audience engagement."

"But what would—"

"Pardon me," said a Southern drawl from just ahead. "I believe you and me have business to conduct."

Zoey prayed that they weren't talking to her, but that particular prayer was almost never answered. She looked up to find a cowboy, an actual dude in full Old West garb, complete with leather vest, chaps, spurs, and a six-gun in a holster slung low on his hips. But it wasn't quite right; the ten-gallon hat on his head was dark and patterned with stars and half-moons. He wore a deep purple cloak and a pair of glowing cowboy boots boasting a pattern so complex that Zoey's brain couldn't quite take it in.

Zoey groaned. "Oh, my god."

Wu, failing to conceal how happy he was to be doing something other than lurking at the periphery of a meeting, said, "Sir, you need to step aside," and Zoey sensed he was kind of hoping the guy wouldn't.

"I am in pursuit of a bounty, but not for either of you, so you can re-lax. The bounty is for Mr. Aviv. But you, miss, are more likely to know his whereabouts than probably anyone, considering the two of you are having relations."

"I don't know where you heard that and I don't know where he is. And I definitely don't have time for whatever high-noon showdown you have planned."

"No showdown is necessary as long as you come with me, where we can have a private conversation about Mr. Aviv's whereabouts."

"She will not be doing that," said Wu, "though if you insist on this course of action, perhaps we should move to a spot with fewer bystanders."

"No need to be concerned about bystanders if you comply. And if you are thinking about trying me, there's something I want to show you that you'll want to see. Are you ready? Look close."

He was now holding his revolver. There had been no visible move-ment; his hand had been at his side and now it was pointing the gun. It happened so fast that it hadn't registered to Wu's eyes, either. When he belatedly realized what was happening, he made a move like he was about to push Zoey out of the way. But then the gun was back in the holster, in a fraction of a blur.

Zoey asked, "Did you seriously have implants installed that would just let you draw your gun faster? Think about all of the things you could have done with that money. You could have gone to school, learned to be an engineer."

"This man," said Wu, "will never be an engineer."

"You are, in effect, harboring a fugitive," said the cowboy, "one who just tried to assassinate the entire family of a political figure. Mr. Aviv is a terrorist of the highest order, as is anyone who shields him from justice."

"I'm sorry," said Zoey, "what's your name, again?"

"You can call me Pistol Wizard."

"Is there . . . something else I can call you?"

"That is my legal name."

"You had your name legally changed to Pistol Wizard?"

"Are you trying to stall for time, miss?"

"No, I just . . . need a moment for that to sink in."

"I know what you're thinking," the man said to Wu, "so let me spell it out. You have many tools at your disposal that you can deploy very quickly, thanks to trained hands and advanced technology. But I can draw and shoot fast enough that even if you're first, it won't matter. My bullet will be through your brain while your projectile is in midair. Do you dare risk it?"

Wu and the man stared each other down and, in the meantime, the one thing Zoey most didn't want to happen was happening: curious spectators were forming a small crowd.

Wu replied, "You are projecting onto me the very doubts that circulate in your own mind. How much faith do you have in this technology? Enough to trust your life to it? I'm sure you have pulled off many quick draws in front of a mirror. But have you tested the accuracy when firing after a draw? At that speed, if the calculations are off by some tiny thousandths of a percentage point, firing just a millisecond too soon or too late, then the bullet goes into your toes, or the twentieth floor of a skyscraper behind me. If some tiny patch of worn leather inside your holster offers one percent more friction on the draw than the system anticipated, then the gun could be seated improperly in your palm, the barrel pointed a few degrees to the right or left, killing Zoey, or a passerby. And before you can notice the mistake and correct, my weapons will be doing their work, denying you your second chance. You see, this is what you cannot replicate when doing dry runs at home or at the shooting range: the risk to yourself, the total and absolute faith in your tools. That can only be perfected by real experience of life-and-death encounters. Unfortunately for both of us, I *do* have that experience."

Zoey said, "Guys, please. If this ends in violence, the only winners will be the rubberneckers who've gathered around us hoping to see some action. Whatever relationship you think I have with Aviv—and please note that I got dumped in the water right along with Damon and his people—it makes perfect sense that I wouldn't know where he is. Even if we were madly in love and carrying on a secret romance worthy of an opera, telling me his hiding spot would only make me a target, as demonstrated by what you're doing right now. So you're in a situation where you can either die for a completely worthless cause in pursuit of a lead that will not, in fact, get you any closer to your bounty, or you can shoot Wu, abduct me, *then* find out I don't have the information you need, right before my people unleash holy vengeance on you and the surrounding landscape. The only good outcome is you walking away."

"You are the one who has not thought this through," replied Pistol Wizard. "For what reaction do you think I was expecting if not the very one I am observing right now? It would be a poor hunter who recoils at the sound of the tiger's roar."

Wu said, "A hunter who finds himself on the receiving end of such a roar has already failed."

"In the name of fairness, I will give you five seconds to stand down and comply. One—URRGGGHHH!!!"

Pistol Wizard collapsed to his knees, though Wu hadn't moved. The cowboy's hands were wrapped around his belly as if he'd been gut-shot.

Standing immediately behind him was the old woman in the gray trench coat and red wide-brimmed hat, the one who'd streamed the boxed-Iris crime scene earlier. She was pressing a folded umbrella into the small of his back.

"That will be quite enough of that nonsense," she said, withdrawing the umbrella from the groaning man.

Wu nodded toward the umbrella. "Is that rigged to fire a projectile, or stun him with fifty thousand volts of electricity?"

"Neither."

There was a wet, farty sound and Pistol Wizard groaned as liquid feces filled his chaps.

"Though I do have those options available to me," she said, "I'm afraid a woman of my age, dress, and profession makes quite the attractive target for muggers in this city, so I have taken steps to arm myself. Speaking of which, I would suggest you take this opportunity to relieve this man of his pistol while he is otherwise occupied."

The bystanders recoiled as another round of explosive diarrhea emitted from the stricken cowboy warlock. Wu took a step forward as if to confiscate the gun from the kneeling, shitting gunslinger.

Suddenly, the man's right hand once again blinked into position, from clutching his stewing guts to pointing a gun right in Wu's face. Only the hand did not contain a gun. Neither did the holster.

The man looked skyward, as did Wu, as did Zoey, as did the old woman. The six-gun was a tiny speck against the crystal-blue sky and white clouds, soaring through the air like a departing rocket, until it vanished from their sight.

"This isn't over!" shouted Pistol Wizard as he stumbled to his feet, his pant legs leaking liquid excrement like a malfunctioning espresso machine. He limped down the sidewalk and somehow it was only then that Zoey saw the vehicle he'd arrived on: a life-sized mechanical horse, built from sinew of black hydraulics and cables and protected in key spots with gleaming white patches of armored skin. The man mounted the beast with tremendous effort, his boots leaving streaks of brown on its white flank.

"YAH!" he shouted as he snatched the reins. Zoey had expected the machine to gallop away and was kind of eager to see that. Instead, its legs remained stiff as it rolled quickly down the sidewalk on tiny wheels contained in its hoofs. Some of the bystanders applauded.

"Thank you, I think," said Zoey to the old woman. "I didn't get your name?"

The old woman was accompanied by her hovering little drone, which, Zoey just now noticed, was wearing a little red hat, a tiny replica of its owner's.

"The name is Margaret Mull. I investigate missing persons. I may have information for you, if there is somewhere private we can speak."

CHAPTER
17

ZOEY WAS NO MORE willing to follow the old woman to another location than she was the magic cowboy, but she offered to walk and talk on their way to Zoey's next destination. That is, if the woman agreed to do it off-stream, which she did. She turned off her little hat-wearing camera drone and stuffed it in her handbag.

"Where are we heading?" asked Margaret as they moved down the sidewalk.

"To that tower over there," said Zoey. "This is going to sound like an obnoxious boast, but that's the closest one with a landing pad and my company helicopter is coming to pick me up. We're going to Catharsis and traffic from the city to the festival is a gauntlet of tribulation."

Said building appeared from the outside to be a cylinder of glass surrounding a snowy cliffside. A hologram scrolling around the exterior branded it as Alpine Climb.

"So are you doing this full time? Going around and doing live crime-scene commentary?"

"Oh, no, just a retirement hobby," replied Margaret while tapping her umbrella on the sidewalk like a cane. "The sponsorship deals you see folks like Charlie Chopra take to make themselves rich seem in such poor taste, considering the subject matter. They'll do live ad reads for drone delivery meals just moments after discussing a child's brutal assault."

"A hobby. So you're doing it for your own enjoyment?"

"Don't think I don't hear the disapproval in your voice, young lady! If it helps, I do not chase lurid details and undressed corpses. My beat is missing persons, I've assisted the police in solving more than thirty cases."

"Oh, wow. That's pretty cool. That kind of makes me feel bad about how I spend my spare time. I want to ask how a person gets into something like that but I have a feeling it's not a happy story."

"If you're expecting me to say I had a beloved child kidnapped or murdered and swore to avenge victims everywhere, I have no such tale, thank god. I think most people's motivations can't be boiled down to something so straightforward. No, I just noticed a generation's talents and smarts were being wasted staring at distractions on various screens and figured all of that time and energy could at least be focused on something useful. As for me, well, I think I just enjoy solving puzzles."

"So you like outsmarting bad guys. You're not worried someone will come after you? Like, if they think you're getting too close?"

Margaret paused for just a moment and Zoey sensed she'd received this as a threat.

"Everyone dies," replied the older woman, "and everyone can die. If we allow that to dissuade us, evil wins before the game even starts."

They stepped through the main doors of Alpine Climb and found themselves at the foot of a sheer cliff. The building was a hollow structure surrounding a three-hundred-foot-tall artificial climbing wall disguised as natural rock, complete with artificial wind and snow. At the top was the Tabula Ra$a Alpine Lodge, a fine-dining restaurant offering dishes of elk, pheasant, goat cheese, and winter vegetables served with the finest and oldest seasoning known to humanity: hunger. Specifically, the hunger that comes from having burned a few thousand calories climbing your way up. Immediately Wu directed Zoey toward a sign that said ELEVATOR.

Margaret gazed upward. "Have you ever wondered what would happen to a society if it became totally impossible to discern fact from fiction?"

After only brief consideration, Zoey said, "Actually, I think we're living in it right now."

"I mean truly unable, to the point where evidence could be falsified so thoroughly that no human sense could detect a forgery, where lies could be created that are identical to the truth, down to the molecule. To the point that all of our forensics and experts would be helpless to determine what is real and what is false. What would people cling to, when searching for truths?"

"They would probably do what they do now: they'd believe whatever they wanted to."

"The technology that makes people strong and turns them into weapons like that strange man back there, some say that's the future. But it seems to me the next frontier, the true power, is in mastering these new, perfect forms of deception. The power to throw a car with your bare hands isn't godlike. There are animals that can do it. The power to create your own reality, that is the power of a god. But you already know that, right?"

They boarded a glass elevator designed to grant riders a view of the snowy climbing wall and the colorful specks that were the tourists inching their way up.

"Are you okay with heights?" asked Zoey as the doors closed. "This ride can be, uh, unpleasant otherwise."

"I am fine with elevators," replied Margaret, "as long as they don't decide to suddenly malfunction in between floors!"

Once the three of them were sealed inside and rising, Zoey said, "If you're hinting that you think the Sex Butcher situation is all an elaborate hoax, we've already come to that conclusion. My problem is that tells us nothing about the condition of the victims. You know, they could be fine, they could be getting tortured, they could be dead. Whatever the thinking is behind the hoax, the big thing is that these women were in fact taken out of society and their loved ones are very worried about them."

"They should be," replied Margaret. "The perpetrator has gone to great expense to make these women *appear* to be dead. If he were to have merely killed them, that would have been unnecessary—a real recording of the corpses would accomplish his goal, if his goal is public infamy. A psychopath who abducts women and fakes their deaths wants the public to stop looking for them, perhaps so that he can keep them for himself, to play with as his toys for as long as he wishes. Months, years, decades."

Zoey understood why this woman had a following. She could spin a chilling tale.

"That's as plausible as anything I've heard so far," said Zoey, "but unless you have some idea who this psychopath is and where they live, it doesn't do much for us aside from inspiring my nightmares for the rest of my life."

"It has not gone unnoticed how hands-on you've been in trying to find these women."

"Well, thank you, but I don't seem to have accomplished much."

"In such a large city, in which so many qualify as one kind of victim or another, you clearly have a vested interest. You were seen on a hundred cameras when Iris turned up in that box. You had just come from a meeting with a prime suspect in full view of a busy street, as if the location had been chosen on purpose. Zoey and the Suits, on the case!"

Zoey felt like she was starting to detect some sarcasm. "You think that's just for show? Because if there's something more I can be doing, tell me, and I'll do it. Hell, I'll skip the music festival tonight, I'd rather be doing this than that."

"It is an objective fact, Ms. Ashe, that you do not take such a hands-on approach to solving all of your problems."

"I'll admit right now, the fact that this is happening when things are at their absolute maximum tension in the city has ratcheted up the urgency. But I do want to find these women and I want to find the guy who took them, if he exists. You can believe what you want about me but I'm telling the truth about that."

"I believe you. But forgive me if I have doubts about your motives. You would be very motivated to resolve this if, say, something about your organization were to come to light if someone else found them first."

Zoey groaned, suddenly feeling like an idiot for letting this woman lure her in. "Ah, here we go. So which conspiracy theory do you subscribe to? Is it the one the angel people were yelling about, claiming we sell women to murderers if they pay a secret fee? What's the evidence for that?"

"The evidence would be the testimony of the three women, if they are recovered, and a possible confession from the perpetrator, if he is caught. I am curious, then: If your people find the victims and their abductor first, will you immediately announce that none survived?"

"So that's the theory you came to offer me? That we're not trying to save these women, that we're trying to find and silence them? But because you have no proof, you told it to me so you could see my reaction? Well, here it is, I guess."

The elevator abruptly jolted to a stop. There were no floors to get off on; the only stop was the restaurant and they were nowhere close to the top.

"Oh, drat," said Margaret. "See? Elevators just hate me."

Wu immediately tensed up, presumably knowing he had to be ready to make the second move because he couldn't make the first one against a little old lady.

"So how does this work?" asked Zoey. "Do you have a gadget in your umbrella there that hacks elevators?"

"She doesn't need one," said Wu, "her comment outside was a signal to her followers to do it for her. She crowdsources her investigations and her fans are happy to help her invade any systems that stand in her way."

They were stuck about two-thirds of the way up, artificial snowflakes sticking to the glass wall of the elevator.

"A flock of talented people dedicated to discovering the truth and delivering justice is a superpower all its own," said Margaret. "In a society that is quickly going mad, they may be the only thing keeping all this from falling to pieces."

"It sounds like another pack of vigilantes to me," replied Zoey. "So let me ask you this: Within your group of talented fans, what's the mechanism for due process? You just watched me talk to a woman who got her face burned off by a pack of true believers who thought *they* were dispensing 'justice.' Is there a process for changing your fans' minds once they've latched onto a target? They're smart enough to hack their way into a hotel elevator, are they smart enough to know when they're wrong? Because I've seen where this road leads otherwise."

"We will accept the truth. I consider myself to be a woman of faith, but what I worship is the truth. I believe that it's our only hope for the future, a movement that considers the truth sacred, that doesn't settle for comforting lies or entertaining illusions. If you are innocent, you have nothing to fear from me."

"And if you or your crowdsourced investigation decide otherwise, what do I have to fear from you, specifically?"

"I am no vigilante. If I determine that you are responsible for the deaths of these women, I will turn you over to the police and hand over all of my information."

"I'm impressed that you have that much faith in the police and prosecutors here. Especially when you're counting on them to take on someone like me."

"Well, that depends on who is in charge of the police a few days from now, doesn't it?"

"Ah. I guess I should have known it was going to come around to that. So we're just going to stay trapped on this elevator until I confess to something I didn't do?"

"Not at all, I assume building maintenance will have it working again in short order. But while I have you, my hope is to impress upon you how important it is that, should your people find the missing women alive, that they remain so until they can be interviewed by the authorities. Just in case you had plans to the contrary."

"Well, then, you wasted your time because I don't. If we can find these women, I'm as eager as anyone to know what they have to say. If the finger points toward someone who works for me or who is allied with me in some way, I promise I'll bring the hammer down on them harder than you or Tabula Rasa PD ever could."

Margaret gave her a long look, as if studying Zoey's expression for signs of cracks in her performance. Behind them, Wu shifted, as if readying one of his many tools. Zoey had a vivid vision of a close-quarters fight that would shatter the elevator glass and send at least one of them tumbling to their death.

Finally, the old woman nodded and, on cue, the elevator jolted itself into motion. They soon arrived at the restaurant, where a pack of sweaty people in climbing gear were looking with disdain at everyone who had taken the easy way up.

"We're heading for the roof," said Zoey. "Are you hungry? Have a meal of mountain-resort food, on me, tell the host to put it on our tab."

"No, thank you. A heavy meal only leaves me drowsy for the rest of the day. And I suspect that I am going to be very busy for the foreseeable future."

"Well, suit yourself," said Zoey as Wu hustled her toward an EM-PLOYEES ONLY door that would take them to the roof. "And thanks for shooting that cowboy with your poop umbrella."

Echo was waiting by the helicopter, rooftop winds whipping around her clothes. She was wearing a split red tunic that hung to her knees, over black leather pants. She spotted them and spread her hands like, *Where have you been?*

Zoey said, "Sorry, we got accosted multiple times on our way back from the noodle joint."

Echo pulled off her sunglasses. "I love how you think you can get confronted by an unstable, augmented wrongcock in public and the rest of us won't know about it. We were all watching, Zoey. The whole thing, including the noodle meeting. We started taking bets on whether or not you'd catch any."

They climbed on board, Wu in the pilot's seat (he wasn't flying it, the helicopter flew itself). Zoey and Echo were alone in the back. The engines whined to life and the cabin leaned and rocked as the helicopter first lifted off, then swept down between two towers. Zoey hated when they did that. Actually, she hated helicopters in general but never voiced that complaint. It was the kind of thing that sounded ridiculous to say out loud.

"Did you bring my concert clothes?"

"In the bag on the floor," said Echo, "next to the restroom door back there. See it? Got your clothes, some headache medicine, that spray for your scalp. I tried to stick one of your cats in there but I think it jumped out."

Zoey leaned back against her seat and sighed. "Did you happen to stick any food in there? You mocked me for being bad at noodles but I really am starving now."

"Check the warming box, maybe the helicopter elves have left you something."

There was an insulated cabinet under a table in the center of the cabin. Zoey opened it to find a white paper bag with a small red-and-blue logo in the center.

"Oh, my god, is this what I think it is?"

She checked. It was.

Two hotdogs from Costco.

"Oh, my god," said Zoey. "I'm gonna cry."

"There are sodas in the refrigerator under the wet bar back there."

"I love you. This is the first good thing that has ever happened to me. Ever, in my life."

Zoey unwrapped a hotdog and ate in a manner that a piranha swarm would find indecent.

Echo said, "What do you say we tell the helicopter to take us to Ibiza? We'll buy a nightclub and just never tell anybody where we went."

"Yes, let's do it. Right now. Leave all this behind. Take me to a place where people are normal, where they do normal things and think normal thoughts. A place where I'll have normal problems, like flat tires and termites."

"How long before you'd get sick of it, do you think? Of being a normal person again?"

"Never. You don't understand, you chose this life. I was thrust into it."

"You really think that?"

"I don't know."

Zoey ate in silence for a bit, watching the gleaming buildings drift by.

After finishing the second hotdog, she said, "I have to make an accusation and I'm not quite sure when to do it or how or who exactly to accuse."

"What do you mean?"

"Lyra said when she asked for Wrexx to be banned from booking appointments, that the manager wouldn't do it, even after it became clear Wrexx was going to hurt somebody, even after there were rumors that he'd just straight-up beheaded a girl in another country."

"Clarence Crockett. That was the manager."

"I thought Axolotl was the manager there? With all the wigs? That's who Will and I talked to at Chalet."

"Axol was brought in after Clarence was fired. And he was fired for not banning Wrexx. He didn't run it up the chain of command, he made that decision himself."

"But he wasn't fired until after the situation blew up and Lyra got burned."

"That's right."

Zoey thought for a moment, then had an idea that made her jolt in her seat. "Wait. This guy worked with all three women. He's a disgruntled employee. He managed sex workers, and his name is *Clarence*. How is he not Sex Butcher suspect number one?"

"He totally was. Budd looked into him, the guy moved to Miami and took a job producing porn. He hasn't been back in the city since, and appears to be speedrunning the rest of his life by spending it drunk and building up debts with the mob."

Zoey sat back, deflated. Of course, it wouldn't be that easy. "I was about to ask why nobody told me about all of that but every time I ask that question, somebody says it was brought up at a meeting where I wasn't paying attention. And it usually turns out they're right."

"You can't micromanage a company this size. It doesn't work like that. You think Lyra was the first sex worker to get hurt?"

Zoey rested her head against the window, letting the vibration of the engines massage her skull.

She closed her eyes and, with them closed, asked, "Am I doing a good job?"

"What? What do you mean?"

"Just, in general. Running things. I feel like nobody thinks they can be honest with me."

"You think Will is afraid to tell you when you've screwed up?"

"I know he is. Not because he's afraid of me, but because he thinks I'm too fragile. He filters everything, like I'm not strong enough to handle it."

"Well, it's not *exactly* that."

"What?"

"It's just that . . . okay, have you ever had a job where some really eager employee comes on board, but they're so eager that they can't stop questioning everything? You're trying to show them how to brew the coffee and they're like, 'Why don't we sell donuts? Why don't we put in more comfortable chairs for the customers? Why don't we get a bigger sign?' Only imagine you had an employee who was like, 'Why do people need coffee to stay awake? Why can't everybody just get the proper amount of sleep?'"

"I'm sorry, hold on. So everybody thinks I'm annoying because I ask questions like, 'Are our businesses ruining lives?' or 'Are we using our enormous influence to make society measurably worse?' So before I came along, nobody asked those questions?"

"It's not that. It's that you are still thinking of it like a game."

"You don't think I take it seriously enough? I feel like I'm the only one who does."

"No, that's not what I mean. How can I put this? When I was a kid, my dad forbid us from playing any video games. Not for the usual reasons—because they were addictive or a waste of time—he said games teach a really bad lesson, which is that every problem has some neat solution. You enter a room, there's a door, that means there must be a key that opens that door, and there's a sword in that room and that must mean you'll need it to kill the dragon later. But in real life, you don't get that. You think there's some perfect way for society to handle sex work, or policing, or just vice in general. That it's just a lock that needs the right key. The real world isn't like that, it's all just a bunch of trade-offs. If you legalize drugs, you get addicts in the park and ruined lives. If you do prohibition, you get jails packed with traffickers and black markets ruled by whoever is the best at murder. You're driving yourself crazy asking where's the exact solution, as if the universe is presenting all of this as a series of obstacles to test you. When in reality, all you can do is manage the problems and minimize damage."

Zoey sighed. "I don't know. I guess I always thought that when you got up to a certain level, with the billionaires and politicians, that you find the people who are making everything bad. Because at least then, it means somebody knows what's going on."

"Guess what: All of the normal people down there, in those buildings? They now think that's us. We're almost out of the city. Last chance to have Wu take us to Ibiza. We can have somebody mail your mom and cats to us."

"No. They'd find me eventually."

CHAPTER
18

THE ONLY THING THAT freaked Zoey out more than massive structures was massive crowds. Granted, she didn't like small crowds, either, but huge New-Years-in-Times-Square-size crowds just seemed unnatural and out of control, like a swarm of locusts blotting out the sun. And when viewed from the sky, the Catharsis music festival was, to Zoey's eyes, an unholy abomination.

The helicopter was taking a route around the periphery of the festival grounds, the sea of bodies stretching out into the horizon. Faint music could be heard within the aircraft, songs fading in and out as they flew from the audio of one stage to the next. The holographic giants undulated and sang on platforms amid the writhing waves of humanity. The crowd was crawling up the bases of the many amplifier towers, the bravest and/or drunkest fans assuming wrongly that if they fell, the revelers below would catch them.

The campgrounds at the center of the stages were a sprawl of color, all of the thousands of tents and tarps. At the center of everything was the two-hundred-foot-tall beehive structure. It was designed to look like it was actively oozing honey, and holographic ads and menus scrolled and danced around the exterior. The "bees" that swarmed in and out were delivery drones ferrying drinks, snacks, and merch to anyone who ordered. There were no lines of customers—the drones would drop your order right into your hand wherever you happened to be on the festival grounds, the charge invisibly sucked from your credit card.

"Who's on the stages?" asked Zoey, just to have something to say.

Without consulting any notes, Echo said, "Vampire Toilet, Jaxx & Joss, The Ginger Triangle, The Parker Sisters, Toenail Fun Gus, and The Fluffy Submarine Collective. That's just on the six main stages, there are smaller acts interspersed in the camping area and unregistered acts are performing outside the gates and in the parking lots."

"Have you memorized the whole schedule? Like, you can name all of the groups if asked? All one hundred–plus of them?"

"Unfortunately, yes. You see the angels? Down there, at the main gate to the north."

From the air, they were just white specks, but Zoey did see them, fluttering around over the heads of revelers streaming in and out of the festival.

Echo said, "Security shoos them away, they come right back, urging the kids to swear off the fornication and pornography of modern music. You won't make them out from up here, but they've also got Liberators interspersed through the campgrounds there in the center, inside the ring of stages. White robes, white masks, the whole bit. Unfortunately, once word got out that the festival was short on security staff, these people unofficially volunteered. They wander from tent to tent, ostensibly to make sure nobody is being sexually assaulted, but they break up anything that looks like sex, just in case."

Zoey was stunned by this. "At a music festival? How do the concertgoers not gang up on them and stuff them into trash cans?"

"A big contingent of those fans down there agree with them. I mean, that's why this place is a flashpoint. One of the headliners tonight is Snowcloak, taking over all three stages on the West side—that's those stages over there. After them it's The Pompeii Sisters and Zenquisition. Those are all pseudo-Christian acts beloved by straight-edge types. That whole side of the grounds over there, where the guys on the middle hologram platform are dressed like goats? That's the West half, those will be all of your conservative kids tonight. They're making a big deal out of picking up all of the trash on their side once it's done. That's where Damon is hoping to recruit a few thousand new voters."

"But these people are from all over, how many can even vote on Tuesday?"

"Not even ten percent. But there's a reason you don't see Damon doing campaign ads about new zoning laws, or fixing the sewers, or addressing the school teacher shortage—nothing is local, everything is broad and universal, ads about housewives scared of street crime, the youth getting sucked into their virtual-reality games instead of learning useful skills, how it's terrible that restaurants need menus in four languages. He could be talking about Tabula Rasa or Chicago or Houston. His audience isn't the voters here, it's everybody, everywhere. Mayor is just his first step up the ladder and you can guess why he picked our city to launch his political career."

Zoey said, "Because it has the most cameras."

They landed on a pad surrounded by conspicuous security armed with what were clearly the scariest-looking guns they could find. Zoey, Wu, and Echo stepped off the aircraft and into the Artists' Retreat (or the Trailer Park, as everyone called it). It was a fenced-off area to the south of the festival where performers stayed in trailers that were nicer than any homes Zoey had even visited as a child (the trailers had to be assembled on-site, as each was large enough that it had to be transported as at least three separate units). Within the retreat was an array of food and drink concessions for VIPs, some of which appeared to be entire upscale restaurants from downtown that had been reassembled as scaled-down food stands to serve the bands and also the various rich people who hung around to bask in the glow of celebrity.

And everything these stands served, Zoey noted as she passed, was free.

On the way, she spotted metal guitarist Guido Balls, folk singer Brenda Shams, and rapper Frannnnnk Williams, all just milling around with their drinks and sushi, laughing and exchanging small talk. You could build a Utopia right here on earth, Zoey thought, as long as the inhabitants were rich enough and surrounded by a tall enough fence.

Zoey's mother was already here, somewhere. Zoey had texted from the helicopter to ask where she was and all Zoey got back was a photo of her mother holding a champagne bottle, arm in arm with a man in a silk shirt and sunglasses who, after inquiring with Echo, Zoey learned was a famous Persian rapper named Biz. Melinda Ashe had always made friends quickly.

Wu nodded toward the luxury trailers. "We're supposed to meet everyone in the temp office. We're at the far end of this row, see the pink one? Shaped like a giant cat?"

"Wait, really? I was joking when I suggested that. How much did that cost? You know what—never mind."

Toni Maiden, a twenty-five-year-old country music star who'd sold something like a hundred million records, walked past carrying a tray of strawberries and cream that looked so amazing that Zoey felt an urge to steal it.

Echo nodded in that direction. "Those are bijin-hime strawberries. Seven hundred dollars each. Not for the tray—that's per strawberry. The best in the world. Is there anybody here you want to meet? You want any autographs, pictures?"

"No, that feels wrong, I think this spot is supposed to be an oasis from all of that. I already feel like I don't belong he—OH, MY GOD IT'S MONKEY SHERIFF!"

She had involuntarily reached out and grabbed Echo's arm, as if to steady herself. It wasn't the entirety of the punk-folk act Monkey Sheriff, just lead singer Shreck Kingley and bassist Speedy Felch. The former had his long, wet hair wrapped up in a towel like he'd just gotten out of the shower, the latter was holding a churro-coated corn dog in each hand and alternately taking bites of each. The trailer parked behind them looked like it had been towed out of an actual rural trailer park, including the standard bullet holes in the door.

"You go on ahead," said Zoey to Wu and Echo. "I'm going to go embarrass myself in front of those guys."

Wu looked them over. "Do you need me?"

"No, go make sure our trailer isn't hiding an ambush. If I get murdered by Monkey Sheriff then you'll all have a funny story to tell for the rest of your lives."

They moved on and Zoey went to approach the two men, urging herself to just bail out and turn around with each step. Shreck was looking at his phone but Speedy was now eyeing Zoey suspiciously while chewing a corn dog, showing the trepidation of a public figure who suspects someone is about to demand something of them.

"Hi, guys, I'm not here to bother you, I just want to say, I'm a huge fan."

"You runnin' for mayor?" asked Shreck, who'd barely glanced up from his phone to say it.

"Oh, no, haha."

"A dude came by earlier, wanted a bunch of pictures, said he was gonna be mayor. I was like, dude, I don't even live here."

"Yeah, it's a whole thing. I just wanted to say, and I guess you get stuff like this all the time, but I got turned onto you guys, believe it or not, when somebody gave me one of your T-shirts, and I had a really hard time last summer, actually went into a mental hospital for a bit, and your song 'Why Go' just hit me like a—well, I just played it over and over. I don't know if that was based on somebody you knew or if it happened to you even, but it meant a lot to me and, haha, I know I'm rambling but I just wanted to say that, thank you for making it, I guess."

Speedy, who was in the middle of biting off some of his right corn dog, said, "It's a cover. From the early nineties."

"Oh. Okay. Well, still! Hope you guys enjoy the festival."

"What do they call that?" He pointed at Zoey.

"Call what?"

"The way you've done your hair. With the bald strip."

"Oh, haha, that's actually the result of an accident. Or I guess it wasn't an accident, somebody was trying to shoot me in the face with a heat ray and it skimmed over my scalp instead."

"Seen a couple chicks with hair like that in the crowd out there."

"Really? Huh. Well, hopefully not for the same reason."

"You shouldn't be photographed with that woman," said a voice from behind Zoey, "if you can avoid it. She and her people will be in prison soon. Human trafficking, sexual assault, charity fraud."

It was Leonidas Damon, approaching with his entourage.

Zoey said, "That's—that's not true, none of that is true."

"Go look her up. Her name is Zoey Ashe, with a 'Y' at the end of the first name and an 'E' after the second. Homeless children have been disappearing around this city for months. Yesterday, they found the DNA of a missing child in the meat from one of her factories. Search for 'Soylent Black,' you'll fall down a rabbit hole. These are nasty people and you won't want anyone to think you've associated with them when they all go down."

"Ignore him!" said Zoey, "This is one of those mayor guys."

Shreck muttered something to Speedy and they headed back inside their shot-up trailer.

Zoey spun to face Damon. "What is your thing with me? Are you obsessed with me? You keep specifically singling me out, is this personal? It feels personal."

"Come with me, to the wine fountain. That's not the name of a restaurant, by the way. It's an actual fountain of wine."

"I'm not going with you anywhere. And it probably has a lot of bugs in it."

He motioned to his assistants, who obeyed the gesture by walking away.

"I'd like to make you an offer," said Leonidas, once it was just the two of them. "Can we go somewhere and talk? The wine fountain is usually a good place because nobody goes there, they don't want to get wine splatters on their clothes."

"Do you have any idea how many times men say that to me? Trying to pry me away from my people so they can sell me on their investment opportunity, or fundraiser, or tell me they want me to stab Will in the back? You're all testing my resolve, I guess?"

"Not your resolve, no. That's not what we sense." He pointed at her. "You know your money is dirty, you know your businesses are dirty— yes, even now—and somewhere, deep down, you want out."

Damon was walking away from the Monkey Sheriff trailer as he spoke and Zoey found herself following him.

"You're not going to sell me on joining up with you and becoming a fascist."

"If hating crime makes me a fascist, then we're living in a country full of fascists, every concerned parent who fears for their child is one. Mine is one of the most universally popular messages in all of politics."

"You don't want to be tough on crime, you want to make it illegal to be a certain type of person. You literally said you want poor people to stop breeding."

"Not poor people. Worthless people. See, rich liberals have this idealized image of the poor, they clutch their pearls at the thought that the world would be better off with fewer of them. You think it's mercy to let them be born incompetent and bumble their way through life, ruining the lives of who knows how many others? As opposed to them not being born at all?"

They had arrived at the wine fountain, a twenty-foot-tall marble sculpture in the shape of several turtles stacked on top of one another, red wine cascading down like blood. At least one bird was trying to bathe in it.

"Have you ever actually visited a prison and talked to the inmates?" asked Leonidas. "I have. I worked as a corrections guard for seven years, that's how I got started as a streamer, showing what those animals do to each other inside. Three-quarters of them are illiterate. They couldn't even have the conversation we're having right now, the whole concept of thinking through hypotheticals, calculating risk, using metaphor and logic, it's so far out of their league you might as well ask a pig to fly a plane. These thugs can't even fill out the forms to get public aid. It's not even that they're evil, it's that their brains don't have the horsepower to process empathy. They're literally not human beings."

"And you think what you just said there passes your empathy test?"

"Some humans cannot govern themselves, Ms. Ashe. Some can. If the world was made up only of those people, we would not need laws or police. It's just biology. We're watching a war between genes, to see which will be passed on and which are doomed to extinction. You know that's all this is, right? You and me, this conflict? It's a race to find out if the genes that create a preference for hedonism and deception win out against those geared toward organization and discipline."

"So you think some humans are just natural lawbreakers?"

"You like cats, right? You know your cats are man-made, they couldn't survive in the wild like that, they were specially bred to be pets. Domesticated. It's the same as with our cattle, our chickens, our pigs—they had to be bred to obey, to stay in their pens, to pull the plow. Well, not too many thousands of years ago, humans had to be domesticated to live in cities. Before that, we were a bunch of nomadic tribes of bloodthirsty hunters. To get a population that can sit in cubicles and resolve conflict with words instead of clubs, we had to be domesticated. That occurred via selective breeding, that's why everything in Biblical times came with the death penalty, they had to filter the savages out of the gene pool."

"It's fascinating to hear the difference between what you say from the podium and what you say now, when you know this is a no-camera zone."

"It wouldn't change a thing, because everyone already believes this, in private. Come on, if you go to the grocery store and see some fat single mom smoking cigarettes while her eight filthy kids run around screaming, you don't get this feeling in the pit of your stomach that something has gone wrong?"

"To be clear, in the picture you're trying to create in my brain, the woman isn't white, is she? I don't know how dumb you think I am, I know the press has made being dumb my whole thing, but even if I suffered severe brain damage I'd still know that as a society we don't have to pick between lawless chaos and a police state where roving packs of government goons purge the streets of the unclean."

"I don't want that, I want a world where that's not necessary because the people naturally govern themselves. Until then, yes, the only way to keep order is to surveil and punish. Every civilization has known that. What do you think religion is? Back in olden times, there were no forensics, no way to catch criminals unless there happened to be a witness. So they made up universal, omniscient witnesses and told everyone they were secretly being watched at all times. It was the only way to make people with weak genes behave. Well, half of us have dropped religion, so we have to make the surveillance real, in the form of a police state. If you don't like it, then you have to get rid of the weak genes. You pick, one or the other: strong genes and weak laws, or weak genes and strong laws."

"And controlling which babies get born means controlling who has sex with who. So it's not just the sex workers you want to ban, it's all sex outside of the purpose of producing a superior race."

"Again, religions had those strict rules for a reason. Have you been to Salt Lake City? Have you seen how clean it is? How clean the people are?"

"I've noticed how white it is. Is that what you mean?"

He just shrugged.

"My answer is no, I'm not switching my endorsement in favor of a dystopian hellscape. Alonzo may be corrupt but we can work with corrupt. If you win, I'll do everything I can to stop you from going any further. And I do mean everything. Goodbye."

Zoey turned her back on Damon and his fountain of blood, heading toward her pink trailer.

To her back, he said, "Your prankster is here, at the festival. If you talk to him, let him know something: My theory of justice cares only about intent, not results. He tried to drown my children, so I'm treating it like he succeeded. His failure to accomplish his goal means nothing to me. What I do to him will send a message to the whole species forward: here's what happens if you come after my family."

Without turning, Zoey said, "That's between you and him. Enjoy the festival, all of the food from the stands has human meat in it, including the vegan dishes."

Zoey made her way back to her pink cat-shaped trailer, stepped inside, and was immediately hit with the annoyed glares of five sets of eyes. She thought the Suits were about to fuss at her for keeping them waiting, then saw that they were standing over a sixth person, who was seated on a garish pink leather sofa.

The Amazing Aviv yelled, "Zoey! You're here! Your people are upset with me for sneaking in but I couldn't wait outside, there are bad guys looking for me. Can I have a word with you alone?"

Before Zoey could answer, Will said, "We have *a lot* to do today."

"I know, I know," she groaned and rubbed her eyes. "Aviv, I assume everyone introduced themselves? This is my bodyguard, Wu, that's Echo Ling, Budd Billingsley, the infamous Will Blackwater, and Andre Knox."

Andre asked, "Hold on, does the infamous label apply to both of us or just Will?"

"And this," said Zoey to the Suits, "is a man who apparently has a death wish. Can you guys all go outside while we have a word? I have to yell at him and I don't want it to get awkward in front of everyone."

No one moved.

Zoey said, "Please, we won't be long."

Everyone started shuffling out. As she passed, Echo gave Zoey a look like, *Really?*

Once everyone was out, Zoey closed the door behind them and spun to face the sofa.

Aviv said, "Cool jacket!"

Zoey was wearing a black leather biker jacket and jeans, her best attempt to fit in at a music festival. Aviv got up from the sofa and made like he was going to try to kiss her. She shoved him back.

"No," she said. "Stop. I am not a prop in your stupid election-season stunt."

She shrugged out of the jacket and angrily threw it on a nearby chair, like she was denying him the one thing he'd chosen to compliment.

"Come on," he said. "It's not like that."

"It's either that or you've decided I represent, what, danger? Risk? Is that what gets you off?"

She angrily removed his jacket, then angrily pulled off his shirt.

He said, "Should we, uh, lock that door?"

"Shut up," replied Zoey as she angrily pulled off her black knee-length boots, then unzipped and pushed down her jeans. "Do you have any idea what would happen to you if you were caught in here? Do you have any idea how many people packed within the surrounding four square miles want to tear you to pieces? Is that what turns you on?"

By the time she finished saying that, their clothes were on the floor and Aviv seemed incapable of answering.

Twenty minutes later, Zoey was staring at the ceiling of the trailer's cramped-but-still-bigger-than-her-old-bedroom bedroom and Aviv was saying, "I swear I didn't come here to do that."

"Why are you here? At the festival, I mean? Are you planning a stunt?"

"I had tickets. All-access pass. I wanted to see you."

"So you did come here to do this. You can get anyone you want, girl or boy, was it really so amazing last time that you had to come back to me?"

"Yes? But just to talk, I swear."

"I would ask how you got in here unnoticed, but the more important question is, what's your plan for getting out? Do you even have one?"

He sat up. "Before we talk business, I want to ask: Was that good for you? Just now? Normally I can last longer . . ."

"It lasted exactly as long as I wanted it to last."

"This may seem like a strange question," he said as he pulled on his pants, "but have you had, like, classes in this? In Kama Sutra stuff?"

"Maybe you've just been screwing beautiful, boring women up to now. Get dressed."

"I feel like I'm getting mixed messages here."

"It's not complicated, Aviv. I know you're bad for me but the hungry, grunting pig-monster that lives inside me doesn't care. It's in charge of my diet, too. It feeds on vice and poops regret."

"Oof."

"And you're changing the subject," she said as she sat up and looked for her bra. "Tell me your plan. Your whole plan. We need to be on the same page or people can literally die. This trailer is parked next to a powder keg, a quarter of a million kids out there who've decided this music festival is the front line of a culture war. This isn't a joke, it's serious."

"What if I told you I think jokes are very serious business? This election is already ridiculous, all I'm doing is pointing it out."

"Well, your serious joke is going to get Leonidas Damon elected."

"If I'm working in his favor, why is he the only candidate who wants me dead?"

"You can't judge your life by whether or not you're making the right people mad," she said as she headed for the bathroom. "If you didn't sneak in just so we could hook up again, why are you here?"

"Well, I thought I would have some information for you, but it hasn't come through yet."

"What information?" she asked through the closed bathroom door.

"I'll tell you when it comes through. There's no point until then."

"Uh-huh. And this isn't all just part of the setup for whatever you have planned?"

"I promise I don't have any stunts planned for tonight."

"Tomorrow?"

"No, no stunts."

"The day after? Election day?"

He paused. "My election-day shenanigans are no more dangerous or chaotic than what the candidates themselves are doing."

"*Aviv* . . ."

She emerged from the bathroom and tried to look stern as she dressed, which actually wasn't easy, considering the contortions that were required to stuff herself into the jeans.

"No chaos," he said, "I promise. I mean, I won't do anything to stop people from voting. I want people to vote, I just wish they didn't have to pick between these two clowns."

"I have to go, we have to prepare for the most stressful thing I've ever done in my entire life, and that includes the several times I've almost died. How are you getting out of here?"

"Leave me, I'll slip out at an opportune time, after the sun goes down."

"The drones out there can see in the dark."

"Zoey, I've been evading authority figures for as long as I've been able to walk. I have a team I can reach out to for help, I'll be just fine."

"So you slip out, and then what? You sneak your way out of the festival, past hundreds of security and thousands of people who hate you?"

"Nope. I'm going to stay and watch the shows. When will I see you again?"

"Never, if you get murdered by vigilantes."

"I'm serious, we should have a normal date sometime."

Zoey was pulling on her boots. "What would that even look like between somebody like you and somebody like me?"

"Honestly? Whatever we want. We could take your jet to Paris and eat the finest pastry in the world for breakfast, fly to Brussels for lunch, Milan for dinner, Berlin for drinks at a club."

"Can we order a bunch of cheap Chinese food and eat it in my bedroom while watching some old, dumb romantic comedy?"

"Sure."

Zoey scoffed and shook her head.

Aviv said, "What?"

"You would be bored to tears. The moment all of this nonsense is over, the moment the danger passes, you'll start browsing for the next thing that gets your heart racing. I've looked around at your social media, I'm not exactly your type."

"Men don't know their type until they put their hands on it."

"Yeah, I'm still waiting to get hit with a punch line at some point."

"See, this is what I'm talking about. You seem to live in this paradox where any guy who shows open interest in you is disqualifying himself, like there must be something wrong with him. Don't you see how crazy that is?"

"I think if you had met me two years ago, with me making coffee behind a counter and you on your way to your next big publicity thing, *maybe* you'd have thought, 'Wow, nice boobs,' if that. Then you'd have walked out and never thought about me again."

"So? Congratulations, you're up here with the famous people now. And I am saying, with one hundred percent sincerity, with no subterfuge, that watching you stand up to these goons day after day, the monsters and the Suits, is the sexiest goddamned thing I've ever seen."

"I've heard that one before, too. And that feeling lasts right up until the man saying it is the one I'm standing up to. Listen: if you get yourself in trouble, if you get caught because you didn't bother to get out of town in time, don't expect me to risk myself or my people to help you. I'm telling you in advance: lay low or get out. Or both. This isn't a game. If you insist on screwing around, I can't help you."

"Stop! I'm getting turned on again."

Zoey found Andre waiting for her outside the trailer, alone.

Before she could ask, he said, "They all took the tunnel to the Green Room. Alonzo is there."

"Wait, he is?"

Andre took off walking in the direction of what was, apparently, the next meeting.

"I got what information I could," said Zoey, weakly maintaining the fiction that she and Aviv had spent their time together in a tense interrogation. "Aviv doesn't have any stunts lined up for the festival. He also says he isn't planning anything outrageous for the election, he doesn't want to mess up the voting."

Andre glanced back at the trailer. "Is he still in there?"

"He'll sneak out at some point."

"I've got to say, him just being here feels like a stunt all its own."

"I could say the same about Alonzo. This wasn't planned, was it?"

"No, but I suppose it was inevitable when he heard the other guy was coming."

"Is this meeting going to be us trying to convince Alonzo to leave? Damon supporters are trashing his offices and burning his campaign signs, what kind of chaos is the presence of the man himself going to trigger?"

Andre seemed to be bracing himself to deliver bad news. "Well . . . I was going to let him tell you, but Alonzo wants the two of you to take the stage together."

"What? No. That throws everything off. It took me months to mentally prepare myself for this."

The Sunday-night onstage appearance had always been her father's tradition. For the locals and out-of-towners alike, the message was clear: "I am the guy who keeps this city fun. If I go away, the party goes dark." Zoey had technically been in charge of the company during last year's festival but she'd only been in the position for a few months at the time. When Will had told her that one of her obligations was a short speech in front of a couple hundred thousand people, she had refused even before he'd finished his sentence. This year, he'd made a convincing case that skipping it wasn't an option. If she wanted to be the face of the company—that is, to convince observers that the company wasn't being secretly run by a shady cabal of criminals—stuff like this was part of it.

They entered the tunnel from the Trailer Park to Green Room East (a temporary building positioned behind the trio of stages—the three West stages had their own, which was inexplicably called Green Room 2). The "tunnel" was not underground; it was a clear polymer tube that Zoey thought looked like a human-sized version of something you'd find in a hamster cage, suspended ten feet off the ground. It was intended to keep them separated from unruly fans as they walked the half mile or so north toward the infield campgrounds. The tube had been cleverly designed with a slick exterior that would make it impossible for anyone to climb on it, so there were only about two hundred revelers sitting atop it as Zoey walked past beneath them. A couple of people slapped the sides and said her name as she passed but, in general, she wasn't nearly as famous as any of the actual bands. To most of the fans perched on the tunnel, she probably just appeared to be somebody's assistant or publicist.

As they approached their destination, Andre said, "You all right?"

"Yeah, why?"

"You seem uncomfortable is all. Didn't know if it was something you wanted to talk about."

"You don't want to hear it."

"No, no, I'm all ears."

"As I walk, it's occurring to me that I could have done a better job cleaning up back there."

Andre had no reply, presumably trying to puzzle through what she meant.

She asked, "Is this tunnel thing soundproof? Can we talk in here?"

"Eh, I just say what I want. I can't live like that, paranoid somebody is picking me up on a camera or a long-range mic from a drone. What kind of life is that?"

"Do you really want Alonzo as mayor or do you just want Damon to lose?"

Andre thought about it. "Honestly? I liked it best when the position was vacant. The various officials had to put their heads together and hammer out decisions. But I think you can make an honest case that Alonzo knows the city on a ground level better than anybody. That charity housing you built in Hambright, you could show up there tomorrow and none of the tenants would know your face. But I can guarantee they all know Alonzo. That has to count for something."

She stayed silent for several steps, then asked, "Have you ever been the victim of a crime?"

Andre raised an eyebrow. "Oh, yeah. We grew up in a not-great neighborhood. Bad enough that my dad moved us out of there when I was still in high school."

"So you know what it's like, right? I mean back when you were helpless, not now, when you're able to do something about it."

"Me, my sisters, my friends, all of us. Our apartment got broken into four times in one year."

"Our various trailers, apartments, and cars got broken into more times than I can count," said Zoey, "and let me tell you, when you're a girl, it's a whole different feeling, seeing how easy it is for somebody to get in. They're usually stealing to sell stuff for drugs but, you know, there was never a guarantee it'd end there. And all of the talk about how you can't blame these guys, that it's their addiction, mental illness, their upbringing—in that moment when you come home from work exhausted and see the glass on the floor, see they've stolen the tablet you'd saved up for six months to buy, knowing it's now in some pawn shop in another state . . . I used to have a fantasy that they'd try to come when one of my mom's boyfriends was there. These were always rough guys—she had a type—and I'd think, 'You know, it'd be worth it to have them break in, so that we could catch them breaking in. Crack their skulls.' All of that talk about bad childhoods and systemic oppression feels pretty ivory tower in that moment."

"You leaning toward Leonidas now?"

"I'm saying I understand his appeal. People are trying to raise kids here. And when you're talking about crime, it's not Robin Hood stuff. You burgle in one of the fancy gated communities around here and you'll get hunted down. But the flimsy barracks they throw together for the migrant laborers, the apartments that don't come with real security? They're easy picking. It's the poor robbing the poor. So it's a little hard to hear Alonzo portray himself as the hero of the lower classes when his attitude toward crime seems to boil down to 'Look, that's the cost of freedom, it's either this or brutal dictator.'"

They had arrived at the door of the Green Room, which was being guarded by a very serious man in a suit and sunglasses.

"If what you're trying to say," said Andre, "is that the poor people here are being forced to pick their poison, either live terrified of a creep crawling through their window or be terrified of a jackboot knocking their teeth out for no reason, well, that's the same choice the people at the bottom have been stuck with for several thousand years."

"I feel like every discussion I have about this just goes in circles."

"And now you know why the very first human cities all had a common ingredient that made them work. We wouldn't have a civilization without it."

"The law?"

"Alcohol." He nodded to the guard and opened the door. "After you."

Zoey passed a K-pop band in blinking plaid suits who were joking to each other about something in their native language. A harried assistant nearby seemed to be frantically trying to repair some problem with a wig. They passed a sofa on which sat the hip-hop duo Brinx and Gumbo, both looking at their phones and ignoring each other. When Zoey passed, they each flicked their eyes up at her, again with that furtive expression of a celebrity quickly checking to see if the approaching suit was about to ask something of them. Zoey wondered how often she had that look herself. She was hustled to a smaller room packed with boxes of various liquor and junk food that had presumably been listed on various acts' concert riders. Will, Echo, and Budd seemed to be in the immediate aftermath of a somewhat tense discussion.

Zoey said, "I made it." To Budd she said, "Echo claims she has the whole band list memorized, off the top of her head."

"It's true. Make her run through the list, it's impressive."

Echo took a deep breath. "On the East stage, it's Cloe's Clown Clones, God's Thong, Dog Juggling, Saanvi Singh's All Jug Band, Dough Ray Meat, Soundturd, 10 Gallon Italian, Yak Jesus, Tiny Little Rat Farts, Lance Dancepants, Funeral Giggles, Cello Mold, Dick Masters and the Dickmasters, Turdvana, The Jessie Stankbones, FOONT!, Beefslap, Live Tuna Sandwich, Beard Cannon, Stinky Geyser, Cornhole Brunch, Beak Soup, DJ Teats, Steve Books and the Readers, Help Us Dolphins, Tangerine Boris and His Ladies, Screaming Morons Vs. The Collective Evil of All Human Society, Cameo 2, Mitch's Vibrating Tits, AquariYUM!, Tennessee Layover, Normal Doug, The Trustworthy Young MFs, The Four Horsemen Trio, Snuffletruck, Richest Bitches, Summer Camp Fingerbang—"

"That's good enough," interrupted Zoey, "I've got the idea."

Will asked Andre, "Did you tell her?"

Zoey answered for him. "That Alonzo wants to turn my festival speech into a joint campaign event? The answer is no."

From the door behind her, Alonzo's booming voice said, "You're not even going to give me a chance to state my case?"

She turned to face him. "If you want to go through the crowd recruiting voters like Damon, be my guest. But my remarks aren't a political appearance. It's one thing for me to tell people I'm voting for you or to donate to your campaign. It's another to make it look like I work for your campaign. Or—and this is how it's going to play in the press—like you work for me. Like you're a puppet of my devious organized-crime family."

"I agree that's how it would look if I took the stage with these hooligans," said Alonzo, sweeping his hand toward Will and the rest of the Suits. "But you, by yourself, in your little biker jacket? The message I see is, 'It's a new day in Tabula Rasa, just like the name says.' And I won't even say anything political, I'll just tell people to enjoy the show, same as you."

"No. You've had weeks to ask for this and you're springing it on me backstage? All of the plans have been made, we have a whole carefully orchestrated security apparatus in place. I mean, why now?"

Will said, "You can guess, if you think about it for a few seconds."

Zoey did. "Ah. Leonidas Damon is doing it."

Alonzo nodded. "Snowcloak is bringing him onstage on the West side, just after they do their opening prayer. Just as a side note, I've gotta say that's the perfect name for what has to be the whitest band that has ever existed."

"Do we know what Damon's going to say?"

Echo said, "We don't, but it's easy to predict. He's going to go up there and repeat his accusation that we all tried to have him killed at the pirate debate. He's going to try to whip his people into a frenzy, to get a riot going."

"So even if he causes the riot, it works in his favor because his official position is anti-riot? How is that fair?"

Andre said, "Tyrants have been using that playbook for longer than we've had words to describe it."

"How about this," offered Alonzo, "I go up with Zoey and make a call for peace. I don't tell people to vote for me, I don't even mention there's an election. I go up, thank the organizers for putting on this beautiful event, then tell everyone to please cool it and to take their anger to the voting booth on Tuesday and keep Catharsis peaceful, etcetera, etcetera."

Zoey looked to Wu. "How does it change the security equation if Alonzo is onstage with me?"

"Well, this is what we were supposed to go over last night. Your angel drones won't chuck blood bombs at you, they can't get in. But there are Liberator activists on the grounds. They won't have bags of blood unless they, I don't know, puncture a vein and fill them on the spot. But if they do that, honestly, they'll have earned it. If one person tries to rush the stage, they'll be tackled by security before they reach you. That's why you're not going to get too close to the edge, there's a piece of yellow tape on the stage, stand behind that."

"That all sounds really straightforward."

"But in the unlikely but always possible event that there is an actual assassination attempt with some kind of projectile weapon, you will go flat. The stage has a slight incline that will make you invisible from wherever the hypothetical shooter is, unless they're ten feet tall. There are no known weapons on the grounds, everyone is scanned when they enter, but of course, a dedicated assassin could have something custom made. Or twenty squirrels could each bring in individual pieces that can be assembled on-site. Use your imagination."

He didn't mean literal squirrels. Some festivalgoers would arrive at the grounds weeks in advance and bury contraband that wouldn't otherwise be allowed through the gates, with the intention of digging it up later. Throughout the festival you'd find kids on their hands and knees digging at any patch of loose soil, hoping to find the booze/drugs/etc. that they or someone else had squirreled away.

Zoey nodded. "Stay behind the line, go flat if someone shoots. Got it. So how does that change if Alonzo is up there with me?"

"Well, I don't have Echo's sophisticated model in front of me but I'd say with two targets onstage, that approximately doubles the chances somebody will try something."

"But it cuts the chances of harm to Zoey in half," said Alonzo, "since they have two targets to pick from. And I have easily twice Zoey's mass—from the front anyway—so that reduces it to thirty-three percent. Hell, that's safer than flying!"

Zoey looked to Will. "What would you do?"

"The better question is, what would Arthur do? I know you don't like asking that question, but his instincts for politics were better than mine. And I think Arthur would let Alonzo onstage but would make it very clear beforehand that Alonzo was deeply, *deeply* in his debt for doing so, and then he'd remind Alonzo of that fact once every forty-eight hours or so for as long as he served as mayor."

Zoey turned to Wu again. "Does this make your life harder? I feel like you complain about me when you're hanging around other bodyguards."

He pondered it, appearing like he was searching for a plausible reason to refuse. "If there are no calls to action to the crowd that they could interpret as permission to rush the stage, then no, we should be all right."

Zoey sighed and said, "Fine," and even before finishing that single syllable knew it was a mistake.

CHAPTER
19

ZOEY AND BUDD HAD huddled in the quietest spot they could find, which turned out to be a control room under the center East stage that looked like the cavernous flight deck of an intergalactic starship. On some level, Zoey had known there had to be a place where experts ran the pyrotechnics and holograms and stuff; what she had not realized, until Budd explained it, was that the entire show was not just planned but *recorded* in advance. Each act—even the low-fi folk groups—had a music director and a live programmer stationed in this room to fill in background vocals and instrumental tracks during the performance. All live singing was tuned and filtered through the mic before it emerged from the amps. Most of what you heard onstage, regardless of the act or genre, was a prerecorded and prescheduled program pumped out from this room, the band just playing along via cues from their earpieces. Was the whole world nothing but orchestrated lies?

There was a tiny soundproof booth just off the control room and the two of them sat knees-to-knees in there, Zoey looking at the padded walls around them and trying not to think of a coffin.

"The control-room people aren't going to get mad at us for intruding?"

"Nah," said Budd, "I know all those guys."

"How do you do it? How do you just instantly connect with people? Will said he once saw you walk up to a cop who was in the act of arresting a homeless man and both of them turned and greeted you by name."

"Well, that's the key, knowing that everybody is different in the details but the same at the core. Every human being has one big, gaping weakness. It's usually one of two things: a sucking hole at their center called 'need' or something they've desperately latched onto to fill that need. Either way, their entire world and personality, all their posturing and bluster, it's all revolving around some central weakness they're trying to cover up."

"So you're just looking for weak points to exploit, like a predator looks at a herd of elk?"

"Oh, no, it don't have to be like that at all. When you see a puppy or a wounded bird, does their weakness make you want to squish them? No, that's when you love 'em the most. When you see even the worst monster among us and realize they're just a needy mammal at heart, it's hard to see anyone as truly bad. Understanding this just takes away the fear of talking to them, that's all."

"Well, it's kind of hard for me to see the frail humanity in the billion-aires who kill so they can add two pennies to their stock price."

"Would you trade places with them?" asked Budd. "Put their hard heart inside you to replace yours?"

"No."

"So you do pity them, because you don't want to be them—even for their money and power, you wouldn't want to become an unfeeling wretch. To be that cut off from your basic humanity has to be a Hell all its own."

"Well, I would ask you what my big insecurity is but everybody in the world knows it."

"Oh, really?"

"Yeah, I worry that I'm not cut out for this world of cutthroat ser-pents."

"You think so? I reckon you're more worried that you *are* cut out for it."

"So, my speech," she said, rapidly changing the subject. "I'll say hello, introduce Alonzo, he'll say whatever he has to say, then . . . what? Is this where you make up a joke for me to tell?"

"Just to be clear, now: I've never made up a joke in my life. All these jokes are older than the hills, some of 'em I heard from my grandpa. He probably heard 'em from his. The skill is in the delivery. That and match-ing joke to audience."

"Can I make a joke about that thing you just said, how everyone I'm forced to meet with every day is a hollow shell of inhumanity?"

"The safest bet is to poke fun at yourself, talk about how your life is a mess. See, that's what soothes the anxiety inside people, hearing that others have got it worse."

"That should be easy, since it's true. I feel like as soon as I adjust to one part of this job, I'm instantly thrust into something new and strange where I look like a crocodile trying to play a piano."

"If only we could transplant into you even half of the irrational confidence of your prankster friend."

"Oh, god. Don't get me started on Aviv, I swear, I can't tell if he's charming or just really tall."

"Does it matter?" asked Budd in an odd tone. "I say, in our world, only one thing counts in romantic relationships, and that's trust. So do you trust him?"

"Not at all."

Budd gave her a curious grin. "You sure? It seems like you treat him like someone you trust."

"I hope not. Will said the most effective con is when you let the mark think they're in on it. For all I know, that's all Aviv is doing with me. 'I trick everybody else, but I'm letting you in on the game.' Hell, you tell me if I should trust him. You're the one who can read everybody."

He shrugged. "I think it's easy to assume males are all sly schemers, when most of us are clumsy oafs, falling on our rears and then tryin' to play it off like we did it on purpose. I think the most common mistake we make in dealing with people is in assuming that while our own feelings are a mess of contradictions, everybody else is operating with a clear agenda and any inconsistencies must be due to some kind of ruse."

"Wait, are you *encouraging* me to start a serious relationship with this daredevil-slash-prankster? I'd almost suspect you're saying this to me as a prank on Will."

"I'm, ah, not so sure that Will wouldn't tell you the same thing. I mean, he wouldn't *tell* you, I'm saying if you could pry open his skull and see his real thoughts, that's what they'd be."

"I don't even know how to respond to that. Everything I learn about that man just makes him more inscrutable. I mean, what's Will's one glaring need or weakness or whatever?"

"You, of all people, should know the answer to that one."

"What do you mean? You know what, I don't want to know."

"I'm just saying, we're all just people, and sometimes our actions make no sense because we're fightin' a battle with needs we don't like or understand. If you're ever wondering how a man feels about you, remember that what he feels and what he wants to feel might be two different things."

"Sure. Ah, okay, we keep getting off the subject, I need a joke for my speech that won't accidentally spark an outrage that helps Leo Damon win the election and have us all thrown into a labor camp."

"I do suppose that outcome would be less than ideal."

"Seriously, though, what specifically happens to us if Damon wins? He can't really put us into prison, right? I'm trying to imagine Will in an orange jumpsuit and it breaks my brain."

Budd raised his eyebrows. "You know Will's done time before, right? All of us have, including Echo. Arthur did, too. A couple years."

Zoey did not, in fact, know this. She leaned back against the padded wall of the booth.

"I don't think I can handle prison, Budd. Is that really what's at stake here?"

"Maybe more than that. Whatever sentence gets handed down, a man like Damon would make sure the key players don't come out in one piece."

"Are you trying to give me a panic attack before I go onstage?"

"You're on the high wire now, Zoey. Be honest with yourself: When you look down, sure you're scared, but maybe you're also a little excited?"

"No. I'm not crazy."

"Women who like danger get called crazy, men get called brave. I can't give you relationship advice—Lord knows my personal life is a damn mess—but I'll say this: If you find a fella who sees you for what you are and doesn't go running for the hills, at least give him a chance."

Zoey thought about it. "When I first showed up here, when everybody just wanted to kill me, you were the first one to say anything positive. I'll never forget that."

He shrugged. "It's no credit to me, seeing what was obviously there.

All right, enough of that. Let's write up some brief remarks that won't precipitate disaster."

The sun had set and Zoey was standing just offstage with Alonzo while The Four Horsemen Trio played yet another encore, the band having already gone twenty minutes over schedule. The music was deafening, the noise of the crowd was impossible. It was simply a sound on a scale Zoey couldn't comprehend. It was nothing that evolution had prepared the brain to process, a mass of voices that crashed across her like ocean waves. Then there were the individual voices in her ear, bugging her with details and reminders that sliced through the cacophony (the little earpieces canceled all other noise the moment someone spoke). This is how she would receive her instructions to go flat or run away in the event disaster struck. She noticed water bottles and other debris were being hurled at the stage, which was making her very nervous.

She asked, "Did we discuss what I do if people throw junk at me? A bottle just barely missed that drummer's head."

"There's a mechanism to repulse projectiles," Wu's voice replied in her ear. She was forced to rely on the earpiece despite the fact that the man was just six feet behind her. "There are vents with compressed air at the edge of the stage, anything thrown, the jets blow it back to the crowd."

"It doesn't look like it's working."

"The band requested it be off, they encourage the projectiles. It will be turned on for you and Alonzo."

The Four Horsemen Trio finished their song and were now goofing around with the crowd, the shirtless lead singer grabbing water bottles and hurling them back at the audience. He found one bottle on the stage half-filled with a yellow liquid, picked it up, and said, "Who threw the piss?" The crowd laughed and cheered, then he tipped it up and drank it. The crowd went wild. The lead guitarist walked off the stage past Zoey, the man absolutely drenched in sweat. When Zoey watched him head down off the stage, she noticed her mother had arrived at some point, looking pleasantly drunk and giving Zoey a nervous thumbs-up.

A voice in Zoey's ear, Echo's, said, "Once they've all left the stage, give the audience a minute or two to calm down. Wu will run one more drone scan for anyone with a threatening posture, anyone who may be concealing a weapon or who seems to be planning something."

Zoey felt her phone buzz with an incoming message and pulled it just far enough from her pocket to check it.

Aviv:

Look to the right, next to the nearest amp tower.

In her ear, Will's voice said, "Stick to the script, don't start doing crowd work, don't improvise. Say what we planned, smile, wave, walk off. Don't create a moment they can use against us."

Zoey didn't bother replying to either of the men. Alonzo stepped up beside her, two assistants messing with his tie and pocket square, respectively.

He waved them off and gave Zoey a sidelong glance. "Can you believe what nonsense this all is?"

Again, despite being right next to her, she was getting him through the earpiece. The band had now all left the stage aside from the drummer, who was out on the edge, looking for two fans to give his drumsticks to. He was crouching over a forest of grasping fingers.

Zoey sighed. "I hate politics."

Alonzo smiled. "So do I."

"Yeah, but the difference is, I'm not running for office. I don't get running on a platform of 'this is all stupid.' I mean, it is all stupid, but why can't we have actual expert politicians who know how to run things well?"

The drummer chucked his drumsticks to the two prettiest girls he could find, then strode off the stage, bumping past Zoey.

In her ear, Echo said, "Just stay where you are for the moment."

"Look," said Alonzo, "what the citizens want couldn't be simpler: They want all evildoers to be instantly apprehended and punished, with perfect accuracy and no inconvenience to the innocent. They want jobs with good pay, flexibility, and low stress but also want all products and services to be available instantly, at all hours, and dirt cheap. They want generous government infrastructure and benefits, but without paying taxes. In other words, they want the impossible. So what they get instead is a show." He gestured to the riggings and the lights above the stage. "Something they can follow like a sport, argue about with their buddies."

In Zoey's ear, Echo said, "Give it another minute or so, we'll tell you when to go on. Wu says there are no obvious assassins in shooting range."

"Thank you, Echo." To Alonzo, she said, "I just want a world where everyone's basic needs are met. That's not impossible and I'm not going to let you or anybody else make me feel like an idiot for wanting it."

"What's a 'basic need'? Does it include a yearly vacation? A yard? Your own car? To get your hair done at a stylist? What about sex? Are they entitled to that?"

"Not if they can't find their own willing partner, no."

"But all that other stuff requires willing partners, too. If everybody is entitled to a home, that means construction workers have to labor for weeks in the hot sun to build 'em. Why is that different from requiring someone to provide sex?"

"For the same reason you'd probably sooner spend an entire year building a house in the sun than five minutes providing unwilling sex to a stranger."

A message chimed and Zoey again checked her phone.

Aviv:
Look for the yellow robot, that's me.

She had no idea what that meant and absolutely had no desire to deal with it at the moment.

"But not everyone agrees," said Alonzo. "Go ask your girls at Chalet if they'd prefer hard labor. At the end of the day, you have to let people choose their lives. For better or worse."

Echo said, "You're up."

Zoey took a deep breath and stepped forward, knowing that if she allowed herself to hesitate for even a moment, she'd just freeze in place. She went out onto the stage and felt her body respond the exact same way it had when she'd jumped into the freezing water during the shipwreck: a visceral convulsion that seemed to purge all the air from her system. Before her was a pulsing sea of humans that faded to a blur of people-pixels that stretched into the distance. She looked down at the first few rows below her and there were the faces of individuals making actual eye contact. Most showed no sign of recognition.

A general cheer went up from the crowd at her appearance, probably just a reflexive reaction to having *something* occurring on the stage. She thought she heard a "Zoey!" shouted somewhere out there, and the word "cat." And then a roar went up and that was for Alonzo, following her out. That cheer from the audience was a high like Zoey had never felt in her life. Good Lord. She could feel that thunder of approval in her shoes, in her gut. The five sentences she was supposed to say, the script she'd memorized by repeating them over and over, utterly vanished from her mind.

A voice in her ear said, "Take a step back," and she had no idea what it meant, then noticed she was beyond the scuffed strip of yellow tape they'd marked as the Safe Zone. Alonzo was waving and, in general, seemed to be waiting for Zoey to say her bit, which was supposed to come first. In the middle of the sea of people was the circular platform with two holograms mimicking Zoey's and Alonzo's movements, giant ghostly doppelgängers towering above the crowd.

Zoey lifted the microphone to her face and her brain just froze up. She cleared her throat and heard it echo across the amp towers. She watched the giant hologram mirror her movements, saw her own fear in its posture. Then a yellow object in the crowd caught her eye and she remembered Aviv's text. It was, in fact, a robot. It was eight feet tall and was actually a walking vending machine, dispensing energy drinks from a cooler on its back, the front branded with a ModoMojo logo made out of animated lightning. Aviv had disguised himself as an object designed to be easily visible for a quarter mile in any direction. The idiot.

A drunk dude in the front row screamed for Zoey to show her boobs and for some reason, that's what broke her paralysis.

"Oh, there we go," said Zoey into the mic. "This guy's asking me to show boobs. People, you can see them any time you want, if you search my name on any platform, it autocompletes to 'boobs.' One request: specifically search for 'Zoey Ashe boobs Cannes,' that's the best clip, I looked really skinny in that one."

Laughs and hoots from the crowd.

"But I know you're not here to see me, so let me get this over quick," she said, back on script. "Thank you for coming out, thank you for your energy, thank you for not utterly destroying all of this stuff my people have taken months to build for you."

A pretty good cheer in response to that. The grin on Zoey's face in response was genuine.

"My company sponsors this here festival," she continued, "against the advice of our accountants—trust me, the ticket prices don't come close to covering the damage you crazies do every year—and I intend to continue this tradition until people stop showing up or I run out of money."

More cheers. And louder. Jesus, had she actually been nervous about this? They were going to have to drag her off the stage. She wanted to feel like this all the time, forever. She again looked to the yellow energy-drink robot suit that Aviv was apparently driving around. It was waving its spindly arms in the air. She wondered if he had bribed the normal vendor to give up the suit or if he'd just stolen it.

"Now," she said when she sensed the roar had dipped somewhat, "here, with what I've been assured is a totally apolitical message, is candidate for mayor Alonzo Dunn."

More cheers, plus a chant Zoey couldn't make out. Probably one of Megaboss Alonzo's campaign slogans. Not that it mattered, people just liked to make noise in unison.

"Settle down, before y'all pull a muscle," said Alonzo, beaming. "She's right, I'm not here to drone on about politics, even the presence of a stiff like me in a suit like this at a party like yours ought to be against the rules. I'm just here to ask everybody to keep the energy pure, keep the future memories happy, enjoy the unifying magic of the music."

A mild cheer from the crowd. For those who knew Alonzo, this wasn't the good stuff. He wasn't playing the hits. But that was the agreed-upon plan.

Zoey raised her mic to tell her joke, say thank you, and then walk off. But Alonzo wasn't done.

"A moment ago, my opponent took the West center stage and got that crowd all riled up about cleaning up the city, then he walked off and that

Christian glam-rock band went into their song about washing away the filth. Or one of 'em, they all kinda sound the same."

Hoots of agreement from the crowd. Alonzo calmly stepped over the yellow tape, nearing the edge of the stage, a couple of feet away from the grasping hands below.

"Well, if you ask me, the world needs a little filth! Let's hear it for the filth!"

The reaction from the audience was a roar that seemed to shake the planet in its orbit.

Zoey just stood there, not knowing what to do with her hands. Was she supposed to be reacting to this? Smiling? Frowning? Keeping her face neutral? What was her face doing right now? Should she just walk off? Would that be seen as a protest? Alonzo had gone off script and there were no good options for reeling him in. She figured that running over and slapping the mic from his hand would probably create an unfavorable narrative in the press.

"So, let me tell you a story," said Alonzo in a soaring tone like he was about to launch into a sermon. "My great granddaddy was a blues musician in Chicago, waaaay back in the olden days. And let me tell you right now: the music you're hearing on these stages, it would not exist without that Chicago blues scene. The Chicago blues gave you Chuck Berry and Chuck gave you the Rolling Stones and so on and so on. And let me tell you about my great granddaddy. He died at age thirty-one, stabbed during a fight in a nightclub. If he'd survived that, I suppose he'd have drank himself to death by forty. But let me tell you, his guitar was the voice of God. I've got his albums at home on the original vinyl and I've never heard a church hymn that made me feel holiness like those chords. See, that's the thing about humans. A lot of time, it's the filth that produces the beauty. So let's hear it for my granddaddy, who'd never have been born in any kind of white eugenicist's utopian society. And let's hear it for all of us who wouldn't be here if people like Leonidas Damon had their way. Here's to the sons and the daughters of the filth!"

The cheer was so loud that it watered Zoey's eyes. Some people chucked bottles toward the stage, which were blasted back by pulses of compressed air as if bouncing off an invisible force field.

In Zoey's ear, Will said, "Just stay back, don't agree or disagree. We're looking for a good moment for you to walk off without it looking like you're storming off in protest."

"Now, I know what they say," said Alonzo, whose body seemed to have been taken over by a powerful, mischievous spirit. "They say, 'Alonzo talks a big game about being a man of the people, but you never see him walk the streets without his security detail!' For one, it's no secret I've got enemies. A man doesn't win this much without leaving a trail of losers in his wake. But if you think I'm afraid to jump into this crowd right now, you don't know me!"

Ravenous cheers. He pointed to a group right at the center of the stage. "You look like you got strong backs! You ready?"

Zoey muttered, "Tell me he's not . . ."

There were voices in her ear, Budd and Will and Echo and Andre, all rapidly discussing what was about to happen. Zoey heard no specific instructions for her.

"And if these fools drop me," shouted Alonzo, "you know what? That's okay. That won't shake my trust in the people, just these particular people. Here we go!"

Alonzo crouched on the edge of the stage, then launched himself, twisting in midair to land backside down. The crowd caught him, for the most part, and clumsily carried him around for a bit and then set him on his feet.

He still had his microphone and, once he gathered himself, said, "Hold on, now!" He made a show of examining his left, bare wrist. "I had a watch! I had a gold Rolex watch! Who's got it?" He allowed for laughter from the crowd, then, "Oh, wait, it's on the other arm. Sorry to have accused you."

Zoey had wandered past the yellow safety line again, entranced by Alonzo's suicidal crowd surf. Some guys in the front row were now beckoning her to jump.

She raised the mic and said, "Not a chance."

This yielded some boos.

In her ear, Echo was saying, "Just come back. Wave and walk off, smile the whole time."

From down among the people, Alonzo said, "Now, come on, if I was her I wouldn't trust you perverts, either. I even felt some of you get handsy with me."

This only triggered the crowd to insist even harder, beckoning Zoey to join them.

"No, he's right," said Zoey. "There's certain parts you're not supposed to touch on a woman without permission and look at me, those parts are, like, sixty percent of my surface area."

Laugher. Jeers. Pleas. The front section of the crowd, with no other entertainment onstage at the moment, had decided they wanted nothing in life more than to get this woman to take the plunge. Everyone was smiling, most were around her age, some beefy drunk guys near the front were insisting they'd catch her. A little ways back, the yellow Aviv-bot was using its spindly robot arms to beckon her forward.

Zoey heard some female voices calling her name and noticed a group of women way off to her left, urging her that way, implying that it was a safe spot to jump and avoid getting groped.

In her ear, Will said, "Zoey, do *not* go into the crowd."

She wasn't sure if she had made her decision prior to hearing that or after, but the decision was made nonetheless. She tossed the mic aside and ran toward the group of female fans. The final words she heard in her ear before she reached the edge was her mother shouting, "Go backward so you land with your butt!"

She tried to obey, flinging herself into the air with abandon, twisting as she went. She landed backward on a bunch of hands and kind of awkwardly rolled off and tumbled to the ground. Then everyone was laughing and helping her up and Zoey was thanking them. Her heart was pounding.

Echo's voice in her ear said, "Wu is heading toward you."

"No," replied Zoey, "tell him to stay put. I'm fine. Just give me a minute."

The crowd's excitement over Zoey's leap dissipated quickly, as apparently the fun was in talking her into it, not the act itself. The stage backdrop was already transforming itself for the next band and the currents of the crowd began mixing as some wandered off to other stages and a wave of new fans washed in for the next act. Alonzo was taking some pictures with supporters and, in general, seemed to have forgotten about

Zoey entirely. The new fans coming in didn't seem to know or care about her either way. These were people from out of town, for the most part, and the audience having convinced some local officials to jump off the stage wasn't in the top thousand weirdest things they'd seen over the last sixty hours or so of the festival.

She was just part of the crowd. Nobody paid any special attention to her other than to smile as they passed.

It was *wonderful*.

Alonzo's security detail and assistants were jumping down off the stage, pushing their way through, trying to get to the candidate. He made a big show of waving them off, he was just chilling with his constituents, all was well.

Finally, Will's voice said, "What's your plan, Zoey?"

"I'm think I'm gonna hang out with the people and enjoy the concert."

There was another pause while Will either exchanged frustrated words with the team over a muted mic or just took a moment to gather himself so he wouldn't start yelling. She thought she may have heard Wu say, "I told you she would do it."

"The issue with that," said Will, restraining himself with all his strength, "is that everyone on the team has a role based around all of this playing out in a certain way. If we have to assign someone to track you, and then many people to come extract you if things go wrong, it throws everything off. You said yourself that you have a responsibility as a boss to not make everyone's jobs harder."

"And you told me that no plan survives contact with the enemy." She actually wasn't sure she'd heard him say that, but it seemed like the kind of thing Will would say. "Things change, I've observed the situation and have decided that I want to spend the concert on this side, with the people. I mean, if the common folk are so dangerous that I can't hang out with them and listen to some music, what society are we even trying to preserve? It sounds to me like the battle is already lost."

There was another pause, during which they apparently had another discussion and decided that Echo was the better intermediary.

"Zoey," said Echo, "the issue isn't that there might be trouble, the issue is that there almost certainly will be. We've talked about this."

"I'll make my way back to you before that. It'll be fine. I have friends out here." She was heading toward the yellow ModoMojo energy-drink robot that Aviv had hijacked. "I'll talk to you later." Before anyone could reply, she pulled out her earpiece and stuffed it in her pocket.

The yellow robot had a tinted portal in its chest that Zoey assumed was for the pilot inside to see out. Between this and the drill machine, Zoey had decided that Aviv's one remarkable trait was a resistance to claustrophobia.

She got as close to the Aviv-bot as she could without it seeming weird. "Is that you?"

Either there was no apparatus for the operator to speak, or Aviv didn't want to give away his identity with his voice. Instead, she got her answer via a text on her phone:

Aviv:

Nice, right? Only had to pay a teenager a few hundred bucks to let me take his shift. I haven't sold many cans of ModoMojo so far though. There's a quota and I don't want the guy to get yelled at.

The robot was rolling through the crowd and Zoey was kind of walking along with it. The drinks were stored in a refrigerated cylinder on its back that swirled with animated slogans. There was a chute that kind of seemed positioned to make it look like the drinks were being dispensed from the robot's butt.

"This is awkward, do people think I'm trying to befriend this vending machine?"

As they talked, kids were coming up and pulling out cans, the system tracking every purchase and invisibly charging their accounts.

Aviv:

Maybe they'll think I took your money without dispensing a can and you're trying to get a refund. Bang on me with your fists, like you're mad.

A roar went up around them. The next act had apparently taken the stage.

Aviv:

Follow me.

The message scrolling across the drink case on the back switched to a flashing red text:

OUT OF STOCK! GOING TO GET MORE! SORRY!

The Aviv-bot headed toward a row of temporary crowd-control barriers marking the thoroughfare that led between the stages. It would take them to the infield campgrounds with its thousands of tents and hundreds of vendors, all at the feet of the towering beehive in the center.

Aviv:

It'll look like I'm going back to get restocked. I have something to show you. Do you want to hold hands?

He extended one of his spindly yellow robot arms. Zoey slapped it away.

"I feel ridiculous."

Aviv:

I'm going to tell you something you'll either find upsetting or liberating: right here, right now, nobody cares what you do.

They made their way to the infield, the trio of East stages now behind them, the three West stages on the other side of the campgrounds. In between was a sprawl of filthy tents and rows of blue plastic portable restrooms. Zoey had no idea how anyone got any sleep with the giant beehive looming overhead. The hundreds of vendor drones swooping in and out of the hexagonal ports did, in fact, create an ominous buzz that could be felt in the air, as if the structure was going to split open and unleash an actual swarm of hornets. Though the delivery drones were not, as she'd hoped, shaped like big fuzzy bees.

As Zoey and the Aviv-bot passed by hordes of filthy and partially clothed festival campers, she noticed a small mountain of trash piled up against one of the apparently nonfunctioning incinerators. She imagined a blinking red dot on that holographic model of the festival grounds, and how that tiny indicator didn't really convey the effect of passing the black cloud of flies swarming around the trash. Or the stench.

"Are we going somewhere in particular?" she asked.

I'm looking for someone, came the reply on her phone.

"Who?"

Aviv:

It's a surprise.

"Am I being lured into an ambush?"

Aviv:

If so, then we both are. Remember earlier when I said I had hoped to have news for you? It's about that. They should be over here, by that pink tent. See it?

She did. As they moved closer, they passed another malfunctioning trash can, another reeking mountain of refuse.

Aviv:

There, see the one in the mask? White tank top?

They were close enough to see four women milling about near a large pink tent, which was as big and garish as a vendor tent but was not marked in any way. That usually meant they were dealing in some kind of contraband. Some drugs were allowed to be dealt on the grounds but only from official sellers, it was too easy to have guys selling mushrooms from plastic bags that did nothing. Still, illegal sellers who'd squirreled away their stock beforehand would come and pitch their tent right on top of the dig and open up for business. A big pink tent like this, though, probably meant sex workers. Only one of the women was wearing a mask, a black germ filter that covered her from the eyes down, the type worn by those who'd developed a cough or who otherwise were concerned about the spread of airborne diseases. Though they were also popular among those who simply preferred not to be tracked on Blink—Zoey noticed this woman also wore sunglasses with hers. The hair above it was cut short, slicked back and buzzed at the sides.

"I see her."

Aviv:

Look at her left ankle.

"We're too far away and it's too dark." From where she stood, all she could verify was that the woman did, in fact, have an ankle.

A new message came through, this time a photo. A close-up of the woman's ankle, apparently taken earlier in the day when the sun was out. She had a thin red band around it, like a tied length of string. No, that wasn't right—it was a tattoo of a red string.

"I see the tattoo, but I don't know what it means."

Aviv:

From your phone, can you access the autopsy report on Violet? The first sex worker who went missing?

"Oh, okay. Yeah, I don't need to. This one has the same tattoo."

Aviv:

Zoey, that's Violet.

CHAPTER
20

ZOEY FROZE.

"Lots of people can have the same tattoo . . ."

Aviv:

It's her. I talked to her. She cut her hair but it's her. I don't know why she's here but she's preparing to do something, she has a small bag of equipment she works very hard to keep out of sight. She dug it up this morning.

"Oh, my god, I have to tell my—" Zoey rummaged in her pocket for her earpiece. "We can't let her leave—"

"It's Zoey Ashe!"

Zoey wasn't sure who'd said it, but it didn't matter—what mattered was that Violet, or the woman Aviv had insisted was Violet, had heard. She turned in Zoey's direction and decided she did not want to be in the vicinity.

"Wait!" said Zoey as Violet jogged away, casting glances back to see if Zoey was in pursuit. "I want to talk to you!"

That, it appeared, was exactly what the fleeing woman was hoping to avoid. She broke into a run, zigzagging between tents, campers, and trash. Zoey did the same.

"Stop!" Zoey looked back and saw Aviv was rolling after them in the yellow ModoMojo robot. Some guys were following him but Zoey wasn't sure if they were participating in the chase or were just trying to get a drink. Violet, apparently seeking out a denser crowd to get lost in, headed for the West stages. She weaved her way through the migration of campers shuffling out to see the headliner shows and Zoey did the same in pursuit, bumping through shoulders and elbows.

She finally found the earpiece in her pocket and stuck it in place. "Can you hear me?"

There was some rustling on the other end, then Echo said, "We've been tracking you on Blink, who are you following?"

"That's Violet! The first supposedly dead woman!" Zoey had to take a moment to catch her breath. "Don't ask me how I know! Track her, I don't know if I can keep up!"

She couldn't, it turned out. Violet, and then Zoey, hopped the low barriers to the thoroughfare that led between the West and Northwest stages, or the middle and top stages as Zoey pictured the layout map in her head. The flowing migration was dense but at least it was moving. Zoey waded in and moved as quickly as the crowd would allow, forcing her way in between hips and shoulders, desperately trying to keep Violet in view. A voice said, "Zoey!" and she turned to see a stranger, a girl who was pointing to her head. She had dark hair and was showing Zoey that she had shaved a stripe in the scalp. Zoey gave her a thumbs-up and kept running.

They passed between the stages, plunging into the crowds on the West side. The band on Zoey's left was ripping their way through some extremely angry song. Zoey stopped because she had lost track of Violet and, to be frank, was already getting winded. Some annoyed people behind her were saying, "Watch it!" as the yellow Aviv ModoMojo beverage mech was rolling up, knocking people aside as gently as it could.

Zoey asked, "Do you see her?" without specifying whom she wanted to answer.

"She's worming her way through the crowd," said Will in her ear. "Heading for the center hologram platform."

Well, at least that was easy to spot: the giant holographic version of the stage show was probably visible from orbit. Zoey made her way in that direction, squeezing through a crowd so dense and tense that it was starting to trigger her anxiety, that feeling like there wasn't enough air for everyone to breathe.

Will said, "She's stolen a hat, a gray beanie, and she's putting it on.

She's found some kind of shirt on the ground, looks like she's assembling a disguise."

"Dark blue flannel," added Echo.

"Got it," replied Zoey.

She now had a stitch in her side, plus there was a throbbing pain in the leg she'd broken not too long ago. God, she'd played basketball in high school and now she felt like she was going to die because she'd jogged across, like, half a mile of music festival.

In her ear, Echo asked, "Are you all right?"

"No, I apparently have the athleticism of a sixty-year-old woman."

"Violet has gotten stalled near the hologram platform, the crowds are really dense there."

The platform was just ahead, at the moment displaying four massive giants playing a power ballad Zoey recognized called "Mommy's Chains." It was written from the point of view of a small child who watches their mother get beaten to death in an alley by a gang of muggers looking to steal her jewelry, only for them to realize afterward that her gold chains are cheap fakes and tossing them to the bloodstained concrete in disdain. The child screams for bystanders to do something, but they just walk past. The song's chorus was the lead singer shrieking,

Why, why won't you stop them
Why, why won't you stop them
Look, her blood is on their hands

The crowd was singing along, bouncing with the drums, whipped into a rage about these fictional villains, their fictional victim and her fictional traumatized child. At this point, they weren't getting out of Zoey's way because there was no place for them to go, just bodies and more bodies.

In her ear, Andre said, "Hey, are you doing that? Or rather, your guy?"

"Doing what?"

It quickly became apparent: the hologram of the band was glitching out, blinking and distorting, though the actual band onstage behind them was continuing to play uninterrupted.

"The hologram? No. Well, I don't think so—" Zoey turned and banged on Aviv's robot suit with her fist. "Hey, are you doing this?"

Aviv:

No.

Then, as if anticipating her skepticism,

I promise. I'd say so if it was me.

"It's not us," said Zoey to the Suits in her ear, "unless we're doing it on accident."

Will said, "It's being hacked, but not remotely. Somebody has to be there at the platform patching into the panel. Do you have any view of that? Is it Violet?"

"I can't see anything, there's, like, a hundred layers of people between us and the platform."

As she spoke, the hologram vanished entirely. The image then reappeared as a jumbled blob and rearranged itself, coalescing into the shape of a panicked young woman in filthy underwear, bleeding from a head wound and trying to free her hands from what looked like leather straps. It was poor quality, the kind of wavy, glitchy hologram you get when recording from a phone in low light. Zoey's first thought was that this was the work of the band; they'd just wrapped up a song about a victimized woman, now here she was. But then Zoey recognized the face. It was, of course, Rose, the third missing sex worker.

"Please!" cried Hologram Rose, her quivering voice emitting from amp towers across the grounds. "Please, can anyone hear me?"

The band had apparently pieced together what was happening and stopped playing.

The lead singer yelled, "Everybody! Cool it! This is not part of the show. What is this?"

"Please!" cried the shimmering figure towering over the crowd. "I don't know if anyone is seeing this, I—I can't tell if I'm getting a signal. I don't have time. He's going to come back. Please listen. My name is Rose. I worked at Chalet, at the mall. I'm locked in this . . . this place, there are no windows, the walls are metal and they're, like, ribbed or something, like one of those shipping containers? I don't know where this is. I feel vibrations, maybe there's some machinery around? I don't know, I don't know. It could be a construction site . . ."

She stopped, whipping her head around like she'd heard a noise. The crowd around Zoey and the Aviv-bot had fallen dead silent. Some were worried about the endangered woman, others still weren't convinced this wasn't a staged drama that had been arranged as part of the festival.

"The man who took me," continued the hologram, "I don't know his name. But he paid for this, he paid to kidnap me, he paid to keep me, to kill me. And there will be others. Please, my phone is dying, I don't even know if this is—"

The hologram went dark, leaving the platform empty.

In Zoey's ear, Will's voice said, "Yeah, it's Violet."

"No," replied Zoey, "that's Rose."

"I'm saying the hologram was uploaded by Violet, that's why she was here, that's what she was waiting to do when you spotted her. There's a maintenance panel, she knew where it was, how to unlock it, and how to reprogram it."

"But why?"

"It would be nice if we could ask her that. But she's heading out of the festival now, toward the back fence and . . . yeah, it looks like she has a getaway ride waiting for her back there, a Vespa."

"Where is she now? Where, exactly?"

"You won't catch her. Instead you need to head toward the platform."

Zoey started heading that way, without asking for a reason. The hologram platform was a disk sitting maybe fifteen feet off the ground. It looked like a landed UFO that was big enough to hold, say, five hundred aliens inside, with comfortable legroom. It was balanced on a single thick leg in the center, specifically designed so it would be all but impossible to climb on it, so Zoey only saw a dozen or so people sitting up there.

Will said, "There's a maintenance panel in the ground covered by a heavy metal door that should have been impossible to open."

"You're sending me to fix your stupid hologram?"

"We're sending you to see if she left a drive or something behind that we can grab and trace back to somebody. Walk forward about thirty paces."

Zoey actually didn't need Will's directions. About, well, thirty paces ahead of her was Margaret Mull in her trench coat and red hat, using her folded umbrella like a cane. She was kneeling over an open panel, examining it with a light emitting from her red-hatted camera drone.

Zoey said, "Somebody beat us here."

"What?"

"The amateur detective who accosted me earlier today, the old woman."

Faintly, in her ear, Zoey heard Andre say, "She's only fifty-nine!"

Zoey's phone chimed with a message she assumed was from Aviv, but she didn't check it. She was approaching Margaret, shouldering past the few people who'd chosen to enjoy the festival from under the platform, including several who were curled up under there either asleep or passed out.

Margaret made eye contact with her and Zoey started to ask what she'd found.

"HEY!" yelled Margaret. "GRAB HER! SOMEONE GRAB THAT WOMAN! THAT'S ZOEY ASHE!"

Zoey was so startled by this that she didn't react at first.

"I . . . what?"

"You need to get out of there," said Echo in her ear. "Any direction, as fast as you can."

A random drunk guy grabbed Zoey by the jacket, though he seemed to have no idea why he was doing it.

"Did she steal something from you?" the drunk asked Margaret, who was hobbling her way toward them.

"Where is she?" Margaret asked, shouting to be heard over the crowd. "Where's Rose?"

"I don't know!" replied Zoey, struggling to free herself from the drunk who had, it turned out, incredible grip strength. "Let's figure it out together!"

Back on the stage, the band's lead singer seemed to be leading the crowd in a prayer for the missing woman. The Aviv-bot rolled up. A frustrated girl was trying to get it to dispense a drink for her.

"Who is he?" Margaret asked.

"Who's *who*?"

"The psycho you sold her to!"

"We didn't!" screamed Zoey. "And in fact, I don't even think she's being held captive! The first one who got taken, whose mutilated body was sprayed across the buildings downtown? She was just here, she ran away! This is a stunt, all of it."

Several onlookers had gathered around now, apparently searching for entertainment since the concert was, at the moment, on hold.

Another text came in and Zoey pulled out her phone. Immediately a bystander wrenched it from her hand.

"Hey! Give that back!"

"She's been messaging somebody!" said the kid who'd taken the phone, gleefully inserting himself into the drama. "Who is 'Aviv'?"

"That," said Margaret, "is the man who tried to kill Leonidas Damon at the debate."

The lack of recognition on the face of the phone thief told Zoey that he had no idea who Leonidas Damon was, or why he was debating, or why someone would try to kill him, or if he'd even heard the old woman correctly. All he knew was that this all seemed very dramatic and important and he definitely wanted to be a part of it.

Zoey yelled, "Everybody calm down! This is all a misunderstanding—"

While she was speaking, the band had apparently decided to continue with the concert, tearing into their next song, "Burn It All." The vocalist howled,

They wear the teeth of the saints like pearls around their necks
The skin of the innocent turned to shoe leather
Their lairs keep tainted, blighted girls, bound for sex
The sins of men, sure they're so clever
Burn it all
Burn it all
We're coming to burn it all down (x12)

Oddly enough, the song didn't seem to bring a calming energy to the situation. The crowd was bouncing again, the music rumbling through the earth at Zoey's feet. It seemed clear that no meaningful conversation was possible at this point.

"What do the messages say?" shouted Margaret to the kid who'd stolen Zoey's phone.

"The last one says 'Climb on.'"

No one had any context for what that could mean, including Zoey. Then she turned to the yellow Aviv-bot, which beckoned to her with its spindly arms.

She ran and jumped onto its back.

The robot took off through the crowd, going way faster than Zoey would have thought possible, or preferred. People were diving out of the way, though at least they could see it coming—the Aviv-bot was heading away from the stage, meeting everyone in the crowd face-first.

"Where are you going?!?" shouted Zoey, though she had no idea if Aviv could hear her from inside the robot and had no means to see his reply if he texted one.

In her ear, she heard Will say, "What is she doing?" to someone else.

Zoey sensed she was being followed by multiple angry pursuers, though it was a little hard to tell because people were getting angry everywhere. "Burn It All" had reached the midpoint's three-minute-long guitar solo, during which the entire stage was engulfed in holographic fire. She and Aviv were rolling past one of the amp towers and fans were climbing up, yanking off hunks of paneling, and peeling plastic shielding from around the poles.

The band blasted into the next verse.

We'll rip down their mansions and splash the gasoline
They'll cry and they will beg, promise to reform
We'll flick down the matches and laugh at the screams
They'll fry in our pit, condemned by the unborn

The harvested plastic shielding made for convenient clubs and members of the audience were indiscriminately smacking each other with them. There was a new cheer from another part of the crowd. From the back of her yellow robot steed, Zoey turned to see the infield campgrounds, now visible between the stages.

Something in there was on fire. Several things, in fact.

The problem, as Zoey vividly remembered from the hologram model of the festival setup, was that they were heading toward the North gate, either because that's where Violet had gone, or because Aviv was just trying to get them out of the developing riot, or both. But leading to the North gate was also the thoroughfare that separated the East and West crowds. As each side was stoked into a frenzy, this is where they would clash and cooler heads, Zoey thought, would almost certainly not prevail. She and Aviv would be rolling right through a war zone.

Fortunately, the song "Burn It All" had run its course, ending with the lead guitarist setting his guitar on fire and smashing it on the stage. Unfortunately, he was quickly tossed a new guitar and then launched into another song called "No One Will Mark Their Graves."

After a haunting intro, the singer crooned,

> One day a child
> With a dirty smile
> Will dig happily in the ground
> And she'll say, "Mommy, look what I have found
> "Strange white stones, of all shapes and sizes
> Thousands, more than I can count"
> Mommy will say, "Those are the bones of the devil's minions,
> The liars and the fornicators, the abortionists and thieves
> Now they lie beneath our golden streets
> Forgotten like discarded tumors, so we could begin again"

Then the guitar kicked in for the chorus, and the energy rippled through the crowd like a wave.

> When justice comes, they will fall like grass
> And no one will mark their graves
> No one will mark their graves
> I said, NO ONE WILL MARK THEIR GRAVES

The crowd-control barriers along the path north had been knocked over and were being torn apart, the thin vertical bars instantly turned into weapons. Revelers were pouring across from west to east and becoming rioters in the process, smacking each other with pieces of the festival they'd salvaged. Zoey and Aviv were rolling right into the flashpoint of the chaos and Zoey noted someone had already set fire to one of the piles of overflowing garbage from the malfunctioning trash cans.

A young man, who seemed simultaneously enraged and enraptured, saw Zoey riding on the vending bot and decided it looked like fun so he jumped on and, immediately after, so did two of his friends. Zoey yelled at them to get off, as if that demand would make sense in any possible context. The weight stalled the Aviv-bot entirely, then the guys all started rocking it until it toppled over, flinging Zoey to the ground in the process. She crawled over and yelled at the robot, asking if it was okay, which probably made the other rioters think she was more drunk than any of them.

They kicked and bashed at the cooler on its back, where the energy drinks were stored.

"Be careful!" she yelled. "There's a guy in there!"

"STOP HER!" came a voice from behind.

Zoey turned to find Margaret Mull rolling toward them on an electric mobility scooter. No one was trying to jump on board *her* thing.

The Aviv-bot used his robot arms to right himself, knocking a few of the drink looters aside. Margaret rolled to a stop.

"Where are you going, dear?" asked Margaret.

"Well, for one," replied Zoey, shouting to be heard over the chaos, "I'm getting out of the riot!"

She got to her feet, trying to calculate what exactly would happen if she tried to jump back on Aviv and take off again. Every possible outcome was some combination of tragic and stupid.

"Then that's what we shall do," said Margaret as loudly as she could manage. "You and I are going to go somewhere we can talk, and you are going to tell me what I need to know. As soon as that poor woman is found and brought home safe, well, we'll work out what needs to be done after that."

She held up a pair of thick black bracelets. They were incapacitation cuffs that, in addition to binding the wrists, could subject a victim to anything from paralysis to extreme pain, depending on what features Margaret had sprung for.

"Turn around, put your hands behind your back."

"Lady, you are not the police, and you are not arresting me."

"I am not going to give you the chance to pull out some gadget and make a break for it."

"And I'm definitely not letting you shackle me in the middle of a massive crowd that wants to tear me to pieces."

There were flailing, shouting rioters all around them, but a specific pack of angry dudes had arrived in Margaret's wake. Well, some of them were angry, some seemed amused; it seemed half of them still weren't sure if this was real or some kind of live role-play thing for Blink, or what. The important thing was that they intended to proceed in the same manner regardless. Back on the stage, the band had exploded into a new song, one Zoey was unfamiliar with. The chorus was something about the fall of Babylon and though she couldn't make out specific words, she felt like she pretty much had the idea at this point.

Margaret made a move toward Zoey, who stepped back. The yellow Aviv-robot quickly rolled over to get in between Zoey and the advancing woman. Margaret tried to step around it and Aviv reached out to grab her with one of the rudimentary, designed-only-to-hold-energy-drinks claws. The detective jerked away and raised her umbrella. She pulled at the handle and out from it emerged a narrow blade, a glint of blue electricity flashing along its length.

She whipped it at the Aviv-bot. *Through* the Aviv-bot.

Sparks flew. A glowing wound of molten plastic had formed across the robot's torso. The animated logos went dark and its spindly arms went limp. It held like that for a moment . . .

And then the top half of the robot slid off and tumbled to the dirt.

The rioters around them cheered the latest destruction.

Zoey screamed.

She rushed over to the severed upper half of the robot on the ground, which made no sense because if half of Aviv was in there then it wasn't like she could render aid. Finding nothing inside, she jumped up to look into the remaining lower section of the yellow vending bot, praying she'd find Aviv crouched down below where his costume had gotten sliced in half.

It was empty. Just smoldering bundles of severed wire and a few cables spurting hydraulic fluid. Aviv was not inside and, presumably, never had been.

A guy near Zoey said, "Dude, was that your robot or something?"

Margaret sheathed her blade, then lunged over and snatched Zoey by the elbow. She tried to slap one cuff around Zoey's left wrist before Zoey yanked it away.

"No! We're not doing this! My people are on their way, you know they are, my bodyguard and all the rest! I don't want to hurt you."

"Your people are bogged down with the riots," said Margaret, "and will continue to be for some time unless they intend on landing a helicopter in the middle of the crowd. So allow me to return the sentiment: *I* don't want to hurt *you*. But I will, if it means saving Rose."

The old woman started to point her umbrella. Zoey shoved Margaret and turned to make a run for it, imagining a slapstick chase in which she would have to run from an old woman pursuing on a mobility scooter. Zoey made it about two steps before slamming into a wall of men who latched onto her, a combination of guys who'd been following the drama and probably some new ones who just saw the young woman in a leather jacket assault an old lady.

"Are you okay?" one of them yelled to Margaret. "What's going on?"

Margaret made some attempt at an explanation, but just then another roar went up in the distance. In the infield, the beehive was now aflame. The light of that blaze would likely be visible for miles, held aloft like a torch in the center of the madness. And with that, it seemed a silent message had gone out to the frenzied crowd: there was no turning back.

The men holding on to Zoey's arms thus didn't need to hear Margaret's story. What they knew was that the festival masses had collectively decided to tear apart the venue and that Zoey was a part of the venue somehow, that one way or another, she represented what it stood for. A voice in her earpiece was offering urgent instructions but Zoey was unable to focus. The rioters had swallowed her up and there was a horrific moment when the drunken-riot hive mind was trying to decide exactly what to do with her. After a shouted, slurred debate that Zoey could in no way understand, a decision was made to drag her off in one direction—toward what, she didn't know. Margaret followed, insisting they turn Zoey over to her, trying to explain she was conducting a citizen's arrest. But the rioters weren't in this for justice, they were in it for fun, and Zoey thought it was kind of weird that the old woman hadn't picked up on that by now. Then Zoey saw where they were dragging her and tried to put her heels down, to skid herself to a stop.

There's a kind of gleeful creativity that manifests in riots, where every individual member feels like, for the first time in their lives, they're acting with impunity, the way calories don't count on vacation. They suddenly have an audience cheering every cruel impulse, so it becomes a rapid-fire contest to see who can come up with the best/worst idea. As such, they were hauling Zoey toward the row of portable toilets, several of which had been overturned in the riot and were spilling raw sewage and blue chemicals into the dirt. She thrashed to get away from them, but that just triggered laughter—her thrashing was part of the game they were playing, the best part. It wouldn't be fun if she *wanted* to go into the swamp of human urine, vomit, and feces.

There was a commotion from behind her and from that direction came approaching lights and a flurry of bodies lunging out of the way. A black motorcycle skidded to a stop and DeeDee leaped off, her yellow eyes glowing.

"Let go of her."

The men stopped dragging Zoey but did not let her go. This was a riot, they were surrounded by a swirling mass of humanity in the act of shouting and breaking things, under the soundtrack of a live band singing a song about pulling down the towers of the wicked. Hadn't this woman in the gleaming black costume gotten the memo? This was the hour of chaos.

DeeDee approached, her hands at her sides, fingers extended and immobile. Margaret shuffled up behind her.

"I'm afraid you'll have to wait in line," said the old woman, "whoever you are."

The detective aimed her umbrella.

DeeDee spun on her. "Who the hell are you?"

"I am just a citizen looking to see that justice is done. I don't want to hurt you, young lady, but I do have the means and I will not leave here without Ms. Ashe in my custody."

Ignoring her, DeeDee gestured to Zoey with her stiff, outstretched fingers. "Come on."

The men holding on to Zoey still didn't let go.

Margaret stepped forward, brandishing the umbrella. "This is your final warning. Don't make me—"

DeeDee raised one hand and swept it through the air, delivering a backhand slap that knocked Margaret to the ground.

She spun back toward Zoey's captors. "Let. Her. Go."

This time, they seemed too stunned to do it.

DeeDee stepped forward and backhanded a dude hard enough that he kind of flipped in midair and landed on his face. Without waiting to see if this changed the rest of the captors' minds, she backhanded another guy, and another, sending them flailing into the dirt.

Now free, Zoey and DeeDee pushed toward DeeDee's motorcycle, DeeDee slapping a path through the crowd. *WHAP! WHAP! WHAP!*

DeeDee jumped onto her motorcycle and Zoey climbed on the back, hanging on for dear life and wondering how DeeDee steered the thing with her nonworking hands. It turned out it just steered itself. They flew through the riot and out the North gate, DeeDee occasionally reaching out with her free hands and slapping fools along the way.

CHAPTER
21

THE FENCE AROUND THE festival grounds did not mark the boundaries of the festivities, only the line between paying and nonpaying attendees. Outside the fence were the tents and RVs of travelers who were happy to experience the vibe from a distance. They were most dense around the North gate, as that's where one could find all of the vendors selling the contraband that wasn't allowed in the festival itself, often intended to be consumed right there at the gate. As DeeDee's motorcycle rolled through it, Zoey thought the haphazard arrangement of dusty vehicles and temporary structures had the look and feel of a postapocalyptic settlement. At the moment, it was welcoming a flood of refugees from the festival who weren't into the riot portion of the evening. Meanwhile, the next bands had taken the stage and were playing right through the chaos.

DeeDee and Zoey rode through the shuffling masses until they arrived at a row of neon-lit trailers surrounded by more pink tents. The "entrance" to the ramshackle-but-festive encampment was marked by a pair of weathered animatronic mannequins portraying women in stripper garb half-heartedly undulating like even they couldn't work up the energy to fake enthusiasm. DeeDee turned in, passing several very tired-looking sex workers who were wearing too little clothing for the chilly night. They sat on the ground and browsed their phones or dozed in lawn chairs. A few stood atop the trailers to get a better vantage point on the riot playing out within the festival grounds, most of them smoking cigarettes and seeming somewhat bored by it.

DeeDee parked and said, "Follow me," as if Zoey had some other option.

"Give me a minute," said Zoey, who stopped and did her breathing, trying to calm nerves that were still humming from having almost been torn to pieces by a deranged riot hive mind.

Zoey tapped her earpiece. "Are you guys there?"

No answer. She couldn't remember the last time she'd heard from the Suits. Maybe the earpiece had gotten broken in the chaos, or maybe they were busy, or maybe everyone was dead. Zoey reached for her phone and then remembered that it'd gotten stolen by some guy in the crowd, who was now either stomping it to pieces or sifting through every message she'd ever sent or received, scouring for any dirt that would be valuable to a tabloid.

Zoey followed DeeDee after properly reassuring herself that her legs worked. They got only mildly curious glances from the sex workers and it seemed clear that DeeDee was familiar to them. They passed the neon-lit trailers and were now walking among makeshift tents, presumably where the residents slept in between shifts. Everything stank of urine and wet trash. All along the ground were discarded Iso patches, purple and pink and red. Slap one on and it would dispense the drug into your bloodstream at perfect intervals to keep the euphoria humming for about eight hours, until it was time for a new patch. Within four hours without one, you'd feel like you had the flu. Four hours after that, your insides would spasm and twist until there was nothing left in your bowels. When you took on an Iso habit, Zoey had been told, it was like you'd had a major organ removed and only those colorful patches could replace its function.

DeeDee said, "I see the disgust on your face. You know, Leo Damon got famous coming to places like this? Getting the trash and human waste on-camera, saying, 'See, look at these subhumans, living like animals, wallowing in filth.' Like anybody wants to live like this, like they're getting away with something."

Zoey said, "You could get a dozen Ivy League lawyers, make them live out on a patch of land cut off from their money, get them hooked on opioid patches, and within a day it'd look just as bad. No trash-pickup services, no running water, no sewer lines. Things turn messy fast."

DeeDee kicked one of the discarded patches with a shiny black boot.

"The dealers are across the way, over in those trucks. The clients come, they pay, the sex workers go right over and buy the patches. The 'circle of life,' as your friend Will likes to call it."

"What are we doing here? Do you think Violet escaped here?"

"She's somewhere around here, hiding from us. So here's the question: How do you feel about the men who come to this camp, the tourists who see visiting the desert whores as part of the exotic Catharsis Music and Arts experience? Would you date a guy who did that?"

"Around here, it's hard to find a guy who *hasn't* paid money for something. If not this, then a dancer in a club who'll throw in a little extra for the right tip, same with the massage parlors. It's just the way it is."

"So how would you feel about a guy who rolled up here and, instead of paying in money, found a woman in a state of withdrawal and offered a patch in exchange for a blow job?"

"No. That's different."

"Is it? A lot of the ones you see here are homeless, when they're done here they'll just move to a different tent, or some scumbag's sofa, or one of the abandoned buildings in the warehouse district. So how would you feel about a man who went there with a bag of fast food and offered to trade it for sex? Or on some cold night in February, he found a teenager on the sidewalk and said he'd offer them a night in his warm apartment if they let him do whatever he wanted?"

"Now you're talking about coercion, people doing things because they don't have a choice."

"But if you pay them in money and they in turn use that to buy food, or shelter, or drugs, then that's fine? Seems to me like you're using the money to hide the reality of what's going on. You know the name Tawny Morris?"

"No."

"Died right over there, last night. The selling point of those Iso patches was that you couldn't overdose and maybe that was true, *if that's all you were doing*. But combine it with almost anything else, like some coke to try to offset the drowsiness, and it can stop your heart, just like that. Tawny died in a puddle of her own mess. No headlines, no outrage, no salacious video blasting from the skyline, no flock of amateur detectives trying to pin blame. Somebody in a city van came and scooped her up, she's probably piled in an overstuffed morgue somewhere. But hey, at least somebody found her before the animals got to the body and chewed it up."

"That's terrible."

"That happens all the time. And it never becomes a citywide obsession like your three white victims. Because these were killed by the system and the system doesn't have a scary mask, it doesn't send letters to taunt the cops. So who cares, right?"

"This all sounds like something I could have heard in one of Leonidas Damon's speeches. Do you want to make sex work illegal? Crack down on the drugs?"

"If some college girl wants to take her clothes off on-camera for beer money, that's none of my business. If some failed actress earns two thousand dollars as an escort for oil sheiks and tech bros, laughing at their jokes for an hour at a restaurant before going up to do the deed, well, she's probably making more than she'd make in any other job she could get. But some of the ones you see here have been hustling since they were ten years old. They've been hooked on synth opioid blends for almost as long and they can't get any other jobs because nobody wants to hire a junkie. You and your people can sit in leather chairs and sip Scotch and talk about supply and demand and the marketplace, but here's the part your man Will Blackwater won't tell you: The people you see out here will likely never be doctors or investors, they'll never be big earners or consumers. They have, according to the rules of the marketplace, negative value. Which means their dying *is the marketplace working as intended.*"

"So what would you do? If it was up to you?"

"Unfortunately, I don't have the privilege of sitting around in fancy rooms dreaming up what I want the whole world to look like. I have real people, flesh-and-blood individuals, with names, who have real, immediate, complicated problems. Individual problems, different from one to the next, that'll take the rest of their lives to solve. They've been buried so many layers deep that you can't fix it by just writing a check or passing some new law. Though writing that check definitely wouldn't hurt."

They arrived at a tent with the entrance closed, guarded by a striking young man in a spectacular wig. He had a long cigarette holder in his teeth and, sitting at his feet, was a filthy, smiling golden retriever.

DeeDee said, "Hey, Shep. We know she's in there. We just need to talk."

"Back off," replied Shep, "or I'm gonna sic my dog on you."

The golden retriever panted, eyes wide, looking back and forth at the strangers to see who would pet him first.

"Will Blackwater isn't here," said DeeDee. "His scary-ass team isn't here. But they're gonna be here. What we have now is Zoey. She's just a regular person, who came here straight from the trailer parks. Zoey, show him your teeth."

Zoey pulled back her lips.

"See?" said DeeDee. "Got trailer-park teeth. She just wants to know what's going on and she'll buy everyone here a shiny new car if you tell her a sad enough story."

Shep was unmoved, but the tent flap behind him was flung open from the inside and Violet stepped out.

"I'll talk to you," said Violet, "but away from here. If the Suits show up, I don't want them disrupting business. Come on."

Violet led them out of the camp, toward as private a spot as she could find. They arrived at a little rocky hill that wasn't ideal for pitching a tent or parking an RV, so they had it to themselves. It also gave them a nice view of the festival, which was now wall-to-wall chaos, lit by a smattering of bonfires and the towering beehive inferno in the center.

"The other two missing women," Zoey asked, "Iris and Rose, are they okay? The message from Rose you just played, that's fake, right?"

"They're physically safe, yes. Or at least they were, until I blew it."

"'Blew it' how? By getting caught, you mean? I don't intend to ruin whatever you're trying to do, I just want to understand it."

"All three of us are in a program, to get us out. We'll get new identities, in another city."

"And this required faking your deaths and freaking out the whole country?"

"If we stayed, what you're seeing in those videos and all that would be real."

"So this is Leo Damon stuff? The whole thing about how sex work exposes women to violence? Is he paying for this?"

Violet scoffed. "Leonidas Damon can go drink a sewer for all I care. This isn't about some abstract threat. We're going into protection because we're being targeted by a specific person."

"Who?"

"You know who."

"Are you implying Rex Wrexx threatened you?"

"I'm not *implying* it. He spelled out in vivid detail what he would do to us. All three of us. He said he was going to give us 'jewelry' to wear. It was made of thin wire, with this buckle thing that pulls the wire tight. He said he'd put them around our necks and when he pushes the right button—"

"It strangles you," said Zoey. "Or worse. I've seen one before."

"He said maybe he'd also have us put them on our wrists and ankles like bracelets, that'd we'd keep them on forever. Tamper with the wire, he said, and it automatically snaps closed, snipping off the hand or foot. The idea was that we'd walk around the rest of our lives, never knowing. That at any moment, if the mood struck him, he could just clip off a limb. Or strangle us, or lop off our heads."

"Jesus Christ."

DeeDee said, "I told you."

"So someone sneaked the three of you to safety."

"Clarence did," replied Violet. "No one else would help us."

"I'm sorry, who is Clarence? There are too many names in my life, I can't keep them straight."

"Clarence Crockett? He was manager at Chalet for a while?"

DeeDee said, "He's the one who got fired after the incident with Lyra."

Ah, thought Zoey, as things became just a little clearer, kind of. This was the guy who'd refused to ban Wrexx, setting this whole nightmare in motion. The guy Zoey had, at one point, thought might be their mysterious psychopath.

"So . . . he helped you because he felt guilty about the Wrexx thing?"

"And because he decided the entire industry is rotten," replied Violet, "and your company, specifically."

"Okay, fine, but why not just have you disappear? Why make a big production out of it? Isn't that just drawing attention?"

"It costs money to make someone disappear, if you don't want them to be spotted on Blink five minutes later. Clarence knew people who could make that happen but in exchange, he wanted to do, well, this. He had a whole storyline planned out. We just wanted to get out of town, Clarence wanted to turn it into a show. He has aspirations in Hollywood, I think. Or something, when he starts talking it's hard to tell whether he's really enthusiastic or just coked to the gills."

"Echo told me he moved away to become a porn star or something."

"Producer, not star. He makes gore porn, that's why he knew how to do all of the effects."

Zoey almost asked what "gore porn" was but figured she could just guess from the name.

She tried to think her way through it. "So . . . I get why this guy hates our company and had Rose basically blaming us in the last broadcast. But who was supposed to be the killer in the final reveal?"

"There wasn't going to be a reveal. Clarence can explain it better than I can, he has a whole pitch. Something about how it's indicting the system, not one bad apple."

"And that this all plays into the hands of the Nazi candidate for mayor, that doesn't bother any of you?"

"As far as I can tell," said Violet as she watched some new object catch fire over at the festival grounds, "politics is just a bunch of people yelling that if you don't do what they want, regardless of whether it's good for you, then that means a monster gets elected. So you have to do whatever they say, just to avoid the monster? No, I'm over that. None of these people care about us."

Zoey wanted to disagree but struggled to think of how.

Instead, she said, "Correct me if I'm wrong, but it seems like this puts my people in a position where we either continue the lie in the name of keeping the three of you safe—a lie that makes us culpable because of this claim that we intentionally sold you into murder—or we expose the truth, which exonerates us but puts you three in danger. Do I have that right?"

"Is that your people now?" said Violet, looking skyward. She was reacting to the sound of a helicopter.

"Yeah. I mean, let's hope so."

The aircraft lowered itself into a hovering position above a clearing not far from the encampment. It fired out from below it a ring of red lights that planted themselves in the ground, forming little holograms that projected a spinning message:

WARNING
STAY BACK
LANDING AREA
RISK OF INJURY OR DEATH

. . . which scattered the spectators who'd gathered there.

As the aircraft landed, Zoey said to Violet, "If you don't feel like talking to them, you might want to get moving."

"What are you going to tell them?" she asked, eyeing the helicopter warily.

"Nothing they don't already know or suspect."

Violet disappeared among the tents, leaving Zoey alone with DeeDee while they watched the helicopter rotors slow to a stop among the cloud of kicked-up dust.

Wu arrived first from the helicopter contingent, holding out a phone for Zoey.

"Oh," she said, "you ran out and got a replacement already?"

"No, that is your phone, I retrieved it."

"You took it from the random guy in that crowd of a quarter-million screaming weirdos?"

"It's a long story."

Zoey thought she detected something in his tone. "Are you mad at me?"

"Would you care if I was?"

"Oh, don't say that. I'm sorry, the moment got the best of me. I'll give you a bonus."

"Do you even know how much you pay me?"

"No. Go to the accounts person and, just, reward yourself a bonus. However much you want."

"It's fine."

"No, it's not. You guys have probably been scrambling ever since I jumped off the stage and now I feel terrible. You must feel like you're protecting a hyperactive child. Do you want a car? You can have one of the fancy cars in the garage."

"You've offered me one before and no, it's fine. It's part of the job."

Will arrived next and said, "Zoey, if he wanted a boring client he'd go find one. So, Violet is alive, I assume the other two are as well?"

"She says so. I'll tell you on the ride back. It appears we have an impossible decision to make. Is my mom on the helicopter?"

"Your mother left to go to an afterparty in the city with the band Vampire Toilet. I know this because her only parting words were, 'Tell Zee I'm going into town with Vampire Toilet.' You can decide yourself how concerned you should be, but at least she's not out in the chaos."

Echo arrived next, eyes fixated on said chaos. Andre was close behind her, his phone in his hand, browsing feeds from within the riot.

DeeDee gave Will a look. "Your little festival has turned into a war zone. Funny how easily even somebody like you can lose control, isn't it?"

Will sipped his drink and said, "It is. This all happened a full twenty-two minutes earlier than our model indicated. The Rose hoax acted as a catalyst."

"Are you really going to pretend this is all part of your grand design?"

Zoey said, "Oh, you have no idea."

Will nodded toward the madness. "The beehive is coated in a flammable material. Easy to light, makes a bright, beautiful flame. The coating burns off after a while and the material that remains is absolutely fireproof, it can't be relit. The objects you see the rioters smacking each other with are panels and pieces of cladding pried from the amp towers and bars taken from the crowd-control barriers. It's all made of a rigid foam that creates a nice, satisfying bonk if you hit somebody with it, but if you swing it hard enough to cause injury, it'll shatter."

"At which point," said DeeDee, "the real thugs will just pull the knives out of their boots."

"There are no knives. Nobody gets through the gate without passing through a backscatter scan that will find any weapon or object that could plausibly be used as one. Anyone whose fists could be used for real damage, anyone with augmentations we can detect or military training, has been removed from the crowd, told they'd won a contest and sent to a 'VIP' area. There's a separate one for sex offenders. Drones are tracking every single attendee, if things get too serious in a spot, security converges and hits everyone with calming foam."

"So you wanted this to happen? You whip these people into a frenzy until they tear each other to pieces?"

"No, they'll tear the *venue* to pieces. For a while. And then we'll put a stop to it."

DeeDee watched the bedlam for a moment, then asked, "And how will you do that?"

Will took a sip of his drink. "Watch."

Zoey rolled her eyes. "DeeDee, you shouldn't just ask Will to explain things to you, he likes it too much."

As they watched, the entire sky in front of them erupted in light. A formation of drones over the festival grounds had fired up floodlights that bathed the world in a harsh blue/white glare. Authoritative female voices blasted from speakers, announcing that due to the rioters' irresponsible behavior, the festival was being shut down and no other acts would be taking the stage.

Then, around the perimeter of the festival grounds, came dots of flashing red and blue lights. The colors were intended to suggest police, even though they were attached to completely privately owned, tank-sized riot drones. Fifty of them rolled into the festival grounds, spraying a stream of white fluid, an extremely cold, sticky concoction that sapped the strength from limbs and, in general, made any kind of vigorous action difficult if not impossible. It also formed a muddy slime on shoe soles that was slicker than ice, allowing for the target to stand or shuffle away at a measured pace, but anything more would cause them to wind up flat on their ass. Zoey knew all of this because of a lengthy presentation she'd been forced to sit through months ago. This included a live demonstration of the "calming foam" conducted in the courtyard of the estate, after Zoey had implied to Andre, who'd been running the presentation, that she didn't see how it could work.

"Oh, nice," said DeeDee as the unmanned vehicles hosed down the crowd, "you're rolling in with the anti-riot tanks we've watched put down protests in pretty much every dictatorship on earth."

"They look like that, yes," said Will. "People *really* hate those things. Andre, do you still have Blink coverage of the riot up on your phone? It'll be hard to see what's happens next from here."

Andre let them gather around his phone so they could watch as the crowds that had been fighting each other instead swarmed the riot tanks. They were not easy to topple, but it could be done if enough strong backs were united in the effort. It required several lifting on one side while others pulled down from the top. It was something the rioters instinctively did because the tanks just looked top-heavy, it was the obvious strategy. It was almost as if these particular vehicles had been designed with that in mind, complete with an obnoxious loudspeaker demanding that the rioters stop what they were doing.

The four of them watched as the first tank toppled over, hilariously spurting anti-riot juice into the air, belching sparks and smoke as if some crucial mechanism had been damaged inside. A cheer went up across the grounds, from both sides. Elsewhere, rioters copied the same technique on another tank, now with renewed confidence that it could be done. All were united in one purpose: to take down the forces that were there to ruin their fun. The rioters' beef was now with the venue, and the vendors, and the security, with the rich jerks who thought they could tell them what to do. The two antagonist factions of the festival, East and West, had found a common enemy. Just as Echo's model had said they would.

"When it's over," said Will, "they'll have won. The riot drones will be trashed, the venue will be a disaster area. But the rioters will be wet, and cold, and hungry. Some will head into the city to find a place to clean up and sleep, or to keep the party going. Those who remain on the grounds will try to straighten up the aftermath to create somewhat clean and warm places where they can collapse for the night. Contrary to the announcements, the next acts will, in fact, take the stage, ostensibly in defiance of festival organizers. The folk act Canterbury Males will play in the West, party rappers Richest Bitches will play in the East. Not a single violent verse between the two."

"What's their hit song again?" asked Zoey. "Richest Bitches?"

"I'm not familiar with any modern music."

"But you know their hit, because we talked about it."

"I don't recall."

"Say it!"

"We're getting off the subject . . ."

"The song," said Zoey, "is 'I Farted My Panties Across the Room Again.'"

DeeDee said, "I feel like I've just listened to a monologue from the devil. So if you climb far enough up the ladder, is it all like this? Are all conflicts just games arranged by the powerful?"

"Boy, wouldn't that be nice," said Will, "to think somebody is in control? No, this is a contained, managed event, created with a tremendous amount of planning and resources." He nodded toward the chaos. "People come from all of the world for this, year after year, and they never regret it."

From behind them, Echo said, "Zero deaths, so far. Five people knocked unconscious but crews removed them from the chaos immediately."

Zoey turned on her recovered phone, swiped to her messages, and found a string of unreads from Aviv, including several informing her that he was not, in fact, inside the energy-drink robot, and then a whole bunch after that, apologizing.

She just turned it off and stuffed it back in her pocket.

Budd arrived last, pointing a thumb over his shoulder. "Shep back there is saying you promised to buy cars for everybody?"

"Sure," said Zoey. "Why not. I'm totally spent, but we need to figure out what in the hell we're going to do with—"

A commotion went up around the entrance of the camp. Not running and screaming but rather the kind of murmuring dread that comes with a surprise visit from an annoying houseguest. And then Zoey felt her soul try to escape through her navel. The giant, transparent luxury tour bus known as the Fish Bowl was rolling up to the neon trailers of the sex workers' camp, blasting music. It was followed by an entourage of SUVs and, overhead, a cloud of spectator drones.

Zoey groaned. "My god, how are some people so good at arriving at the exact wrong time?"

Will took a drink from his flask. Zoey gave him a look and he silently handed it to her. She downed quite a bit of what remained.

"All right," she said, "let's go over there."

"Haha!" shouted Wrexx at the sight of Zoey and her crew. "You're alive! When you and Alonzo jumped into the crowd! Whoa! That was tit-chili supreme."

Zoey didn't reply, and neither did anyone else. Some of Wrexx's crew were wheeling hand trucks of boxes out of the Fish Bowl and the entourage vehicles. A camera drone hovered in front of Wrexx's face and he got into character.

"Hey, welcome to the members of the Wrexx Army who are tuning in, for the rest of you, we've been having a wild, wild, wiiiiiiild day here at Catharsis, but the energy turned a little too extreme for us so we rolled on out of there. We came right up here among some of the nomads, the hustlers out here keeping it real in tents and campers, on their business 24/7, making a buck to keep food on the table. My crew are rolling out free cases of coffee and donuts and, of course, Wrexx-branded sweatshirts and heated blankets for chilly nights like these. These folks out here, the working girls and the working dudes, they're the real heart and soul of this city."

He was edging closer to Zoey and the Suits as he spoke. Zoey shot a glance toward DeeDee, wondering if she would attack the man on-camera. She saw only her back—DeeDee was storming away, wanting no part of Wrexx's publicity shoot. Echo noticed and went off after her, probably to make sure DeeDee wasn't going to come roaring back to run over Wrexx with her motorcycle.

"It just stinks that they have to spend tonight out here in these cold tents," Wrexx was saying, "but, what can you do? Oh, wait, there is something. What I have here are vouchers for a night in Libertine Suites, downtown! That's in the Livingston Towers complex but let's be real: it's Zoey Towers now. Me and Zoey want to make sure these hustlers have a warm, clean place to sleep tonight, or whenever they want it. You're gonna say this is all political, but me and my girl here . . ."

He put an arm around Zoey's shoulder.

"Our only political position is that it's the people who make this city work, not politicians or clergy or anybody else out there trying to tell others how to live their lives. We have to look out for each other, nobody else is gonna do it."

He paused, clearly waiting for Zoey to chime in.

"I, uh, agree that they should be protected at all costs," said Zoey, "and they should be protected from every direction, from police, from violent customers—"

"Exactly," said Wrexx. "As for Rose, the lovely young woman who we saw in that terrifying live feed tonight, I'd ask all of you out there to send your most positive energy her way, if you have any knowledge about where she's being held or who is behind it, please contact the police, or if you actually want something done, hit me up with a message. Now let's get busy handing out the goods here."

He went off to grab a stack of merch to hand out, followed by his swarm of viewer drones. Well, most of them. Several hung over Zoey, buzzing and pulsing, waiting to see if she would join in the charity effort.

Budd came up behind her and in a grim voice said, "Ms. Ashe, we have an emergency meeting back at HQ to deal with this festival disaster. We need you there. We'll dispatch staff to finish up here."

Zoey nodded and tried to act like she was only reluctantly allowing herself to be hustled away to the helicopter.

As they were lifting off, Zoey said, "Had Wrexx been planning this? Trying to pin me down somewhere so he could get shots of the two of us arm in arm?"

"I don't know," replied Will, "but it tells us one thing very clearly: Wrexx very much thinks you want him dead."

"Well," sighed Zoey, "at least he knows how to read people."

CHAPTER
22

IT TURNED OUT THAT the reason the Suits had gone out of contact with Zoey for a bit was because they were in the process of evacuating themselves, making a public show of escaping the chaos that had, at least from the rioters' point of view, grown out of their control. The key to keeping the ambitions of a mob contained is to provide the illusion that containment has been lost.

This was all planned but was part of what Zoey had missed by avoiding the security briefing twenty-four hours earlier. It had been established years ago that managing the riot portion of the Catharsis festival had to be done off-site, for the same reason that it's hard to steer an ocean liner if you're tied to the propeller. The fenced-off Artists' Retreat, with all of its luxury trailers, would, according to Echo's models, be overrun by rioters about twenty to thirty minutes after order had totally broken down. The trailers were all designed to be destroyed or, at least, taken over, the commoners rejoicing at ransacking the enclave of the elites. All bands and vendors were offered evacuation prior to the point, though some always chose to stay behind and join the riot.

The Suits had thus moved to the remote office, aka the nearest of their businesses with a meeting space: Andre's barbecue restaurant, Carnivore-Tex, located in the trendy East Village neighborhood. It boasted five stories of dining with a whirling column of fire whooshing up through a glass tube in the center of each floor, the flames slow-cooking meat in rotating racks in view of the diners. The ventilation was designed to spread the appetizing scent of roasting meat for three blocks in every direction.

The restaurant had been closed to customers but Andre insisted he knew how to make the best items on the menu himself. So at midnight, Zoey was watching riot cleanup on a series of monitoring tools while eating a fire cloud burger: a hamburger patty covered in the restaurant's custom chili sauce, topped with raw chopped onions, melted butter, and marshmallow creme. Zoey had discovered a rule in Tabula Ra$a, which was that if a menu item sounded like a disgusting prank, it was probably pretty good.

Zoey had scrolled through all of the messages from Aviv, twenty of them, finally ending with,

Aviv:

Please understand the whole thing happened because I decided you were right, I couldn't stay at the festival, I couldn't stay in TR. I had to get out of town but I wanted to spend time with you at the festival and I had another one of my bad ideas.

She replied,

Stop messaging me. I have a one-strike rule for guys who make me the butt of a joke in public.

Then she put away her phone.

"Leo Damon is about to give a speech," said Budd. "From the festival grounds."

"In the middle of the night?" asked Zoey from around her burger. "Do tourists think the city's 'sleepless playground' bit is fun? Because it's not! It takes years off your life!"

"He has to do the appearance now," said Andre, "while the grounds are still a mess. It'll be too clean in the morning. He can't let his followers know that there are ways to clean up litter without exterminating the litterers."

"And there are even more viewers up and watching now than on a normal Sunday-night-slash-Monday-morning," added Budd. "The roving packs of expelled refugee revelers who normally alight on the city's bars and strip clubs have all decided to drunkenly scour the city for Rose. They're crawling over any facility that has shipping containers, trying to find one that contains a captive missing woman, generally making a mess wherever they go."

"How long," said Zoey, "until they latch onto some random citizen and declare him to be the Sex Butcher and stone him to death in the street?"

"Our model says there's a fifty percent chance of that happening by sunrise," said Andre.

"Is that a joke?"

"You'll never know."

"I keep thinking I'm going to get to go to bed at some point, but that's not going to happen, is it? It sounds like we're in crisis mode until further notice. Can somebody show me where the coffee machine is?"

Andre gave Zoey a hard stare. "This establishment has a very good coffee machine. It's a commercial Bunn model, the best they make. If anyone is to use it, it will be me."

"Sure, I'm good either way."

"No. You say that, but whenever I hand you a cup of coffee that you didn't make yourself, you take a sip and get this little disapproving look on your face."

"I do not!"

Budd said, "You do. It's, like, 'Ew, these beans were grown at the wrong elevation and breathed on by a depressed donkey.'"

Andre gave her a solemn expression. "This has been a long day and I will gladly crank up the Bunn. But you have to promise not to make a face when you drink it."

"Can't you just turn your back to me?"

"No. I'll feel it in the room, it's a disapproving energy you put out."

Budd said, "It's true. You're just like your old man was with cigars."

"I'll do my best," she said, then looked around the room. "Did we ever hear from Echo?"

"Just the one cryptic message," replied Will, "telling us to leave without her."

"Is she with DeeDee?"

"The message was so cryptic that I don't even know that. It only implied that she would be here at some point and that we should be ready when she arrived."

"Ready for what?"

"It didn't say."

"All right," said Budd, "I know we all feel wrung out right now, but here's Leonidas Damon, who's about to make everything worse."

Budd brought up the feed on the row of wall monitors that, on a normal day, would presumably be blasting a series of sporting events. Damon was speaking to a pack of reporters and a crowd of supporters somewhere on the East side of the festival grounds, surrounded by debris and the orange glow of smoldering trash-fire aftermath.

"First of all," he began, "I want to thank all of the volunteers who have stayed behind to try to clean up this mess. I know it's dark, but you can see around me what condition this place has been left in. If you want to know my opponent's vision for this city, just take a look around. The party is great while it lasts but in the end, you're just left with carnage. Waiting just over there are bulldozers, ready to come in here and push all of this away, where it will be hauled off to the incinerators to provide heat to the city. Well, in this election, that's us. We're the bulldozers."

A big cheer from the smattering of gathered fans.

Zoey heard her phone chime. No doubt a reply text from Aviv, which she ignored.

"What is our city known for?" continued Damon. "As a freak show of crime, of women who are bought and sold like animals, butchered like animals? I can only imagine what the family of young Rose is going through, watching her ordeal turned into entertainment for social media. Because it's all part of the show, isn't it? Well, not on my watch. If you elect me, I will put a thousand new police officers on the street. It's time to put an end to this bloodbath."

More cheers.

"Further, I will close down the artificial-meat plants until inspectors have had an opportunity to examine every step of the production. Families should know what they are feeding their children! And I guarantee, if any nonanimal tissue is discovered, it will be DNA tested and cross-checked with our database of missing crime victims so that we can get closure to some of these families."

"Wait," said Zoey, nearly dropping her burger. "Did he just invent a new conspiracy theory?"

Andre, who was returning with a mug of coffee for Zoey and a huge chunk of peach cobbler for himself, said, "Yeah, he's been testing that one today. Combining the missing girls and the Soylent Black conspiracy into one nonsense stew."

"It's testing very well for him," added Will. "His lead may be double digits at this point."

"With, what is it, thirty hours until the polls open?" said Zoey. "How in the world are we going to submarine his popularity in one day?"

Will didn't reply. Only drank.

"Speaking of which," continued Zoey, "months ago, I seem to remember you guaranteeing that his candidacy wouldn't go anywhere. You said you had dirt on all of the probable candidates."

"We did. But Damon pulled a move that is genuinely hard to counter, from a PR perspective. He tells a story of growing up in a life of crime, addicted to drugs and sex, even hinting that he'd assaulted multiple women before seeing the light and achieving his current moral perfection. The big scandal is that he's lying: his past is as vanilla as they come. He is an utterly unremarkable man who has lived an unremarkable life. He's a newcomer to politics so he has no record, no scandals. He just hasn't done anything, really. Good or bad."

"Echo said my problem is I'm a pie-in-the-sky idealist who always expects some neat way to solve problems. So is this one of those examples where I just have to accept that we're going to lose? Because it kind of seems like Leonidas Damon has us boxed in."

Budd said, "If you're looking for a ray of hope, there's always the chance that there's a gap between what people will tell a pollster and how they'll actually vote. They may not like the sound of hearing themselves say they're voting for chaos and human meat in the burgers, but might vote that way on Tuesday. Which is tomorrow, as of a few minutes ago."

"The problem," said Will, "is that there are two very different factions in Damon's supporter base. There's the hard-core authoritarians, who want crime crushed at all costs and actually like his vision, then there's the normal people, who assume the hard rhetoric is just talk but that he'll still be tough on crime and generally make the streets safer for the innocent children. In other words, the second group assumes he simply isn't competent enough to be a tyrant, whether he wants to be one or not. So if you try to make him look incompetent, it actually helps with that second group. If you try to make him look a crazy wannabe dictator, it helps him with the first."

Zoey felt her exhaustion turning into despair. "It kind of sounds like our problem is that this is a democracy and more people want Damon to be mayor than Alonzo."

"Maybe," replied Budd. "He's convinced them they're caught in a trap so that they'll chew off their own legs."

"If you could fast-forward them into the future to see what kind of world Damon wants," said Andre, "they'd lose their enthusiasm fast."

"So how far are we willing to go to stop him," asked Zoey, "if nothing else works?"

Will looked like he was about to answer but was interrupted by a banging at the rear door, from the alley. They all went back there and in from the door burst Echo Ling, who was as close to frantic as Zoey had ever seen her.

"Quick," said Echo breathlessly. "Help us get him inside."

Everyone in the room knew not to bog down the process with questions or demands for explanation. If someone on the team insisted they needed your immediate assistance, you assisted. Explanations could come later.

Will, Zoey, and Budd followed her into the alley, where DeeDee was waiting next to a hotel shuttle that they had presumably stolen and/or hijacked. She opened the side door and lying across the seat in the back was Rex Wrexx, bound and gagged. Will took exactly three seconds to absorb what he was seeing, process how it changed their situation, and recover. He and Budd quickly dragged Wrexx inside and restrained him in a chair in the kitchen, which was the room farthest from any windows.

They left Budd to watch him, then everyone else gathered in the dining room, out of earshot.

Will said, "Andre, Wu, would you mind going out and making sure nobody followed them here?"

This was a perfectly sensible idea, but Zoey silently noted that Will also had a tendency to get Wu out of the area whenever he suspected a crime was about to occur. Wu's job was to guarantee Zoey's safety, not to participate in any kind of criminal conspiracy.

After the two left, Echo said, "Wrexx left the camp with a sex worker named Danza, told his team he'd be back before sunrise. We have that long before his people and his fans notice he's late, then some very brief amount of time after that before they start actively looking for him."

"Okay," said Will, seeming to take a moment to calibrate his next words to not sound like criticism. "So, tell me why exactly he is here."

"He was going to kill her," replied DeeDee. "We tailed him when he left. He took Danza to a hotel room—the same joint he was giving out vouchers for—and puts this around her neck."

She handed him a loop of thin, black wire, big enough to be slipped over a head. It was, of course, identical to what Lyra had shown Zoey at the noodle joint.

"It looks like you all know what this is."

"It's a constrictor wire," said Will. "It can be controlled remotely, you activate it and that buckle pulls it tight."

"'Pulls it tight.' Yeah, that's one way to put it. The tiny little power plant in that buckle is tech Arthur brought into the world. The wire is some kind of space-age material."

"It's a nano-filament braid. And we didn't make this, it's something that got out onto the black market. I also think it was extremely convenient that Wrexx chose to go after a new victim on tonight of all nights, right in front of you."

"It was a setup, so what? All Danza did was ask if he was interested."

"On your instruction."

"On her own desire to see Wrexx taken down."

"So after setting up your own sting operation, without running it past anyone, you then kicked in the door of his hotel room with the intention of . . . ?"

"Slapping Wrexx's head clean off his body."

"And I suppose Echo convinced you otherwise."

"I told her," said Echo, "that we'd have no chance of disposing of the body if we did it there, that one way or another, it was to her advantage to get the rest of the team involved, in a less public place."

"I told him I'd kill him unless he took that wire off Danza," said DeeDee. "He refused. We had to get it off her ourselves, after Wrexx was subdued. We had to rig software that would bounce back its signal. See, it's set to check in once every second off Wrexx's vital signs. And could only be loosened based off a deactivation signal from him."

"In other words, it was set to go off if Wrexx were to be killed. Insurance, against us. Something he could hold over our heads if we threatened him. We had to spoof a signal to get it off her or else just tampering with it would have triggered the mechanism and Danza would be dead."

DeeDee said, "So what more do you need?"

"You've sent your message," replied Will. "He knows we can get to him. We tell him to back off, that he's not to indulge this impulse any further."

"You, of all people, should know that a guy like this can't be reasoned with."

Will closed his eyes and touched his forehead with his fingers, a show of exasperation that Zoey had never seen before and that she didn't think was a performance. Just now, for the first time, she understood how utterly exhausted he was.

"DeeDee," he began quietly, "this is our only option. Do you want power? Do you want to affect change, real change? This is what it looks like, it's the long game. You have to think bigger than the monster that's in front of you. Let's go back into the kitchen as a united front."

"Do you think I'm doing this out of mindless rage? I'm doing it on behalf of justice. So what happens if, in the name of justice, I go back there and slap his head clean off his body?"

"You are a member of Alonzo's family. If you kill this guy and that turns his fans against Alonzo, then Damon wins and then who knows what happens after that. We'll have launched a ship that can be very hard to turn around."

"How do you know that losing the election would even stop him?"

"Because it's the one reputation Damon can't have. Nothing else sticks to him—call him a racist, a sexist, a fascist, those words don't mean anything to his supporters. But the one thing he can't be is a loser. And he definitely can't be seen losing to someone like Alonzo. That's the one outcome that would smother his political career in the crib. So now we have to go back there and convince Wrexx to clean up his act and to keep boosting Alonzo for the next two days."

"He's not leaving this restaurant."

"Why? You can't wait two days to go after him?"

"No. Because after the election is over, you'll say I need to give it a bit of time so tensions can calm down. Then once tensions calm down—if they ever do—you'll say, 'don't do it now, we just got people calmed down again.' Then after that, you'll say, 'you can't do it now, it's almost time for the next election.' People like you have been putting off people like me for hundreds of years that way. It'll never be the right time."

Zoey asked, "Echo, if you could magically program Wrexx into your threat-assessment software, what would it say are the odds he kills a woman in the future, if he hasn't already?"

Before she could answer, Will said, "What if we could do the same with Damon, see what happens to women like Violet, and Iris, and Rose once he's in power? Because we do have a model showing we can't win without Wrexx's help. Hell, at this point, it's a stretch that we can win *with* his help."

DeeDee leaned close to Will. "If Wrexx had hurt someone you cared about, he'd already be dead. Do you want to know how I know that?"

"And do you want to know how many times I've resisted the urge for payback in favor of playing the long game?"

"Do *you* know how many of my people have died waiting for your people to play your long game?"

"We can't let you do this, DeeDee. You know we can't. Alonzo knows. Do you think we installed your implants without adding a fail-safe to shut them down?"

"Do you think I allowed you to install these implants without overriding your fail-safe? Your unfailing assumption that you're smarter than everyone else is going to be what gets you killed someday. Maybe soon."

They stared each other down. Zoey held her breath.

"Well, hold on now," said Budd, who had at some point silently emerged from the kitchen. "Are you two so dug in that you can't see that you've already arrived at an agreement? Will asked for two days, or at least that's what I heard, after which DeeDee can do whatever she wants. Further, DeeDee just established that even if Will were to renege, he can't physically prevent her from acting. All he can do is shake his fist and call her mean names. So there we go: DeeDee holds off for at least two days, at which point no one can stop her from doing as she sees fit. Now, DeeDee, I get that you don't trust Will here, but you trust Zoey, right? If you have a guarantee from her, would that be good enough?"

"During that two days," said DeeDee, "Wrexx will be watched every second. *Every second*. And if he steps out of line—"

"Then nobody here will try to stop you. Are we all agreed?"

Zoey, DeeDee, Will, Echo, and Budd piled into the kitchen and found Wrexx watching the door, looking amused. He was clearly already thinking about how he'd be able to squeeze literally years of content out of this incident.

"Feels good, doesn't it?" said Wrexx as they entered. "Got me tied to a chair, helpless, now you all get to loom over me and feel powerful. There's no high like it, the high of domination. You girls must especially be getting off on this, spending your whole life scared some guy is going to murder you if you set him off, now my hands are tied and you can say anything you want, do anything you want, and I can't strike back." He smirked. "Or can I?"

Budd said, "Can we untie your hands? Are you going to act like a fool?"

"I'll be good."

Echo cut him loose and Wrexx rubbed his wrists.

Will held up the constrictor wire. "We'll make this quick. *This*, has to stop."

A chair had been set legs-up on the counter next to Will. He looped the wire over one of the legs, as if intending to use it as a visual aid.

"We're not asking," said Will. "The women are terrified of you and this . . . *predilection* of yours threatens everything if it gets out. The cops in this city can't be trusted to enforce an order of protection but we're implementing our own, right now. Stay away from the sex workers in this city, just stay away. Whatever need you're fulfilling by playing these games with them, work it out with your therapist. This is not a lot to ask, considering all we're asking you to do is nothing."

Wrexx's gaze shifted from Will to Zoey to DeeDee. Working through something in his head.

He grinned. "The three women, the ones you accused me of abducting, they're alive, aren't they?"

"We're still working that," replied Will, "but they don't concern you one way or the other, not after tonight. Understood? Just go out there, keep doing your thing, and we won't have Leo Goddamn Damon as our mayor when we wake up Wednesday. Can you do that? Can you control this?"

"You accused me of abducting and murdering those women. If they're still alive, you owe me an apology."

"We never accused you of anything," said Budd. "We inquired, the same as we've inquired with dozens of folks in an effort to find our missing employees. What matters now is what you do going forward."

"Then why have I been brought here and treated like an animal?"

DeeDee said, "That loop of wire we pulled off of Danza, do you think we don't know what that's for?"

"It has many uses."

"But for you, it has only one."

Wrexx nodded, always just a hint of that smirk playing across his lips. "I know that was Violet you people were trying to chase down at the festival. I'm thinking that not only are the three whores alive, but that you've been talking to them."

"I'm telling you," said Will, "that line of inquiry is a dead end. If they're still around, you're not going to bother them."

"I never bother anyone who hasn't hurt me first. Who arranged their fake murders? And this thing with Rose, is she just acting all that out in a studio somewhere? There are worried people looking all over for her."

"So we're in agreement?" asked Echo.

"What happens if we're not?"

"Then," interjected Budd, "you will be creating tension and conflict on our side at exactly the time when we should be united against Leonidas Damon. You actively campaigned against him, if he takes office, you don't think he'll find some reason to come after you? We all want the same thing here, unless you want to hurt women, which you've just said you don't want to do, on account of how much offense the mere accusation triggers in your heart. We say hands off, you say you have no urges otherwise." He held out his hands and smiled. "So where's the disagreement?"

"And when he says 'hands off,'" said DeeDee, "he means all women, everywhere on earth. You need to change your ways."

"And if I don't do this to your satisfaction?" asked Wrexx.

"Then one day, you may walk into a shadowy place and not come out of the other side."

"You guys heard her just threaten me, right? What am I supposed to think? You drag me in here, practically kidnapping me, throwing these crazy accusations in my face, and we're supposed to be friends?"

"We're not friends," said Zoey before she was able to stop herself. "I think you're a narcissist and a sadist, I think you've intentionally put yourself into a position where you can hurt women and get away with it. And where it really seems like my father could solve all of his problems by making the right people disappear, I am apparently not allowed to do that. So this is what we're doing instead. We're giving you a second chance."

"And yet, all it takes is another woman with a grudge to falsely accuse me and you'll send your attack dog after me. No trial, no due process."

"I would appreciate it if you stopped treating us like we're stupid. I've been dealing with men like you my whole life, long before I moved out here. I don't want to hear any more pleading and I definitely don't want to hear you playing victim."

"And regardless," added Will, "we're not relying on your better nature to come through. We're relying on you to make a rational decision that this vice of yours threatens to undo your life in many ways. We are also relying on you to recognize that if *we* are making rational decisions, then it is not in our interest to harm you."

"But I've already been harmed. Dragging me in here, accusing me in public. I've been traumatized, my reputation has been damaged."

"To prevent us from just talkin' in circles for the rest of the night," said Budd, "why don't you just tell us what you want. You already know what we want, so what's your demands?"

"I want an apology."

DeeDee scoffed and turned, leaving the room, presumably because it was either that or slap Wrexx's skull right off his body. Once again, Echo followed. Zoey felt herself about to say something and, this time, physically bit her tongue.

Will, in the inflectionless tone that Zoey always found chilling, said, "On behalf of myself and our entire organization, I apologize if you have found tonight's events upsetting."

"No," said Wrexx. "Not from you. I want an apology from the three women, for putting on this charade, for spreading slander about me."

Will had to take a moment to gather himself.

Quickly, Budd said, "But they're not here, so we can't make any promises on their behalf, can we? I assure you, if we find them alive, and if they feel they have something to apologize for, we will do whatever we can to facilitate that. But this is the last day of the campaign. We have events planned from five in the morning until the final votes are counted. Some of us are gonna be awake for more than forty straight hours. If we cry, our tears will smell of dark roast. I know for a fact that you, Wrexx, will be just as busy registering last-minute voters, pushing your people to punch the right name on the ballot, trying to avert the very dark timeline in which Leonidas Damon gets a foothold in politics. Can we go our separate ways, in peace, and do that important work without this other situation getting in our way?"

"We can," said Wrexx. "Just know that I don't consider this resolved until the accusations are cleared up. A man's reputation is all he has."

"Well, now, there's where I do have to disagree. A man's *character* is all he has. If reputation is the only thing keeping a man in line, well, then all he has to do is build himself up a following that'll turn a blind eye to anything but an atrocity committed live in front of their eyes, and maybe even that. And, as we prepare to depart from here in peace, you may have a lingering thought that it's your reputation that will save you, regardless of your actions, that maybe you've got enough fans and guards to keep someone like DeeDee at bay. But you should be aware that I know the names of every single man and woman in your security detail. I know the names of their wives and husbands and girlfriends. I know which ones are loyal to you and which are in it for a paycheck. And what I don't know, I can find out. See, you heard Will's threat there about the metaphorical restraining order and I can see in your eyes that it just makes you more excited, the thrill of defying him and knowing you got away with it. That's part of the fantasy, isn't it? But I am telling you, *we see all*. Whether you go to a hotel, or an alley, or in a cave in the Himalayas, we will know your intentions even before you do. Whatever you got away with when Arthur was in charge, things are different now. Maybe Arthur didn't care too much about the girls getting hurt as long as the money kept flowing. But Zoey is in charge now and when these people get hurt, she's not happy. And when Zoey isn't happy, Will isn't happy. And when Will isn't happy, ain't nobody happy, until things get put right."

It seemed like maybe Wrexx was trying to formulate a comeback so he could have the satisfaction of the last word. And it seemed like Will was ready to respond to whatever Wrexx said by popping his head off his body like a champagne cork.

Before anyone could speak, Wu reentered the room, apparently having finished his lookout and/or decided that the immediate potential for criminal conspiracy had passed.

"All right," said Will. He turned to Wu. "Do we know where DeeDee went?"

"She and Echo are out on the sidewalk having cigarettes, trying to calm each other down."

Will nodded. "All right. Budd, we need to transport Wrexx here back to the festival grounds, or the hotel, or wherever his transparent bus happens to be. You and he will come up with a very reasonable cover story he can give his people or anyone who may have seen him get abducted from the hotel."

"Sounds easy enough."

"That means it won't be. I'm going to go talk to Echo, see if she'll go with you."

Will left the room.

Budd directed Wrexx to stand and said, "My car is down the street. The door is behind you."

Instead of moving in that direction, Wrexx stared down Zoey.

"You know, it seems to me like I've been doing my part in rallying my people to Alonzo's cause. But the last time I checked, he's still running behind. Since it's you people who supposedly run this city, it kind of seems to me like you're the ones who're dropping the ball and trying to put the blame at my feet. If you have something planned that can turn this around, maybe you should let me in on it."

Budd smiled. "It's funny, I've been thinking about that. And I've got an id—"

Zoey never heard the noise that interrupted Budd's words. The blast wave traveled faster than the sound.

CHAPTER
23

ZOEY COUGHED HERSELF AWAKE to find she was in total darkness.

She was lying awkwardly, her face pressed into the floor, her legs twisted around, one arm pinned under her. The air was thick with destruction dust—ash, concrete, and plaster. She thought she could hear trickling water somewhere, but there were no other sounds, aside from the ringing of her ears.

"Hello?" The word came out as a rasp. She coughed again.

She tried to roll over. Something heavy was lying on top of her. Something metal, or wood, or plaster, or all three. Her whole body hurt. She tasted blood in her mouth. She blinked and tried to adjust her eyes to the darkness, still saw nothing. Was she blind? Was she dead?

"Is anyone here?" she said a little louder. "Hello?"

What had happened? Where was she? What day was it?

With time and dedicated effort, she was able to roll over onto her back. The floor under her was concrete. Lying on top of her was, it seemed, a hunk of ceiling and a light fixture. She could move it a little, but couldn't lift it off herself. She thought she might be able to scoot out from under it as there seemed to be some room around her, but in the darkness, she wasn't sure where she would go, or if there weren't worse dangers waiting in the shadows.

That's when she felt the panic start to creep in.

"Hello?!?" she rasped as loudly as she could manage.

No response.

She had been in Andre's restaurant. In the kitchen. But others had been there with her, and now all was silent. Zoey was certain, in that moment, that everyone else was dead.

She wanted to cry but couldn't work up the energy or the moisture. So she just lay there for a moment, feeling around with her hands, seeing if her body was intact. It seemed to be. Her face was wet and sticky. She suspected she had a bloody nose, or a bloody something.

"Hello? Anybody?"

No response. She couldn't think of anything else to say or do.

She sucked in as much air as she could and screamed as loud as she was able. "HELP! SOMEBODY! I'M STUCK IN HERE!"

The last word trailed off into a coughing fit. She tried to think. Who knew she was here? Anyone? What had even happened? Some kind of attack? An earthquake? Did they have those in Utah? Was the whole building wrecked? The whole city? Had there been a nuclear war? How long ago did it happen? Five minutes? Five hours? Five days?

She felt her breath getting short and remembered the woman trapped in the glass box.

Wait.

She heard something. A voice?

She said, "Hello?"

She heard rustling, metal scraping.

And then, "Zoey?"

She couldn't recognize the voice. The word was slurred, mumbled.

"Yes! I'm here! Who is that?"

"Wu." He sounded close.

"Are you okay? What happened?"

"I am . . ." He seemed to be checking something. "I am not bleeding. Not externally anyway." There was some hissing and spitting as he tried to form the words and Zoey thought about Lyra, trying to talk through mangled lips. "Sorry, I am missing some teeth." *Teef.* "Are you bleeding?"

"Uh, a little, I don't think it's bad. I can't see anything. Can you?"

"No. Feel your clothes and floor, for blood."

She did. "Seems all dry. Got some blood on my face but that's not a new feeling for me."

"Can you move? I'm pinned to the floor. There is something on my legs, I think a refrigerator."

"There is some ceiling lying over me but it's not superheavy. I mean, it's not light, either, but I can scoot out from under it, if I have a reason to. I'm able to move all of my limbs."

"Do you have your phone?"

She couldn't believe that question hadn't occurred to her before now. She searched her pockets and the floor nearby.

"No. I think I had it in my hand when whatever happened happened. So it probably went flying."

"Hold on."

She faintly heard rustling again, then her field of vision became about ten percent brighter. She looked to her left and saw light behind a narrow gap, between fallen appliances and hunks of plaster.

"Ooh!" she said. "I can see you, sort of. You're only maybe, seven or eight feet away. Can you call someone?"

"I'm not using the light on my phone, this is a flashlight I keep on my belt. My phone is smashed. It was in my pocket."

"Do you know what happened?"

"Let us see if we can figure it out together. I hear no sounds from the street, which tells me there are many layers of solid material between us and the outside. The refrigerator that is currently crushing my left leg was on the opposite side of the room prior to the event, at least twenty feet away. Which means there was an explosion capable of propelling it that far that originated from the other side of it, which means the alley out back. So that tells me there was a detonation from the alley, perhaps from a car. Either the entire building collapsed on us, or it has partially collapsed and the rest is teetering above us, ready to fall the rest of the way at any moment."

Zoey absorbed all of this and again tried to smother her panic before it could take hold.

"All right," she said. "Do you have any idea of what happened to everyone else? Who else was in the room with us?"

"Rex Wrexx, Budd . . . I believe Will had left the room. Some had gone outside . . ."

"Do you see any sign of anyone else?"

"I see . . . there are human remains nearby, but it is impossible to say whose. It is more than one person."

Zoey stopped breathing. "Wu, nobody else responded when I yelled out, other than you. Is it possible—is it possible that we're the only ones?"

"There is no use in speculating," he said after a suspicious pause. "All we can do is assess our situation. We have breathable air, neither of us have wounds that need immediate treatment, or at least, that can be treated with what we have on hand. We know that emergency crews will be here soon, but do not know how quickly they can excavate us from the rubble, and we have no way of knowing if or when this space we are occupying will become unstable. If the building has collapsed above us—and considering I'm looking at the remains of load-bearing walls, I assume it either has, or is about to—then that means you and I are probably in a spot where two fallen walls have formed a triangle, like a tent, creating this pocket of space. But there are millions of pounds of brick and cement above us, and if things shift, those walls could go flat on top of us."

"Well, now, hold on. If they come to dig us out with bulldozers or whatever, couldn't that accidentally cause the same thing to happen?"

"Yes. I have been on the scene for multiple building collapses and while it is not unheard of to retrieve survivors from the wreckage, the odds are not in their favor. The rescue efforts must be done in a very slow and deliberate fashion, specifically for that reason. It can take days. I heard a story of a man in Haiti who survived for two weeks after an earthquake collapsed his building. But generally, the rules of survival are very clear: If you can get out, do it. Find a window, find a gap, find something. Then once you are out of the building, get as far away from it as you can."

"Okay. Well. You've got the flashlight, so tell me where we're going."

Another suspicious pause.

"Zoey. My left femur is pulverized. My right foot is facing the wrong way. Even if I were to get out, I likely would never walk again. Look my direction, you see the light?"

"Yes?"

"Keep looking." The light shifted around, then streaked across the concrete floor. Wu had slid the flashlight toward her. Zoey had to scoot that way to get in grabbing distance. The light was a tiny little thing, like you'd put on a keychain.

She said, "Got it."

"You will want to move the opposite direction from me, out of the kitchen, away from the source of the blast—"

"Wait, why? Wouldn't the bomb have made a giant hole in the building?"

"The bomb would have created a pile of rubble. But I am more concerned about a secondary device."

"Why would there be a second one?"

"It is very common, the first bomb is intended to draw a crowd of first responders and bystanders, then the second bomb takes them all out after they arrive."

"Jesus, that's evil."

"The farthest from the blast is also where you are most likely to find intact building, including clear doors and windows. That is your best chance. Move that direction, first look for the door to the dining area, then keep going straight until you can feel cool air from outside, or hear street noises. Find a way to mark the floor, or leave a trail of something, if you fear getting turned around."

"And what happens to you?"

"My body will go into shock soon. If you can get out and speak to rescue crews when they arrive, perhaps you can direct them to me."

"And in the meantime, the building could collapse on you. Or another bomb could go off, like you said."

"Just hours ago, I heard you have a discussion about how sometimes there are no perfect solutions. My job is to protect you. I was not able to prevent this attack but I remained alive and conscious long enough to give you these instructions. And that will have to do."

"Oh. So you think you're going to die."

"That is simply the reality of the situation. You don't work in this field without the explicit understanding that this is how you may go. I took on one of the most dangerous assignments in the country, replacing a friend who died in the line of duty. If you make it out, tell Mei that my final act was to try to get you to safety."

"Okay."

"That's my wife."

"I know that. I'm not leaving you to lie there, alone, in total darkness, waiting to get crushed like a bug under a billion tons of bricks."

"Then we both probably die and you will turn my final act into a failure. Go. Now. The longer you wait, the more you put both of us at risk."

Zoey was crying now, silently, trying not to make a big production of it.

She took a deep breath and said, "Okay."

"*Go.*"

"Okay."

"Goodbye, Zoey. Working for you has been . . . interesting."

She took a breath, steadied herself, dried her eyes, made her decision.

"All right. I'm going."

She clicked the flashlight, shining it around to try to get a sense of her surroundings. Then she crawled out from under the hunk of ceiling that had been resting on top of her. It was slow going, propelling herself with her elbows, her body not exactly the ideal shape for sliding along on her belly. She put the flashlight in her mouth to try to keep some kind of clear view of what was ahead.

As she crawled, she felt new pains awakening in her body. It felt like she'd sprained or maybe even broken her ankle, her ears were still ringing from the blast. Her sinuses were burning, her eyes were burning. She felt pain in her scalp and then remembered, almost with amusement, that this was the preexisting wound from the butterfly-witch attack.

She crawled until she reached a dead end, a gap between fallen debris and appliances barely large enough to fit her hand into. She investigated with the light and made a left turn, curled around a fallen hunk of countertop . . .

Then encountered a human arm.

She reached out and shook it.

"You awake?"

Wu startled. "Zoey, you went the wrong direction. Your better chance is—"

"Shut up. I'm not leaving you."

Wu's face was an unrecognizable mess of swelling and blood, it looked like he had been thrown and caught the landing impact face-first.

"Zoey—"

"Shut up. Look, I know how men let their emotions get away from them in situations like this, but in your hysterics you have wound up with this crazy idea that my life is more valuable than yours, when *you have two children waiting for you at home.*"

"I have three children."

"Three! And your plan was to sacrifice yourself because, what, I employ you to do that? Good god, what has capitalism done to our brains?"

"Zoey, look at my leg—"

"Yeah, it's squished, you have, like, a thousand pounds of restaurant-grade refrigerator on it, full of who knows how much additional weight in coleslaw and potato salad and cobbler. Life is full of these little problems we have to overcome. But don't give me that nonsense about how you'll never walk again, considering that my company owns technology that can give you super-legs that will allow you to kick an entire moose across a golf course."

Zoey scooted around so that she was lying next to him. She reached down and found his hand. She squeezed it. He squeezed back.

She said, "Are you scared?"

The longest, most suspicious pause yet.

"Yes."

"So am I. And now I can sense a new fear entering your brain, that you might have to spend your final hours with *the most annoying woman you have ever met.*"

Incredibly, he laughed. Weakly, but enough to send himself into a coughing fit.

"I do not think of you that way."

"Yes, you do, I can hear it in your laugh!"

And so they lay there, in the dark, waiting. Zoey glanced around with the flashlight to see if there was anything useful nearby and happened to notice a length of thin, black wire: the constrictor device DeeDee had taken off Wrexx's would-be victim. It was no longer in a loop, having pulled itself all the way through the buckle. It sat in a pool of splinters next to the hunk of chair leg it had severed, the wood looking like it'd been hacked off in one swing by a strong man with a very sharp axe.

At some point, Zoey fell asleep or passed out. All she knew was that she felt like some amount of time had passed and her body felt different: some new aches, some new numbness, and she was now *incredibly* thirsty. She had the same ringing in her ears.

Wu's hand had gone limp in hers.

She squeezed his fingers. "Hey. You still there?"

No response.

How much time had passed? Why hadn't anyone come? If she had decided to leave Wu, could she have come back with help by now? Should she go ahead and go? Should she check if he is—

She became aware of a noise that, in retrospect, was probably what had woken her up: the sound of rocks bouncing off other rocks. It was growing in volume and frequency, from above them, all around them.

The rubble was shifting.

Zoey held her breath. She felt like she should be doing something, finding a table to crawl under, anything other than just lying still and waiting to be flattened. She clicked the flashlight. Nothing happened. She stupidly clicked the button over and over, shaking it, slapping it.

The rumbling petered out into silence.

Zoey tried to shake Wu awake again. No response. She kept trying.

Nothing.

She cried, forced herself to cut it short.

What now? If Wu was . . . gone, should she leave? Was it already too late? She had no light now and no idea if there was even a clear path to crawl in any direction. She was so thirsty. She had a headache. And somehow, it was the ringing in her ears that was killing her, making her whole body vibrate, as if it was coming up from the floor . . .

She was assaulted by a new, hellish noise. Bricks fell and shattered, sounding like an army was riddling the rickety structure with bullets and grenades. There were pops and cracks and rolls of thunder. Zoey realized that she was screaming, pushing herself up against Wu for comfort, but he was not moving, and somehow that ringing in her ears persisted through it all, growing under the chaos, over the chaos, until the grinding shriek took over the world.

And then light pierced the darkness, blinding her, and the wreckage to her left was pulsing and swirling and flying, like everything was getting flushed down a giant toilet. Concrete dust choked the air. Debris sprayed her face like buckshot.

Out of the swirling chaos came a single headlight in the center of a mass of whirling blades. Aviv's ridiculous basement-drilling machine rolled to a stop about two feet from her legs. The front end clicked open and she expected Aviv to poke his stupid face out. Instead, it swung wide to reveal the interior of the machine was empty aside from a cell phone and a shoebox-sized case covered in warning stickers.

A voice from the phone said, "Zoey?"

She crawled over and grabbed the phone. "Who is this?"

"It's Echo."

"Oh, my god. Oh, my god. Who else made it out?"

"Zoey, digging in has destabilized the structure, our model is saying this space could go flat at any moment. The scan showed Wu was pinned under something, is that right?"

"Yes."

"Is he—is he in a condition to move if you can lift the object?"

"I don't know, Echo. I don't know." She was crying again. "But I want to get him out. I don't want him to get pulverized. I want . . . I want to get him out in a condition where his family can see him."

"Grab that box," replied Echo, knowing better than to argue. "There are instructions on the lid." More bricks rumbled overhead. "Hurry."

Zoey took the phone and the box, then swung the drill door closed so she could see by its headlight. She crawled back toward Wu and popped open the box, which contained a rolled bundle of red canvas and a small black device with vents on it. A crude diagram instructed her to unspool the canvas and slide it under the object she wanted to lift. There were a bunch of warnings she didn't have time to read. She pushed the strip of red canvas under the fallen refrigerator, and hit the one button on the attached device, unsure of what was supposed to happen next.

The device whirred to life, producing a shrill whine that was possibly louder than the drill had been. It was an air pump. The canvas inflated and kept inflating, filling the space under the fallen appliance. It seemed extremely stupid and pointless, you weren't going to lift several hundred pounds of steel and potato salad with a freaking balloon. But then the appliance shifted and yeah, apparently, if you can move enough air, hard enough, you can lift anything. There was suddenly an inch of clearance above Wu's messed-up leg and Zoey was elated, before she realized she had not even a vague idea of how to accomplish Step 2. She needed to drag Wu out and into the boring machine but he was probably a hundred and seventy pounds of dead weight and she barely had room to stand up—

Debris rumbled overhead. Somewhere, something hard and heavy landed on something equally hard and heavy. Everything shook in the aftermath.

The phone, which she'd left on the floor somewhere behind her, was urging her to get out.

Zoey awkwardly tried to crouch and grab Wu under his armpits. She pulled backward with all her weight—

There was an abrupt gasp and a terrible scream.

Wu's eyes flew open.

"Wha—what is happening?!?"

He blinked, disoriented, clearly no idea where he was.

"We have to move! I got the fridge off you! There's an escape vehicle right over there! But I can't lift you!"

Wu did not ask any questions. He started pushing himself back with his hands, scooting along the floor at an excruciating pace.

Something overhead exploded.

Zoey tried to help propel the man along the floor as he scooted backward on his butt, pulling his ruined left leg out from under the refrigerator. He then rolled over and crawled on his elbows, his right foot twisted at a disgusting angle. The two of them moved along like a couple of dying caterpillars until Wu was able to pull himself into the drill, dragging his battered legs behind him. Every step of the way, the cell phone on the floor was yelling at them in Echo's voice to move faster, that the structure was coming down, as if this was somehow more apparent from Echo's vantage point than it was from theirs. It sounded like the very columns that kept the heavens aloft were collapsing.

Zoey, totally oblivious to Wu's howls of pain, had to shove his legs in the last bit to clear the hatch. Wu pushed himself to the side as well as he could and said, "COME ON!"

It had actually not occurred to Zoey until that moment that she also needed to cram herself in there, it didn't look like there was half as much room as needed for that. But he was right: there wasn't going to be time for a second trip.

She crawled in and it was like she was being born in reverse, pushing herself into a narrow canal that had Wu on one side and the thin padding of the cramped drill machine's interior on the other. She wormed her way in, realizing only after she was mostly inside that she should have gone feetfirst so she could close the hatch. But just as the hatch had opened on its own, it now closed on its own, pushing her feet the rest of the way in. Zoey was pressed up against Wu so tightly that she couldn't expand her chest to breathe. A series of electronic voices spoke but she could not hear them, as it now sounded like they were inside an avalanche.

The machine vibrated and the motors whined and Zoey wondered if it would have to turn around to drill them out, but of course, it was made to go both directions. The spinning array of bits on the other end went to work. The interior was soundproofed as well as could probably be expected, but the combined cacophony of the falling building and the grinding drill was still deafening. Worse, the trip seemed to be taking an eternity. Had they gotten stuck? Had the mechanism failed? Had the entire building now fallen on them, creating a mountain of concrete that would take weeks for the machine to grind through, if its batteries even had that much charge? Zoey couldn't breathe, her chest was too restricted, and it felt like there was simply no air inside the sealed tube.

Then, after some interminable amount of time, the noises faded and the engines wound down. She heard voices and the Aviv-drill was opened, this time at the head end. Hands were helping pull her free and she tried to look around, to count everyone, to see if everybody had made it out. She knew almost immediately that not everyone had.

CHAPTER
24

ZOEY EMERGED TO FIND herself inside a fancy liquor store, surrounded by bottles of expensive whiskey stacked on spiral oak shelves three stories tall. She was disoriented by that until she figured out that they had drilled their way across the alley and well into the building next door.

Echo ran up, looking haggard and exhausted, which to Zoey was like seeing the Statue of Liberty on fire. She handed Zoey a bottle of water.

Zoey gasped, "Where's Will? Who all—"

No one was listening. Paramedics had swarmed in and Wu was immediately loaded onto a gurney and hustled away to an ambulance waiting outside. Across the room was Aviv, holding a tablet full of holographic menus. He was pale and sweaty, looking like he had just delivered a baby in the back of a taxi. DeeDee was crouched on the floor nearby. At her feet was a glowing hologram of what looked like a pile of trash. It was a scan of the rubble next door, a red blob indicating the space where Zoey and Wu had been located.

"Hey," Zoey said to anyone who would listen. "Where's Will? Did he—"

Echo was now talking to a guy in a high-vis vest who was telling her about building integrity, how the liquor store wasn't safe if the rest of the other building collapsed that direction. Another ambulance had pulled up at some point, presumably for Zoey—she had no intention of going to the hospital—and it joined a whole lot of flashing lights already on the scene. Those were Tabula Ra$a PD, as apparently, blowing up a whole building was enough to get attention from their thinly stretched staff.

"Hey," she said. "Echo. Hey. Where's Will?"

Echo finally pulled herself away, put her hands on Zoey's shoulders. "Do you need to go to the—"

"No." Her ankle was killing her but that meant nothing right now.

"Are you sure? You shouldn't even be standing."

"Where's . . ."

Zoey trailed off as she scanned the room. She saw Andre walk by outside, on his phone . . .

Echo said, "Hey," and moved to make sure she was making eye contact with her. "You should sit down. You're unsteady, I can see it. Let me find you a chair—"

"Who didn't make it?"

Echo didn't answer for a moment. Tears were welling in her eyes.

"Echo. *Who didn't make it out?*"

In a trembling voice, she said, "Budd didn't make it."

Zoey just stared.

"But . . ." She turned back toward the stupid miniature tunneling machine and the wall they'd just drilled through. "If we survived, maybe he—"

"No. He was—" she took a breath, "he was standing right on the other side of the wall from the blast. He never knew what happened, he wouldn't have even heard it."

Zoey found herself sitting on the floor, having never consciously made the decision to sit.

"That's . . . are you sure?"

"They've—they've found, ah, a lot of him."

Echo gestured toward DeeDee and her hologram. DeeDee swiped some controls and another patch of red appeared, only this one was fragmented. Scattered.

DeeDee muttered, "Doppler scan. It's how we found you."

Echo sat down next to Zoey and only then did Zoey realize Echo had been crying, a lot. Zoey had never seen her do it before.

From across the room, DeeDee said, "Wrexx, too. The explosion, or debris, it tore him in half." She swiped again. Two red splotches appeared. Zoey realized what she was hearing in DeeDee's voice wasn't sadness about Wrexx's passing, but disappointment. Aviv was still standing over by the wall with his control pad, looking as uncomfortable as a man can look.

Zoey could only shake her head. "It's a miracle that Wu and I got out."

"No," DeeDee replied. "You were just standing in the right spot."

"Has anyone talked to my mom? Does she know what happened?"

"Not yet," said Echo. "Will didn't want to bother her until he knew—until he knew your condition, one way or the other."

"What happened? Do we even know? Was this some kind of attack from Damon's people?"

Echo got a look on her face that Zoey couldn't quite identify. She clenched her jaw, shot a look to outside, to the paramedics. It's like she was annoyed, or embarrassed, or otherwise about to say words she didn't want to feel passing over her mouth.

DeeDee answered for her. "It was Harmonia."

The word meant nothing to Zoey. For a moment she thought it was an unfamiliar adjective.

"The woman with the butterflies?" clarified Echo. "At the meat factory? She either overloaded her implants or got hold of a device. But it was on purpose, she left behind a video that she'd set to go up after the deed was done. She'd been hiding on the roof, who knows how long, and when the time came she dropped down into the alley and detonated herself, like a bomb from a plane. That's why Wu and Andre hadn't spotted her when they went out."

Zoey heard all of those words but processed none of them.

"So," said Zoey, feeling like she was trying to take a quiz while someone was punching her in the gut, "she somehow found out we were here and came to blow us up? Or did Damon send her?"

"No. She, uh . . . well, according to her broadcast manifesto, she didn't know anybody was here. She thought she was blowing up the walk-in freezer where the, uh—"

"Where the human meat was stored," finished Zoey. "Jesus Christ, I am going to have a stroke. Where's Will?"

"Outside, fending off the police. Listen, the world doesn't know what happened here. I mean, that there was an explosion is already news. Who was inside when it happened, and why, is not."

"What about Wrexx? Nobody knows he was in there, do they?"

"No. But we have only hours until they figure it out. Maybe less. Are you sure you don't want to go to the hospital? Logically, I shouldn't even be asking you but I know better than to try to force it."

"No. And if you want to do something for me, make sure nobody else asks me that."

Zoey pulled off her shoe and sock to examine the bad ankle. It was purple with bruising but she had full range of movement. So probably not broken.

Echo wiped her eyes, sighed, and said, "This doesn't seem real. There are people literally all over the world who knew Budd. In Shanghai and Moscow and Australia, friends who'll be devastated by this, who still don't know. So many that we don't even know who they all are, who to contact. Probably some on every continent. There are mob bosses and senators and actual royalty who'll cry when they get this news. People who won't be at his funeral because they can't admit they knew him. People who owed him but will never be able to pay him back. My god. This is, I think, the worst night of my life."

Andre entered, looked shocked, and said, "Nobody told me Zoey was out! I was on the phone, how come nobody came to get me?"

He kneeled down and hugged her.

"Why have they got you on the floor?" he asked. "Nobody could find Zoey a chair? She has to sit on the dirty floor?"

"How are you holding up?" asked Zoey.

"Been notifying Budd's loved ones as best I can. I just got off the phone with one of his partners. And I can already see the question on your face, but basically, Budd was in a relationship with several women at once—or at least the ones I know about were all women—and it's difficult to discern from the outside which partners knew about each other. A few lived in the same house, but not all. It's made for a somewhat delicate notification process."

"But *how are you holding up*?"

"I don't know, man. Grief is funny in a situation like this. When it's sudden, I mean. Out of the blue. At first, it's just shock, like an ambush. But once that's passed, you realize the ambush isn't really over, the grief hides and waits, ready to jump out at the most random times, for years and years."

"I guess it's just that, of all the ways to go, to have no idea it was coming . . ." Zoey shook her head. "This doesn't seem right. Everybody who didn't know they'd talked to him for the last time, no chance to say goodbye . . ."

"Budd was one of those types who'd come to the party, then at some point would just vanish, probably to go to another party. The man lived with his pedal to the floor, slept three hours a night. If you'd asked him how he wanted to go—not that any of us are going to get to choose, probably—but if you asked him, I think he'd choose something quick and painless that makes headlines all around the world. A spectacular crime, the details of which remain mysterious? Yeah, this is what he'd have wanted, if immortality wasn't on the table."

Echo said to her, "I think Aviv has been waiting to talk to you this whole time but he's scared that if he comes over here, you'll have him killed on the spot."

Zoey sighed. "Send him over, I guess."

Echo got up and made a quick hand gesture to Aviv, which he apparently took as a signal that it was safe to approach. Andre and Echo gave them their space.

Aviv shuffled over and, standing over Zoey like a skyscraper, muttered, "Hey, there. How are you doing?"

"So you didn't really leave town. So that also was a lie."

"And it was a good thing I didn't! Will tracked me down, god only knows how. He says, 'Meet me at the estate, we're packing up your drill.' Believe it or not, we lost another hour charging the battery. And even then we couldn't charge it up all the way, it was down to three percent when you came blasting through the wall there."

Zoey shook her head. "I have such a stupid life."

"So, I know nobody cares about this now, but it matters to me. So, uh, there was no way I could stay at the concert with the bounty out there. But I really did want to be with you, in a crowd, like normal people. I had this fantasy of just hanging out. It didn't work and I'll say it right now, my team told me it was a bad idea, the thing with the drink robot. Particularly Sig, she said it was the worst idea she'd ever heard and that you'd never speak to me again. I thought you'd find it charming but I guess other women have an eye for this kind of thing."

"I can't imagine dating somebody else who has a 'team.'"

"It frees up so much time!"

Four police officers entered the room.

Aviv glanced their direction. "So, I'm about to be arrested. There was no way for us to get here with the drill without showing up on all sorts of cameras. There's a whole network of observers who just monitor which vehicles come and go from your estate, did you know that? Anyway, your team convinced them to hold off until we completed the rescue. That's what Will has been doing out there."

"Arrested for . . . ?"

"The pirate-ship incident? Tell me you haven't already forgotten about that."

"It just feels like so long ago. And I don't know if you're new in town or what, but if you don't want to be arrested, tell Will, and you won't be."

Aviv gave her a tired grin. "Zoey, think about who you're talking to. If I don't want their little jail cell downtown to hold me, do you really think it can? No, when something like this happens, you just incorporate it into the narrative."

"Based on what you just said, I have a feeling you and Will could be best friends."

"If you don't want me to contact you after I've served my time, I'll respect that. I'm not a stalker, I'm just not very good at all this. But I'm sure you're in no mood to think about it right now."

"Well, you've got that right. If you go away for twenty years, maybe by then I'll be in the mood."

The cops arrested Aviv in the polite manner in which wealthy celebrities are taken into custody. He was hustled out and Zoey felt like she should be feeling something about it, but at this point that was like asking for a melody from a smashed guitar.

And now here was Will, striding in from outside. He somehow did not have a drink in his hand even though he was surrounded by ten thousand bottles of the stuff. He was instead holding a blue blanket that he'd apparently borrowed/stolen from the paramedics.

Zoey got to her feet, rather than make Will force her, and tried to ready

herself for whatever plan he'd come up with while she was holding everything up by selfishly getting buried in a building collapse.

She said, "I suppose it's time for another emergency meeting."

Instead of answering, he draped the blanket over Zoey like a cape,
pulling it over her shoulders. Then he reached around, like he was adjust-
ing the blanket or something back there, and he kept doing it, reaching
farther around her back, and Zoey finally realized that Will was hugging
her. She got her arms free and hugged him back and he squeezed her so
hard that it kind of hurt her ribs, but she didn't say anything and they
stayed like that for a while.

After he let her go, he swallowed and said, "You should be in the hospital."

Zoey didn't even acknowledge this. "Echo told me what happened. After everything, of all the enemies you've taken on, Budd is gone forever
because this mentally ill woman blew him up by accident?"

"No." Will stabbed a finger at her. "No. Don't think that. Don't ever
think that. Damon's people leaked this narrative, they fed it, they made
it trend. He and his backers are who fed Harmonia's neurosis and paid
for her implants. I said it before: they have a whole dark-money fund to
sow chaos just like this. They didn't even care what happened, it was
like throwing a grenade into a crowd. No, Zoey, Budd died to the most
powerful weapon in the known universe: a compelling lie. Don't ever un-
derestimate it. That is the dragon that sits atop the mountain, the one that
threatens to burn the world."

"I want to go to bed."

A pause from Will, then, "You can if you want to."

"But you're not."

"No. There's work to do."

"I don't care about all that. The election, I don't care about any of it.
I just want to go hug my mom, and my cats. I want to soak in a tub until
my entire body doesn't hurt anymore. I want to go to sleep and when I get
up I want to go to the hospital and sit outside Wu's room, where I can be
there with him without being close enough to bother him."

Will didn't reply.

"I mean, I just got pulled out from under a building. My ankle is killing me and I probably have injuries I don't even know about yet because my nervous system is too traumatized to tell me about them."

Will still didn't reply.

"There is no reasonable person on earth who would ask me to keep going," she continued. "No boss, no platoon leader. If they pull a soldier out from under a building, they don't send him back to the front lines. They fly him out."

Still, nothing from Will. He just looked at her, no expression to indicate he was prodding her one way or the other.

"But we don't have much time, do we?"

Quietly, Will replied, "No. We don't."

"To do what, though? What can we even do?"

"We are going to sit down somewhere safe, clear our heads, and think through our options."

"Then let's go, before the crowds show up."

Will said, "We can't go yet. There's press out there. We need to go out and make a statement. The street streamers were leaking rumors of your death the whole time you were under there, we need to correct the record. Or, you know, correct it to our version of the truth."

Zoey felt dread flowing in. "And by 'we' you mean . . ."

"You and I. You're our most sympathetic face. The statement will be simple: we lost our close associate Budd Billingsley, and almost lost you and your personal security, to a terrorist bombing by a pro-Damon supporter. And that nobody else was in the building." He looked to DeeDee. "No one can know Wrexx was here, agreed?"

"What exactly do you have in mind?" asked DeeDee in a tone that suggested she was very frightened of the answer.

He shook his head. "Only the broadest of strokes." He thought for a moment, then said to Zoey, "And then say that the police will be able to thoroughly investigate the scene *after* we've had a chance to recover Budd's remains."

Andre shook his head. "Man, Budd would not want anyone risking their safety just to gather up his parts for cremation."

"I know," said Will. "But we're going to tell them that anyway."

CHAPTER
25

ZOEY LAY ON HER side in her bed being clutched tightly from behind by her mother, Zoey herself clutching her two very confused cats. Her left foot was in a carbon-fiber walking boot and her toes had gone numb, as the device administered steady blasts of cold to keep the swelling down. A full medical team had been waiting at the house when she'd arrived, summoned by Will via an obscenely expensive service that specialized in house calls and discretion. Zoey sensed the operation wasn't totally above-board (for example, the doctor just dispensed the pain medication from his pockets) but she wasn't going to question it.

"I used to read about Arthur," whispered her mother, "when he was getting big, making all of his money, turning up on TV for this scandal or other, and I would think, 'There's somebody who's never going to be an old man, he's going to burn out too fast.' He had this voracious appetite, like he was trying to eat the world, and I thought one day he's just gonna pop. He'll wreck one of his million-dollar sports cars, or die in a shoot-out with a rival, or OD. But I always thought that on some level, he'd deserve it. Not because he was bad, but because that was the life he chose, to keep biting off more and more. But that's not you. You wouldn't deserve it. Don't they know that?"

Her mother pressed her face into Zoey's hair.

"Whatever you have to go off and do," she said to Zoey, "I'm not going to try to talk you out of it, I know better. I just . . . I don't know, I just hope you don't get addicted to it. To this life."

"Me, too."

"So what can I do to help?"

"Vote tomorrow. Convince other people to do the same. And not for Leonidas Damon, just to be clear."

Zoey's phone alarm went off.

"What's that?"

"I scheduled exactly twenty minutes for us to be traumatized together. Now it's time to get back to work. The rest of the team is waiting."

Zoey had told the Suits she was in no mood for the Buffalo Room so they were meeting in the conference room instead. Then she regretted it the moment she entered and was greeted with the empty chair in Budd's spot. Will, Echo, and Andre were already watching a monitor on which Leonidas Damon was giving an impromptu press conference in front of the rubble at Carnivore-Tex. They were three exhausted people, plus Zoey, who felt like she was operating at about twelve percent capacity. It didn't look like they'd be capable of preparing a nice dinner, let alone, well, whatever the hell they were about to do.

"Of course, details are still hazy," Damon was saying on the monitor, "and will probably remain so, knowing who is involved. But what is clear is that one particular woman in this city was simply pushed past her breaking point. Of course, I don't condone an act like this. But what do you expect? This citizen, who called herself Harmonia, sacrificed herself because the depravity of this city drove her to it. That you can't even trust the food at restaurants like this one to not contain the very flesh of our neighbors, our children? Outcomes like this were inevitable. How much can the citizens be expected to tolerate before they say, 'enough'?"

Zoey asked, "Why does this guy get to make a speech uninterrupted, when the reporters who accosted me outside the restaurant kept shouting questions at me like this was all my fault? I had blood on my face!"

Echo said, "You did well, considering."

"I mumbled something about how Damon sucks and I honestly don't remember what I said after that."

"Specifically," said Andre, "you said that you hoped Leonidas loses tomorrow and then, quote, 'has his scrotum pecked away by crows, so that he can't reproduce, oh wait, I guess he already has kids, doesn't he, well, whatever, I'm going to go take a bath.' We've all watched the video."

"Many times," added Echo.

"Now, as you know," continued Damon on the screen, "there was an attempt on my life, and on the lives of my family, on Saturday night. I am pleased to say that the man responsible has been arrested and hopefully will be prosecuted to the fullest extent of the law. He, along with everyone who collaborated with him, everyone who enabled him, everyone whose wrong-doing would have gone unpunished had he succeeded. Tomorrow, we're going to send a message that the grown-ups are back in charge, that you can once again feel safe walking these streets and eating from these estab-lishments. That newcomers can feel safe moving here with their children, knowing they won't be snatched away to be sold on the streets or ground up and sold for food."

Zoey said, "So that's his whole campaign now? The cannibalism stuff?"

Will sipped his drink and said, "With the bombing, it's now dominat-ing the news. You can't talk about the bombing without talking about the bomber, and the bomber was Soylent Black. At that point, it's just a matter of spinning it so that we don't get sympathy as victims."

"Which we won't, because we're having this conversation in a hundred-million-dollar estate built with crime money. Is there any update on Wu?"

"Still in surgery," replied Echo. "And, ah, I'm told he will be for some time. There's a lot to fix."

"We're going to get him back to normal even if we have to saw off my legs and sew them on him. Or Will's legs. I guess mine wouldn't look right."

"These people," continued Damon in a tone like he was building toward some kind of climax, "they mistake our charity and goodness for weak-ness. But we'll show them. We'll show them how hard and how quickly we can strike when it's our very civilization at stake!"

That drew some hoots and hollers from supporters as Damon raised his fist and walked off. The news feed cut to another story, showing candles and flowers placed around a dumpster near the bombing site, the pave-ment around it scattered with brick fragments.

"An odd footnote to tonight's tragedy," said the voice of the news streamer, "fans have gathered around the trash bins outside of the blast site to mourn Bandito the raccoon, who became a major Blink celebrity after a local teenager attached a harness and camera so that fans could track the animal's adventures around the city. Bandito was known to raid the garbage cans outside of Carnivore-Tex for scraps and fans say he was just feet away from the woman when she detonated her device."

Andre suddenly looked up. "Ah, man, not Bandito! He used to come eat out of our bins, the little guy drummed up a ton of business for us. People would see the rib bones in the garbage and say, 'Must be pretty good, no meat left on 'em.'"

"You might not feel so positively toward him," said Echo, "when you hear that Bandito's death is now trending higher than anything else involved with the explosion. And Budd's name barely comes up."

"Nah, Budd would have thought that was hilarious."

"To be clear," said a new voice from the doorway, "I do not work for you."

"DeeDee!" said Andre. "You came! Yes, the empty chair you see was Budd's and no, there's not some big symbolic meaning if you choose to sit in it. When Zoey showed up after Arthur passed, she sat in his old chair and nobody thought twice about it."

"I'll stand, thank you."

She wasn't in her vigilante costume but the black vest she wore over her sweatshirt looked tactical. Zoey wondered if DeeDee wasn't always wearing something that could stop a bullet or a blade.

Zoey said, "The coffee is brewing, if you couldn't smell it. You know it'll be good because I pushed the button myself."

"All right, so what exactly do you people do? We have to create a story, right, to swing the election and save the future? Something that can fool a whole city? A whole country?"

"That's right," replied Will. "I'm giving us thirty minutes to come up with it."

"If Arthur was alive," said Echo, "the strategy would be obvious. In fact, he'd say the easy play had been handed to us on a silver platter the moment the bomb went off." She looked to Will. "Right?"

Will nodded. "It was somebody on Damon's side who killed Wrexx.

If we go public with Wrexx's death, it rallies Wrexx's people to our side, motivates them to turn out higher than they're polling. That could be enough to turn it."

"And all that requires," said Zoey, "is for us to turn sadistic sex monster Rex Wrexx into a martyr, a symbol for our cause. So all of the women he's hurt, the ones he drove into hiding, and DeeDee here, they all sit and watch us go on-camera and sing Wrexx's praises, talk about this hero to the working folk who was cruelly taken from us by the evil puritan radicals."

"That's what *Arthur* would have done," said Echo. "Nobody said that's what we're going to do."

"But then we're stuck. Wrexx's people are going to figure out he's missing. When they go looking, somebody is going to find out DeeDee snatched him—for good reason, DeeDee, I agree with you—but then when it comes out that he's dead, it's going to get pinned on her, which means it gets pinned on Alonzo, and his fans are going to revolt, and Damon will win by twenty points."

"One day," said Will. "We have one entire day, during which Damon is going to use the Catharsis riots and the Carnivore-Tex explosion to feed a narrative of a city out of control."

"Okay," replied Zoey, "so we have to blow all of that off the headlines, somehow. We have to give the world a better story. Something nobody on either side can take their eyes off of. And we need to come up with it in the next, oh, twenty-six minutes or so. Is the coffee done yet?"

Andre shouted some commands and a holographic drawing board appeared in the center of the conference table. He drew five letters with his finger and they hovered in midair, in glowing orange script:

AIDAS

"Since we have somebody new, here's a quick intro to selling anything, including an idea. You lead your customer through five steps: Attention, Interest, Desire, Action, and hopefully, Satisfaction. If you've got yourself a billboard on the side of the highway, you hope to get the customer's attention and then have them follow all of those steps to buying your car or wristwatch or what have you."

Echo said, "In our world, we work backward. Start from the state of mind we want the voters to be in at this time tomorrow, how do we want them to feel about Damon, and Alonzo, and themselves. Then we work back to what action they can take to bring that about, what desire would cause them to take that action, and so on."

DeeDee sighed. "Already this sounds like I'm being taught the dark arts by minions of Lucifer himself."

"Now you're getting it," said Andre as Zoey handed him a mug of coffee.

"All right," said Echo to an exhausted room, thirty-four minutes later. "Here's the shopping list I've written down. Two high-end, ultra-realistic female sex dolls. Two pig carcasses. Several hundred large white feathers. The lower half of one male human cadaver. As many white robes and identical masks as we can find. At least a gallon of fake blood—"

"It has to be real," interjected Will.

"At least a gallon of real blood. The list of machinery and parts that Andre has written on this napkin. And finally, a group of competent people to help us put the project together, who can be trusted to keep a secret to the death, who happen to be available right now. And that's what we need to, just let me double-check here, swing a mayoral election by several points. Am I missing anything?"

Before anyone could answer, Zoey's phone chimed with a message from an unknown number:

Hi, Aviv gave me your contact, hope that's ok. I'm Sig, Aviv's projects coordinator. A is in big trouble and we're all pretty scared here. No, this is not part of the act, none of this is.

Zoey replied,

I was there when he was arrested, he had the chance to avoid it but said he was giving up willingly. It all seemed pretty polite.

Sig:

Haven't you heard? He never made it to the police station.

Zoey:

He escaped already?

Sig:

No. Someone came and took him. And we don't know where he is.

The Suits and DeeDee saw Zoey's reaction and, with some trepidation, Echo asked what was wrong.

"The Amazing Aviv is once again trying to make it all about him, this time by getting disappeared at the hands of, I don't know, Damon's people? Somebody trying to cash in on the bounty? His team is insisting it's not a stunt."

Zoey thought Will would be exasperated by the prospect of another crisis crowding its way onto their to-do list, but instead he looked oddly intrigued.

Will said, "News of it has to have made the rounds by now, at the very least among other bounty hunters who've lost out on the payday."

Echo and Andre both took to their phones, seemingly in a race to see who could come up with it first.

Andre apparently won. "Who's Pistol Wizard?"

Zoey covered her face with her hands. "Oh, my god."

Echo said, "He broke Aviv out of police custody. And by 'broke him out' I mean the cops pulled the paddy wagon over and allowed this idiot to take Aviv in exchange for some amount of money smaller than the bounty."

Zoey let out a theatrical sigh. "Where is he holding him?"

"Unknown."

"So what do we do?"

Will said, "Pistol Wizard may be doing it for the bounty but posting the bounty itself was insurance. The idea is that if Damon loses, a city run by Alonzo would make the charges go away."

"In other words, if Damon loses, he quietly has this guy kill Aviv."

"Actually," said Andre, "I assume that if Damon detects that we're screwing with him and senses that we've gotten the upper hand, he'll tell the vigilante to kill Aviv out of spite. Or he'll try to use that as leverage, if he feels backed into a corner."

Zoey turned to Will, who was doing a poor job of hiding the fact that he regarded all of this as possible good news. "I take it you think this guy is doing us a favor by keeping Aviv off the table and unable to do whatever nonsense he had planned for tomorrow? And if he dies, that's just a minor side effect?"

"Zoey, we've spent this whole meeting lamenting that we're short on people. Aviv has support staff."

"Ah."

She composed a reply to Sig.

Zoey:

How many people does Aviv have on his team? And are they busy right now?

CHAPTER
26

AT ABOUT FOUR-THIRTY A.M. on Monday, Zoey and Andre arrived at a huddle of three abandoned hangars next to an expanse of weedy neglected pavement. The facility was, at one time, the Beaver Municipal Airport, belonging to one of the small towns that had been swallowed up by the blob of urban sprawl that was Tabula Ra$a. The pair were driving a borrowed van bearing the logo of a mobile pet-grooming service, and sitting atop the vehicle was an animatronic dog with holographic flies and stink lines hovering above it. The big doors of the center hangar had been left open just enough for one vehicle to slip through.

DeeDee was waiting for them inside, still in inconspicuous street clothes. She pushed the huge sliding doors closed behind them.

"Are they all here?" asked Andre as soon as he exited the van.

DeeDee nodded. "They said they'd listen but that's all the guarantee you're going to get."

Inside the hangar was a faded shipping container—Rose's supposed prison, presumably—and a battered RV that looked like it'd been all over the world. Scattered around was filmmaking equipment: cables and lights, plus a lot of stacked black cases for the gear. Zoey spotted a makeup station and a card table piled with junk food and a coffee machine.

DeeDee led them to the RV, Zoey clomping across the concrete floor in her walking boot. At the moment, her pain was being kept at bay with a patch that administered medication and she tried not to think about the colorful patches littering the ground at the sex-worker encampment.

DeeDee glanced back and, noticing the conspicuous empty spot where

Zoey's bodyguard should be, asked, "Are you traveling without personal security?"

"For the moment," Zoey replied. "Will said we could get somebody new but I don't like the idea of just swapping out Wu like a broken part. I feel like I deserve to be unprotected for a while."

If DeeDee disagreed with this logic, she showed no sign of it.

Instead, she asked, "Will he regain use of his legs?"

"We have the best possible people on the job," replied Zoey, knowing that wasn't a real answer. "If not, we'll take care of him, one way or the other. Him and his family both."

DeeDee shot a glance back at Zoey. "You'd better. It's the least people like you can do for people like him."

When they reached the RV, they found Violet standing directly inside the door, looking like she'd been nervously practicing the next interaction for hours. Seated at a tiny table in the kitchenette behind her was Rose, dunking a tea bag in a mug of hot water and picking bits off a store-bought muffin.

"So," began Violet. "That's Rose, Iris is in the back, asleep. I can get Clarence on the phone, he said he'd take the call but that's as far as I got."

Zoey said, "You guys aren't worried about being discovered? You've got a whole city full of idiots trying to find you."

"They're not trying to find us," said Rose. "They're trying to find a killer's rape dungeon. This place has been shut down for years, there's barely any Blink coverage out here, nobody has reasons to fly drones over it."

"I guess I was assuming you'd gotten out of town and were doing all of this from Mexico or something."

"I can tell you've never been on the run," replied Violet. "It's traveling that gets you caught, getting away from your people, buying train or bus tickets. And some of this stunt needed us to be local."

"You're filming all of it here? The whole serial-killer story arc?"

"Ah, yeah. I mean, it's done now, we're hauling away all of the stuff later today, or whenever we can get a clear path out. Without getting caught on a camera, I mean."

Andre looked to Rose. "You gave a good performance with the thing at the festival. It got the whole city looking for you."

Rose shrugged. "He made me do it thirty times to get it right, then I think he wound up using the first take anyway."

"She wants to be an actor," said Violet. "The only one of us with experience, so he gave her the part with all the lines."

"When you say 'he' you're talking about Clarence, right?" asked Zoey. "The former manager at Chalet who's running all this?"

Rose said, "He was always directing on the side, he used to promise pros at Chalet that he'd put them in his movies."

"Forgive me for being slow, but I'm extremely sleepy: our info was that he'd moved to Miami and never came back."

"That's right. He did all this remotely, we have a monitor where his big sweaty face would come up and shout directions. All of the props that had to be bought, all the gear that had to be rented, he'd have it delivered to an empty house down the street, then I had to haul it out here. It was a huge pain."

Andre asked, "Where did you get the dead body? The one that played you in the first video?"

"It was an unclaimed body from the morgue. It was set to be cremated. The morgue freezers are always so jammed up with unclaimed bodies that you can take one without even a bribe. Just come and say you're a friend of the deceased and there you go, you've got yourself a corpse. Way cheaper than having a full mock-up done."

"So," asked Zoey, "how was this supposed to play out? What was the next release? Has it been filmed already?"

Violet said, "Our part is over, we were to move to another safe house after the broadcast at Catharsis and start prepping to leave town. In a few days, the cops were to get a note from the supposed killer, pointing them to my dead body. They were to find my skeleton in a burned-out car. It's from the same corpse we used for the video, we have a guy who can make the teeth match the dental records. The killer was going to leave a note on the skeleton, saying that he would continue to hunt sex workers. And I mean the note was going to be directly on the skeleton, carved into the skull."

"So the supposed killer would forever remain a monster," said Andre, "lurking in the shadows. Never to be caught, because he was never real."

"Sex workers go missing all the time," added DeeDee. "So with every unsolved, people would think maybe the Sex Butcher got her."

Zoey nodded. "And the tabloids would go crazy for it."

"Just like Jack the Ripper," said Andre. "Remember Damon bringing him up in his speech? There was something like a dozen supposed victims but they think maybe only five were from the same killer, the rest may have been copycats or random victims. Who knows, right? That's why he became a legend, because of the mystery."

Zoey sighed. "Well, if I know how this game is played, I'm guessing that if Leo Damon wins, exactly four years from now he'll have his storm-troopers shoot some vagrant and declare him to be the Sex Butcher. It'll happen just in time for his reelection campaign."

Rose's phone rang. "That's Clarence," she said while chewing some muffin.

She set the phone on the table and a hologram of Clarence's face popped up. It was weird because Zoey couldn't see him from the neck down but somehow knew just from his face that he was wearing a Hawaiian shirt.

"Let me make this very clear," Clarence began, his head bobbing in a way that suggested he was pressing a pointed finger into the table for emphasis, "if you blow the lid on this, all three of these women will have big fat targets on their backs. I'm sure you and your people aren't too happy with me right now, but I personally don't give a rat's ass who or what Will Blackwater is or isn't happy with. I got friends down here, mob friends, so if you come after me, there'll be consequences. *Capisce?*"

Rose rolled her eyes.

"We actually need your help," said Zoey. "A lot has happened and there isn't much time. As for the three women, they can remain as alive or dead in the public's imagination as they want. We have another, bigger problem."

"My help, as in you need me to go public and confess to the hoax? Because I'm not—"

"Oh, god, no," interrupted Zoey. "In fact, we need you to never do that. We need you to shoot something else for us."

"Let me take a guess," said Clarence, "you want a new twist in the Sex Butcher saga that absolves your organization of all involvement."

"Nope. Whatever negative reputation my company has, it is well de-served. We have obscene wealth, we don't need public adulation on top of it."

Andre asked, "But we do have to ask: Why did you add the Secret Menu conspiracy stuff? In Rose's final bit, she said the killer had paid for the right to do it. That's never been true, Clarence, and you know it."

"I *don't* know it. I got thrown under the bus over that whole Wrexx situation."

"You refused to ban him," said Zoey. "After Lyra reported him. Did that order come from above or not? If it did, tell me who gave it to you and I'll get rid of them."

"You don't get it. *They didn't have to specifically say I couldn't ban him.* All they had to do was make it very clear that per-store revenue goals had to be met, no excuses. No, I couldn't lose an influencer customer who could swing my average review score by three stars with a single video. Not when I was trying to meet a number that was based on paying eight-figure rent at the mall. Real cute how that works, isn't it? Nobody has to come out and say anything about keeping Wrexx as a client, they just set the conditions so that nothing else can happen. Then when disaster strikes, they shrug their shoulders and say, 'Not our fault, that was an underling who went rogue, for absolutely no reason.' So as far as I'm con-cerned, yeah, Wrexx *did* pay for the right to indulge his psychopathy."

"But why did you—you know what? Never mind, I don't care. You have a right to be disgruntled. As for the new video, we want to kill Rex Wrexx."

"On-camera?" asked Iris, who had appeared at the door to the back at some point, wearing flannel pajamas. "Like a snuff film?"

Violet said, "She wasn't really asleep back there, she just didn't want to talk to you."

"I'd be down for murdering Wrexx on-camera," said Rose through another bite of muffin.

"Well," replied Zoey, "the first thing you should know is that Rex is already dead. The world doesn't know it yet."

This brought stunned silence to the room. Four mouths fell open and they all exchanged glances, even Clarence's holographic head.

"He is?" asked Violet. "How?"

"If I told you, it would just raise more questions. And that's the problem: if the circumstances of his death remain mysterious, his crazy fans could do something horrific in retaliation. So we need to re-kill him, live, on-camera. With Wrexx gone, you should be safe, *if* we can take the heat off of you with his weirdo fans by giving them a new story, a new reality. If we do it right, you should be free to do whatever you want, under your own identity or another. All three of you."

"What about me?" asked Clarence's digital floating head.

"What do you want?" asked Andre, sounding like he was bracing himself for the response.

"I need enough to pay back what I borrowed for this project."

Iris smiled. "Did you say 'borrowed,' Clarence?" She looked to Zoey. "He got the money to do this by skimming from a movie production. He got mob investors to make a high-end slasher porno and spent most of it doing this instead. Soon they're going to ask why their big-ticket gore porn looks like it was shot with amateurs in a two-bedroom apartment and a bottle of ketchup."

Zoey said, "We can do that. If we get your word that you'll never talk about this."

"If I talk about this," replied Clarence, "the guys I skimmed the money from will cut off my nuts and feed the rest of me to the gators."

Zoey noticed that these were the same people Clarence had just boasted as friends a minute ago, but chose to not mention it.

"And just to be clear," said DeeDee to the three women, "Zoey and her people aren't doing this out of a sense of charity. It's politics and about making sure Alonzo wins tomorrow, for their own interests."

Violet tried to puzzle it out. "But how does this stunt help with that?"

Iris said, "It's obvious, dummy. Rex is their guy, they want to stage some heroic last stand." Iris did a theatrical dying rasp and said, "All you Wrexxicans out there, honor my memory by voting for Alonzo!"

"No," said Zoey. "Wrexx doesn't deserve that. And that would make it obvious that it was a stunt, if it was that self-serving. People would start digging into it. An operation like this, well, it's complicated. And I mean, it's complicated by design."

"To the point that we're not completely sure *we* understand it," added Andre.

"What I'm saying," said DeeDee, "is don't agree to do this without a gigantic paycheck. Trust me, she can afford it."

"She's right," said Zoey. "Tell me what you—"

"I want to be an actor," replied Rose. "A real one, not in porn."

Zoey looked to Andre. "Well, I don't think we specifically are in that industry . . ."

Andre said, "We produce advertisements for our businesses, we are friendly with investors in film, we have influence with many influencers. We can't make them give you an Oscar but yeah, we can line you up with paying work. Stuff that will get you seen."

Of the other two women, Zoey asked, "What about you guys?"

"I want an apartment," replied Iris. "One that I own outright, in the city. And I want a position as a high-end escort. Meaning I can pick my clients, can pick my terms. I've seen the ones you have doing that, they're not any cuter than I am, they can just afford better hair and makeup."

"You want to keep doing sex work?"

"Why not? I'm good at it, I like meeting new people, I like eating and drinking at fancy restaurants. And a lot of these guys don't even want sex, they just want a pretty girl to laugh at their jokes."

Andre said, "We can set you up. We can't force customers to come your way but we can do the other bits."

"And I want it all under a new identity, new paperwork, new backstory. I'll change my hair."

"That won't fool any stalker tracking you on Blink," said Zoey. "You'd need surgery . . ."

"Ooh, good point. I want sharper cheekbones, bigger eyes, with that eye-widening thing they do. I also want height surgery, the thing where they lengthen the bones in your legs? I want to be two inches taller."

"Not only can we get you that but I might make an appointment of my own. Violet?"

Without hesitation, Violet said, "I want eff-you money. Enough to get away, enough to never have to work, enough to get all the therapy I'll need to start sleeping through the night again. New identity, new life.

This city is Hell, this line of work is dehumanizing, and I pray that everyone who made it like this will have to face judgment for it. I'll take your money. But I'll use it to advocate for others who've been forced into this life, to get them out."

"We can work that out. And I'm not offended."

"I didn't ask if you were."

CHAPTER
27

AROUND SUNRISE, ZOEY AND Andre pulled up to a nondescript ware-house in an industrial park that was full of similar structures, plus one giant blackened crater where one used to be. They were in a borrowed pest-control truck shaped like a giant cockroach and arrived to find a semi–tractor trailer had already pulled up to one of the loading docks.

They'd just gotten off the phone with Will, who insisted his own appointment had gone according to plan. He and DeeDee had visited the Fish Bowl and demanded to talk to Wrexx. They needed to maintain the illusion that the Suits knew nothing about his status as a man who had recently tied the record for Deadest Person in the Universe. This meant acting out their extreme annoyance that Wrexx hadn't appeared at any of the campaign-event prep. Will interrogated Wrexx's entourage for any information they might have about where he tended to land after a bender, but whatever information they had, they were largely unwilling to share. Will left them with a rude message to relay to Wrexx whenever he turned up, if Will wasn't able to find the man first.

Zoey and Andre entered the warehouse and rolled up the loading-bay door from the inside to find the back of the semi contained six people Zoey had never met. Wait, was Aviv's "team" larger than hers?

A tiny woman with a black bowl cut extended a hand and said, "Hi, I'm Sig," then quickly gestured to the other five in turn, saying, "that's my brother Gunnar, this here is Magnus, our prop builder, that's Kris, Jo, and the straggler lingering in the back is Thelma."

Zoey immediately forgot most of those. She was never great at remembering names but Sig—she remembered that one—also talked a hundred miles an hour.

"We know time is short, so first thing's first," said Sig, spraying it out as one long word. "Have you found out where Aviv is being held?"

Andre said, "Our man Will is working on that. If he doesn't know already, he will by the time we ask."

Sig nodded, then stepped farther into the warehouse and surveyed her surroundings. The hulking machines around them could have been mistaken for woodworking equipment, if one didn't know better—it was all blades, motors, hooks, and clamps. Each device was designed to do immediate and decisive violence to whatever was fed into its maw.

Andre gestured at the machinery. "This is all gear harvested from a meatpacking plant that got converted into a creepy cultured-beef lab, all of it supposed to go up for auction next month. We've got lift-assist carts for the heavy ones, and they're all heavy ones. We'll start with that bandsaw thing right there, the green one." Two of the biggest, burliest dudes in Aviv's crew immediately marched that direction with no questions or complaints. "When you get to the airport, it's the middle hangar. Knowing Aviv's line of work, I assume you have tools to evade Blink drones when you need to?"

Sig wouldn't even dignify that with an answer.

Zoey asked, "Did you by any chance have any luck finding the feathers?"

One of the people still in the truck, the woman who'd lingered behind, wordlessly held up a clear plastic bag packed with large, pure-white feathers.

"They're fake," she muttered, "it's all we could get."

"Perfect. All right, we have to go, we'll be back to help when this is done."

Andre said, "We've got to go meet with the devil."

Leonidas Damon agreed to talk to Zoey at his campaign headquarters. She much preferred this to meeting at his home—there presumably was less chance of any kind of nudity—but the circumstances of this one were much more difficult. Zoey was there to lie, and she hated it. Specifically, she hated that her life had become a diabolical conundrum in which success meant becoming good at lying, but at the incalculable cost to her soul that came with being good at it. Still, Will had told her that as deception goes, this was the easy stuff. There was no story to memorize, nothing that a smart opponent could sift through for contradictions. She merely needed to feign ignorance and to play up her outrage toward Damon, which in theory, should be easy because she always felt ignorant and was outraged about the sheer fact that Leonidas Damon existed.

The campaign office was a sprawling cubicle beehive, a space packed with the most ambitious, relentless, and energetic strivers in the city on the most stressful day of their lives. Zoey entered alone, finding Damon standing among a huddle of staffers. He made eye contact with Zoey, then motioned for her to follow him to a private, glassed-in office. Once inside, he did not draw the blinds. Zoey followed slowly and awkwardly on her protected ankle, playing up her wounded vulnerability. Considering how the ankle throbbed, it didn't require a whole lot of acting.

"Quite an eventful twenty-four hours," said Damon. "You look like you've aged twenty-four years."

"I'll make this short," said Zoey. "I want this to end."

"What, specifically? The world?"

"The chaos. Half of the people I care about are missing, maimed, or dead. The whole city out there feels like it's under siege. Hundreds of drunks spent the night trying and failing to rescue a woman who, for all they know, has now been tortured to death. I want it to be over."

"I don't doubt that you blame me for the attack on your friend's restaurant. Here's where it helps to step back and look at the big picture. Why did that crazy woman have access to the unregulated technology that would allow her to even do such a thing? Why was she out on the streets, instead of in the custody of a criminal justice system? What set of social and economic conditions convinced her that what she did was a reasonable course of action? You're tired of the chaos, but I did not give birth to it. If anything, it's a blessing that now you can see its inevitable outcome."

"Who has Aviv?"

"It was my understanding that the police had him."

"You know that's not the case. A vigilante scooped him up to collect on your bounty."

"My bounty? I hope you have evidence for such a serious accusation."

"You're saying you don't know where he is?"

"I do not. But I'll definitely keep an eye out, I can see that he means a lot to you."

Damon said that with a horrible little smirk. Zoey gave him nothing in return.

"And what about Rex Wrexx?" she asked. "Do you happen to know his whereabouts? Maybe in the same place as Aviv?"

"This is the first I'm hearing that he's gone missing."

"No, it isn't. He's not showing up to any of his appearances. He was supposed to be rallying voters for Alonzo, all day today, all night tonight."

"Maybe he got spooked by the bombing of your restaurant. Maybe he's decided to leave town in search of more peaceful pastures. Can you blame him?"

"You approached me at Catharsis with the intent of convincing me to do something. What, specifically?"

"Why do you ask now? Because your statistical models show that I'm going to win tomorrow, barring some kind of black-swan event on the scale of Christ returning to earth?"

"I could turn that question right around: If you are that confident, why did you approach me at all?"

"I don't want to win in a nail-biter. I want a unified city, and to take office with an overwhelming mandate from the public. Especially here, where any kind of close result would immediately be cast into doubt, thanks to the city's reputation for corruption."

"So you want me to campaign for you today?"

"Oh, no. That would give some the impression that I sold out to you rather than the other way around. I simply need you to not push for Alonzo. No dirty tricks, none of the old Arthur Livingston strong-arm tactics, no blanketing neighborhoods with thugs forcing voters to switch to Alonzo tomorrow. No disruption of the process, no crazy stunts to sew chaos."

"And in exchange, my people don't go to prison if you win."

"They won't go to prison for past crimes. Once I take office, and I mean that very minute, everything counts. It'll take time to get the criminal justice system properly staffed up, but any illicit operations that continue after I'm in charge can and absolutely will be prosecuted. Unfortunately, I cannot promise the same for your man Aviv. He will get what he has coming to him. No more, no less."

Zoey made a show of digesting this information and struggling not to choke on it.

Damon said, "Considering you were treating my possible victory as your own personal apocalypse, you're taking this well."

"I had time to think about it while I was suffocating under several million pounds of concrete and brick. Also, I know you won't be mayor for long."

"Now, see, that sounds like a threat."

"No, that sounds like me knowing that you will use your four years in office here to build a résumé for either governor or the senate, then after a couple of years of that, you'll run for president. You probably plan to make your name with a run in the party's primary, and then four years after that, take it all."

"It's good to have goals, don't you think?"

"I also think that once you get that job, you don't intend to leave it." Zoey stood. "But that will be someone else's problem."

She stood up to leave.

"I am very happy to be certain people's 'problem.' Do you understand how unselfish I'm being? I could have embarked on a path that drew only adulation, telling everyone what they want to hear. You may disagree with me, but you cannot say I don't stand by my convictions."

Zoey knew she should just end the conversation, she'd done what she needed to do.

Instead, she turned at the door and said, "I'm curious about something. My mother is kind and supportive but has been poor her whole life. My father was a ruthless shark but created thousands of jobs and single-handedly altered the economy of an entire state. They came together under circumstances involving extremely questionable morality and consent. In your perfect society, I already know *I* wouldn't exist. But which parent would you have prevented from breeding?"

"Let me answer your question with a question: Have you ever noticed that when you refer to people you see as having fundamentally broken values, you describe them as some kind of animal? You just called your father a shark, you've called me a snake." Damon grinned and pointed at her. "Maybe you should think about the instincts that are coming to the surface when you use those words. Thanks for coming, I hope I can count on your vote tomorrow."

Zoey slid into the sedan with Andre.

He handed her a coffee. "Is he on board?"

"He doesn't trust me, that's clear. But he doesn't know Wrexx is dead, I'm sure of it. And that's what matters."

As they pulled into traffic, Andre said, "So . . . did he tell you the news?"

"What news? And give me a moment to brace myself before you answer that question."

"I don't know quite how to say it, because it's real bad if true and nothing if it's not."

"Just tell me."

"It's trending on Blink that—and there's no confirmation, mind you—but it's trending that Aviv has been killed."

Zoey just stared at him, in the way you do when you're not quite sure you heard what you just heard.

"But . . . how?"

"Shot by the Pistol guy while getting transported to wherever he was planning on keeping him. Again, just a rumor, no witnesses or video. Sounds like something was leaked to the street streamers."

"I—okay. Okay. I mean, what do we do?"

"I don't think there's anything you and I can do, other than what's already on our lengthy list. But I wanted you to know."

"Yeah. Right."

"Are you all right? Do you need a minute?"

"No. I mean, it's just a rumor."

"Right."

ZOEY IS TOO DRUNK FOR THIS DYSTOPIA   317

"And it's not like I've spent months in the trenches with Aviv, we just met."

"Uh-huh."

"But still, if this Pistol idiot shot him, that will be the last bullet he ever fires."

CHAPTER
28

SEVERAL STOPS LATER, ZOEY and Andre finally arrived back at the estate at noon, in a borrowed mobile pedicure stand shaped like a giant woman's foot. They found everyone in the ballroom, aka Santa's Workshop. Echo was at the fabricators, where it appeared she had recruited Carlton to help, the latter holding on to a long, curved piece of white carbon fiber as it was slowly spat out of the giant mechacaterpillar's mouth.

Echo shot a look at Zoey over her shoulder and, as a greeting, said, "You got the feathers?"

Zoey held up the bag she'd gotten from Aviv's team. "What do we know about Aviv?" she asked, trying to make the question seem almost casual. "Is he okay? His murder is the top trend on Blink but it's all just street streamers speculating."

Will, who was at a long banquet table examining what looked like plastic eyes the size of dinner plates, said, "I planted that story, which isn't true, unless it's true by coincidence. The rumor will force the man holding Aviv to issue some kind of proof of life soon and no matter how hard he tries to hide it, that will wind up revealing Aviv's location."

"Ah. So you weren't concerned about Aviv's loved ones who might be traumatized by that kind of news? You know, like, I don't know, his grandmother or something? What if she heard that and worried herself sick that her precious boy had died?"

"Well, that'll teach her not to get her news from Blink. Normally, Budd would hit somebody up for the information but in his absence, we're forced to do it my way. And I have too many other places to be, I just finished meeting with Axol."

"Will they do it?"

"In exchange for enough money to retire, yes."

Echo approached, wiping her hands. "Wrapping Wrexx's digital face around somebody else's body for the feed is actually the easy part, Clarence says he has to do it for his porn all the time, which I frankly don't want to think about. The quality depends on how much source material you have to work with, but Rex Wrexx happens to be one of the most photographed people on the planet, there are more hours of footage to pick from than there are hours in Wrexx's life. About ten times more, in fact. Even then, this wouldn't hold up under forensic analysis."

"It doesn't have to," said Will, "the physical evidence will render the video evidence moot."

"Unless," rebutted Zoey, "somebody theorizes that we did exactly what we're planning to do."

"Please," said Andre. "What kind of sick bastard even thinks that way?"

Zoey looked over at Echo. "I can't believe you're so energetic, have you had any sleep at all? Are you just running on pure caffeine at this point?"

"Sure," replied Echo in a deadpan tone. "What I've been taking is . . . caffeine. Absolutely."

"All right," announced a new, gruff voice from behind them, speaking over a drumbeat of determined footsteps. "It wasn't easy, but I got 'em."

It was former detective Hank Kowalski.

"Got what?" asked Zoey.

"A pair of adult male legs, of roughly the height you need, from a naturally deceased corpse who I'm sure would've been fine with donating his body to science fiction."

"Will they match?" asked Andre, looking skeptical.

"They don't have to be perfect," replied Will. "Not if we do this right. We need to get them into the refrigerator truck with the rest."

Echo was looking at her phone. "All right, here we go."

Will glanced over. "It's about time. Get it up on the monitor."

Pistol Wizard had gone live on his own Blink account, standing in what appeared to be a combination restaurant/zoo. There were tables and chairs set up right in the middle of animal enclosures, as if the lions, tigers, and bears would be prowling around seated customers as they dined. The facility was, however, empty of both customers and animals at the moment, aside from the vigilante and his captive.

"I am coming to you live from the former Action Safari French Bistro, which was the finest eating establishment in this city before it was so cruelly closed down by the damned lawyers. In response to rumors that the so-called Amazing Aviv has been killed, I present him to you now, in the flesh."

Aviv was behind him in one of the animal enclosures, this one painted to look like snow and ice, as if a polar bear had once called it home. Aviv had some visible cuts and bruises that suggested there'd been a scuffle at some point but otherwise appeared unharmed. Oddly, there was no fence or bars around him, the enclosure was entirely open, seemingly leaving the man free to walk out the moment he didn't fear getting shot by the magical cowboy.

Aviv smiled and waved to the camera.

"Say something," said Pistol Wizard, "so that they can verify your voice and know that this isn't some kind of trickery."

Aviv said, "I am well, though my phone has been taken from me and there is nothing here I can use to entertain myself. If there are any Aviv fans out there, if you can come throw me a book, a ball I can bounce off the wall, something—"

"That'll be enough from you. Now, before any of you out there get any grand ideas of doing a jailbreak, maybe in order to collect the bounty yourselves, you should know that he has been fitted with a constrictor cable that will trigger the moment he passes the boundary of this building. It also triggers if the mechanism is tampered with, or if I am tampered with—if I die, the device goes off. If you're thinking you can put a weapon to my head and force me to disarm it, think again. I can't do it even if I wanted to, which I don't. The device will self-disarm in forty-eight hours, after this blasted election is over and all votes have been counted. Until then, Mr. Aviv cannot be removed from these premises in one piece. If you think this is an empty threat, shall we ask Mr. Aviv?"

Aviv said, "It's true, he even demonstrated that it worked, used it on a pineapple. The wire sliced it like butter. And having spent several hours with the man, I can absolutely attest that he does not know how to deactivate this device, or anything else."

"So there you have it. If the voters of this city do the right thing and put a law-and-order mayor into office, I will happily turn Mr. Aviv over to the authorities so that justice can be served. If not, well, I will see to it that justice is served regardless. Pistol Wizard out!"

He cut the feed.

Zoey put her head in her hands and groaned, then asked Echo, "Have you ever wanted to rescue someone just so you could be the one to strangle them?"

Before Echo could answer, Will said, "We told Aviv's team we'd go get him, that was the deal."

"Yeah, but we didn't say I wouldn't strangle him afterward."

"That's cold," said Andre. "The man just drilled you out of a fallen building!"

"Will made him do that."

"Not that it's relevant," said Will, "but I wouldn't have found him if he hadn't wanted to be found. Do we have a plan for this scenario? His body being booby-trapped?"

"Well, DeeDee managed to get one of those constrictor wires off the sex worker she rescued from Rex, right?"

Echo shook her head. "That was almost an hour of careful hacking, with privacy, while the guy holding the activation code wasn't actively trying to trigger it. The only way that'd be possible here is if somebody distracted this idiot for that long, in a space with no rooms or walls to separate him from the attempt. Aside from the restrooms, the restaurant's space is totally open, including the kitchen. You can see into it from the dining zoo."

"And what is that place, again?" asked Zoey. "The Safari something?"

"The Action Safari French Bistro," said Andre. "Up north, around where they've put in all of the new hotels and the family-friendly stuff? It closed down before your time but it was cool when it was open. It had robotic wild animals that stalked around the restaurant using AI that was just randomized enough to make their movements look kind of natural. I ate there once, they had a black panther prowling around our table while we ate. The thing looked like it had actual sharp teeth and every once in a while, it would growl and lunge at a diner, its mechanical jaws snapping at us, programmed to always stop just inches away. Everybody in the place would scream and get a good laugh from it. Especially when it jumped at a kid, they always reacted the best. A portion of every dollar spent went to wildlife preservation or something like that. It closed in the wake of several lawsuits, the aftermath of a pretty gruesome incident."

"Oh, god. Do I even have to ask what the incident was?"

Andre shook his head and took on a grave tone. "There was a big group of customers, a children's birthday party, in the leopard enclosure. It was a long table, with two of the leopards prowling around behind the kids. Six children, between the ages of seven and nine, all wound up in the hospital, some in critical condition. And yeah, it's exactly what you're probably thinking: they all got sick after a cook got drunk and took a shit in the beef stew."

Echo said, "Wrexx's people are starting to panic. We've planted a rumor that he was seen in a few of the casinos, in camera-free zones, heavily implying that he'd lost a huge amount of money and was bouncing from one blackjack table to the next trying to win it back. It's keeping his fans occupied but his people aren't buying it, they're starting to get suspicious. But if anything, they're waiting for somebody to go public with a ransom demand."

Zoey asked, "Why wouldn't they eventually connect him to the building explosion?"

"Because DeeDee is good at what she does. Wrexx's associates track him through his phone and thanks to her setup, his 'phone' kept checking in with inscrutable messages from the hotel for hours after we took him out of there. Those continued even after the bombing. The final message said he was turning off tracking for privacy, so he could get his head right."

"Okay," said Will, checking his watch. "Damon is doing his big, final rally tonight, less than eight hours from now. That's when our curtain goes up, whether we're ready or not. We'll rotate everyone to get in a couple of hours of sleep where we can find it, but between here and there, we've got a whole bunch of props and costumes to make."

CHAPTER
29

ZOEY HAD FOUND THAT in any arduous project, there is a specific point about eighty percent of the way through when it feels like the entire enterprise was doomed to failure from the start. Thus, at about six P.M., she stood in the ballroom, her ankle throbbing, holding an untouched cup of half-assed Beansomnia coffee, and feeling her gut fill with doubt. She was watching Andre, Echo, and Will try to fit a piece of the ridiculous machine they'd made through the too-narrow door and into the back of a panel truck they'd borrowed from the pool company, the whole time wondering why they'd ever thought any of this was a good idea.

After they'd finished loading it, doing only minor damage to the device in the process, the truck pulled away and Will returned to Zoey.

He brushed off a bit of feather that was stuck to his pants and asked, "Are you clear on your role?"

"Yes, but in a way that is only alerting me to how convoluted this plan is. You and I have to stay here while they finish up at the hangar, right?"

"And you're capable of doing all of it? With your ankle and . . . everything? Everything that's happened? Your head is in the right place?"

"Is this your way of asking how I'm doing, Will?"

"Only to say," he hesitated, "just that there'll be time, when this is over. To think through all of it and work out your feelings. We just have to power through this part."

"I know."

"I don't want you to think that I'm ignorant of what people are going through. There's just a lot to do, is all."

"How are *you* doing?" she asked.

"About how you'd expect."

"I have no expectations about your mental state, in any situation."

"I am swimming to stay ahead of a dark thing slithering through the water behind me."

Zoey looked at him, temporarily speechless.

Then she said, "Come on, I want to go to the kitchen and make a proper espresso."

Will easily outpaced Zoey as she clomped her way down the hall in her ankle-healing boot.

"Hey, wait up."

Will looked back over his shoulder, clearly not understanding why it was necessary for them to walk abreast to the kitchen.

He let her catch up and she said, "You know . . ." She probed herself for the words. "You know that wasn't your fault, right? The restaurant, all of it? I know Wu would say the same."

Offering this kind of sentiment to Will always felt like offering a bouquet of flowers to a wildfire. But she felt it was worth trying anyway.

After showing no reaction, he asked, "If something were to happen to me, could you run the show?"

He wasn't being maudlin or dwelling on his mortality. It was a challenge, a rhetorical question to which the unspoken answer was "no."

"Not yet," replied Zoey. "But you couldn't do it, either, when you were at my experience level."

"That's not what I'm saying. When the incident happened at Montana Skies, when it became clear that we'd screwed up, gotten sloppy, I tried to blame everyone on earth but myself. Budd missed the intel, Wu blew the security scan, you didn't adhere to protocol. But everyone reports to me, everyone takes their cues from me. And the truth is, I had my priorities elsewhere and, as a result, so did everyone else. That's all it takes to let something slip through."

"Oh, so you do blame yourself. You know that's just vanity, right? This assumption that you're the only responsible adult in the world?"

"All you have to do is observe any team member's behavior and you'll see the reality of it. I'm the backstop."

"The what?"

"In any group," he said, "in any company or household or platoon, there's one person who acts as the last resort. If anybody else runs into a situation so tangled that they can't untangle it, there's always this one person who'll know what to do. That was your father, when he was alive. I didn't fully appreciate that, not until he was gone. See, the thing about being the backstop is *you don't have one*. You can't hand off your problems to anybody, you're the last line of defense. If something gets past you, somebody dies. And when things go wrong, there's nobody else to blame."

"Okay, but it kind of seems like you imposed that title and burden on yourself. There's nothing stopping you from saying, 'Hey, gang, I can't handle this all on my own, let's just join together and face this problem as equals.' You act like you've been thrust into this role but if somebody else tried to horn in on it, you'd set them on fire."

"There's no such thing as a leaderless group, humans don't work that way. Someone is filling that role, it's just a matter of whether the nature of the group allows for titles to make it official. Everyone wants to operate with a backstop, because the stress is unbearable otherwise. You have to know that if certain choices become impossible that there's always someone who'll take the responsibility. It's just," he shook his head, "it's just the way it is, Zoey."

"So how do you deal with it when disaster strikes?"

"I channel myself into defeating whoever made it happen. It doesn't bring back the dead, but in this world, that's usually all you get."

"There was a moment when I was under the rubble when I thought maybe everyone had been killed but me. And I asked myself, what would I do, if I got out as the sole survivor? And the answer I arrived at was that it wouldn't matter what I did, because the wolves in this city would come eat me alive. Without my people around me, there's nothing between me and them. So I do get it, I know what the team does for me. And I know what you do for me."

Will, thoroughly hating this kind of conversation, didn't reply, probably in hopes it would just die on the vine. He started to walk a little quicker.

"But," she said, dashing those hopes, "what I can't take is this package deal where the guy in this protector role, this backstop or whatever, says, 'If you want me to keep the wolves from the door, then that means I set the rules, we all operate according to my values now.'"

Will's eyes went wide, like he was on the brink of literally gasping in disbelief. "Zoey, we have totally remade this organization based on your morals. Billions of dollars have shifted from here to there because you weren't comfortable with some aspects of the business."

"I know and appreciate that. I do. But I guess I'm saying this to myself as much as I'm saying it to you. Because if one day you should go off the rails, start getting paranoid and dangerous? I'd have to stop you."

"Of course you would. The rest of the team would join you."

"But what I'm saying is, well, I'm saying it would be hard for me. To make myself do that, like, no matter how crazy things got, I think I'd always be saying, 'Well, that's Will, that's our backstop,' like you said. Because I do notice what you do and it does matter to me. I don't know. I'm not making sense."

"Yes, you are."

"You look exhausted."

"I haven't slept for more than an hour at a time, not since Montana Skies. What almost happened there, I imagine living the rest of my life with the knowledge I'd let it happen and I, well, I *can't* imagine it." He shook his head. "It's unthinkable."

"I guess I just want you to know that I know. You know? Let me try that again: I know that your enemies would try to use it against you, if they knew that you, you know, cared about me. And I know that that means you can't show it. And I know that puts you in a really lonely place and I know that me knowing that probably doesn't make it less lonely but that's all I know to say. That I know."

Jesus, that whole monologue had been a total disaster. Thank god they were almost to the kitchen.

"Anyway," she said, "I just wanted to say that, even though I know it didn't help."

"No. It did."

They entered the kitchen to find Zoey's mother leaning on the beverage bar, engrossed in her phone.

She glanced up. "Hey, Zee! I'm just about to head out!"

"Be careful out there, there are fights and stuff breaking out among campaign volunteers."

"The ones starting fires and turning over cars don't work for the campaigns! They're just idiots who wanted to start fires and turn over cars! They do it when the wrong sports team wins. I'll be fine. How are you doing, Will?"

Zoey said, "Don't ask him that, it's a whole thing. You're working through the night?"

"That's the plan. I had thought the canvassing was just knocking on doors, talking to everybody. But Echo's software targets popular people, the ones who have a lot of friends, or Blink followers. It even assigns charisma scores to everyday folks, the ones who can sway opinions at the last minute. Kind of crazy. Especially when you go look up your own score, it turns out mine is way up there!"

"She says Damon's staff has the same data, instead of targeting everyone, you just hit the influencers. Humans are social animals, we imitate what the cool people are doing, make their same choices."

"Well, I've recruited all of my friends to help, we'll do what we can. Right up until the polls close. We're mapping out a route."

Zoey leaned closer to see her mother's phone screen, which was playing a collage of raccoon videos.

"Are your friends raccoons?"

"Oh, ha, no. Did you hear about Bandito? Poor thing. Everybody's talking about him because of all the pro-Alonzo or anti-Damon phrases we've tried to get trending, the one that's spread the fastest by far is 'Justice for Bandito.'"

"Of course." Zoey sighed. "Andre says Budd would have thought that was hilarious."

"You know what's sad? You never got to tell his joke at the concert, Alonzo disrupted your flow."

"Oh, right, I guess I didn't."

"What was it?"

"The joke? Oh, it was this thing where I talk about how I was living out in the boondocks when I inherited my money, and when I got here a rich guy at a party asked, 'What's your net worth?' and I said, 'Not much, it's got a bunch of holes in it, the fish swim right through.'"

"Hmm, I'm not sure I get it."

"Yeah, I think that was always the point. Good luck out there."

"You, too. It sounds like you're going to need it more."

Leonidas Damon's largest and final rally was being held on the shores of the Atlantis Recreation Complex, positioned so the cameras would capture the wreck of the pirate ship in the background. Supporters had packed the beaches around him, boats had flocked in the water behind. Zoey watched from her kitchen as Damon took the lectern at precisely eight P.M. Monday night to a roar from the crowd that was similar but not identical to the sound she heard when she took the stage at Catharsis: an unchecked zeal, an army feeling the kind of mutual bond normally found only in a bunker. Only these voices had a darker, bitter edge. Distilled hatred bottled with love on the label.

"Thank you," said Damon to the throng. "Thank you. What you're feeling right now is what heroes feel just before victory. The thrill of knowing you're about to save the world."

A huge cheer greeted the end of that line, though Zoey felt like the crowd was ready to cheer any sequence of noises from the candidate. The loudest cries came from the front row, where a dozen of the white-robed Liberators sounded like they were chanting their slogans through tears of joy, though it was hard to tell through the masks.

"I thought this would be an appropriate spot for our final little get-together, the place where they tried to kill our movement, only for it to rise from the cold depths, alive and well. The polls open a little less than twelve hours from now. What happens after that will be written about in history books. How does that feel? To know you're inscribing the pages of history in real time?"

Zoey looked to Will. "If this extremely stupid plan of ours doesn't work, you'll deal with Damon somehow, right? He'll have a mysterious, fatal accident while in office? Maybe make it look like he accidentally strangled himself to death while jerking off?"

"You're not worried that that's just proving him right? That the whole game is about eliminating the undesirables?"

"Are you being sarcastic? I mean, it's a last resort, but it is a resort. I understand your whole bit about how killing the man doesn't kill the movement, but, you know."

"No, he needs to lose."

"That might not be on the table."

"And he needs to lose so hard that he looks ridiculous."

"That," said Zoey, "is by all appearances impossible."

"We'll see." Will dialed his phone and as soon as the other end picked up, said, "Go."

CHAPTER
30

WHEN A HIGHLY ANTICIPATED Blink feed went live, its spread was almost instantaneous. The entire addictive appeal of the network wasn't in the God's-eye level of voyeurism (well, it wasn't *just* that) but in the promise of being *current*, of being perfectly in sync with drama as it unfolded, regardless of location or circumstance. Thus, if a new development occurred in an ongoing story you'd been following, Blink would interrupt whatever you happened to be watching to take you there. So when Rose turned on her camera inside the shipping container, speaking to her audience with well-practiced panic, the viewers didn't have to make the choice to tune in—the software made the choice for them. That meant that within three seconds of going live, Rose had fifty thousand viewers. Within ten seconds, it was half a million. It wasn't just curiosity that drew all of those eyeballs, but an acute fear of being out of the loop, which had been trained into the audience by the algorithm and dopamine.

"Is anyone out there?" Rose said into her camera. "The signal is so weak. Wherever he put me, it's somewhere that the signal can't get to, not very well. Especially not now." She broke down in tears.

Zoey watched this on a split screen with Damon's rally on the other side, both feeds displaying concurrent viewer counts at the bottom so she could watch his audience get pulled away in real time. It turned out she didn't need the numbers; journalists at the Damon rally received the alerts and could be seen looking down to tune into the Rose feed. Stump speeches weren't likely to become news events, barring some kind of gaffe or an assassination attempt. New developments in the Sex Butcher case, on the other hand, were audience-engagement gold. Soon, it was Damon's own supporters in the audience who were checking the alerts popping up on their phones. Leonidas proceeded through his talking points but felt the energy in his crowd dissipating, noting that the last applause line had landed like a mid-eulogy fart.

"Listen," pled Rose in a shaky voice, "if you're out there. He came back. He told me I would never see him again. Then I heard noises, like machines. I went to work on the lock and . . ." She broke down into sobs. "Look."

The camera spun around and Rose pulled open the door to reveal a wall of compacted dirt.

"He buried me! I think this box, I think it's underground, somewhere. I don't know where. I don't know. But I can feel it getting harder to breathe. I'm going to suffocate in here. Please, if you're out there, if this signal is even getting out, find me. Please. It's—it's somewhere with freshly dug soil, large enough to bury something big like this. There'll be construction equipment, bulldozers or diggers. Please. If I don't make it, you have to stop him. It's Rex Wrexx, he did this, he's done it with others, he'll do it again. Rex is sick. And he's gone off the edge. Please—"

The broadcast ended, as if the signal had died.

Back at the Damon rally, the candidate allowed his remarks to peter out, finishing with, "I understand there has been a development in the horrific crime spree gripping this city, I'm going to go huddle with my team to see what we can do to help . . ."

No one was listening to him.

Will looked at Zoey. "You ready?"

She took a deep breath. "I guess so."

She went to the kitchen sink and sprayed water on her hair, cinched her bathrobe closed, and looked into her phone. She opened her rarely used Blink account that, despite her nonexistent posting schedule, still had nearly a million followers.

"Uh, hey," she said into her camera, "I just watched that Rose stream along with you, I'm not much for press conferences so, uh, I guess consider this my statement. I'm going to stand here for a moment and give the audience a moment to trickle in."

The little viewer count at the lower right of her screen jumped from five to six figures in a single frame. She was standing so that her kitchen was plainly viewable in the background. As she talked, she walked into the hall, establishing that she was in her home and caught unaware when this all occurred.

"As of right now," she continued, "at this moment, I do not care about this stupid election. I have associated myself with Megaboss Alonzo and we both welcomed Wrexx and the pull he has with his fans. Politics is about making deals with devils but I have to say, I'm done. Whoever finds Rose gets five million dollars, whoever finds Wrexx, and stops him, gets another five. Uh, million, I mean, not another five dollars, that would be stupid. I'm asking everybody, Damon supporters, Alonzo supporters, tourists in town for the festival, all of you people like me who are just sick of seeing political ads on every surface and every screen: if you're available to help, please do. If you have a vehicle or two working feet, if you have access to a drone or aircraft, please, help us find Rose and the monster keeping her. And whoever else he may have taken. Thanks."

She cut the stream.

She looked to Will. "How was that?"

"Fine."

"I still think we should have dropped some hints to the location."

"They'll find it. We just have to hope they find the right one. Or, you know, the wrong one. The hive mind never misses with something like this. Finding the juiciest story, I mean, not the truth. Let's go. We're going to need to do four vehicle switches if we're going to make it there without being tracked."

It only took about half an hour for the Blink hive mind to nail down Rose's supposed location. There was only one that perfectly fit the description she had given that could also plausibly fit all of the known facts: an under-construction Combat Motocross Association track just outside the city, to the northwest.

It was a sprawling complex of curves, hills, and dips, where riders on dirt bikes would tear around the track, firing at each other with whimsical weapons, such as guided missiles filled with piss. Wrexx owned a CMA team and was one of the early investors in the sport. He was also one of the backers of the new track and, as such, would have had access to the grounds. The entire site was covered by canvas tents to keep the finished product a surprise to curious onlookers, so he'd have had some measure of privacy. Could he have transported an entire screaming shipping container to the facility and had it buried by the earth-moving equipment parked around the site while remaining undetected? Probably not. Was the location just plausible enough to become the focus of the streaming audience's collective curiosity? Absolutely.

So after thousands of drones and millions of viewers scoured every square foot of the Tabula Ra$a metro area and several miles of the surrounding Utah countryside, and after several hundred false leads and rumors were dismissed, the Combat Motocross track was declared to be the secret lair of the Sex Butcher, aka Rex Wrexx. The first wave of vigilantes, street streamers, concerned citizens, and even a couple of actual cops gathered to find that none of the backhoes and bulldozers on the site could be commandeered thanks to anti-theft mechanisms that had been thoroughly locked down by Echo. So the people began to dig with shovels and spades they brought from home, some using their bare hands. More and more citizens arrived to help over time, some bringing water and food or gear to assist the search, like floodlights and generators. All were unified in the task of saving a woman who was, in reality, about seven miles away, sitting in a chair with a cup of coffee and having bloody wounds applied to her face. Not wound makeup— that wouldn't work for a live audience. Actual wounds. Clarence knew the process well and directed the steps from the monitor in excruciating detail.

The dig site quickly took on a carnival atmosphere, as did any gathering in Tabula Ra$a involving more than, say, three people. The food trucks came and someone was playing music. In this spot, no one cared about politics or religion or any of the thousands of tribal markers that would otherwise have kept these individuals from attending the same party. Every Blink influencer with any sense of ambition in their soul was on the scene, moving about the area to figure out which individual digger in the sprawling complex was in the right spot, everyone wanting to catch the first sound of a shovel hitting metal.

Zoey and Will, meanwhile, were in the middle of a vehicle swap to head out of town when Echo popped up on Zoey's phone.

"Okay," said her perfect little holographic face, "I have good news and bad news. The good news is all of the street streamers have converged on the Combat Motocross track, including your friend Margaret Mull."

It turned out that Margaret had not, as Zoey had worried, succumbed to a lethal dose of DeeDee backhand. She was, in fact, still on the case, and of all the street-crime influencers, she was the one the Suits were most interested in keeping distracted. Three times now, Zoey had arrived at a location to find this woman already waiting, as if remaining one step ahead of events as they played out. And that absolutely could not continue.

"The bad news," continued Echo from the phone, "is that Ms. Mull is currently in the process of leaving the track and we don't know why. She said nothing on her stream, just packed up and walked off."

"Is there any sign that she's sniffed out the real location?"

"No, but if she's sniffed out that the race track isn't it, that seems somewhat inevitable."

Zoey turned to Will. "So what happens if she figures it out?"

Will kept his eyes fixed on the road. "Then she'll have a decision to make."

"*She'll* have a decision to make?"

He gave a tiny, almost imperceptible nod. "If she's as smart as I think she is, she'll also figure out that we can't allow her to blow the lid on this."

"Yeah, but, what would we do if she tries?"

"The day you truly become the boss," replied Will, "is the day you realize that decision is yours, not mine."

CHAPTER
31

THE SUITS ALLOWED THE concerned-citizen mob to dig for about two hours, long enough for several arguments to break out regarding whether or not they were digging correctly, or in the right spot, or if they should just wait for heavy equipment to arrive. Those following the drama needed regular updates and plot twists, with steadily rising stakes; when Rose's buried torture chamber wasn't immediately found, the hive mind started to get antsy.

It was clearly time for Act II.

Zoey, Will, and Andre were now huddled around Echo near the back door of the hangar at the old airfield, watching the feed. All four of them were wearing white plastic overalls over their clothes along with rubber gloves that, to Zoey, didn't seem quite sturdy enough for the task. Once they confirmed that there were no possible witnesses within a mile of the facility, Echo started a new stream.

Faking a "live" stream with recorded footage was the oldest trick in the Blink hoax playbook, because there really was no way to detect it—the tool Echo was using was just a slightly more convoluted method of pointing a live camera at a monitor playing the pre-recorded events. The way such feeds were debunked was by other witnesses with cameras of their own physically going to the location and verifying if events were playing out as portrayed. That meant the team had a narrow window in which to act.

Echo's stream—ostensibly live but playing footage recorded hours ago—did not immediately catch on. This was no surprise; whenever

there's a big trending event like this, there are always false leads, streamers attempting to drum up a following by faking some new development.
So when this one began, only a few hundred users tuned in to watch a
small group of figures in white robes and creepy doll-like masks try to
bang down the side door of an abandoned airplane hangar. But just as
Echo had predicted, it slowly gained traction as viewers who'd grown
bored with the Combat Motocross dig began browsing around for alternatives. As the audience tuned in to the fake live feed, first as a trickle and
then as a flood, this is what they saw:

The video wasn't great quality, the product of the cheapest, last-model,
button-sized camera they had on hand, one with poor night-vision capabilities. It opened on a pack of five figures in robes and masks attempting
to shoulder-tackle their way through the locked side door of a large structure. The camera operator, who spoke in a voice that some would recognize as that of Lyra Connor, pointed her camera toward another figure in
an identical robe and mask and asked for an update.

They answered in a voice that repeat customers of the Chalet Intimacy
Parlor might have recognized as that of fill-in manager Axolotl. "We are,
as all of you know, the Liberationists."

Axol was saying this from behind a mask that wasn't exactly like those
used by the Liberators, but close enough. It was a porcelain-doll mask,
white with red-painted lips and dark shadows around the eyes. It was the
best the Suits could find on short notice.

"This whole town has decided to look for Rex at his motorcycle track
or whatever, but our drone, Azalea, has done its work . . ."

Axol gestured into the sky, where a white blur was hovering high up
at the edge of the frame. According to the script, the name of the drone
was "Azrael," but either Axol had forgotten it or, more likely, just decided
they liked "Azalea" better.

". . . and has traced poor Rose's location to here, in this old-ass haunted
airport. If Wrexx is in there, well, either he'll surrender himself for judgment or we'll deliver judgment of our own, on the spot."

Axol held up an object that even a caveman could have identified as a blunt weapon.

"I got it! Here . . ." said another voice from off-camera.

Another Liberationist had run up, handing a tool to Axol about the size and shape of a battery-operated drill. Axol pressed it to the door. The device was a cutting tool, slicing through the door as quickly as Axol could move it, as easily as a marker drawing a line. They carved out the part of the door containing the knob and deadbolt, then kicked it open.

The wearer of the camera pushed through the door and the view swung around the room. The space was much more cluttered than the first time Zoey had seen it, and it was a lot to take in for any casual viewer who'd dropped into the feed out of curiosity. One would glimpse machines and large glass vats, hints of stray blood and meat on the floor. But then the camera settled on the shipping container, now with a giant pile of dirt pushed up against the door on the end. And with that, the follower count instantly exploded.

Lyra, who'd actually refused payment for her performance until Zoey insisted, pointed toward the container. "There! It wasn't buried at all, he just pushed some dirt up against the door to keep her from getting out! We have to clear the dirt away!"

The Liberationists ran over as if to claw away the dirt with their bare hands.

Axol said, "No, I can slice through the side!"

Axol ran up and banged on the side of the container with open palms. "You hear me in there, Rose?"

A faint, frantic voice answered in the affirmative.

"Go all the way to the back!" shouted Axol through the wall. "As far from the door end as you can go. This cutter sprays sparks and molten bits of metal all over the place." That aspect of the cutting tool was, in fact, something they'd discovered when they'd run through this part during rehearsal, when Axol had accidentally set Andre's shirt on fire. "Yell when you're safe!"

Axol cut into the wall of the container and by the time Rose was pulled through the smoking hole, wearing the same filthy underwear she'd worn for her broadcast at Catharsis, theirs was the most popular Blink feed, in any category, in the English-speaking world. They asked Rose if she was okay, if she knew where any other victims might be. Rose found herself too stunned to answer. That's because she was gawping at what surrounded her in the hangar, seeing the Sex Butcher's operation for the first time. The Liberationists looked around them and then they, too, were stunned into silence.

Hulking meat-slicing and -chopping machines, stained with old blood. Plastic-wheeled carts full of butchered remains. And three vertical glass vats, one empty, two occupied with unthinkable horrors.

Axol muttered, "What the f . . ."

The camera zoomed in to reveal what the two occupied vats contained: a Frankenstein combination of women and pigs, mismatched human and swine limbs stitched together for some unknowable purpose. They had no heads; at the stumps of their necks were bundles of wires and clear tubes pumping blood, as if to keep the bodies alive absent a brain to maintain those functions. In response to this sight, Rose delivered, in a trembling whisper, her longest section of dialogue and also the bit she'd struggled with the most during filming. The take Clarence Crockett went with in the final cut never quite felt authentic to Zoey, but maybe that was just the scrutiny that came from having seen it several dozen times.

"He was turning them into sex slaves," said Rose. "He told me, he joked about it, about how he wanted to slice off the useless parts of a woman and keep the rest. I didn't know what he meant, but I think he was trying to find a way to make new bodies and keep them alive, so he could do what he wanted with them. He had some kind of AI that would stimulate the muscles and control the limbs, cause them to go through the motions, react while he had sex with them."

Zoey had never liked that part, she felt like it was overexplaining, that there was no reason Rose would have this much information about Rex "Sex Butcher" Wrexx's devious plan. But Clarence the Director insisted average viewers didn't mind that kind of thing, that the pure, visceral shock value would override the logic centers of their brains. Will pointed out that the holes in this little stunt would no doubt reveal themselves in the weeks and months ahead, but only after everyone had moved on from the story. They only needed the illusion to hold up for the next twenty-four hours or so.

One of the other white-robed figures, a woman saying her only line, asked, "What are all of these machines for?"

"The failed attempts," replied Rose, "the ones that didn't work, that must be how he disposed of them. Look—that's a machine for grinding hamburger. He must have been grinding them up and, I don't know. I don't want to know."

"We have to get out of here before he gets back!" screamed Lyra from behind her mask.

"No!" shouted Rose. "I can't leave them like this!"

She was referring to the two headless zombie-pig sex-slave cyborgs in the vats. Rather than argue—which had actually been scripted but cut for time—Axol strode over to the vats with the club and smashed the glass, allowing the liquid inside to rush onto the floor.

"Burn them," said Rose, gesturing toward a row of red gas cans over by the wall. Echo had pointed out during filming that there would have been no reason for the Sex Butcher to have a bunch of containers of accelerant just sitting around but Clarence had, again, said it wouldn't matter. If you try to make a video for the nitpickers, the effort will be missed by the average viewer and the nitpickers still won't be happy because they're incapable of happiness in general.

While the Liberationists splashed gasoline around the Sex Butcher's cyber-monster sex-slave cannibal lair, a voice from off-camera asked, "What are you doing?"

The camera swung over to find Rex Wrexx himself standing in the very doorway that Axol had just kicked in minutes earlier. Tens of millions of Blink viewers all over the world gasped in front of their screens at, again, something they believed was occurring live.

Will had reluctantly played the part of Wrexx because he was the only one of them whose build roughly matched (Will was two inches taller in real life but that wasn't the kind of thing anyone would notice right away). He wore the actual jacket Wrexx had been wearing the night he died, recovered from the rubble at Carnivore-Tex. Will said the lines in his own voice, which was then redubbed in Wrexx's voice, built by an AI via analysis of millions of words the man had spoken on-camera over the years.

"Wrexx" strode into the room, brandishing a gun. "Whatever she said, it's a lie! Rose came here on her own free will." His voice had been calibrated to sound deranged, the tone of a man who was on a thirty-hour bender with no end in sight, a psychopath who'd reached the final, careless stage, the serial murderer becoming a spree killer. His physical mannerisms matched perfectly because the man playing the role was, himself, mentally strung out nearly to the point of collapse.

"That's not true!" shouted Rose.

"As for them," he sneered, gesturing toward the pig-women in the vats, "I found them like that. I don't even know what they are."

"Just put that down," replied Axol. "If you're really innocent, let the cops decide." Axol had struggled to deliver that part without sounding sarcastic, but they used the best take they had.

"If you destroy them," he said of the vat monstrosities, "you'll be the murderers. They're as alive now as they were before. Because that's all they were, when they were alive. Receptacles. Just like all of you."

Wrexx ran over, grabbing for Rose as if he intended to leave with her. An altercation ensued that wasn't perfectly convincing to Zoey's eyes, but she knew real fights never looked like the movies anyway so the awkwardness would sell it as authentic, if anything.

Wrexx fired his gun, missing everyone. Axol swung their club and connected with his arm, causing him to drop his weapon. Enraged, Wrexx grabbed Rose by the neck and shoved her toward the largest of the meat-processing machines. He kicked a red button with his foot and the machine roared to life, metal teeth spinning inside a feed chute large enough to swallow an entire side of beef.

"This is your fault!" he screamed over the machine. "All you've tried to do is bring me down!"

He twisted a shrieking Rose toward the meat grinder and her shrieks sounded very genuine, probably because she really had been terrified of the thing. Wrexx grabbed her hair and made like he was going to push her face into it.

"STOP!" said a new voice, and the camera swung around to find DeeDee in full vigilante garb.

She ran up and, with her flattened hand, smacked Wrexx in the head. This moment had been another point of bitter contention, with DeeDee insisting that she be allowed to smack Wrexx's head clean off his body. But there was A) no way to do the effect convincingly and B) no way to make that work with the rest of the program, which would, in fact, be performed live for an audience. So instead, the blow was only enough to cause Wrexx to stumble and let go of Rose.

The rest of the Liberationists rushed in to pull Rose away while DeeDee and Axol advanced on Wrexx together. They pushed him toward the whirring machine as he struggled against them, growling threats about all the ways he would torture them once he'd gotten free. Lyra screamed, "Grind him up!" from behind the camera, something that had not been scripted, but she'd seemed to have gotten lost in the scenario a bit, spending the rest of the scene uttering curses toward "Wrexx," some of which Zoey had never heard before. The fake Wrexx put one foot up on the grinding machine, trying to use his leg to push himself away from the chute and the whirring blades that awaited within. At this point, the camera swung away, as if the wearer had spun away from the scene either in revulsion or maybe just to avoid the splatter. The audio, however, still captured the gruesome sound of a man's legs being fed into an industrial-grade hamburger grinder, which the team had created by feeding a man's legs into an industrial-grade hamburger grinder.

The video then cut out, as if the camera had been shut off.

The fake video feed that had taken nearly twenty people several hours to put together ran for only seven minutes and forty seconds. The finished product still wasn't exactly what they'd planned. For example, they'd originally hoped to shoot the events from multiple angles, since the idea that such a group would show up with only one camera was significantly less believable than the existence of the Sex Butcher dungeon itself. But there was no time to make a second or third feed perfect, so they'd scrapped it. Regardless, now the live portion was about to begin.

The issue, as always, would be time. The Suits knew that the moment Echo's fake feed appeared interesting, real people would be heading to the airfield as quickly as they could get there, at which point the locked fence around the facility would hopefully buy the Suits a few more minutes. It's true that the shovel-wielding mob at the motocross track were easily an hour away, even on a good traffic day, but the fake feed needed to completely play itself out before *anyone* laid eyes on the interior of the hangar. Any Blink user who happened to be right next door or driving past could show up early and spoil the party. So the Suits frantically working inside the hangar had one ticking clock—to be finished and out of there long before the seven minutes and forty seconds of pre-recorded feed elapsed—and then separately had to hope that no witnesses showed up to the scene within that window.

Thus, while the world watched the "Liberationists" burst into the door of the hangar via Blink, Echo was saying, "Go, go, go" to Zoey, Andre, and Will, who all rushed out the back door to a borrowed catering truck they'd parked just outside. That truck contained a refrigerator section and a warming section, which was probably great for making sure the roasted chicken and bean salad were both at the perfect temperature for a wedding reception. In the Suits' case, they'd been hauling around two halves of two separate corpses in the refrigerated section to halt decomposition. About an hour earlier, they had gone through the messy process of dragging them across the truck to the warming section. They'd left them in long enough to heat to just over one hundred degrees, so that the parts would be at roughly human body temperature when or if the first bystanders on the scene felt the need to touch them. These, Will was fond of pointing out, were the little details that, if overlooked, could screw up a PSYOP and alter the course of history.

The legs—which Kowalski had provided from a corpse—had already been fed into the hamburger grinder as the final step of filming the fake feed. Now they were carefully pulling out the other half: the severed torso of Rex Wrexx that they had recovered from the bomb site. It had oozed all over the truck and Zoey made a point of telling Will that she didn't want it ever used to haul food again. They hustled the leaking torso into the hangar and put it into position in the hamburger-grinder chute, the arms dangling out in such a way as to prevent it from sliding in further. They splashed around some blood so that it would still be wet for whoever arrived first, wiped up any fluids they'd spilled on the way in. Then they turned on the meat grinder, made sure the Liberationists and DeeDee were in the right positions, then got the hell out of there.

They had cut it terrifyingly close. The first bystander on the scene was a passing farmer who was totally unaware of the Blink drama but was set to receive alerts regarding proximity to any violent crime in progress (he kept a pump shotgun in his truck for just such occurrences). He arrived at the fence before the video had even ended but stopped at the gate. Ramming through chain link with a pickup truck looks easy in an action movie but at best is going to scratch the hell out of your front end, and the farmer still had seven years of payments left. Instead, he laboriously climbed over and, even with that delay, breached the hangar a mere forty seconds after the pre-recorded stream had ended. If he'd had a camera, or had just thought to look, he'd have seen the Suits racing away in their catering truck, but that wasn't his focus; he arrived with an understanding that a woman was being rescued from her captor and that the heroes doing the rescuing may need help.

He had thus burst into the hangar and found the masked Liberationists standing around the whirring meat grinder, gore scattered at their feet. Axol punched the off button on the machine and the farmer observed that on the output end was a spray of chopped-up muscle, skin, and bone. Lying in the machine's mechanical mouth was the actual, intact torso of Rex Wrexx. It was clear what had happened and would be even clearer to someone who'd been watching the supposed live feed: the Sex Butcher had, ironically, been butchered, turned into hamburger, feetfirst. If the farmer had touched the torso, like, to check for a pulse, he'd have discovered that it was exactly as warm as one would expect a freshly dead corpse to be. But neither he nor anyone else would feel the need to do that, so the whole effort to make sure the partial corpse was the correct temperature had been a total waste of time.

Instead, the farmer walked close enough to the corpse to see that it was, in fact, the famous Blink influencer Rex Wrexx, but not so close that he would be standing in the slain man's blood. Only the farmer had no idea who Rex Wrexx was, so that detail was also lost on him, and he backed away so as not to contaminate a crime scene. The farmer asked everyone present if they were all right, assuring them that help was on the way.

Sure enough, two more witnesses soon popped in the door behind the farmer: a young couple who very much did know who Wrexx was and who were at least a little familiar with the Sex Butcher case. They also approached just close enough to confirm that what they'd heard on the stream had taken place in real life; that Wrexx had died via partial hamburgerfication and that the extremely identifiable top half of him lay in the machine's bloody feed chute. They took plenty of pictures and video and no amount of analysis would ever find that the corpse they recorded was not, in fact, exactly who it appeared to be. A pair of camera drones then buzzed in, creating additional verification. No amount of interrogation of the witnesses or analysis of their captured footage would reveal any inconsistencies: Wrexx's torso was wearing the tailored shirt and jacket he'd been wearing when last seen, his fingers bore his custom-made jewelry, the necklace given to him by his grandmother hung around his neck. Unassailable third-party records of the aftermath had been created. A new truth had been birthed into the world.

One of the newly arrived drones, Zoey noticed while watching from their fleeing vehicle, was wearing a tiny red hat.

At this point, Rose, who'd had to make herself cry a second time to match the physical state she'd been in at the end of the pre-recorded video, asked the newcomers to back away. In a state of determined, righteous rage that she had to perform live and with no second takes, she borrowed the laser cutter from Axol and used it to ignite the gasoline that had been splashed on every object in the vicinity. It actually took several tries to ignite it and Zoey held her breath the entire time. But then it caught and the Sex Butcher's lair went up in flames.

CHAPTER
32

IT WAS HARD TO anticipate, Will had said, how a devoted fan base would react to a scandal, in the same way that it's hard to know how a cult's followers would react to a fallen leader. But it usually depended on the offense. A professional athlete will never lose his fans over charges of tax evasion, but evidence of rigging games is lethal. A teen heartthrob can probably survive accusations of cheating on his girlfriend but not, say, getting caught on-camera strangling a dog. It all comes down to how uncomfortable it becomes for fans to express support publicly. As Echo had noted earlier, humans are social creatures who instinctively want others' approval of their tastes. It thus takes a special kind of scandal to make fans burn their idol's merchandise in the streets, knowing they can never again be seen wearing it in public.

It said quite a bit about Rex Wrexx's fans that, with each suggestion of how to stage his ignominious death, Will had shaken his head and said, "No. It has to be stranger." When, at the conference-room brainstorming session, Zoey had finally suggested what *she* thought the Sex Butcher's lair should look like, everyone agreed it would probably work and then kind of avoided talking to her for a while after that. Sure enough, in the couple of hours since the event, there didn't seem to be a lot of Wrexx defenders making their voices heard. Hurting sex workers was one thing, but what he was doing was just *weird*.

This, of course, did nothing to help Alonzo's poll numbers. Any hope for that, if there ever was any hope at all, would come in the morning, with Act III. For now, news of what occurred out at the old airport needed to percolate and marinate in the zeitgeist. As such, way down the list of trending topics, a single word kept coming up, ascending on the wings of rumor and the occasional sightings of an odd shape in the sky:

Azalea.

Sure, it wasn't trending above "Justice for Bandito," but it was slowly gaining steam.

It was now the wee hours of the morning and Zoey was in one of the white sedans with Andre, heading toward the former Action Safari French Bistro. She'd been texting with her mother, who was still doing her canvassing among those on the contact list who were known to be up overnight. In this city, that was no small number of people.

Zoey said, "I can't get over what my mom told me about how their vote-canvassing plan was all about picking out this small group of voters who actually matter."

"Well," replied Andre, "it's not that they matter more as human beings, they're just the types who spend more time and energy socializing and keeping on top of trends, that kind of thing. Most normal folk don't have time for that nonsense, they're too busy working their jobs and raising their kids. So when they want to know what to do, what to wear, what to eat, they look to the whales."

"The what?"

"Come on, now. You've owned enough casinos to know what a whale is."

"Oh, right. A big shot."

"Well, a big spender. A heavy user. About a quarter of the city's gambling revenue is from this tiny group of rich, obsessive players. We're talking the top one half of one percent. You can pick any vice, you'll get the same. Alcohol, your real profit comes from the top ten percent of drunks, the guys who down seventy-five drinks a week. Opinions about politics are like that: a sliver of the population forms strong opinions and everybody else just looks to them to decide what they should think. Let me give you a tip, should you ever find yourself in such a position: if you want to run a city, focus on the whales."

"You mean the rich donors? I'm pretty sure politics has worked like that forever."

"No, I mean the whales in all areas, not just money. Like crime. About seventy percent of this city's armed violence is done by the same group of a few hundred people, we're talking literally two hundred and fifty or three hundred individuals. Instead of treating crime like it's this looming dark cloud of evil, or blaming a whole race or demographic, you zero in on the tiny pack of individuals capable of carrying out these acts and intervene. Go right to the whales."

"I'm starving, but I feel like it's inappropriate for me to stop and eat. I've been obsessed with getting a fancy corn dog ever since I ran into Monkey Sheriff at Catharsis."

"There'll be people serving food at the Safari Bistro."

"I don't think it's still a working restaurant."

"No, but in this city, where there are crowds, there are food trucks."

"Crowds?"

Traffic was at a standstill blocks away from the abandoned bistro. Sleepless curiosity-seekers were choking the sidewalks and streets, even clogging the parking lots of the surrounding businesses. Zoey had assumed Aviv had fans—it'd have been a tragedy if all of that cost and risk was for, like, thirty people—but it somehow hadn't occurred to her that his arrest and subsequent abduction would draw a crowd. She had been told that some were holding a "vigil" outside of the restaurant but wasn't expecting *this*.

Zoey asked, "Does no one in this city have to get up for work in a few hours?"

"Lots of businesses close on election day," said Andre. "It's got something of a party atmosphere. But also, pretty much everyone on Blink following this story thinks this is all the prelude for one of Aviv's patented stunts. They think the arrest, getting snatched up by this guy, that it's the equivalent of a stage musician making a big show of getting chained up in a straightjacket before he's lowered into a tank of water. Not just that he'll get out, but that he'll do it with *style*."

"Well, he's not."

Andre didn't reply.

"I mean, his team told me that directly and they'd have to be in on it if he had anything planned."

Still nothing from Andre.

"We're about to risk everything to get him out," said Zoey, who intended to just keep saying things until Andre responded. "He had to know we'd try to come get him. If this is part of a stunt and he intentionally didn't tell me, that's purposefully lying in a way that could get people hurt. I'd never forgive him."

More silence for a moment, then Zoey said, "Just say it."

"Certain guys, they see everybody else as audience, so they get it in their heads that all will be forgiven if the show is good enough. Like his bit with the yellow robot, he'd probably imagined some cutesy reveal that would leave you mad but a little dazzled at the same time. I'm not saying that's what's happening here. I'm just saying. Let's go."

The two of them made their way through the crowd, Zoey feeling Wu's absence as she pushed through a field of sleeves. Andre could probably fend off an attack from any normal assailant, but Zoey fully believed Wu could extract her even if every member of this crowd turned on her at once. It wasn't just that he was capable, it was that he was willing, and that thought almost made Zoey tear up again. She hadn't visited him in the hospital yet, though her presence would probably have just annoyed patient and staff alike. She also decided that her snap decision to plunge into the crowd at Catharsis without Wu at her side was probably the dumbest of her entire life.

She was holding a clear plastic shopping bag. They wanted the contents easily viewable and noted as innocuous by even the dumbest guard. The "B" team of this operation wasn't visible from their viewpoint but that was by design. Sig and the two biggest and burliest members of Aviv's support crew were two blocks away in a borrowed ambulance, dressed as paramedics. The disguises only pertained to their employer, not their qualifications: Aviv's team were, in fact, trained in all manner of emergency medicine, as they were almost always the first response in cases of stunts gone awry. Zoey assumed they had no contingency for, say, reattaching a head freshly severed by high-tech cheese wire, but they were here for a charade, not medical intervention. At least, that was the hope.

The Safari Beef Bonanza or whatever it was called had a roof but no walls to speak of. Thin columns supported an overhead platform on which wild animals full of gears, hydraulics, and circuit boards used to prowl about and lean over the edge to menace arriving customers. It had probably looked pretty cool in its day, but the now deactivated frozen animals up there had been exposed to wind and rain for a couple of years, their fur having molded and sloughed away, leaving them looking like cybernetic zombie predators. Below them was the expanse of faded animal enclosures and tables. The chairs had all been sold or stolen, it appeared.

Aviv was lying on one of the tables and whistling a mournful prison song. The Pistol Wizard was stalking around the perimeter, twirling his gun around his finger, waiting for somebody to try something. The only barrier between him and the crowd was an old, flimsy orange plastic fence, erected long ago in a token effort to keep curiosity-seekers and vandals out of the closed business. What kept the audience at a distance right now was the fear of an augmented armed idiot and the knowledge that any attempt to encroach on the situation would result in a gruesome outcome for their hero. A girl shouted at Zoey and pointed to her head—she, too, had shaved a Zoey stripe in it. Also, Zoey did note that Andre was right about the food trucks; she passed one doing bustling business selling a variety of food, but none of it was corn dogs.

Zoey and Andre shouldered their way to the front of the crowd. Pistol Wizard spotted them immediately and strode over, gun in hand, a smirk on his face.

"Did you come here to buy your boyfriend's freedom?" asked Pistol Wizard, projecting his voice so the crowd could hear. "Because this cowboy ain't for sale."

Zoey held up the bag. "We got here as fast as we could. You don't have to let us in, you don't even have to let us talk to him. But he needs this."

Pistol barked a laugh. "How dumb do you think I am?"

"It's his seizure medication," said Andre. "Sealed in the package, you can have an expert examine it, if you've got one on hand. But the man needs it. Those instructions were given to the cops but we're guessing you didn't listen when they tried to tell you that. If they even bothered."

"Whatever his supposed seizure problems," answered Pistol Wizard, "I'm sure they can wait one day. Now, you two can just git on outta here."

Zoey shot a look to Aviv, who was still lying on the table but now making eye contact with her. They hadn't discussed this plan with him in advance, of course—they'd never had the chance—but he had to have overheard the word "seizure" by now and it didn't require a particularly nimble mind to put together what that plan was.

"Listen," said Zoey, "this isn't just for his safety, it's for yours. Seizures are more likely when the patient is tired and hungry. Look it up. If Aviv has one, you have to get him to a hospital. But you can't get him to a hospital without killing him. If he dies because of your stupid contraption, then the rabid fans you see around me will have no reason to stay back. The invisible wall keeping them away from you will have dissolved."

Pistol Wizard held up his revolver. "I've got my invisible wall right here."

"You've got six bullets in there," said Andre. "Against an enraged crowd, that's just going to make them madder."

"See, I don't think so. Because in that whole crowd, each one is gonna wait for someone else to go first, to absorb the bullets. And I'm guessing they won't find any takers."

"You're being a dick for no reason," said Zoey. "Just look in the box. Or let me open it and show you the contents. But that's all this is, some medicine. And he said he was bored, so I brought him this."

She held up what, hopefully to Aviv's eyes, was a red rubber ball. This one was from Wu's inventory and Zoey had zero practice using one. And they did only have one.

In a blur of movement, Pistol brought up his gun so that it was pointed directly in her face. "Get. Back."

"If he doesn't get this, he could have a seizure any minute. The medicine, I mean, not the ball. Do you understand? *Any minute.*"

If Aviv hadn't gotten the cue by now, Zoey thought, he never would. With an expression on his face that Zoey interpreted as curious concern, he hopped down from the table and approached. Pistol Wizard spun on him with his revolver.

"STOP RIGHT THERE. Get back on the table." He spun back to Zoey. "Go away."

Andre had in his pocket a tiny little device that, DeeDee had claimed, would spoof the "all is well" signal to Aviv's constrictor wire collar. But to work, it needed to be close—as in, just inches away from the wire—and that was only the first step to extracting Aviv from the situation. All they needed right now was a pretense to get close to him, as if administering emergency first aid—

"Don't," said Aviv to Zoey, smiling as he approached. "I thought you guys might try something like this, because you are the coolest, but there's no need."

When he got close, Zoey noticed for the first time that she actually couldn't see a wire around his neck.

Aviv looked to the sky. "Sig, if you're listening, and I assume you are, call it off! I love you guys, but you don't have to do this. I'm fine."

He backed off and Pistol lowered his weapon. Aviv headed back to his table but instead of lying down, he hopped up onto it, standing tall as if about to give a speech. It turned out that's because he was.

"Can everybody hear me? Can I have quiet? Thanks. So, I've had some time to think here, while being a captive of one of this city's superpowered weirdos. And I have an honest question: Who out there just wants things to be, you know, normal? Not a dark theocratic dystopia, not a superhuman freak show, just a fun city where you can live your life without waking up to another nightmarish headline. It can't just be me, right?"

The response from the crowd indicated that it was not, in fact, just him. Zoey and Andre exchanged a look that combined confusion, dread, and utter exhaustion.

"I know this is last minute," shouted Aviv from his perch, "but this city has the best, most advanced voting system in the world, so I think we can make it work. I hereby throw my hat into the ring for the position of mayor of Tabula Rasa. Now, it is too late to get my name officially on the ballot, but on your voting app, all you have to do is scroll down and fill in my name in the write-in blank. The Amazing Aviv is my legal name, you do have to spell it right for it to count."

The crowd went wild. Zoey put her face in her hands. She really, really just wanted to go to bed.

"Voting starts in a few hours!" shouted Aviv. "I know most normal folks are asleep right now but when they wake up, I want them to find our write-in campaign as the top trending topic! Toss the clowns in the lake, both of them. The Amazing Aviv for mayor! Oh, and Justice for Bandito!"

Zoey muttered to Andre, "Get me out of here or I'm going to kill him myself."

CHAPTER
33

ZOEY WATCHED THE FISH Bowl burn from inside her shower.

She had, reluctantly, switched the shower's interior screens from "outdoor shower on tropical beach" to a news feed. That's where she found out that Aviv had not, in fact, gotten his write-in mayoral bid to be the top trending subject, but it was way up there. It was just hard to top people waking up to find that one of the world's most popular streaming influencers had turned out to be a serial murderer who was experimenting with headless porcine sex zombies. The ensuing discussion had even dredged up some forgotten allegations about Wrexx's connection to a headless corpse in Bali and, it turned out, similar cases in at least three other countries.

So she bathed and watched Wrexx's transparent tour bus being consumed by flames that had been ignited by his own fans. His security entourage, who presumably were only waiting for their final paychecks to clear, did nothing to stop it. It wasn't clear who, specifically, had started the fire, as it was very much a group effort. Many of the most loyal Wrexx disciples were eager to be seen on-camera publicly rejecting the man and all he had stood for, as were his allied influencers. Zoey turned off the feed and finished the bathing and drying process in peace, then made a conscious decision not to bother with the robe. Her outfit for the day was a tailored white jacket and skirt that was supposed to have some kind of symbolic significance but soon she found herself standing in front of it and thinking about how vividly it would show bloodstains, if this was to be a day for such a thing.

Her phone chimed in a message.

Zoey had texted Wu earlier to ask how he was doing but wasn't expecting a response. It just felt weird to not at least ask. So she was caught off guard when it turned out the message was from the man himself:

Wu:

ZOEY THANK YOU FOR YOUR MESSAGE

A pause, as if he was struggling to type.

Wu:

UNFORTUNATELY IT IS CLEAR NOW THAT I AM GOING TO DIE

She felt her heart sink. Could she even get to the hospital to be with him in person? Would his family even allow her in?

Wu was still typing, ever so slowly.

Wu:

OF BOREDOM.

Zoey groaned and replied,

You almost gave me a heart attack.

Have you had your surgery yet?

After a very long pause, during which Zoey was afraid Wu had fallen asleep, he replied,

TWELVE HOURS OF COMBINED SURGERY ON THE CRUSHED LEG

TRAUMA SURGERY AND THEN ORTHOPEDIC

STILL NEED ONE MORE AND THEN SURGERY ON ANKLE.

Zoey replied with a frowny face.

Wu:

BUT THE BOREDOM IS THE WORST.

Zoey:

Well just focus on getting better!

There was another pause long enough for Zoey to assume the conversation was over. She set herself to getting dressed, deciding on the white suit because she didn't want to devote the energy to finding something else. Then,

Wu:

THE DOCTORS SAY I WON'T BE ABLE TO WALK

For the second time, Zoey's heart sank. Surely there was something that could be—

Wu:

NORMALLY UNTIL I'VE HAD MONTHS OF PHYSICAL THERAPY.

Zoey:

Hey would you mind waiting until you have the entire message typed up before sending it?

Wu:

NO

Pause.

Wu:

PROBLEM.

Zoey sighed, tossed her phone onto the bed, and got ready for Act III.

She had made everyone meet in the kitchen for the morning "let's all gather to see what fresh Hell awaits us" activity. Only after arriving in the kitchen, fully dressed in her symbolic white suit, did she realize she was starving (they had not, in fact, hit up any of the food trucks at the scene of the Aviv fiasco, and she'd collapsed into bed upon her return to the estate). Her hunger had been awakened by the heavenly, unmistakable scent of Carlton's waffle iron doing its work. She entered the kitchen to find Andre at the food bar talking to someone on the phone, his tone conveying that he was in overdrive trying to charm them into doing something they presumably did not want to do. Budd's spot next to him was conspicuously vacant. Will was deep in conversation with Echo, and neither of them looked up at her when she entered. No Wu, no Budd, no one to talk to.

She went to the bar next to Andre and asked Carlton what was for breakfast. Next to him was a wire rack onto which he had arranged the thick, finished waffles so that they would take on a curved shape, like taco shells.

"Korean street waffles," said Carlton. "A favorite of Arthur's when he was anticipating a particularly hard day. A crispy warm waffle, folded to hold a generous filling of cream cheese, honey, and whipped cream, in layers."

"Oh, god."

"Arthur used to say that the dish did nothing to make the events of the day turn out well but that for a few minutes, at least, all would seem right with the world."

A moment later, Will came over and saw Zoey about to ram her face into the cream-and-waffle taco. He nodded toward her spotless, white suit.

"You might want to eat that with a knife and fork."

"You can use a knife and fork to eat a butt. What's the status of all the simultaneous horrors happening in our world?"

"Damon has scheduled his morning press conference at eight, after he makes a big show of using the app to cast his vote. We—or rather, the Liberationists—have scheduled a press conference that is to occur immediately after Damon finishes his. So for right now, it's Damon's move."

Zoey's mother burst into the room. "Ooh! Waffle tacos! Honey, you should be wearing a bib, that shirt is, like, five thousand dollars."

It had, Zoey knew, actually cost a lot more than that. Zoey's mother was wearing a presumably less expensive T-shirt that said "JUSTICE FOR BANDITO" around an animated graphic of a sassy-looking raccoon with a halo and angel wings.

Echo said, "He's apparently on his way to the lectern now."

Zoey's mother asked, "When will we know who's winning?"

"That's a little complicated. No one has the right to see the vote counts in real time, as that could skew the results. But when people vote on the app, they get the option to report their choice publicly, without their name, of course. It kind of works as an instant exit poll. And that does update in real time."

"The problem," said Andre, who'd apparently finished his call, "is that you get into all sorts of game-theory nonsense. Maybe Alonzo voters are reporting their votes as Damon, to boost his numbers and motivate other Alonzo voters to punch their ballot, to catch up. Or maybe one candidate appeals to a certain personality type that's more likely to tell the world who they support."

Zoey bit into the waffle and tried to suppress the indecent noises she wanted to make upon tasting it.

"So," said Zoey, wiping a full tablespoon of whipped cream from her face, "what you're saying is that we have data, but it's bad data."

"Which," added Will after sipping his drink, "is worse than no data at all."

"I think the show is about to begin," said Andre, taking a street waffle from Carlton. "Everybody cross your fingers and hope he takes the bait."

Since there were no official polling places, Leonidas Damon decided to hold his ceremonial vote and speech at the scene of Wrexx's burned-out tour bus, smoke still wafting from smoldering embers. The man liked having apocalyptic ruins in the backdrop of his public events.

"I won't keep you long," began Damon, "I know that most of you, my supporters especially, have work to get to, children to take to school, business to conduct. And at this point in the campaign, what is left to say? We are on the winning side of history and our people are already proving it. We will burn out the poison that flows through the veins of this city. They call me a dictator but I am not the one who is going to cleanse Tabula Rasa. You will."

He gestured to the crowd, specifically to the row of white robes who'd been given their usual, conspicuous spot in the front.

"It's the citizens who are rising up, fighting back. That's what we've seen over these last few days, a populace that thirsts for justice. All I want to do is harness that energy, to say, 'What can we, as a government, do to help?' When I take office and the predators of this city cower in fear, it won't be me they see in their nightmares, it will be you!"

A clamor of approval from the crowd.

"Societies can't be reformed from the top down," he continued, "it has to happen on the streets, on every corner, in every alley. Change comes from every citizen who sees wrongdoing and says, 'No! Not in my town, scumbag!'"

A roar from the crowd, but a bigger roar from the white robes in front.

"Now go vote! Let's send a message!"

The feed ended. Will took a deep breath, finished the rest of his drink, then looked to Echo.

"Tell them we're a go."

The knockoff Liberators group, the "Liberationists," had been Zoey's idea. She'd had some trouble putting her finger on exactly what bothered her about Leonidas Damon, aside from the hundreds of obvious things that bothered her. She finally decided that it was how he tried to have it both ways: he wanted the benefits of a like-minded gang roaming the streets to enforce his rules but without the drawbacks of accountability. His connection to them was, by design, nebulous and unspoken, an association that existed in the minds of the voters but on no documentation or payrolls. If they stop a crime, he takes credit. If they screw up, they take the hit. It would be a shame, Zoey had said, if someone were to exploit that ambiguity somehow.

So the press conference they'd put together for the Liberationists included no fewer than fifty members in white robes and doll masks—the sum total of all the costumes that could be found or made on short notice, and all of the associates they could convince to wear them in exchange for a nice payday. It was enough to give the impression to even the mildly informed voter that this was the largest and thus most important faction of the white-robed enforcers. Hell, who was to say these weren't the originals?

They'd positioned themselves in front of the main entrance of the giant crystal-donut mall, the one that housed the Chalet Intimacy Parlor among hundreds of other businesses. Axolotl had not been asked to act as the leader of the knockoff Liberators group but had simply assumed the role and refused to discuss it further. So, backed by this gang of masked and robed angelic crusaders, Axol stood before a crowd of press, street streamers, curious onlookers, and camera drones. It was a galaxy of eyeballs vastly larger than the one Leonidas Damon had just addressed.

"Everybody be quiet!" yelled the masked Axol to an already quiet crowd. "We're not looking to get famous, we're just here to let everybody know how things are gonna be from now on. You all have seen by now how things went with Rex and his freaky sex-monster dungeon. As Leon Damon just said, we will rid this city of evil. And this time next year, none of y'all will ever leave your house in fear. You will never walk down a dark alley, never cross a parking lot without the knowledge that there is an angel nearby. You will know it, and the freaky deviants who walk these streets will know it. They will know that a powerful, all-seeing eye will spot their sins and someone will intervene, right then and there. Gird your loins, folks, because this," dramatic pause, "is Azalea."

They'd had it hovering just out of sight, behind the donut mall. On cue, Azalea floated up into view through the center hole of the building, descending over the crowd until it was just overhead, the motors issuing forth a deep rumble at a frequency of 17 Hz, which Will had said was scientifically known to induce dread in the human brain. Every face in the crowd turned skyward. Every mouth gasped. Azalea—or Azrael, as it was supposed to have been called—was a drone built to resemble a Biblically accurate angel. It had been Will who'd pointed out that these holy messengers from the Lord were never depicted as women with harps and two wings on their back. In the book of Ezekiel, they're described as a "wheel intersecting a wheel . . . full of eyes all around." In Revelation, one is depicted as having six wings and is said to be "covered with eyes all around, even under its wings."

As such, Azalea was a twenty-foot-wide, winged, thrumming monstrosity. The rumbling engines were embedded in a feathered abdomen that sprouted six white wings. The whole apparatus was then surrounded by three intersecting rotating wheels, all of it fabricated in Santa's Workshop. There were huge, red, terrifying eyes glued to every surface that could hold them. In the center, on the main body containing the engines, was a seven-foot-wide eye the color of blood with a white feathered eyelid that occasionally blinked. As Azalea hovered, always present was that deep thrum felt in the gut, a noise like the guttural growl of a hulking predator. It could be felt from two blocks away.

"You've seen our angels around," continued Axol, "this here is the next step. See, Azalea doesn't just look out for crime, it looks for *sinners*, so that they can be stopped before crime happens. Azalea can detect bad intentions instantly—it scans facial expressions, posture, and other scientific markers of bad character. High testosterone, that sort of thing. It instantly recognizes any face, then accesses criminal records, flagging predators in advance."

The crowd actually seemed kind of impressed so far.

"And this is the amazing part," continued Axol, "this here drone, and all of the others we'll be filling the sky with, scans Blink for any history of sinfulness, with the unclean instantly flagged in the system. It will know if you have been dishonest in your business dealings, when you have had sexual intercourse outside of marriage and, thanks to voice and face scans, when you have told a lie. Any history of taking a bad tone with a stranger, arguing on the sidewalk, or telling offensive jokes—everything will be noted and logged."

Some muttering from the crowd. This seemed like a step too far, to those paying attention.

"It can also detect deviant sexuality in an instant," continued Axol. "Eye-tracking technology tells it exactly where your gaze is pointing at all times. It measures microscopic changes in blood flow to the face and heat signatures to the genitals, which signal arousal. That means if you are a married man ogling the body of a woman who is not your wife, you will be publicly flagged in the system as an adulterer, for the Bible says that you have committed adultery in your heart."

A couple of people in the audience laughed, thinking this was a joke.

"Laugh it up while you can," said Axol. "Anyone who shows signs of sexual arousal at the sight of anyone more than seven years younger than themselves will be publicly flagged as a predator and a groomer. Would you like a demonstration? There is a young lady here in the front row wearing a tight T-shirt. In the course of this gathering, fourteen men and three women have committed adultery in their hearts at the sight of her. They have all been flagged."

Some people in the crowd were actively talking back now. Axol ignored them.

"For example, you, sir." Axol pointed to a middle-aged man in the crowd. "Thanks to Azalea's detection system, we can say with one hundred percent accuracy that you, a married, forty-six-year-old man, are having an affair with your twenty-five-year-old coworker. Not only are you an adulterer, but the age difference means you are a predator. Your wife and coworkers have been notified."

Every nearby camera turned on the man, who was instantly in a panic. "That's—that's not true! We're just friends! It was her idea!"

The guy, of course, was a plant, paid to play this role.

"Azalea, tag this man."

The audience had presumably assumed that all of the mentioned markings and flaggings were to be done in some kind of software that would be opt-in for the viewer, and probably continued believing that as the feathery mass of spinning eyes descended on the man. Then the crimson center eye split and opened. From inside came a spray of fluorescent green that painted the man from head to toe. Everyone around him recoiled to avoid the splatter.

"That dye glows in the dark and stays on the skin for five years. You can't wash it off." This wasn't true, but it's not like such a chemical would be impossible to create. "All sinners will be marked and publicly shamed."

Azalea rose and loomed over the uncertain faces below, slowly rotating as if scanning their faces, reading their minds, weighing their souls. Then it locked into position, as if it had found another target.

"You, sir," said Axol, pointing to a random man in the crowd, one who was absolutely *not* in on it. "You just had an explicit sexual fantasy about a young woman who just walked past wearing tight shorts and a tank top. You, too, have been flagged as an adulterer and a predator. You shall be marked."

He sputtered a denial in much the same way the previous man had, then tried to run. Azalea easily caught up and painted him a bright shade of Sinner Green. Zoey noticed a few bystanders got paint splatters on their clothes and frantically tried to rub it off.

"And, of course," continued Axol, "Azalea will know if you have had an abortion, or facilitated one for a partner, and will flag you in the system, and real life, as a murderer."

The crowd was now yelling back. It seemed a line had been crossed.

Zoey held her breath.

In the rear of the pack of Liberationists, some of the white robes were slipping away, backing through the doors of the mall. This was their escape plan if the audience got out of control. That is, if this all went exactly according to plan.

"But that's not all," shouted Axol, who was standing firm over their objections, "the system also tracks associations via Blink, so that all who continue to employ, work with, or befriend the tagged sinners will also be tagged as sin enablers. You will be named and shamed, cut off from employment and opportunity, until morality returns to this city and this countr—"

Axol ducked to avoid a thrown shoe.

"Destroy that thing!" shouted someone from the crowd. It was the first painted man.

A chair was flung at the rumbling Azalea drone, knocking off a cloud of feathers. A shoe bounced off its blinking eye, followed by a briefcase that had been hurled with impressive force. Most of the mob was now focused on trying to slay the robotic angel. *Most* of them. The rest had decided to go after Axol and the remaining Liberationists. One guy rushed the lectern. Axol punched him in the jaw, knocking him out cold.

Then came a noise loud enough to make the clouds tremble. It was a trumpet, emitting from the spinning angel drone. It was a sound simultaneously regal and terrifying, the signal that a royal avenger had been aroused.

The first painted man, the one who'd been secretly paid to play this role, slumped over onto the pavement, as if dead. His hands and feet twitched, which Zoey thought was a bit over the top. Then, Azalea spoke in a voice that had been calibrated by their software to inspire pure dread:

"THIS MAN HAS BEEN DESIGNATED A VIOLENT THREAT AND EXECUTED. EVERYONE IN THE VICINITY WHO DOES NOT RELENT AND REPENT WILL SUFFER THE SAME FATE."

The feathered machine then revved its motors, its intersecting rings of eyes spinning faster.

Each member of the mob below now had a decision to make. We often boil this choice down to "fight or flight," but Zoey knew from personal experience that there was a third common reaction: "freeze." As Azalea readied its next attack, Zoey found all three in the mob below. Some ran for their lives, some froze in place, as if waiting for instructions. What the plan needed was for that third "fight" group to focus entirely on the flying machine.

Azalea opened its red eye and its green dye sprayed forth, only now it rotated so that all were being sprayed and tagged. As it sprayed, it lowered itself closer to the people, low enough that it seemed well within range of attack. A woman in the audience who was walking on crutches swung one of them, bonking the outer ring of eyes.

"Get it!" someone shouted.

The fighters fought and the freezers watched as Azalea was battered with projectiles until it wobbled and started to fall, screaming louder and angrier warnings that only added fuel to the mob's rage. Axol and the rest of the Liberationists were now quickly retreating into the mall behind them, ditching their robes and disappearing into the bustling swirl of shoppers and tourists. Axol was the last one in, locking the mall doors to prevent pursuit from the rioters.

Soon, the mechanical angel of judgment tumbled to the pavement. Just moments later, the second man to be dyed green stood atop it and, with a primal howl of rage, smashed its center red eye with a cinder block.

CHAPTER
34

MEGABOSS ALONZO DUNN WAS awaiting vote results at a bustling barbecue held in the downtown park. Thousands of supporters and random hungry people would wash in and out of the event through the day, grabbing a rib or chicken leg and, hopefully, casting a vote with their phone. As with everything Alonzo did, it was loose and casual and also carefully calculated. It was a beautiful day with temperatures in the sixties and you couldn't beat the vibe of tens of thousands of smiling folks enjoying free food while old-timey blues music wafted from speakers. Alonzo intended to spend the day mingling with the crowd, taking pictures, and shaking hands. The unspoken message was clear: "This is all most people want: to enjoy their lives and to be left alone." And in case the unspoken message wasn't conveyed, it would also be spoken by Alonzo, loudly, several dozen times.

Zoey and the Suits had intended to spend much of election day at the park barbecue, not onstage but simply among the citizens, making it clear whose side they were on. There, they could wait for any crises to break out and respond as needed.

Around lunchtime, Zoey was in the park eating a barbecued chicken wing when Will came along. He looked disapprovingly at the wing and then glanced at Zoey's white lapel for stains.

Zoey said, "It's a chicken wing, Will, it's either this, or you can feed it to me so I can keep my hands clean."

"We need to leave."

"What's happened?"

Echo, who was close behind, answered for him. "All of the streaming viewers are on Aviv's event and, while I know we said we weren't looking at the exit polls, it's clear that he's moving votes."

"So? I don't see how Aviv would be any worse than the candidates we have now."

"Do you even know his politics?" asked Will. "You understand that we're not just supporting Alonzo based on a general vibe, right? He has specific government appointments to make and specific laws to get passed and enforced. But even then, the problem isn't that Aviv will win. There isn't enough time to get the largest block of votes, most of the city won't even have heard of him by the time polls close. The problem is it doesn't take much to swing the election and he can easily peel off enough to do that."

"How do we know he won't swing it to us?"

"We don't," replied Echo, "and we can't model the outcome either way. He's appealing to those who weren't going to vote at all because they hate both candidates, plus some who just want chaos. Identifying exactly who those voters are, how many of them exist, and how they'll behave is difficult to impossible."

"So what are we supposed to do about that?"

"We go to the Safari Bistro," said Will, "and you try to convince him to scrap his write-in campaign and throw his support to Alonzo."

"What makes you think he'll listen to me?"

Will and Echo just stared in response.

"All right, let me finish my wing. Somebody get me a damp towel."

Zoey had been taken aback by the size of the crowd when they'd had their aborted breakout several hours earlier, but that turned out to be a mere beachhead for the main assault. The Safari Bistro throng was now engulfing several city blocks and was more raucous than either of the other two candidate gatherings. Many weren't there because they wanted Aviv to be mayor but for the reason Andre had mentioned earlier: they thought it was a stunt, the final act of Aviv's election-prank trilogy. After months of brutal negative campaigning between the two known mayor candidates, here was a charismatic agent of chaos stealing the spotlight from both in a way that surely infuriated them. It had thus become publicly safe and beneficial to be known as an Aviv fan; he was filling a void in the zeitgeist. It also came at the perfect time, since the Catharsis festival was over, as was the Sex Butcher hunt. Residents and tourists alike were looking for the Next Weird Thing. Were they about to see a grand escape from a devious trap? Were they about to see a man gruesomely die in the attempt? If you wanted to know, you didn't dare look away.

It was almost, Zoey thought, like Aviv had planned it from the start.

Getting through the crowd this time was going to require the opposite of stealth. They took the flashiest company helicopter and landed on the only building with a pad on the roof—still a few blocks away—and made a show of flying the aircraft low over the crowd on their approach. Zoey and her entire surviving team then made their way down the sidewalk toward the zoo restaurant, creating quite a stir in the process. Zoey at one point had to stop and sign an autograph for a girl who, once again, had shaved a stripe in her scalp to approximate the bald spot Zoey had just that morning tried desperately to hide with a side part. She also noticed that they kept passing people eating exotic corn dogs, one guy munching on a hot dog enshrouded in a coating of french fries, another on one that seemed to be enrobed by a sliced-open Twinkie and then deep-fried. The elusive corn-dog truck was surely nearby but, in one more cruel irony, Zoey was now in no mood to patronize it.

As they reached the densest part of the crowd, Aviv stood atop a table and shouted, "Let her through! That's Zoey Ashe! And her scary entourage! Let them through!"

By the time Zoey, Will, Andre, and Echo arrived at the orange fence around the old open-air restaurant, they were being tracked by seemingly every flying camera in the city, everyone assuming that their appearance was part of the stunt. Aviv approached the fence with a huge smile on his face.

"Don't smile at me," growled Zoey. "I'm coming in there."

She climbed over the fence. Pistol Wizard rushed over, his six-gun at the ready.

"Get back, missy!"

She did not. She stumbled into the restricted area, rolled to the ground, then got up and brushed dirt off her skirt.

"If you shoot me," she told Pistol Wizard, "my people will kill you and everybody you know. I have to talk to Aviv, in private."

She grabbed Aviv's elbow and pulled him toward the only enclosed space: the restrooms off to their left. Pistol Wizard fired a shot into the air. Zoey flinched, but kept walking.

Pistol Wizard chased after them, weakly shouting, "Hey!"

"All you have to do is wait outside," said Zoey, not even turning to address him. "Aviv clearly doesn't want to escape, so I can't imagine what you're afraid is going to happen in here."

Before Pistol could even respond, they reached the restroom and Zoey shoved Aviv inside, then closed and locked the door behind them.

Aviv grinned. "You look amazing."

"I could strangle you right now. It's just lies on top of lies. You don't care about me, you care about your fame and selling branded merchandise."

"No, we can't do that," he said, stopping Zoey's hands. She had taken off her jacket and had been in the process of unbuttoning her shirt. "I mean, I want to, but we physically can't. You have to know why."

"Because your idiot captor could barge in on us?"

"No, because of the constrictor wire."

"What wire?" She pulled his collar away from his neck. "You don't even have one on."

"I very much do."

"Where?"

Aviv just stared, a strange smile on his face.

Zoey said, "You can't be serious."

"It's partially my fault," said Aviv, unbuttoning his pants. "The loop was too small to go around my head and Pistol Wizard didn't know how to loosen it. So while he was struggling with it, I might have sarcastically suggested an alternate placement for it and he might have decided from that that it was a good idea. See?"

He pulled his pants down and showed her.

"I can't slide it off," he noted, "because it's behind my—"

"Shut up. Aviv, I've only known you for, like, two days but I am confident in saying that this is the kind of thing that could only happen to you."

"I know, right?"

Zoey sighed and squeezed her eyes while Aviv buttoned up his pants. "This thing, your run for mayor, this was your plan all along, wasn't it?"

"Yes! That was the election-day stunt, I was going to put in my name and we were going to rig the screens downtown to display 'Vote for Aviv' slogans. Stuff like that. The voting app makes it really easy to do write-ins, if enough people write in a name, the software starts auto-suggesting it in that field as the day goes on. We tested it and—"

"You looked me right in the face and told me you weren't going to do this."

"I said I wouldn't do anything to disrupt voting! And I'm not, I'm running as a write-in. Nobody is being tricked, they can choose to vote for me or not."

"And what's your plan if you win?"

"I won't win, come on. Novelty write-in candidates don't actually win elections."

"In a normal city, no. Have you honestly not—"

She was interrupted by a roar from the crowd outside.

"Oh, god," she asked, "what is it now?"

She stepped back out of the restroom and found the crowd outside the orange fence was parting for a new arrival. Zoey suspected she knew who that new arrival was, mainly because there was only one person who could truly make the situation exponentially worse and, according to the rules of the ancient curse that this city apparently lived under, that's who it had to be.

Leonidas Damon and an entourage that included his wife and assistants made their way through the crowd, Damon smiling his fake smile and waving as if he was among friendly supporters, though here he most definitely was not. He forced his way toward the spot in the fence where the rest of the Suits were waiting for Zoey to return.

"So now all becomes clear," announced Damon as he reached the fence, using his stump-speech voice. "The corrupt puppeteers of this city put together a scheme to try to thwart the will of the people. Honestly, it's insulting that you think it's so easy to manipulate the public."

Andre said, "Did any of this look *easy*?"

Zoey approached the fence. "I promise you that not only did we not ask Aviv to run, but I am officially asking him, in front of all the cameras and all these people, to please drop this write-in campaign. It's just confusing the voters." She said this while awkwardly trying to re-button her shirt. "And what exactly do you think we planned? Do you think we blew up our own building? Do you think *that* guy," she gestured toward Pistol Wizard, "is on the payroll? Look at him!"

"He won't drop out," replied Damon with a sneer. "No, he's still got one big stunt left. I don't know what it is, but I bet you do."

"We definitely do not," insisted Zoey. "And considering the horrors that have played out over the last couple of days, the acts of terror, the gruesome deaths, the tensions around the city . . ." she had turned toward Aviv and raised her voice to make it extremely clear who exactly needed to hear this, ". . . I can't imagine what kind of 'whimsical' stunt wouldn't be *incredibly* inappropriate."

Leonidas Damon shook his head. "You people have nothing to offer the world but distractions. Is that what you want on your tombstone, Zoey? That all you did was feed wasteful habits, selling brief amusements and cheap gratification? Our whole civilization is amusing itself right into the dustbin of history."

Andre, who had somehow acquired a corn dog that seemed to be encrusted with Cheetos, said, "Hey, this city was built on cheap gratification!"

Will said, "We give people ways to relieve their boredom before it congeals into sadistic cruelty."

"Whoa, am I missing the party?!?" came a booming voice from behind them, the crowd once again parting for its arrival.

That was, of course, Megaboss Alonzo, who along with his entourage was pushing his way through to the front, where every camera was now pointing. He apparently had heard that the other key players—and all of the streaming traffic—was converging on this spot and didn't want to be left out. "Are we having an impromptu debate? We never got to finish the last one."

Damon smirked. "I'm sure you'd like us all to believe that you—"

"OH, MY GOD!" screamed Zoey, "SHUT. UP. All of you, shut up! Shut up! Shut up! My head is pounding. I am so sick of listening to men talk and talk and talk and talk."

She bent over, her hands on her knees, trying to breathe and settle herself before she said something she didn't mean.

She stood, took one more slow, calming breath, and said, "No bull has ever shit as much bullshit as you bullshitters shit. Honestly? Of course, there are more qualified mayors out there than Alonzo. *I'm* probably more qualified to be mayor, and I have no idea what specifically a mayor even does. But *you*," she stabbed a finger at Damon, "I look at you and all I see is a smooth, paved road that leads gently downhill into a mass grave. You don't care about humanity. You don't love people. You look at this," she swept her hand across the crowd, "and you see an infestation, a mess that needs to be cleaned up so that you can finally have a perfect, orderly society of people who are exactly like you, because you're so narrow in your thinking that you're sure you're the only true human being and that everyone else is trying to be you and just failing to various degrees. And the irony is that if I could somehow breed a destructive personality trait out of humanity, that kind of murderous tribalism would be at the top of the list!"

Damon said, "We are going to win. One way or the other."

"Now, here's the other thing: I can't even tell if you know what's lurking beneath your skin. I think you've dressed up your whole deal in so many pretty words and academic ideas that you can't see the tribal animal inside, whispering in your ear. You think you've been blessed by evolution to tame the jungle? I *hate* that people like you force us into this choice, where we just have to pick some other option based purely on the fact that they're not *you*. I could spend the rest of the day criticizing Alonzo but I don't dare, because any criticism of him risks steering history into a mountain of human skulls."

Damon smirked. "Are you finished? Because what people like you don't under—"

"NO. I am NOT finished."

Zoey pointed a finger at Aviv who, at the moment, was stripping off his shirt with a smug expression like he was just dying for Zoey to ask him why. She refused.

"You," she said to Aviv, "people like you stand on the sidelines and point out what's wrong with the system, getting applause because you throw pies in faces. But if you were put in charge, the whole thing would collapse in a day! You don't have any solution beyond what a toddler would offer. 'Everyone should have everything they want, for free, all the time!' Well, guess what, there's more collective wants than there is collective stuff, so now what? You don't know, because criticizing the system without taking the risk of offering alternatives is *nothing*. It's a dog barking at thunder."

Aviv had already taken off his shoes and socks and was now removing his pants.

Echo muttered, "Why is he—"

"DON'T ASK! That's just what he wants. He has some kind of stunt in mind and he's not going to be deterred. It's best that we just ignore him. Everybody, just vote your conscience. Ignore all of the sideshow, stop following politics like it's a sport designed to entertain you. Do what you think is right, then regular folks, rank-and-file humans grinding away in cubicles will try to make it work, like always."

"She's right," declared Aviv.

Zoey turned to find he was now standing in the Safari Bistro, totally nude, to cheers and hoots from the crowd.

Damon sneered and said, "Don't make a fool of yourself."

"Too late," replied Aviv. "Thank all of you for your support and thank you for coming out here and keeping me company during my imprisonment. But I've grown tired of this and I think we're done here. So, yeah, if you want to vote for me, do it. If you want to vote for somebody else, that's okay, too. But let me leave you with this final statement. Here is what the future will look like under Leonidas Damon."

Aviv got down into a sprinter's stance. The crowd went dead silent. He took several deep breaths, like he was bracing himself.

Echo whispered, "What is he doing?"

Will said, "I can tell you with all sincerity that I have no fucking idea."

Aviv took off toward them, sprinting toward the orange fence. Pistol

Wizard made some noise about stopping or he'd shoot, but he seemed as confused as anyone else. Zoey backed up, as did the rest of the crowd, gawkers munching on their corn dogs, eager to see what was about to happen next.

Aviv ran with determination, as if running from his own mortality, as if chasing down a destiny that was just as determined to evade him. He was heading for the dining table that happened to be the closest to the orange fence.

He reached the table, leaped onto it, then jumped off the table, both arms in the air.

The nude man *almost* cleared the fence.

Instead, his ankles hooked the top of the fence, causing his body to flip end-over-end, his momentum pushing him past the invisible barrier that would activate the constrictor wire. There was an almost inaudible, wet *squinch,* and Aviv, his eyes suddenly wide, had birthed a spray of crimson from his groin. His body pinwheeled toward the crowd, causing his severed genitalia to soar ungracefully through the air, the momentum of Aviv's spinning body launching the member like a trebuchet. The elongated wad of undulating flesh floated through the air until it smacked Leonidas Damon square in the face, leaving a red splatter on his cheek.

Aviv flopped to the ground. There were gasps from the crowd. Confusion froze everyone in place. Echo had her hand over her mouth. Andre had been in the middle of chewing his corn dog, then spat it out.

Will, his expression unchanged, said, "Huh."

Four figures emerged from the crowd at full speed, one of them carrying a white medical-grade cooler. Zoey thought this was awfully convenient, but of course, the cooler bearer was Sig and the other three were members of Aviv's support team/trauma unit. One of them flipped open a briefcase that unfolded itself into a stretcher and, with practiced efficiency, they staunched the bleeding on the man's groin and gathered up his severed part to put it on ice. They raced through the crowd with the wounded man on the stretcher, down the sidewalk, until they were met by an ambulance that had, again, been conveniently waiting in the exact right spot.

There was a smattering of uncertain applause. Leonidas Damon was forcing one of his assistants to clean his face with a disinfectant wipe. Nearby, a crying child vomited.

Pistol Wizard stood, his gun at his side, watching the ambulance race away, sirens blaring, hopefully to the nearest hospital.

He scrunched up his brow and said, "What in the *hell* was that?"

Zoey sighed. "Democracy, apparently. I'm going home."

CHAPTER
35

ZOEY:

Hey would you mind if I came up to see you? It's fine if you're not feeling up to it.

Wu:

NO.

Zoey:

No, you don't want me to come or no you wouldn't mind?

Wu:

DON'T COME

Zoey:

Okay, I understand. Do you mind if I ask how are you doing?

Wu:

WITHOUT BRINGING FOOD

SOMETHING SOFT

BECAUSE OF MY TEETH.

Zoey:

Done.

Wu:

WHO WON MAYOR?

Zoey:

The polls are just about to close, we'll find out together!

* * *

She arrived at the top floor of the hospital with an assortment of dishes from food trucks outside, including bingsu (hair-thin, creamy ice noodles), kakigori (shaved ice with the texture of packed snow, soaked with heavy coconut cream and mango sauce), and a layered milkshake cocktail that would phase through five different flavors as you made your way down.

She was greeted in the hallway by Wu's wife, Mei. Zoey braced herself. Zoey had always gotten the impression that Mei hated her, mainly because the woman made little effort to hide it. The circumstances of this meeting—that Zoey had gotten her husband buried in an exploded building—had her preparing herself for anything up to and including a physical assault. Mei spotted her and Zoey instinctively turned to hand off her tray of treats to Andre, just in case.

It was a good thing she did. The woman raced up to Zoey and gave her an aggressive hug.

"Uh, hi," said Zoey.

"He told me how you stayed with him. My goodness, what a story. It must have been terrifying."

"I've barely had time to dwell on it. I suspect when my schedule frees up, all of the trauma will catch up to me at once."

"Well, we'll be praying for you."

Wu's teenage children were parked on a bench in the hall, each playing games on their phones. One of them was wearing a Justice for Bandito T-shirt. Outside Wu's room—a full suite in the rich-people section of the facility—were two men in pink suits who Zoey knew were on loan from her own private security company, there in case some bad guys came after Wu and sent more than the three or so he could handle himself from the hospital bed. When she entered the room and saw him, she burst into tears.

Wu's left leg was in a cylindrical black cage with various tubes running off of it. His right ankle was in a plastic cast similar to the one Zoey still wore on her sprain. His face was swollen almost beyond recognition; black and purple bruises covered his jaw.

"It looks worse than it is," he slurred, then immediately shifted his gaze to Andre. "Ooh, give me the one with the straw."

The monitor in his room was already on, currently showing street-streamer Charlie Chopra, who was covering the smashing of Liberator angel drones. Angry mobs were also downing any drones that sort of looked angelic, including those belonging to a flower-delivery company who'd chosen devices that looked like Cupid. Zoey swiped it to election coverage.

She asked, "How long does it take them to count the votes?"

"Zero seconds," said Echo, who'd arrived in the hall behind her. "It's all electronic so there's nothing to be counted, it just holds off on announcing the results until the last person has voted."

"Your boyfriend just got out of surgery," said Wu. "He's down the hall."

Echo added, "They think the video of his, ah, accident will set the record for fastest-spreading clip in Blink history. Specifically, the version someone posted that was in extreme slow motion."

Zoey sighed. "Please tell me I'm not visible in the clip that's going around."

"You are," Echo replied, failing to hide her glee, "and the slowed-down zoom on your facial expression is really something. You can see several emotions playing out on your face at once."

"What, were you guys watching it in the car on the way over?"

"I had intended to watch it once, just to understand what, exactly, had occurred. But it bothered Will so much that I wound up replaying it a few dozen times."

"Do we have results yet?" That was Will, who'd joined Echo in the hall. They both shuffled into the room so they could see the monitor.

Zoey looked to Wu. "Do you hate it when your hospital room is all crowded like this? I always hated it."

"It will be fine until the pain medication wears off. Then I become very irritable."

Zoey's mother arrived next, squeezing into the room. "Have I missed it? What happened?"

Will shushed everyone—the vote results were in. A news talking head standing in front of city hall went live. He said the results would be read as they were released, in no particular order. Zoey clinched her fist as she waited, and then the first results appeared on-screen as the reporter read along:

"Megaboss" Alonzo Dunn: 28%

Everyone in Wu's hospital room groaned. Someone down the hall, presumably a Leonidas Damon supporter, cheered and clapped. Zoey scanned the faces around her and saw only uniform dread as more results rolled in:

(Write-In) Zoey Ashe: 12%

Zoey's mother hooted and clapped, then suddenly stopped after a sharp look from her daughter. The Suits had known some would write in Zoey's name and her canvassers had been told specifically to discourage that, as any such support would be taken directly from Alonzo. But they hadn't spent a lot of time thinking about, or planning for, this result.

"Still," muttered her mother, "it's nice that people like you!"

Zoey didn't reply. With a sick feeling, she watched the rest of the numbers arrive.

(Write-In) Bandito the Raccoon: 13%
(Write-In) Aviv: 5%
(Write-In) Amazing Aviv: 6%
(Write-In) The Amazing Aviv: 4%

Zoey shook her head. "I knew allowing write-ins was a bad idea. I feel like I'm in a nightmare."

(Write-In) Aviv's Flying Severed Dingus: 1%
Other Write-In: 4%

Will and Echo exchanged looks, rapidly trying to do the math in their heads. Before they could work through it, the talking head read out the answer at the same time it appeared on the screen:

Leonidas Damon: 27%

"Wait," said Zoey, "did we win?"

"We did," replied Will, "though if you combined their votes, the actual winner was Aviv, Aviv's dick, and an exploded raccoon."

"It's so close between Alonzo and Damon," said Zoey's mother. "Will he demand a recount?"

Echo shrugged. "There's nothing to recount. It's a database, that data was entered directly by the voters."

The feed cut to Alonzo's election-night party in the park, where the crowd was cheering and weeping. It then cut to Leonidas Damon's gathering, where everyone just seemed incredibly confused.

Zoey looked to Will. "So, did this play out exactly according to your secret plan you came up with months ago?"

He sighed and said, "Sure, why not."

Contrary to what Wu had said, Aviv was not, in fact, "down the hall" but was located in an adjacent tower connected by two elevators, a sky bridge, six hallways, and three helpful staff who redirected Zoey when she got lost. The whole complex seemed like a prank hospital somebody had built just to mock her. But finally she found a room packed with so many balloons and flowers that it had to have violated some hospital regulations. She knocked on the doorframe and Aviv, who was covered in a blanket but seemed to have a lot of tubes and wires snaking out from under there, lit up at the sight of her.

"Hey!" he proclaimed. "It looks like I'm gonna be okay! They did a surgery I guess to temporarily reattach things and get the blood flowing, but the real surgery is tomorrow to connect all of the nerves and such at a micro level. They're having a world-famous surgeon from Hong Kong do it remotely with those robot arms. Isn't that wild?"

Sig was seated next to the bed, looking exceptionally cranky. Though Zoey thought she was one of those people who just had a cranky resting face.

"She doesn't want to hear the gory details," said Sig. "I think you're lucky she stopped by at all."

"Ah, Sig is squeamish about this stuff."

Sig leveled a disbelieving gaze at him. "*I picked it up with my hands and put it in a cooler.*"

"And I've told you how much I appreciate it!" To Zoey, he said, "I had my team on hand in case the trap went off. What I did at the end there, that was spontaneous! I just came up with it on the spot."

"I'm going to be frank," replied Zoey, "it didn't look planned. And as a piece of political performance art, I also have to admit I'm not at all clear on the message."

"Maybe that was my intent."

"So what happens when you get out, do you move on to the next city, plan your next stunt?"

"Even if so, I could still come back to see you, or you could see me. You have your own helicopter! And because it'll take time for me to, you know, recover, we could actually just hang out and spend time together, actually get to know each other. Talk."

"Uh-huh. So how long will it take you to, uh, recover?"

"Well, the doctor said six weeks, but when I told him it was you, he was like, oh, three months at least. She'll pull it right off."

Sig threw up her hands and left the room.

"She's had a rough few days," said Aviv. "So your guy won the election, right?"

"Eh, the monster didn't win, which is what matters. In my world, that's about the best we can manage. I have to go, my foot is killing me. I want to go home and knock myself out with pain meds."

"When I get out, we'll get a room, a cheap one, order some Chinese food and watch a romantic comedy."

"Aviv, we don't even know if we can tolerate each other's company for longer than it takes to have sex and get dressed."

"Let's find out!"

She sighed and said, "Sure, why not. But just to be clear, you and I have nothing in common."

"Of course not! It would be outrageous for me to even suggest such a thing. That's why we should get together, so you can find out we have nothing in common. Then you can move on."

He delivered all of this with a toothy grin. God, the guy was so sure he was great at this.

"Whatever," sighed Zoey. "In the time it takes you to get out of here, you'll probably meet some hotter girl and forget all about me."

At some point in the conversation, Zoey's body had moved closer to the bed and it was now holding hands with Aviv. She studied all of the wires and tubes and wondered if they would get damaged if she were to climb onto the bed and snuggle her face into Aviv's neck.

"And, uh, I'm sorry," said Aviv, "about your friend Budd, I mean. I know he meant a lot to you guys. There was a time right at the start, when we were getting my drill and the rest of your team were doing scans and all that, when we thought we could get everybody out, we thought maybe you'd all survived. So I was there when the news came. It sounds like the guy was a legend."

"Now that he's gone, I think he'll literally be that. A legend. Nobody will believe he's actually dead."

She released his hand, wiped her eyes, and said, "All right, I'll get out of here and let you rest." She slapped his thigh. "You're going to need it."

Zoey left his room and felt like maybe, finally, somehow she was done with tense meetings for a while. She couldn't remember the last time she hadn't had some strategy session or debate or *something* on her calendar that tied her guts in knots. As she headed down the hospital hall she almost felt weightless. She studied signs to try to figure out how to get back to Aviv's room, took what she thought was the right elevator and, one floor down, it opened to let on another passenger:

Streamer and amateur detective Margaret Mull.

Zoey said, "Oh, *come on.*"

"I won't stop this one," said Margaret, both hands perched atop her umbrella as the doors closed. "Do you know who I trailed to wind up here? Lyra Connor, who had an appointment to discuss reconstructive surgery on her face."

"I guess that's good," said Zoey, "as it seems like that will get results for her quicker than waiting for all of society to stop judging women based purely on appearance."

"I also wanted to let you know that I was there, when you were doing your show at the airport. Well, my camera was. You use software to detect feeds but as with anything, it's an arms race between detection and evasion. The feed wasn't public, it was just for me. So I could understand."

"I saw it when it hovered into the room," said Zoey. "And I assumed it hadn't just arrived there. But I didn't tell my team that."

Margaret had to pause a moment to process this. "I'm working on the unsolved Wrexx cases. The ones overseas, I mean. It would be nice to bring closure to those families."

"Oh. That's good."

"How did he die? Really?"

"I don't know what you're talking about."

There was a pause, then Margaret said, "Well, I'm glad the three women are safe."

"Are the other two safe? That's good news."

Margaret nodded. "Before coming here, Lyra met all three of the women for celebratory drinks, in very cursory disguises. A lot of smiles, a lot of laughter. They seemed to be planning new financial futures for themselves."

Zoey just watched the floors count down.

"It appears you're determined not to say anything to me," said Margaret, "and I understand, though I wish I had the answer to just one question. Why not simply tell the truth?"

"I still don't know what you're talking about, but somebody once told me that sometimes, the truth looks like a lie and the only way you can set things straight is to tell a lie that looks more like the truth than the truth."

"That sounds like something a lawyer would say. Or a politician."

"And what nobody had to tell me, because I figured it out myself, is that people are just people but celebrities are an idea. If you want to stop one, you can't just kill the person, you have to kill the idea."

The look on Margaret's face indicated that she had, in fact, gotten the answer she was seeking.

The elevator dinged, the door opened, and they both stepped off.

"So," continued Zoey upon finding the hallway empty of eavesdroppers, "you're saying you know something the public doesn't. Are you obligated to share that information?"

"I am not a journalist. I seek justice for victims who have been failed by the system. That keeps me quite busy in a city that barely has a system at all."

"Are you sure? You could get quite a bit of publicity for your streams by blowing the lid on, well, whatever you believe we've done here."

"My dear, if fame was my goal, I would have learned to sing. Some of us do just want to see the right thing done. I would say most of us, in fact."

"Do you think I'm one of you? One of the good guys?"

"Time will tell," replied the older woman as she shuffled down the hall. "I'll be watching either way."

Zoey watched her go, then surveyed the unfamiliar surroundings and realized she had, in fact, gotten on the wrong elevator.

CHAPTER
36

BUDD BILLINGSLEY'S FUNERAL WAS strange in that nothing at the event openly marked it as being for Budd, or being a funeral. It was held late at night in Frisco, a genuine Old West ghost town about a half hour west of the city. Budd had apparently bought the land that used to be Frisco, which at the time of purchase had contained mainly a collection of dilapidated shacks and fenced-over mineshafts. The genuine buildings had since been roped off for preservation, and around them was built an open-air bar/grill/nightclub. The music was low, the lighting soft, a gentle breeze rustled the scrub brush. Attendees instinctively kept their voices calm, as if this was a sacred place in which the dead were trying to rest.

Hundreds showed up and Zoey knew none of them. Andre introduced one fancy guest after another, with connections and relationships stated only in vague terms. There were a lot of "associates" and "friends," faces from all around the world (she heard at least four different languages spoken in the conversations she passed), and she knew there was a whole collection of prominent figures who couldn't come, or who couldn't be seen attending. Instead, the Suits had set up an area for flowers and other gifts, one so inundated with colorful displays that it looked like a Rose Parade float had crashed there. Many of the gifts, Andre had said, came with unsigned cards and cryptic messages that only those close to Budd would understand. Virtually none included his name.

She and Andre then ran into Alonzo and DeeDee, the former in a black suit and the latter in a stunning gown designed to look like she was enshrouded by gleaming black eels with bright red pinprick eyes.

Andre said, "Good evening, Mr. Mayor."

"Man, don't even use that word," replied Alonzo. "I had DeeDee spend the last week helping me put together a to-do list for my first hundred days and just looking at it gave me a heart attack. I say to her, 'This is a nightmare, whose idea was this?' The desk in the mayor's office has seven drawers, I'll need at least five of them for alcohol."

DeeDee just shook her head. "I told you."

"Do you have an official position?" Zoey asked her. "Comptroller? Chamber of commerce? I'm just throwing out words I remember seeing on yard signs."

"Oh, don't think I didn't ask," said Alonzo. "She's got it in her head that she'd wind up getting stuck with all the work. No, she's got something far more ambitious in mind. She wants to unionize the sex workers."

"Now, that's interesting."

"All the powerless can do is gather together," said DeeDee, "organize, and gain some power in numbers."

Alonzo shook his head. "Good luck with that. Impose too many rules and girls will just work outside the organization. Try to stop them and you're right back where you started, with prohibition."

"This is a world of infuriatingly imperfect solutions. But you'll find that out soon enough."

Zoey looked around. "Do you know where Will is?"

Andre pointed. "Old graveyard. You'll see it, over in that direction."

On the way, Zoey found Echo, wearing a tight black floor-length dress with a slit up to her hip. She was being hit on by a man with the build and composure of an NFL quarterback. Echo spotted Zoey and used it as an excuse to break away, pretending like she had some urgent business to discuss.

"How are you holding up?" asked Echo once they were on their own.

"Hospitals, funerals, conversations with strangers in suits. My last week has been a buffet of all my least favorite things."

"Let's get away to a beach somewhere. A private one. Just the two of us. Or just you, if you want to be alone."

"No, I'd need you as my social buffer, you know I can't talk to people. Just tell me when and I'll follow you to the airport. How are *you* holding up?"

"This is the worst it's ever been for me. Losing someone, I mean. When I came on board, Budd was the one who tried to bring me into the fold, no one else knew what I was even doing here. He was the one who said, 'Around here, you make your own role.' Then he showed me how."

"So this is worse than when my father died? Just before I got here?"

Echo had to think about that for a moment.

"I don't know. My relationship with Arthur was, ah, complicated. He was the king but he liked the idea of me more than he liked me—you know how men are. And he became weird and distant at the end. We sensed he was, I don't know. On a dark path. Like we didn't know what was going to happen but we were all preparing for *something*. It's hard to explain."

"How is Will doing?"

"Go ask, he's right over there. I'll set a date for our beach thing and if you try to back out, I'll sedate you and drag you onto the plane myself."

"Sounds good."

Echo broke off and Zoey found Will Blackwater standing alone at a wrought-iron fence surrounding an ancient cemetery full of crooked tombstones so weathered that some names were no longer legible. Memories literally erased by time.

"Do you have your flask?" she asked him.

"Left it at home," answered Will without looking at her. "I'm trying to cut back."

"You know the weirdest part? I still expect to find out that this was all an op, that Budd is going to pop out of the shadows, explaining that this was a ruse for some purpose or other."

"I wish. But if you're seriously asking, no, we wouldn't have left you out of the loop on something like that."

"I know you're still blaming yourself and I've accepted that nothing I say will stop you from doing that, so I guess I'll just leave it be."

Will just kind of grunted.

"So who's buried here? Old-timey prospectors?"

Will nodded. "In the late 1800s, some guys found this mine, sold it for twenty-five thousand dollars, thinking they'd won the lottery. The next owners would go on to extract fifty million dollars' worth of silver and gold. A thriving little town grew up around it, then the mine collapsed and that was that. The town dried up and blew away like dead grass. If you look at those tombstones, you see a lot of birth and death years close together, sometimes the same year. Children, babies. Dead of disease, starvation, violence, horrible injuries. And now people like us mingle over their bones and sip champagne."

He pulled out his flask and took a drink. He tried to put it back inside his jacket but Zoey yanked it away.

He said, "You know every swallow of that is about four thousand dollars, right?"

"There's one thing still bothering me," she said as she used her dress to wipe the spit off Will's flask. "You've talked about how my dad's romantic partners were always a security threat, that you had to do a quick vetting of them almost on the fly to make sure whatever floozy he was bringing home wasn't an assassin, or somebody trying to get in to do corporate espionage or blackmail. When Aviv drilled his way into the house, then spent hours with me unsupervised, that should have been an absolute crisis. Especially with the election. But you barely cared."

"There was a lot going on."

Zoey took a long drink from the flask and then handed it back to him. Then she said, "I think you had vetted him already."

"We looked into him, since he had publicly stated his goal was to get into the estate, if that's what you mean."

"I think you knew he was going to get into the house that night. Maybe you didn't know exactly how, but you knew he was going to succeed."

Will didn't answer.

"Even weirder," added Zoey, "you kept the team away from the house that night, with the security stuff at the festival. They said you kept delaying them."

"Once again, I sense that you're accusing me of something but I can't begin to guess what."

"Uh-huh. So, total change of subject: When you vetted women for my father, did you ever get proactive? Like, you found a woman, dug into her background, and set him up with her in order to keep him from going after some other, worse women?"

"I can't even imagine how Arthur would have reacted to finding out I'd done something like that."

"What an interesting answer. So how long would you say we need to stay at this event before we ditch it for some smoky bar where you can bend my ear with Budd Billingsley stories while we get incredibly drunk?"

"I would say the time it takes us to walk across the party and get to the car. Are you talking about just you and me, or the whole team?"

"Whole team."

He nodded. "Andre knows more stories than I do."

"I mean, if it was just you and me getting plastered together, I think that could be dangerous."

Will didn't reply but didn't look like he needed clarification, either. "All right, let's get the hell out of here."

"No, no, that's not what I'm saying," slurred Andre around a cigar. "I'm not a religious man, I'm not saying I believe it. I'm saying that the Bible itself says God is a cheat. If he came into one of our joints we'd have to kick him out."

Zoey was gazing vacantly at the city lights sprawled out behind tendrils of smoke. They were at a rooftop cigar lounge that Budd had frequented and possibly owned. Golden braziers kept the chill at bay and the most beautiful man Zoey had ever seen was tinkling away on a grand piano at the center of the space. Zoey suspected her hair would stink like aged tobacco for a month.

"You know the bit in the New Testament where Jesus resurrected that guy?" continued Andre. "What was his name?"

"Lazarus," said Echo.

"Yeah. Budd told me one time—and Budd grew up religious, you know—he told me one time that that bit was the one that stuck with him. Because Jesus finds out his friend has died, and Jesus is God incarnate, but this man, this man who was also God, he goes and when he sees the corpse, you know what he does? He cries."

"'Jesus wept,'" muttered Echo. "In Sunday school we had to memorize a verse and I picked that one because it's only two words long." She glanced over at Zoey. "Your cigar has gone out."

"Yeah, I think mine is defective."

"You're supposed to take a puff every minute or so," noted Will. "It won't just burn itself down."

"Eh, the wet end is getting gross anyway."

"I'm still talking," said Andre as a server set a fresh drink on the table in front of him. "And listen, because this is meaningful. So, ah, Jesus cries at the sight of death, is my point. And that's crazy, because he's God, he's all-knowing and all-powerful, but even he, *even he*, when he sees the dead body of a friend in front of him, crumbles. He can't handle it. See, they don't have that up in Heaven, the dying. He cried because until that moment, *he didn't know*. Do you see what I'm saying? Until he saw it, God didn't know what death was. Not really. He had to experience it like we do. And when he finally did, his ass couldn't handle it."

"And then he undid it," added Echo.

Andre nodded in the exaggerated manner of a drunk telling a story and realizing someone has actually been listening.

"Yes! Exactly. Exactly. He resurrects his friend, which is against the rules! Nobody else gets to do that. For us, death is forever, but when it was Jesus's own pal, he said no. I don't accept this. I can't. So while the dealer wasn't looking, he pulled new cards outta his sleeve. And that was where Budd landed on God, that he may be all-powerful, he may be all-knowing, but when he came down here to *our* world and tried to play *our* game, he couldn't hack it. He couldn't take the thing he saddles us with every day, this death, this losing people. This never getting to say goodbye. When he came down and tried to play the game *he* created, the sheer random cruelty of it knocked him flat."

"That drone is circling, I think it's press." That was Wu, less than two days removed from his most recent surgery and trying not to create a trip hazard with his armored right leg. "My cigar has also gone out, but it's fine. It's been giving me a lightheaded feeling ever since Will told me what it cost."

Will shot a glance toward the whirring machine orbiting the building. "If somebody out there thinks we're that interesting, I feel like they're the true victims."

"In fact," said Echo, "all he did was cheat. When Jesus got a huge crowd together and didn't plan any kind of food for them to eat, he just makes loaves and fishes appear out of thin air. He didn't want to deal with the logistics, finding reputable fish and loaf dealers, rationing out everything so there'll be enough for the folks in the back, keeping the hungry crowd calm. He just turns on the Infinite Food cheat code."

"Yes!" proclaimed Andre as he slapped the table with an open palm. "Exactly! So if Budd is standing for judgment right now, and I know it's been several days but who knows what the wait times are like up there, but if he's being judged, I think he'd say, 'All I did when I was on earth is what you did when you were visiting: I saw what I needed to accomplish and if rules stood in the way, I found a way around.'"

"You think that would fly?" asked Will through a Scotch glass. "With the guy who set up the whole trick with the apple?"

"Ooh, are we talking about God?" asked Zoey's mother, who'd just shown up, wearing a dress Zoey wouldn't have the confidence to wear even in private. "What would your ideal afterlife be? If you got to choose?"

"This right here," replied Andre, pointing down at the table. "Send me back to earth, reincarnate me or whatever, give me another go-around. Only maybe having retained what I learned this time."

"Well, you know," said Echo, "in the Bible Heaven isn't even described as this vacation paradise in the clouds, it's all action and political intrigue. Angels fighting armies of demons with flaming swords. If so, I'll take that. Imagine you're old and dying in your hospital bed, then you open your eyes and you've got a new, muscular body. Then Gabriel is like, 'Good, you're here. Take this flaming longsword, a dragon got loose and we've gotta go take it down.'"

"I think I'd take the vacation paradise," said Wu. "But I'd first ask to have my personality altered into the kind of person who enjoys vacations. Turn off the hypervigilance."

"Wait, do we get to change our personalities?" asked Zoey. "Man, I wouldn't even know where to start, in that case. If I can turn myself into the kind of person who enjoys anything, then why do I even need a Heaven? Turn me into a happier person and just send me back here, like Andre. Or just send me back as Andre. What's your Heaven like, Mom? Just a big club where everybody is really hot?"

"Hmm. I think I'd love just talking to all the people. All the ancient rulers and thinkers and rock stars. Think of the amazing stories they'd have to tell!"

"If you want the most interesting stories," muttered Will, "you probably need to go to the other place."

"Nah, everybody goes to Heaven. Budd would have agreed. So what's your perfect afterlife, Will?"

Will thought about it but showed no sign of enjoying those thoughts. "When you get to the point that you've lost as many people as I have, seeing them again would be enough. Well, that and I would have some very hard questions for the boss."

"*Will*," said Echo, forcing the words around her cigar. "You're bringing down the mood. It's just a thought experiment, what would your perfect situation be, if you could have any possible situation?"

Zoey raised her hand. "I bet I can answer for him. Seriously, I bet I can."

Will seemed skeptical. "I'm almost afraid to hear what you're going to say."

"You get to Heaven, only to find it's all burned down. They had an electrical fire or something. And Saint Peter says, 'It's all gone, it's all burned to the ground. And *we need you to be in charge of rebuilding it*.'"

"That's . . . yeah, that's pretty much it. I think that's just about it, exactly."

"Then as soon as he's finished," said Echo, "I'll burn it all down again with my flaming sword. Wait, how would Heaven work if the only thing that makes me happy is ruining Will's thing?"

Wu was still watching the harmless drone as if silently wishing it would try something. "I'm thinking you've just stumbled across the reason the whole thing couldn't work."

Zoey groaned. "Aaaand another friendly conversation descends into an existential crisis. God, don't you people ever just sit around and talk about sports or something? Wait, where are you going?"

Will had stood and was putting on his hat. "Got an early morning meeting. You guys stay and relax, this place never closes."

"So that's how it is, huh? Just always onto the next threat, dealing with this one while preparing for that one, probably while already thinking about the one after that?"

"Yep."

He grabbed Zoey's half-full glass from in front of her and downed the rest of the contents.

"And it never ends?" she asked, staring into the empty glass.

"Nope. Well, it ends eventually."

Zoey shook her head. "It's exhausting. How do you keep yourself going?"

"You pick up the torch the departed are no longer able to carry, and you press on, in their memory." He shrugged. "But to be honest, seeing what's next is the best part. And I bet deep down, you agree. See you tomorrow."

He patted her shoulder and headed off. Zoey leaned back and sighed, watching ghostly tendrils of smoke rise up and dissolve among the stars.

TURN THE PAGE FOR A SNEAK PEEK AT
JASON PARGIN'S NEW NOVEL

I'M STARTING TO WORRY ABOUT THIS BLACK BOX OF DOOM

Available Now

Abbott

Abbott Coburn had spent much of his twenty-six years dreading the wrong things, in the wrong amounts, for the wrong reasons. So it was appropriate that in his final hours before achieving international infamy, he was dreading a routine trip he'd accepted as a driver for the rideshare service Lyft. The passenger had ordered a ride from Victorville, California, to Los Angeles International Airport, a facility Abbott believed had been designed to make every traveler feel like they were doing it wrong.

He rolled up to the pickup spot—the parking lot of a Circle K convenience store—to find a woman sitting on a black box, one large enough that she probably could've mailed herself to her destination with the addition of some breathing holes and a piss drain. It had wheels and she was rolling herself back and forth a few inches in each direction with her feet, working out nervous energy. The millions of strangers who'd become obsessed with that box in the coming days would usually describe it incorrectly, calling it everything from a "footlocker" to an "armored munitions crate." What the woman was actually sitting on was a road case, the type musicians use to transport concert gear. This one was covered in band stickers, a detail that would have been inconsequential in a rational society but turned out to be extremely consequential in ours.

Abbott rolled down the window and braced himself, doing his usual scan for reassuring signs that the passenger is Normal (he'd developed a sixth sense for the weirdos who, for example, wanted to sit in the front). The woman on the box wore green cargo pants and a dazzling orange hoodie that looked to Abbott like high-visibility work gear. Though, if she was on the job, the bosses weren't strict about the dress code: She wore a faded trucker cap that said, WELCOME TO THE SHITSHOW. Below that was a pair of oversize sunglasses with lime-green plastic frames and, below that, smeared lipstick that looked like it had been hurriedly applied in the dark. Her hair was short enough that it looked like it had been shaved without a mirror while driving down a bumpy road. It did not occur to Abbott that all of this would be an excellent way to thwart security cameras and facial recognition software.

Abbott, his nervous system already hovering a finger over its big red Fight-or-Flight button, asked, "You got the Lyft to LAX?"

He was hopeful she'd say no, but there was no one else in the vicinity aside from a rail-thin man by the tire air machine having a tense argument via either Bluetooth or psychosis.

"Oh my god," said the woman on the box, "I have a huge favor to ask you. HUGE. I am in so much trouble with my employer."

She removed her green sunglasses, as if the situation had become much too serious for such eyewear. Her eyes were bloodshot and Abbott thought she'd either been recently smoking weed or recently crying, though he knew from personal experience that it was possible to do both simultaneously. He was now absolutely certain that the favor she was about to ask was going to be illegal, impossible, or just a string of nonsense words. He wasn't sure how to respond without accidentally agreeing, so he just stared.

"Okay," she said, after realizing it was still her turn to talk. "Yes, I ordered a trip to LAX, but in the time I've been waiting, I found out that's not going to work. This is a big problem. BIG problem."

Her voice was shaky and Abbott decided that she had, in fact, been crying. He instantly sensed two opposing instincts in his brain quietly begin to go to war with each other.

"This box I'm sitting on?" she continued. "The guy who hired me has to have it by Monday, the Fourth of July. I can't ship it, because I can't let it out of my sight—I have to stay with it, wherever it goes. And I can't fly, for reasons that would take all day to explain. Now, I'm going to ask you a question. It's going to sound like a hypothetical or a joke, but it's an actual question. Okay? Okay. So, how much would you charge to drive me to Washington, DC?"

Abbott took a moment to make sure he'd heard her right before replying, "Oh, that's not something you can do in a Lyft, the maximum trip is only—"

"No, no. You'd clock out of your app or however you do it. I'm asking you, personally, as a citizen with a beautiful working car—what is this, an Escalade?"

"A, uh, Lincoln Navigator. It actually belongs to—"

"I'm asking what you would charge to take me all the way across the country. And your reflex is going to be to say no amount of money because I'm talking about totally putting your life on hold for more than a week, without notice. Restaurants, hotels, lost business, canceled Fourth of July plans, additional stress—it's a lot to ask. But I'm willing to pay a lot. Or rather, my employer is willing to pay a lot. Look."

She twisted around and dug into a tattered duffel bag that Abbott hadn't previously noticed. When she came back around, she was holding two thick folds of cash, each bound with rubber bands. He physically recoiled at the sight of it, mainly because not a single reasonable person has ever carried money that way.

"This is one hundred thousand dollars," she said, waving the cash around like a mind control amulet. "The guy who hired me has this kind of money to throw around and no, he's not a criminal, he's a legitimate rich guy, if such a thing exists. No, I can't tell you who he is. All I can tell you is that he needs this box by the Fourth at the latest and it has to be kept quiet. Today is Thursday.

We can make it easily, we don't even have to travel overnight. Four days of leisurely driving and we'll get there Sunday evening, no problem. One hundred K is my starting offer for you to make this drive. Make me a counteroffer."

At this stage, Abbott was considering this request in the exact same way he'd have considered a request to be transported to Venus in exchange for a baggie of rat turds: he just wanted out of the crazy conversation as quickly and safely as possible.

He said, "I'm sure there are plenty of people within a few miles of here, probably a million of them, who'd love to take you up on this. But I really can't. I'm sorry."

She shook her head. "No. No, you're perfect for this, I can tell already. And I can't keep asking people, I have to get on the road and I have to do it now. The more drivers I have to ask, the more people know about this, and that's bad. Secrecy is part of what I'm paying for. And I'm not crazy, I know how I look. Though I will have to tell you about the worms at some point. But no, I'm dressed like this for a reason. How about one fifty?"

A third fold of cash was added and Abbott had to force himself to look away from it. He prided himself on not being enslaved to mindless greed, but way back at the rear of his noisy brain was a tiny voice pointing out that this amount of money would let him move out on his own and tell his father to fuck off (though it would definitely have to be done in that order). It would be *freedom*, for literally the first time in his life. Abbott imagined a factory farm pig escaping into a sunny green pasture and seeing the clear blue sky for the first time. Though he was having trouble imagining the pig looking up. Could pigs do that? He'd have to google it later. Wait, what did she say about worms?

The woman grinned and sat up straighter, the posture of an angler who's just seen the bobber plop under the surface. It kind of made Abbott want to refuse just to spite her.

"But there are rules," she said, a finger in the air. "You can't look in the box. You can't ask me what's in the box. And you can't tell anyone where we're going until it's over. After that, you can tell anyone anything you like. But no one can come looking for us."

"Well, there's certainly nothing weird or suspicious about that. So, why don't you just rent a car and drive yourself?"

"No driver's license. I used to have one, but the government took it away. They said, 'You're too good of a driver, it's making the other drivers look bad, you're hurting their self-esteem.'"

"I just . . . I really can't, sorry. You say I'm perfect for this, but I assure you I'm the absolute perfect person to not do it. That's, what, like, fifty hours of driving? I don't even like to drive for *one* hour."

"You drive for a living!"

"Oh, I just started doing this a couple months ago to—"

"I'm just teasing you, I know you probably didn't grow up dressing as a Lyft driver for Halloween. But no, you're my guy. You're not married, right? I don't see a ring. No kids, I can see it on your face. If you have another job, it's one you can walk away from, it's not a 401K and health insurance situation. You probably live with a parent, so even if you have pets, there's somebody to feed them while you're away. You're old enough that nobody's going to assume you were abducted. You're, what, twenty-four? Around there?"

"Twenty-six. Did you just deduce all that on the fly?"

She smiled again and made a show of leaning forward, narrowing her eyes as if to examine him. "Ah, see, there's something you need to know about me: I can *read minds*. I can tell you're skeptical, so let me give it a shot. Ready?"

She narrowed her eyes further, comically exaggerating her concentration. At this point, Abbott was 99 percent of the way to driving off and marking the ride as canceled.

"You have trouble getting to sleep at night," she began, "because you can't turn off your brain. Usually it's replaying something stressful that happened in the past or rehearsing something stressful that could possibly happen in the future. You then have to down constant caffeine just to function through the day—I bet you've got one of those big energy drinks in the center console right now. You sometimes get really good ideas in the shower. You can't navigate even your own city without software that gives you turn-by-turn directions. You get an actual, physical sense of panic if you can't find your phone, even if you know it's still somewhere in your home."

She was rocking in her seat, rolling the trunk's tiny wheels back and forth, back and forth.

"You don't have a girlfriend or a boyfriend," she continued, before Abbott could interrupt. "You've never had a long-term relationship and, at least once in your life, you thought you were dating someone while the whole time *they* thought you were just friends. You actually don't have any close friends. Maybe you did when you were in school, but you don't keep in touch. You've replaced them with a whole bunch of internet acquaintances—maybe you're all members of the same fandom or a guild in a video game—but you'd be traumatized if any of them suddenly showed up at your front door unannounced. Sometimes, out of the blue, you'll physically cringe at something you said or did when you were a teenager. When you use porn, you may have to sort through two hundred pics or videos before you find one that will get you off. You're sure that humanity is doomed and feel like you were cursed to be born when you were. Am I close?"

Abbott had to take a moment to gather himself. Forcing a dismissive tone with all his might, he said, "Congratulations, you've just described everyone I know."

"Exactly. It describes everyone *you know*."

"I really do have to get back to work, I don't—"

"Don't get offended, please, none of that was intended as an insult. I'm only saying that I know you're an outsider, just like me! I think the universe brought us together. But I'm not done, because this is the big one: The reason you're hesitating to make this trip, even for a life-changing amount of money, isn't because you're worried that I'm a scammer or that my employer is a drug lord and this box is full of heroin. No, what you fear above all is *humiliation at the hands of the unfamiliar*. What if you get a flat tire on a highway in Tennessee, do you even know how to change it? What if we wind up the wrong lane at a toll road and the lady in the booth yells at you? What if you get a speeding ticket in Ohio, how do you even pay it? What if you get into a fender bender and the other driver is a big, scary guy who doesn't speak English? Then there's the absolutely *terrifying* prospect of spending dozens of hours in an enclosed space with some weird woman. What if you embarrass yourself? Or, worse, what if I say something that makes you embarrassed on my behalf? You'll have no mute or block button, just unfettered raw-dog, face-to-face contact, with no escape for days on end. What if I'm so unhinged that we literally have nothing to talk about, no shared jokes, no way to break the tension? What if, what if, what if—all of these scenarios that humanity deals with a billion times a day but that you find so terrifying that you wouldn't even risk them for a hundred and fifty thousand dollars in cash. So the question is: Would you do it for two hundred?"

She fished out a fourth hunk of bills. The escalating amounts actually didn't make an impression on Abbott; at this point, the dollar figures all registered as equally impossible sums of money. But the hand that held the cash was trembling and he sensed the thrum of desperation inside the woman, the vibe of one who has exhausted every reasonable option and is now trying the stupid ones.

"A hundred now," she said, "and a hundred after we arrive in DC. If you think it's a trick, that we'll get there and I'll steal back the money at knifepoint, we can swing by somewhere and you can drop off the first payment. You can even take it to your bank, let the teller do the counterfeit test on the bills. If we hurry."

"How do you know I wouldn't do that and then just refuse to drive you?"

"Because *I can see into your soul*. You would never do that. Not just because it's wrong, but because you'd be torn apart by the awkwardness of that conversation, of having to see the look on my face when I found out you'd double-crossed me. Also, you'd soon realize that you wouldn't just be screwing me, but my employer. And even if he's not a criminal, you can guess that's probably a pretty bad idea. He could send guys in suits to your house to demand the money back and just think how awkward *that* would be."

Abbott heard himself say "Can I have time to think about it?" and knew that his automated avoidance mechanism had kicked in. He'd been developing this apparatus since his first day in kindergarten when the Smelly Girl had asked him to play with her and, in a panic, he'd had to come up with a plausible excuse not to (he told her his family's religion forbade touching plastic dinosaurs). These days, it was pure reflex: if an acquaintance invited him to trivia night at the bar, a ready-made, ironclad excuse would fly from his lips before he'd even given it a thought.

Sure, sometimes he'd find himself wondering if maybe he should be filtering these invitations before they were routed directly into the trash. Here, for example: on some level he knew this offer deserved more consideration. But his request for time wasn't about that, it was just one of the stock phrases he deployed to get to a safe distance where plans could be easily canceled via text or, even better, by simply avoiding that person for the rest of his life. Sure, this woman was in some kind of distress, but that would be no burden to him once she was out of sight—

"No, you can't have time to think about it," said the woman on the box. "I meant it when I said we have to leave right now. *Maybe* we can swing by your place to pack up some clothes and whatever medications you're on—you're on a few, right?—and to tell the parent or grandparent you live with that you'll be back late next week. But it has to be real quick, in and out."

"I can't even tell my dad where I'm going?"

"You'll tell him that a friend needs you to help with a job that pays a bundle, that it's being done on behalf of a celebrity and has to be kept quiet so the press doesn't sniff it out. And that it's nothing illegal. That's, like, ninety percent true. Or eighty percent. It's mostly true."

"Is your employer a celebrity?"

"He's not a movie star or anything, if you're trying to guess who he is. But your dad shouldn't question it." She waved a hand in the vague direction of Los Angeles. "Out there, you've probably got a hundred professional fixer types doing jobs like this as we speak."

"Then go find one of them. If you think I'm such a loser, what makes you think I can even get us there?"

"All right, enough of that." She stood and put on her lime-green sunglasses. "You don't even have your heart in it anymore. Come on, help me load the box, it's really heavy. We've been sitting out here too long and people are starting to stare."

In the coming days, many words would be spent speculating as to why Abbott had agreed to the trip. Was it the money? Or did he genuinely want to help this woman he'd never met? The truth was, not even Abbott himself knew. Maybe it was just that by the time she was lugging the box toward the rear of the Navigator, it'd have simply been too awkward to stop her.

Malort

Considering he was two hundred and seventy-five pounds, bald, covered in tattoos, and wearing mirrored sunglasses, Malort could have wound up with many nicknames. But, a drunken bet in a Milwaukee dive bar decades earlier had resulted in a bicep tattoo of a Jeppson's Malört bottle, the Chicago-area liquor so infamously bitter that the label featured a lengthy paragraph apologizing for the taste. His friends had all agreed the tattoo and nickname fit him, but never dared to explain their rationale in his presence. He did have to drop the little dots above the O in recent years as nobody knew how to add those in text messages.

The man they called Malort rolled up to find that the Apple Valley fire department had apparently arrived just in time to turn the shack in the desert from a smoldering ruin into a wet smoldering ruin. Only two and a half walls of the flimsy structure were still upright, exposing the charred interior like a diorama. It told a fairly simple story of a loner hiding from and/or rooting for the Apocalypse. From where he sat, there was no sign of the black box and he had a sinking feeling it was long gone.

He stepped out of his metallic red Buick Grand National and approached a young man whose build and face made him look like a kid who'd dressed up in his dad's helmet and turnout coat. He was hosing down the aftermath to cool the embers and looked like he would have a stroke if two thoughts appeared in his brain simultaneously. He noticed Malort and a beam of curiosity pierced his haze.

"This your property?" asked the kid.

It was a dumb question, thought Malort. The type of guy who sets up in a wilderness survival shack probably doesn't get around in a sparkly Buick that surely lists at least one pimp in its Carfax report. He took the dumbness of the question as a good sign. Instead of answering, Malort pulled out his phone and pointed the camera at the scene, acting like he had an important job to do. Generally, if you can project enough confidence and purpose, all the uncertain nerds of the world will just part like the Red Sea.

He stepped toward the smoldering structure with his phone and, without looking at the kid, grumbled, "Is there propane?"

"There was, it already popped, that's what blew out the sides here. The ruptured tank is on the floor, there's some kind of apparatus attached. Maybe a booby trap, or maybe they were trying to deep-fry a turkey? You ever seen one of those go wrong? Nightmare. So, uh, are you a friend? One of the neighbors?"

Malort peered into the half-standing structure from afar, trying to stay out of the hose splatter. The other firefighters hadn't seemed to register his presence, most of them distracted by the task of spraying down the landscape to keep stray sparks from triggering a brushfire.

"The strangest thing just happened," rumbled Malort. "You know the big house over the hill there, behind the fence with all the barbed wire? The crazy bastard who lived there owns all this, it's all his property. So, I was chasing an intruder through that house, then they went 'round a corner and vanished into thin air. I looked all around, saw neither hide nor hair of 'em. A few minutes later, I looked out the window and noticed the smoke over here."

"Oh, really?" said the kid, who didn't seem to understand what that had to do with this.

"Nobody dead in there, I take it?"

"No, sir. Looks to me like they either left the propane to blow on purpose or left it unattended on accident."

"So there's no corpse in *there,* but if you go over the hill and look in that house behind the barbed wire, you'll see the owner is dead on the floor of a workshop where he was making Lord-knows-what. Though I wouldn't advise poking your head in unless you've got a strong stomach. They'll have to identify him by his teeth and prints, considering the condition his face is in."

Malort studied the smoking remains of a bed, now just a blackened frame and springs. The morning sunlight and the spray of the hose was decorating the scene with a festive little rainbow.

"Is that true?" asked the kid, trying to piece together the implications. "Did you call it in?"

"I'm not much for callin' things in. Though you should tell your people to wear protective gear when they go over there. I don't know what the guy had in his shop, but there were homemade radiation warning signs on the door. You can decide for yourself whether a homemade radiation sign is scarier than an official one." Malort studied the shack's exposed ashy guts and asked, "Have you seen any sign of a road case? One of them black boxes with aluminum trim, about the size of a footlocker?"

"No, sir. I mean, we haven't dug around inside there, but I haven't seen anything like that. Hey, uh, Bomb and Arson are on their way, you should tell them about the dead body."

"Nobody has come to take anything from the scene?"

"Not since I been here. I didn't catch your name?"

"And nobody saw the occupant leave? Or what vehicle they were driving? Might have been a blue pickup."

"No, sir." The kid was glancing around now, presumably for someone senior to come to his rescue.

Malort zoomed in with his camera, focusing on the bit of intact wall at the foot of the bed. There was a schizoid scatter of pictures and drawings pinned to the wall, blackened and curled. The residue of a mind gone to batshit. He snapped a photo. He then studied the floor around the bed. . . .

"Point your hose away," growled Malort. "I'm gonna check somethin'."

He stomped toward the shack, kicked over the burned-out bed fame, and yanked away a waterlogged rug underneath. There it was: a hatch that opened with a metal ring.

"Huh," said the kid as Malort yanked the hatch open. "They got a basement?"

"They've got a tunnel and a bomb shelter. Follow it back a hundred yards or so and you'll wind up under that house behind the fence. It turned out my intruder didn't vanish, they slipped into a bedroom closet, climbed down a ladder, ran over, popped out here."

Then, thought Malort, they'd rigged it so he'd get a face full of propane tank shrapnel if he tried to follow.

The kid looked amazed. "Damn. Is this like a cartel operation? I have a buddy who said they busted a place that had tunnels running all through the neighborhood—"

"Sir!" shouted a new voice from behind the kid. "What's your business here?"

It was the older guy, coming to assert his authority. Malort tensed up. The dude was in his fifties or sixties but that only put him in the same range as himself. And you generally didn't want to tangle with a firefighter; they had muscles from hauling gear and bad attitudes from breathing toxic chemicals and remembering the screams of burning children.

"He's looking for a big box," said the kid. "He says the old guy who owns this land is dead over in that house behind the fence. And now he's found a secret tunnel under the Unabomber hut. And the house is radioactive, maybe."

"Who are you?" asked the older man, ignoring the kid completely.

Malort put his phone away. "I was just leavin'."

"No, you're not. I'm gonna need to see ID. Hey!"

Malort ignored him and made his way back to the Buick.

The senior fireman was talking into a radio now, hurrying to get himself between Malort and his car.

"You just wait right here."

He put a hand on Malort's chest. Malort stopped, looked slowly down at the gloved hand, then back up to meet the old guy's eyes. There he detected the same apprehension he'd seen on the faces of authority figures since his growth spurt in middle school. He decided that, if things continued to progress in this fashion, he would open with forearm blows to the head and then delegate the closing argument to his boots. No doubt the other firemen would try to jump in, but you can't waste your life worrying about stuff that's not gonna happen until thirty seconds from now.

"Everybody," announced Malort, "get out your phones and start recording, because if this old fuck doesn't get out of my way, what happens next should really be somethin' to see."

He balled his fists and his heart revved into another gear. As stimulants go, an early-morning ass-kicking was only a notch below speed. The old man gave him a perfunctory hard look and then backed down, allowing Malort to get behind the wheel of the Grand National unimpeded. The old man made a big show of photographing the license plate to save face.

As Malort backed up, he leaned out his window and said, "Never challenge a man in a Buick. He's got nothin' to lose."

As he headed back to the main road, he pulled up the pic of the shack's interior and zoomed in on the charred paranoia collage. Written on a handmade banner above the darkened scraps were three words:

THE FORBIDDEN NUMBERS

ABOUT THE AUTHOR

Jason Pargin is the *New York Times* bestselling author of the John Dies at the End series as well as the award-winning Zoey Ashe novels. He previously published under the pseudonym David Wong. His essays for Cracked.com and other outlets have been enjoyed by tens of millions of readers around the world.